THE DRAGON RIDERS

COWBOYS AND DRAGONS

BOOK 2

ANTHONY A. KERR

Copyright © 2016 by Anthony A. Kerr
Cover Design by Anthony A. Kerr

All rights reserved. No part of this publication may be reproduced, distributed, or transmitted in any form or by any means, including photocopying, recording, or other electronic or mechanical methods, without the prior written permission of the publisher, except in the case of brief quotations embodied in critical reviews and certain other noncommercial uses permitted by copyright law. For permission requests, please write to the publisher at the following email address: *permissions@thundermountainbooks.com*.

This is a work of fiction. Names, characters, businesses, places, events and incidents are either the products of the author's imagination or used in a fictitious manner. Any resemblance to actual persons, living or dead, or actual events is purely coincidental.

Published by Thunder Mountain Books, Co.
ISBN 978-0-9968565-2-2 (paperback)
ISBN 978-0-9968565-3-9 (ebook)

For more information, please visit *www.aakerr.com*, and sign up for updates.

Thank you for reading.

*To Jenifer:
Your optimism and encouragement
inspire me to reach for new heights.*

CONTENTS

1	The Warehouse	1
2	Trapped	9
3	Too Much of a Good Thing	15
4	Not Far From the Tree	24
5	Tempest	30
6	Dream Walking	40
7	Twenty Questions in a Tub	48
8	The Chief	56
9	People of the Unseen Land	65
10	City of the Ancients	75
11	The Temple	83
12	The First One	93
13	The Tale of River	101
14	Grandpa Stone's Magic Putter	110
15	Reinforcements	119
16	Retreat	127
17	Recharge	134
18	Tabrati	143
19	The Call of Destiny	150
20	A New Lead	157
21	The Ancient One	162
22	Quest of the Dragon Riders	173
23	The Dragons of Latin America	179
24	Lord DeSoto	187
25	Leyla	194
26	X Marks the Spot	204
27	The Deal	212
28	Temple of the Spear	223
29	Trial by Lightning and Fire	229

CONTENTS

30	The Temple Sanctuary	235
31	Higher Calling	244
32	Out of the Frying Pan…	252
33	… Into the Fire	259
34	Capture the Talisman	268
35	Reckoning	276
36	Reconciliation	284
37	Lord Ddraig	292
38	The Dragon Riders	300
	Glossary	315

MAP OF THE CITY OF THE ANCIENTS

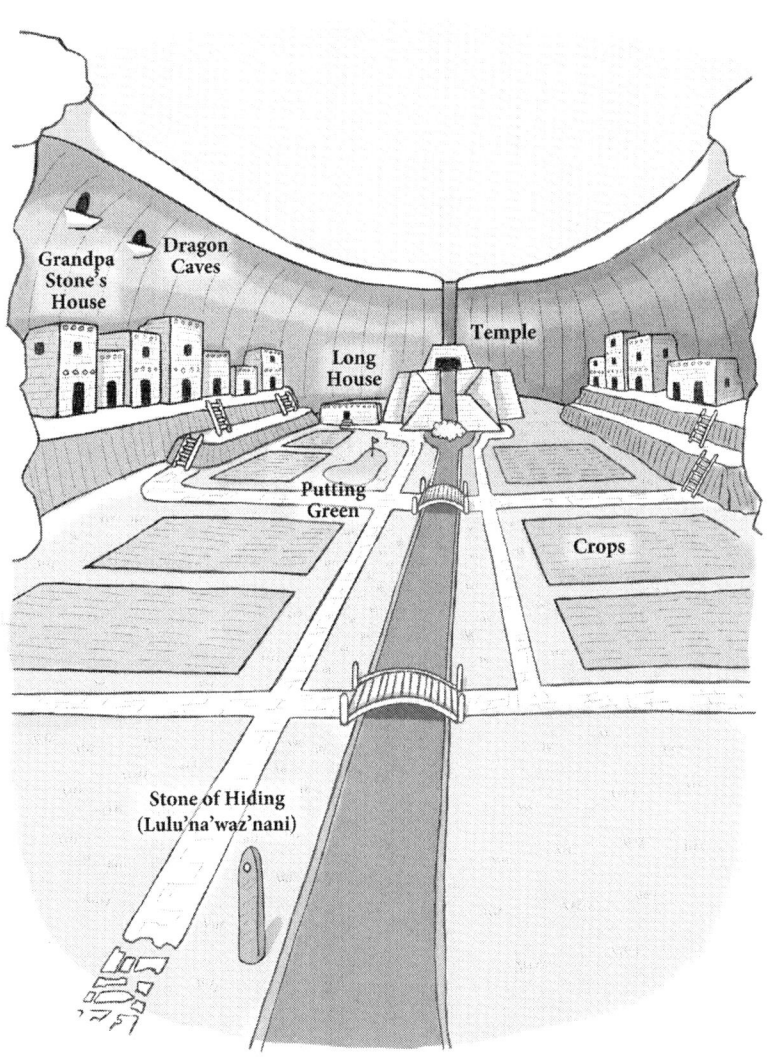

CHAPTER 1

MIRANDA
The Warehouse

MIRANDA JERKED AWAKE as static burst over her helmet speaker. She frantically grasped the saddle's horn, sucking in several quick breaths in an attempt to calm her racing heart. *Thank you, safety harness!* she thought.

"*Are you okay, Lady McAdelind?*" asked Indigo, the juvenile blue dragon she was riding, her smoky voice resonating in Miranda's mind.

"*Yeah, fine. I'm just tired,*" Miranda replied telepathically. "*And please, call me Miranda.*"

"Keep sharp everyone," Mr. O'Faron's voice crackled over Miranda's helmet speaker. "We're almost there."

Miranda gazed ahead to where an eerie orange light illuminated the clouds they were soaring above. She reached up and turned a knob on her helmet radio control panel until she was on a private channel with her brother. "Is that Denver, already?"

"Yes. Did you doze off too?" Justin said through a yawn.

"This has been the longest day of my life. I could have really used a good night's sleep."

"I agree, but we needed to do this tonight," Miranda said. This had easily been the longest day of her life too. It had begun with her sneaking off to the Warren to let Storm know that the old dragon's former mistress, and Miranda and Justin's aunt, Em, was alive, then quickly turned into a fight for her life against a half-dozen wyverns and draconians. A chill shot down her spine at the thought of the vile lizard-men and their scorpion-tailed mounts. Yet here she was, heading directly into another encounter, and maybe another battle, with the same terrifying enemies.

"Remind me again why this couldn't have waited until tomorrow night?" Justin asked.

"Because there's a good chance the dracs would have disappeared by then. We need to strike while we know where they are." During dinner Grandpa McAdelind—or Grandpa Mac, as Miranda and Justin had started calling him—had decided to raid the only known draconian hideout for information: the warehouse where Mr. O'Faron had met with the draconians after picking up Miranda and Justin from the Denver airport only a few weeks before. So much had happened in such a short time. Their home and their life back in Manhattan seemed like a dream now. And yet here they were, riding dragons through the night sky. "Should be pretty simple," Miranda added.

"Nothing is going to be simple on this idiot of a beast," Justin grunted, and shook his head at the very young grayish-blue dragon he was riding, Steel. "I really miss Red."

Miranda glanced down at the inexperienced blue dragon she was riding and wished Storm was with her as well. In just a short time, they had been through so much together, and Miranda knew, without a doubt, that the fierce dragon would always do everything in her power to protect her.

But Red and Storm were both recovering from their battle with the wyverns, and despite their unrelenting protests, Grandpa Mac had decided the best thing for them to do was to recuperate. Breathing fire and lightning to fight against an overwhelming force—something no domestic dragon had ever done before—had taken a lot out of them both, and until Grandpa declared both dragons healthy again, they were grounded.

Plus, according to Mr. O'Faron's information, there would only be a handful of draconians at the warehouse anyway, so five dragons should be more than enough to overpower them.

Even so, Miranda still couldn't help but wish that Red and Storm, and… O'Faron's son, Billy were with them now too.

She felt her face flush slightly at the thought of the handsome older boy. He was still a little mad at her and Justin for thinking he had been the person stealing from their family. Despite his feelings, he had insisted on coming along. But his arm was still healing from a fight with Justin, during which her brother had managed to smash Billy's elbow with a can of bear mace, and Mrs. Lóng, Grandpa Mac's mysterious cook and confidante, had said it would be another day or two before he could ride again.

"We're almost there, Indigo! Ready to bust some heads?" Miranda said.

The blue dragon shuddered. *I'm hoping that if we ask politely the draconians will just cooperate with us.*

Justin laughed. "A diplomatic dragon. Nice."

"*Well, I'm ready to bust their heads, boss,*" Steel chimed in enthusiastically. "*You give the word, and I'll tear those filthy lizards into smithereens.*"

"Looks like we got the wrong dragons, Justin. Want to switch?" Miranda teased.

"I wish. Next time, I get to pick my dragon first."

Mr. O'Faron held up one arm to signal that he was about to make his descent, and Miranda hurriedly switched back to the main radio channel. "Okay, here we go!" he called, lowering his arm. Thunder, his blue dragon, banked into a steep dive and vanished into the clouds.

"All right, kids. Once we get to the warehouse, wait for my signal that it's all clear before entering. Understand?" Grandpa Mac said. Seeing that Justin and Miranda had both nodded, he guided Argo, his massive gold dragon, after Thunder.

Then less than a heartbeat later they were followed by the young dragon trainer, Miss Ddraig, on her red dragon, Flare.

"Okay, Steel," Justin said sternly. *"Let's keep it simple. Follow the other dragons down to the warehouse. Nice and easy."*

"Sure thing, boss-man!" the young blue replied, sounding excited.

Justin let out a high-pitched yell as Steel tucked into a tight barrel roll and dove into the thick clouds below.

"All right. Our turn," Miranda said, leaning forward to direct Indigo to dive, but the dragon's only response was to shake uncontrollably.

Miranda sighed. *"Come on, Indigo. This will be a breeze. You have nothing to worry about."*

She could feel the young dragon's hesitation. *"But what if it's worse than we expect? What if there are twice as many draconians as we think?"*

"Then we'll deal with all of them," Miranda said, with more confidence than she felt, and patted Indigo's rough, scaly neck reassuringly. *"Don't worry. I won't let anything happen to you. I promise."*

The dragon nodded once before drifting slowly downward into the clouds.

Miranda had always imagined clouds to be warm and soft like pillows, but passing through them felt more like being in a cold carwash with all the windows down. Before she knew it, she was soaked to the bone and shivering uncontrollably.

After what seemed like an hour, Indigo spread her wings out like a pair of giant sails and landed softly on the gravel-covered roof near the four other dragons.

Something was wrong. Everyone had their helmets off, worried looks darkening their faces.

"I said slowly, you oaf!" Justin whispered harshly to the slinking Steel. "Your clumsy landing alerted everyone inside that we're here."

"Are you positive?" Grandpa Mac asked.

Justin closed his eyes, as if reading signals only he could detect, then nodded. "Yep. They're running around, thinking about... fire. That's weird."

"They must be burning any evidence we might be able to use to find Robin, Kaya, and Em. We have to go in now before they destroy everything. Remember, our goal is to grab anything that will lead us to the imprisoned members of our family. William, on the count of three," Grandpa Mac whispered, and held up one finger, then two. As soon as his third finger went up, both he and Mr. O'Faron gave their mounts a slight kick.

As if they had rehearsed this many times before, the two dragons each slammed one massive clawed forepaw into the roof and started peeling the corrugated metal back as if they were unwrapping a huge Christmas present. When the hole was big enough for a dragon to squeeze through, Argo launched himself in, followed immediately by Thunder.

A weird droning sound erupted from inside the warehouse—the creepy chanting the draconians seemed to love. The plan was to wait for a signal indicating it was safe to enter, but there was so much noise, Miranda couldn't make out a single word.

Justin had his eyes closed again, and his head cocked to

the side. When he frowned, Miranda asked, "What's wrong?"

"I'm not totally sure. The dracs aren't surprised or scared. And their thoughts are… hard to read. I can't even get anything from Argo or Thunder to see what's happening."

Miranda closed her eyes and tried to connect with the dragons' minds. If Justin were having difficulties sensing the dracs, it would be even harder for her. Her brother had a knack for reading the thoughts and intentions of both dragons and draconians. But Miranda couldn't see or feel anything but a big black spot, as if they were intentionally being blocked. Her eyes shot open. "Something's wrong, Justin. We're being *jammed*!"

"How is that even possible?" Justin asked.

Miranda shrugged. "How is *any* of this possible?"

Steel was dancing impatiently back and forth, and then as if the waiting had just become too much for him to handle, he crouched at the edge of the hole. *"We're missing out on all the fun. I'm going in."*

"Oh, no you don't! We're supposed to wait for the signal, you stupid dragon!" Justin screeched, as Steel leaped into the warehouse, disappearing into the darkness below.

Miranda turned to Miss D. "What do we do now?"

The dragon trainer smiled wickedly and shrugged. "If you think I am missin' any of this, you're mental, you are." She urged the hesitant Flare into the opening.

Indigo started to rapidly back away from the hole. *"I don't think this is a good idea. Not a good idea at all. We need to wait for the signal. I have a bad feeling about this."*

Miranda agreed with the trembling dragon, but if they didn't move now, any evidence leading them to her parents and aunt would be destroyed. "I need to find out what those dirty lizards know. So I'm going in, with or without you."

"Oh, no, no, no! Lady McAdelind, it is my duty to protect you, and this is far too dangerous. We should just wait here a little

while longer."

A wave of heat shot up through the hole in the roof, followed by screaming and shouting.

"We need to go. Now!" Miranda yelled and kicked Indigo with both heels to spur the beast into action. The dragon hesitantly jumped forward and plunged down into the warehouse.

Intense heat hit Miranda and took her breath away. Indigo swerved hard to the left and away from the source of the blistering air. The dragon landed on a tower of metal scaffolding at the far end of the warehouse. She turned to give Miranda a better look at the chaotic scene unfolding below.

The structure was much larger than Miranda had expected. Not nearly as big as the Grand Corral in the Warren on Grandpa's ranch, but close to the size of a football stadium and several stories tall. Crates and metal enclosures of all sizes had been pushed and stacked haphazardly around the edges of the warehouse. Miranda had expected to see the draconians burning any evidence they may have had, but instead she saw Grandpa Mac, Mr. O'Faron, Miss Ddraig, and Justin all trapped in a cage constructed completely out of green fire. The entire center of the warehouse had obviously been cleared for just this purpose. The dracs must somehow have anticipated their arrival. It was a trap.

Miranda coughed and tried to take in a deep breath, but the fire was quickly consuming the oxygen within the warehouse. Not only that, but there was a strong odor, like rotten eggs, that almost knocked her out of her saddle.

Miranda grabbed her nose. "Pee-yew! Do you smell that?"

Indigo looked around nervously. *"Yes. It smells like gas. I told you this was a bad idea. We need to get out of here immediately. I need to get you to safety."*

"No! We need to save everyone!" Miranda shouted back.

But she wasn't sure how she was going to do that just yet. Surrounding the cage of fire were hundreds of robed draconians chanting, their arms held out, palms facing the flames. Not just five or ten, as they had thought. And there were still more dracs, about a dozen, not taking part in the chanting but busy doing something around a large brass urn that stood next to a heavy wooden table stacked with items of various sizes that Miranda could not identify. Destroying papers and other evidence maybe? A few steps away from the urn she also saw several large wooden crates, placed too near to be there by accident. And what could be in those? she wondered.

Miranda's eyes narrowed on this group of lizard-men. She had to stop them first.

"I think if we knock a section of the roof down, we might be able to crush some of the draconians and create a breach in the fire trap," Indigo stammered.

"Good idea," Miranda said, not taking her eyes of the dracs in the corner. "But we need to stop those creeps over there first."

"But what about the others? They need our help. I thought you said we needed to save them."

"And we will. But we need to stop those filthy lizards from destroying any clues about where my family might be located. That is our primary mission and what we came here for."

Indigo swung her head toward the spot Miranda was indicating. "There are more than ten draconians. I can't fight all of them by myself."

"Sure you can," Miranda said, cracking her knuckles. "I have an idea. How do you feel about… lightning?"

CHAPTER 2

JUSTIN
Trapped

"I TOLD YOU TO WAIT FOR THE SIGNAL!" Justin yelled in frustration.

As soon as Steel had landed near Argo and Thunder on the warehouse's concrete floor, Justin knew they were in a trap. From outside the building he had only been able to sense a couple of dracs, but after surveying the massive interior of the structure, he estimated there were more like a hundred spread out in a large circle surrounding them.

A second later, Flare landed beside Steel.

The draconians' chanting intensified. Suddenly the net of green fire spread up and over them, like a giant woven dome of flames, cutting off their escape.

"And now we're trapped. Smooth move, Steel," Justin scolded.

But the dragon did not respond. Something down here was definitely messing with Justin's ability to communicate with the dragons and sense the draconians.

Justin leaned over and placed a hand on Steel's neck. *"Can you hear me?"* he said mentally, projecting his thoughts toward the dragon, but Steel just stared back at him blankly.

Justin frowned. "You can't hear my thoughts, can you?" he shouted.

Steel shook his head and looked around nervously.

"Well, this isn't good," Justin yelled to his grandfather over the chanting and the roaring flames. "I can't communicate with the dragons except out loud."

Grandpa Mac nodded. "Then we'll have to do this old-school. At least your sister listened and didn't get caught in—*this*," he said, waving his weathered hand at the net of fire.

Justin tried to see through the flames but couldn't see anything. "Yeah, but where is she? We could really use her help right about now."

Suddenly the draconians' chanting changed, becoming more urgent, and the dragons instinctively moved away from the flames to huddle tightly together in the center.

Justin unhitched himself from his safety harness and slid down to the ground next to Steel. He took a couple of steps toward the fiery wall, spinning around in a circle to examine the glowing tendrils of flame as they moved and swayed like giant cobras readying to strike. Justin found the motion very hypnotic, almost relaxing. Unconsciously, he began to emulate the fire's movement, feeling the raw energy pulse around him.

"Justin! What in Sam Hill are you doing? Get back on your mount!" Grandpa Mac bellowed, snapping Justin out of his trance. "As soon as we figure out a way through this, we need to move quickly."

"I'm not sure we can pass through the fire alive, sir," Mr. O'Faron said, scanning all around them. He looked down. "We might be able to go under the ground, though."

Grandpa Mac followed his gaze to the concrete floor. "Worth a shot. Argo, Thunder, Flare, and Steel! Start digging."

Justin watched in awe as Argo made a fist and punched

down hard into the slab, cracking it. Thunder followed with another strike, causing a big chunk of the floor to tilt upward. Together, Steel and Flare grabbed the loose piece and hauled it out of the ground.

Argo looked at the concrete slab, the size of a refrigerator, for a moment, gripping it with all his foreclaws, then launched it at the nearest draconians.

They didn't even flinch. As soon as the huge chunk of the floor came in contact with the flaming net, it instantly vaporized.

Grandpa Mac patted Argo on the shoulder. "Nice thought, old friend. Now keep digging!" he shouted.

The chanting intensified, and Justin began to feel dizzy. Then suddenly a sharp pain erupted in his brain. He grabbed both sides of his head, screaming.

A steadying hand rested on his shoulder. "Are you okay, son?" his grandfather asked.

Justin tried to speak but couldn't find the words. The pressure was too intense. His brain felt as if it were in a vice. The chanting grew louder and louder until Justin could hear nothing else.

But then something deep inside Justin started to push back. Even with his eyes shut tightly, he could still see the interlocking flames swaying and dancing in his mind's eye. He concentrated on that feeling as the fire began to move closer. The circle was shrinking, closing in on them.

"Justin. Can you hear me?" Grandpa Mac asked again, shaking the boy slightly.

Justin nodded, still struggling to form words. "Stay close to Argo. They're tightening the net."

His grandfather looked around. "You're right, it's moving toward us. Wait, where are you going?"

"There isn't a lot of time before this kills us, but I think I can fight back." Justin didn't dare to look at his grandfather before he started walking straight toward the wall of flame, afraid that if he did, he might lose his nerve.

Justin felt a burning sensation on his thigh, and he looked down to see the stone shard his parents had given him before putting him and his sister on the plane, a fragment from some ancient tablet, glowing through his jeans.

A distant voice whispered in his mind, *"You can't fight back. You are not special. You are not important. You are not... her."*

"We'll see who's special," Justin muttered under his breath. He closed his eyes, concentrating on the motion of the flames. He could feel the fire moving, shifting, dancing: it seemed to be alive. When he had unlocked Red's ability to breathe fire, Justin had felt something similar within the dragon, and he reasoned now that if he could feel it, maybe he could control it too.

Justin reached his arms up and drew the fingertips of both hands slowly apart, as if trying to force two of the snaking tendrils to separate with his mind. If he could open a gap wide enough, they could all escape to safety.

But nothing happened.

Justin took a deep breath and tried again, forcing his will to focus on the trap. At first nothing changed, but then the flames flared in intensity. That wasn't what he had wanted to happen, but he knew he had caused the fire to do *something*. Maybe if he tried the opposite gesture, he could get the flames to die down.

Justin threw his arms out toward the fire again, this time bringing his hands together. There was a rushing sound as the flaming tendrils flared in all directions in a massive burst of heat. Justin felt like screaming in frustration.

Nothing seemed to be working. He could still feel the fire, but no matter how hard he tried to control it, the more it would do the opposite of what he intended.

Justin thought back to how Miranda had absorbed the

lightning that two wild blue dragons had shot at her during their attack, when he and his sister were returning Azuria's egg. Somehow, she had managed to redirect the breath weapon back at their assailants. Maybe Justin needed to do something similar now.

Justin focused all his effort on trying to bring the fire *to* him. And at first, it seemed to work. The flames leaped toward him, but at the same time, they expanded outward as well, growing in size and intensity.

The draconians chanted with even more urgency as the wall of flames surged toward them like a circular tidal wave of fire.

Justin could hear their screams of pain as several draconians burst into flames. Not what he had intended, but maybe he could get this to work to his advantage. The draconians' chanting had to be some sort of spell. If he could just keep pushing the flames at the dracs, he was pretty sure he could break the magic. He just needed to try harder.

Justin reached out with his mind, drawing the fire to him again. The more he gathered, the faster the dracs chanted, trying to resist him.

Justin threw all of his will at the net of green fire. The chanting was suddenly replaced with screams of pain from all sides as the fire around him exploded outward, incinerating most of the draconians.

And that's when everything went wrong.

The fire wasn't just moving outward toward their enemies but also collapsing in all around him.

Yelling and shouting drew Justin's attention back to his grandfather. The old man looked terrified, pointing frantically all around the warehouse. The whole place was on fire. Justin felt like throwing up.

There was a screeching sound as several of the steel girders supporting the roof broke away and crashed to the ground nearby. It was only a matter of minutes before the entire ceiling would collapse in on top of them. They needed to get out of the building—*now*.

Justin started sprinting back to his grandfather but skidded to a stop when he realized the hopelessness of their situation. The dragons had formed a protective ring around their human companions in the middle of the inferno, trying to shelter them from the intense heat. And even though the people were safe for the moment, the dragons shielding them were not so lucky. Justin could see the pained expressions on their faces as the out-of-control blaze began to blister their wings and scales.

Oh no! What have I done?

CHAPTER 3

Miranda
Too Much of a Good Thing

"Are you ready?" Miranda asked the timid dragon.

Indigo shook her head emphatically. "*I still don't believe this is the best course of action, Lady... er... Miranda. We should try to free Lord McAdelind first.*"

Miranda surveyed the green inferno blazing out of control and gritted her teeth. She should help the others, but she also needed to stop the dracs before they burned the evidence. "No, we need to keep the draconians from destroying anything else. That is our primary mission, and what Grandpa Mac wants us to do."

"*But if domestic dragons were supposed to use breath weapons, we would be born with the ability to use them on our own. There has to be another way.*"

"If there is, we don't have time to figure it out. It's now or never, and I'm not going to let my family rot in some cell because you're scared." Miranda was a little surprised at how harsh those words came out, but that was how she felt. Her parents and aunt were out there somewhere—imprisoned, hurt, alone, maybe even tortured—she needed to do something.

"Yes, Lady McAdelind," Indigo said, with a mix of shame and defeat.

Miranda felt sorry for putting the young dragon in a situation like this, but she also knew it was the only way. She leaned forward and touched the back of the dragon's neck with both hands, pushing her will into the creature's mind.

Indigo was terrified of everything. Scared of fighting, scared of being outside, scared of being discovered by humans, scared of cattle, and scared of letting Miranda down. Fear clouded every aspect of her life. She wasn't like Storm at all. The older blue was fearless, with only one thought on her mind, to protect the people she loved. But right now Indigo was fighting hard against the desire to run, to escape.

Miranda searched but couldn't even find the spot to access Indigo's latent ability to breathe lightning, and she began to feel frustrated. Everything would be lost if she couldn't figure this out.

Then a thought struck her as she remembered what Justin had told her about Red finding *his* fire. The red dragon, unlike Storm, kept his insecurity buried deep beneath his conscious thoughts, hiding his fears from everyone—even from himself. What if Indigo was the exact opposite, what if the fear that shrouded her was the thing holding her back? On a hunch, Miranda decided to show the dragon a series of memories—but not her own.

"Indigo, I need to show you something," Miranda said and began to remember the vividly detailed experience of sharing Storm's recollections of the night she had lost her beloved mistress, Miranda's aunt Em. She showed Indigo how Storm was so scared that she forgot the plan they were supposed to execute, and how her hesitation had caused her mistress to suffer. Then she showed her the devastating consequences of that decision, how her grandfather had fallen to his knees and cried to the sky for his daughter. Next Miranda remembered the picture of her aunt still alive, followed by the image of Storm breathing lightning on the wyverns, destroying the creatures that had taken Em from her.

Miranda could feel the dragon's fear dissipating, replaced by a single-minded purpose to help. Only then could she feel the mysterious force preventing the dragon from using her breath weapon. Miranda pushed with her will against that force and felt it beginning to crack—but that still wasn't enough.

"Indigo. I can't do this without you. I need your help." She felt the dragon beneath her still holding back.

"I'm scared of what might happen," Indigo said.

"I know, but don't worry. I won't let anything bad happen to you. I promise."

With that, Indigo herself directed everything she had at the inner wall, and it came crashing down.

Miranda opened her eyes in time to see the arcing electricity collect from Indigo's shimmering scales and gather at her head, then explode from her mouth with a deafening thunderclap. Miranda shielded her eyes too late from the blast, and her vision flashed with afterimages of the lightning strike's fractal path.

To Miranda's dismay, the lightning only struck down half of the draconians gathered around the table and the flaming brass urn, leaving the other half safe to redouble their efforts. "They're still destroying everything. We need to hit them again!" Miranda yelled.

Indigo wobbled underneath her. *"I... don't think... I can. I... feel like I'm... going to... pass out."*

Miranda saw the draconians grab something big from the table and begin it drag it over to the urn. "We have to do it now."

Indigo sunk to her knees. *"I'm... too weak... my Lady."*

A feeling of dread crept up Miranda's spine; this could be their only chance of recovering any clue they might need to find the hostages. Then she looked to the right and saw that the massive wall of green flame was moving closer toward the chanting dracs. If she didn't act fast, either the draconians the urn or the expanding ring of fire would destroy everything. She closed her eyes and reached further into the exhausted dragon's mind.

"I'm sorry, Indigo, but we have to try." Miranda exerted all her will at the small spark of energy that remained deep inside the blue dragon.

She felt Indigo begin to panic as the electricity formed, arcing now all around them both. Miranda was amazed to see the glittering sparks dancing over her own body, yet leaving her unharmed, as if she and the dragon were united as one.

"Lady McAdelind... Please stop... I can't do... another blast."

But Miranda continued to wrap the energy around her. She could feel the lightning pulsing with a life of its own.

"I'm... too weak," Indigo pleaded. *"Please... Miranda, stop!"*

Miranda could feel Indigo's fear and exhaustion but knew that one more blast would finish the dracs off completely, and then she could grab what they were trying to destroy. Just when the energy was getting too much for Miranda to contain, she thrust it outward herself, shouting "Now!"

Indigo managed another blast of lightning—not as strong as the first, but enough to knock the remaining draconians gathered around the urn backward into the surging wall of green flames behind them, and vaporizing them instantly.

"We did it!" Miranda yelled and jumped off the dragon's back.

Indigo let out a rattling breath as her eyes rolled back into her head and she slumped unconscious to the ground.

"Indigo?" Miranda whispered and gently touched the dragon's face. Her chest was barely rising and falling with each shallow breath. Miranda had pushed her too hard. She needed to call for help, but there was no one to help her. *What have I done?* she thought.

"Grandpa! Miss D! I need help!" She was looking around for any way to reach the others when her gaze fell back to the brass urn where the dracs had been hurriedly burning things. The out-of-control inferno was rushing toward it. This was it, her only chance; everyone else was trapped. If Miranda didn't get down there now, everything they have done tonight, every sacrifice, would be for nothing.

Miranda hesitated, fearing that if she left the young unconscious dragon helpless in the face of the growing dangers all around, she would be leaving her to certain death. But the mission had to succeed—they needed to get any information there was before it was too late. Miranda made up her mind.

She sprinted down a flight of metal stairs, leaping down the last five steps. When she got to the table, Miranda saw nothing left but an old rolled-up piece of parchment and some ripped-up bits of cardboard lying on it, plus small pieces of wood scattered around the foot of the brass urn containing the unnatural green flames, still licking upward like serpents.

"No!" Miranda screamed. The draconians had been using the cardboard and wood to keep the small fire going, she realized, and the scroll must contain some sort of spell to create the deadly trap. She slammed her fist down on the table, tears of frustration filling her eyes. There had to be more than just this. She looked around the table: nothing. This was their best and only shot at finding any information. Miranda couldn't leave empty-handed. She snatched up the old scroll and jammed it into her pocket. A fire spell was better than nothing and might come in handy sometime in the future. She then sprang over to the nearest crate and jerked the top open. Inside, she saw a bunch of small canisters of propane, like for a camping stove or something. She ran over to another crate; its contents were the same. As her eyes caught sight of the warning label pasted on all of the canisters, she sucked in a quick breath as she read:

DANGER! EXTREMELY FLAMMABLE. FIRE / EXPLOSION HAZARD

Miranda's eyes darted back to the rows of steel industrial shelving that lined the interior walls of the warehouse on all sides. They were stacked with more canisters of propane, piles and piles of them. This was the gas she had smelled. The entire warehouse was the trap. At some point—in mere seconds—the fire would cause a massive explosion as soon as it reached the crates and the shelving, killing everyone, including the dragons.

But Miranda wasn't trapped in the ring of green fire with the others, she realized. The dracs must have been watching, waiting for her to fly in after the rest of her team, and when she didn't, they had no choice but to close the trap around them without her.

Miranda needed to act swiftly to stop the flames. But how?

Spinning around to catch sight of anything she could use, she saw a fire extinguisher not far away hanging from a hook attached to one of the steel pillars that held up the roof. She grabbed it, unclipped the nozzle, and pressed the trigger hard, spraying a jet of white foam at the wall of flames moving ever closer to the crates of propane. But nothing happened: the foam simply vaporized, like everything else the fire touched. "It has to be some form of magic," Miranda muttered to herself, staring up at the cage made of green fire.

She turned to the brass urn. "Definitely magic," she whispered, racing over to the urn and covering it with thick white spray.

As soon as the foam snuffed out the fire in the urn, the entire torrent of flames behind her vanished instantly with a whooshing sound. Well, that was one disaster evaded. But the feeling of victory disappeared instantly when the whine of thick metal bending past its breaking point drew Miranda's attention to the warehouse roof, ablaze with red, orange, and white flames—normal fire, not magical fire. They had to get out of there before a section of the crumbling ceiling collapsed on the propane canisters and set off a deadly chain-reaction.

Miranda ran over to the circle of dragons, all curled together to protect their human companions. "Grandpa! We need to get out of here, now. There are propane gas canisters all over the warehouse. If those flames hit just one, we'll all be goners for sure."

Her grandfather nodded grimly and said, "Mount up. Let's move."

Miranda looked back over to where Indigo was lying still on the scaffolding, and her heart sank. "Oh no." She motioned to Miss Ddraig. "Miss D! I need your help. Indigo is hurt."

The dragon trainer looked to where Miranda was pointing, then motioned for Flare. "Climb aboard," Miss D said, hauling herself up into the saddle.

Miranda scrambled up and scrunched in behind Miss D. *Fortunately, this will be a short hop*, she thought, wrapping her arms tightly around the trainer. And after a few flaps of

Flare's massive wings, the two were soon springing down from the dragon's back as she perched at the edge of the scaffolding, gently sniffing Indigo.

"What did those dirty dracs do to our little girl?" Miss D exclaimed.

"It was the lightning," Miranda said, not wanting to let the dragon trainer know Indigo was like this because she herself had pushed her too hard.

While Miss D checked the young blue's vitals, Miranda knelt down next to Indigo's head, stroking her cold cheek. "I'm so sorry," she whispered.

"She's alive, but barely." Miss D said, and whistled to Flare. "Okay, girl. We need to get this one up an' out of here, right quick. Do you think you can manage?"

Flare nodded. *"I can do it, Gwen, I can. You just wait an' see."* The petite red dragon grabbed Indigo gently but firmly around her neck and the base of her tail with her forepaws and held her tightly. Flare looked up at the ever-widening hole in the roof and with a mighty leap sprang into the air, carrying the unconscious juvenile dragon to safety.

Miss D grabbed Miranda by the arm, and together they raced down the steel staircase inside the scaffolding to where the others were anxiously awaiting their return.

Justin was already up on Steel, a look of deep shame on his face. What could he have possibly done? *It's not like he almost killed a dragon that trusted him*, Miranda thought ruefully.

Miranda reached up and grabbed Justin's hand, and he helped her swing up behind him into the saddle. It was only then that she noticed the burns covering one side of the young dragon's back. She looked around at the other dragons. Thunder and Argo had similar wounds. "What happened to the dragons?"

"I… happened," Justin said, and his voice broke slightly. He touched Steel gently on the back, making the dragon flinch and flooding Miranda with a wave of intense empathetic pain.

The young blue dragon launched them into the air, and with every beat of his wings Miranda could feel his pain renewed. When they finally cleared the roof of the warehouse, Miranda saw that her grandfather had joined Mr. O'Faron on Thunder, and Flare and Miss D had secured Indigo on Argo's broad back. Next to the massive gold dragon, Indigo looked so… fragile.

The dragons cleared the burning warehouse mere seconds before it exploded in a massive fireball. The hot blast of the shockwave buffeted them around as they made their way back into the protective safety of the clouds.

"That was way too close," Justin said, then motioned to Indigo. "Will she be all right?"

"I don't know," Miranda said. But her thoughts weren't with the injured dragon—all her attention was focused on the burning warehouse. Their one lead had quite literally just gone up in flames. She wanted to scream as guilt and rage flooded into her heart.

She had failed.

CHAPTER 4

JUSTIN
Not Far From the Tree

JUSTIN FOLLOWED THE SLOW PROCESSION of wounded dragons into the Warren. Each plodding step they took sent waves of their pain through his mind. Part of him wished he could shut it out, make the pain go away, not only for himself but also for all of the dragons he had inadvertently hurt. But a bigger part of him felt his own suffering was just what he deserved for losing control of the fire. He had been so caught up in the fact that he could feel the flames, it had seemed a foregone conclusion that controlling the fire would come just as naturally to him. And he couldn't have been more wrong.

Justin looked over at his sister as she walked anxiously behind Argo's lumbering form. The massive gold dragon was laboring under the added weight from the still unconscious Indigo, who was strapped securely to his back with silvery ropes. Justin knew his sister blamed herself for what had happened to the young dragon, but he also knew she had done what she could to save them all.

Justin walked faster to catch up to Miranda. "I know you're blaming yourself, sis, but it's not your fault. The dragons get exhausted when they use breath weapons; we learned this the hard way. Indigo was probably just too young."

Miranda didn't turn to look at him but nodded slightly in acknowledgement.

"At least you didn't screw up like I did. You came and saved us. You're a hero—."

Miranda spun on him, an angry look in her eyes. "I am no *hero*. I failed. The trail to our kidnapped family members ended in a trap," she said and turned her focus back to the injured dragon.

"You really know how to talk to the ladies," a deep smoky voice said from the shadowy mouth of a corridor they were passing on their left.

Justin stopped, letting the other humans and dragons get farther down the hall before he turned to Red. "First of all… that's not a lady, that's my sister. And second, she did save all of us."

Red tilted his head. *"Saved you from what? What happened?"*

Justin averted his eyes. "Mainly she saved everyone from me. It was a trap. The dracs were waiting for us. There were about a hundred of them around us in a circle, chanting. Then a net, or web, of green flames spread over us. Well, most of us. Miranda and Indigo didn't get caught." He looked down at his hands. "I could feel the fire, Red. I mean, inside me somehow. Like it was alive, but when I tried to push it back away from all of us, I made it grow and spread in all directions. The dracs got incinerated, but I couldn't control it. I set the warehouse on fire and almost got everyone killed."

"What is up with you and fire, kid?"

"It's not a joke. I hurt the dragons. Burned them. They're in a lot of pain, because of me."

Red stepped gingerly over to Justin. He was still healing

from their fight with the wyverns and dracs only the day before. *"Well, at least you didn't crash any of the dragons into something. That's quite an improvement from your usual tactics."*

Justin tried to stay mad, but a smile forced its way to his lips. "It's not funny. The dragons are the only reason that Grandpa, Mr. O'Faron and Miss D are still alive. They used their bodies as shields. I... I hurt them."

Red shrugged. *"Or saved them. You got rid of all those draconians in one move. Remember yesterday, when we had trouble with just one? That seems like a good thing to me."*

"But—"

"But nothing. Fighting's a messy business. You can't come out untouched. Even when you win. And yes, sometimes you get hurt." He tapped Justin on the shoulder with one massive front claw, almost sending the boy to the floor. *"But we're warriors, remember. Take no prisoner cowboy-dudes. We take the good with the bad, because it all comes with that title. And it's only going to get harder, kid. Do you think this is the worst Tiamat is going to throw at us? Not even close. We can't lose focus. We've got to keep on going."*

Justin remembered the image he had seen of Tiamat, the huge and terrifying serpent goddess, depicted in a mosaic in a hidden chamber that he, Miranda, and Grandpa Mac had discovered above the trophy room. He shuddered. Then he looked the big red dragon in the eyes for a moment and nodded. "Okay. What do we do now, heroic warrior-dude?"

"First. I need you to come with me. We have a little problem I need you to solve before we do anything else."

"What is it?" Justin asked, curiosity overriding his guilt.

Red frowned. *"You'll see. Come on. It's in my lair."*

* * *

Justin was staring at a large steel door at the end of one of the long halls in the massive underground complex. There was nothing remarkable or unique about this particular door, save for the fact it was painted bright red, and supposedly belonged to a dragon renowned for never staying in his lair. But it wasn't until Justin unlocked Red's ability to breathe fire that he had understood why the dragon never wanted to stay inside his cavelike home. When Red was nothing more than a juvenile, Justin's father had left in search of his missing sister, Justin's aunt Em, leaving the young dragon all alone and feeling abandoned. Somehow, being inside his lair had made the dragon anxious ever since.

"You're actually staying in here now? Why?"

"*My reason for keeping away from this place doesn't matter any longer. I have a part of my human family back,*" he said, bowing his head slightly toward Justin. "*But the lair isn't what I wanted you to see. It's what's inside that I need your help with.*"

Justin walked over to the door, slid it back a crack, and peered inside. The lair was a little larger than the others he had seen, and quite a bit warmer. Not seeing anything he should be worried about, Justin pulled the door all the way open and walked inside. The room shimmered beneath the soft lighting cast by recessed fixtures spaced evenly all around the outside edge of the ceiling, a glow that reflected off the surface of a small pool in the center of the room. Off to one side was a large mound of fine gravel.

Red stalked in silently behind Justin and whispered, "*Hmmm. That's odd. She was just here—*"

Justin felt the presence of another dragon only a second before it tackled him to the ground. He rolled over and was quickly crab-walking away as fast as he could when the dragon pounced again, pinning him to the cool stone floor.

A small blue-scaled face appeared in front of him and

cocked its head to one side. *"Dada!"* it said enthusiastically in Justin's mind and started to nuzzle into him hard, scraping his side with its sharp stubby horns. *"Dada..."* it cooed again, resting its head on Justin's lap.

Justin looked up at Red for help, but the big dragon was just letting out a series of short, weird-sounding hisses Justin had not heard a dragon make before. He looked at Red quizzically. "Are you... laughing?" he asked. "It's *not* funny. What's going on?"

"Don't you know, Dada?" Red said, laughing again.

The small blue dragon spun around as if noticing Red for the first time and leapt up at him to nuzzle his massive leg. *"Mama!"* it said, cooing again. Red almost fell over backward trying to get away from the over-affectionate baby dragon.

"Oh my gosh. Is this the wyrmling we saved in Denver?" Now it was Justin's turn to laugh. He stood up, dusted himself off, and walked over to the young dragon. "What's she doing here? I thought she was down in the nursery."

Red was trying unsuccessfully to unwrap the clingy little beast from his leg. *"She's supposed to be, but she keeps breaking out and sneaking in here. We dragons have an exceptional sense of smell, of course, and lucky me, this little worm remembered my scent."*

"And she thinks you're her mommy. That is priceless. I really wish I had a video of this touching moment."

"Yeah, keep laughing, Dada. She needs to go," Red said. *"I finally decide to settle in for some well-deserved rest, and I can't sleep more than a couple of minutes without her jumping on me, or biting my tail."* He unfurled one massive paw to gently pin the squirming wyrmling to the ground. *"I think she'll listen to you, so I need you to throw some of those dragon-whisperer thoughts into her head, and tell the infant she needs to stay in the nursery."*

Justin pushed Red's paw off the small dragon and started

scratching her under her chin. "Mean old Mommy wants you to leave," Justin said in a cute baby-talk voice. "But I think Mommy has been alone for so long, having a companion to keep her company is really the best idea. Yes, I do."

"*Are you going to talk to her, or what? If you don't solve this soon, I'm going to have to eat her.*"

Justin continued to ignore the older dragon. "She needs a name. Oh! How about *Redamina,* after Mommy."

Red flopped down on the ground and sighed. "*Or we can call her Idiot, after Daddy. Redamina isn't even a real name. Come on, man. I need sleep. She's a sneaky little thing, always creeping up and pouncing on me. Do you know how much it stinks being scared awake?*"

Justin snapped his fingers. "That's it. Red, you're a genius. We'll call her Bloo. B-L-O-O. Get it? We combine Blue with *Boo!*: Bloo."

Red covered his eyes with his front paws. "*You are definitely your father's son. That's a* terrible *name.*"

"Okay, *Red,*" Justin quipped.

"*My point exactly. Now are you going to help me or not?*"

Justin closed his eyes and sent reassuring thoughts to the young dragon. About her being safe nearby, about letting Red get some rest so he could get better quickly; then he ended with an image of Red playing a game of chase with her. Bloo bounced around excitedly. "Come on girl, let's get out of here and let grumpy old Mama get some rest."

Red sighed. "*Thank you.*"

"As a matter of fact, let's get you settled in *right* next door to Mama in one of these cozy empty lairs! You can have your own crib, and visit whenever you like!"

"*I hate you. You know that, right?*"

CHAPTER 5

MIRANDA
Tempest

MIRANDA ROLLED OVER and looked at the clock on her nightstand: 12:40 p.m. She hugged her pillow tightly, not wanting to get out of bed just yet. She had stayed in the Warren through the night, sitting up next to the unconscious Indigo.

In the subterranean complex, you could lose any sense of day and night. Most of the time, the lights were dimmed at sunset and came back on full at sunrise. But the night before, in the examination room, the lights had stayed on as Miss D, Mr. O'Faron, and Grandpa Mac had cleaned the burned dragons' wounds and tried everything they could think of to wake the comatose blue.

At some time around five in the morning, her grandfather had ordered Miranda back home to get some rest. She had protested, maybe even yelled a little, but in the end, she had relented and gone to bed. Miranda felt convinced there was no way she could fall asleep feeling this angry, but now it appeared she had been wrong about that as well. The last thing she had wanted to do was get anyone hurt, but she needed answers. She had to find something, anything, even just one clue that would lead to finding her parents and her aunt.

Well, I'm not going to find anything in my bedroom, Miranda thought and slid out of bed. After a quick shower, she got dressed, grabbed the package her parents had sent to her and Justin, and headed downstairs to snatch some food before going to the Warren. She thought maybe she could find something that might lead somewhere either in the documents her parents had sent or in Mr. O'Faron's secret room, where she and Justin had discovered a kind of homemade memorial shrine to Aunt Em.

When Miranda walked through the swinging door into the kitchen, she almost ran straight into Mrs. Lóng. The strange cook was just smiling at her with a baseball bat in her hands.

Miranda jumped back quickly. "Okay, you're being creepy again."

Mrs. Lóng laughed merrily. "Oh, my dear child. This is nothing," she said and in an instant her smile had disappeared and she was staring menacingly at Miranda, swinging the bat down repeatedly and smacking it into her open palm.

This is it, Miranda said inwardly, the old lady has finally lost her mind for good. Miranda was getting ready to run for it when Mrs. Lóng started laughing again. "Calm yourself, dear, I am only teasing. The bat is your brother's. I was just about to take it up to his room."

Miranda pushed past Mrs. Lóng to get to the pantry. As she grabbed a couple of trail-mix bars and a small bag of chips, she said, "You know this whole creepy thing you've got going on really isn't that endearing, and it's not very funny to anyone but yourself." When there was no response, Miranda turned to find the kitchen empty. "Whatever," she said and shut the pantry door. She went to the refrigerator, took a cold bottle of water from it and turned around. Mrs. Lóng was standing there again. Miranda screamed and dropped the water.

Faster than Miranda could even perceive, the old cook reached out and caught the bottle in midair before it touched the ground. "Here you go, dear. Were you saying something?"

Miranda noticed that Mrs. Lóng was no longer holding the bat. She looked around the kitchen for it, but it wasn't anywhere. "Where's the baseball bat you just had?"

Mrs. Lóng shook her head disapprovingly. "Teenagers. So caught up in their inner torment that they don't pay attention to what other people say. I took the bat up to Justin's room. He left it outside last night." Mrs. Lóng snapped her fingers and smiled. "I almost forgot. Your grandfather wants you to check on the wild blue's egg you found alive and see how it's progressing."

"Why me? I don't know anything about dragon eggs or baby dragons."

"Because, dear, wild dragons normally won't let anyone near their young. But you seem to have a special bond with this particular dragon," the old cook said, giving her a sly smile.

Miranda let out a dry laugh. "If you call trying to kill me—twice—a special bond, then I suppose we do."

For weeks, Azuria, the wild blue dragon that had shot lightening at Miranda, had believed that Miranda had stolen her egg. But the thief had been Francisco DeSoto, the former head of security for Thunderbird Ranch, who had used one of Miranda's T-shirts to confuse the dragon's acute sense of smell into thinking she was the culprit.

"I think you know that is not the case. After your performance yesterday, the wilds are either terrified of you or they respect you deeply—probably both. As a matter of fact, I believe you may be the only person in the world who could walk into the wilds' section of the Warren right now and come out alive. Your grandfather is very concerned for the egg's safety and has the utmost faith in you, so get moving."

"Are you sure this isn't just one of your jokes, and as soon as I walk into the wild dragon's corral, all the dragons are going to attack me?"

Mrs. Lóng looked hurt. "No, I wouldn't let harm come to you, you're too important. This is no joke, child. Now be on your way, time is of the essence," she said and shooed Miranda toward the swinging door.

Miranda was getting ready to exit the kitchen when she remembered something. "Wait a minute. How did you get upstairs and back down here so quickly. And Justin doesn't even play baseball." But when she turned around, Mrs. Lóng was nowhere to be seen.

"All right, that's super creepy," she said and looked around the kitchen one more time before shaking her head and heading toward the Warren.

* * *

Miranda placed her hand on a glossy black panel at the entryway to the wild dragons' section of the Warren. A red light scanned up and down her palm once, verifying her identity. The door made several loud clicking noises as a series of magnetic locks disengaged. She pushed open the door, stepped inside, and pulled the door shut behind her. Loud clanking sounds echoed in the cavernous space as the locks reengaged, cutting her off from a quick escape. She felt trapped and alone.

The vast corral, a twin to the one the domestic dragons

use for exercise in their section of the Warren, was empty. *Great.* Miranda had no idea where Azuria's lair was. She had hoped someone would be here, so she could ask how to find the big blue. Miranda could go back and try to find her grandfather, but she didn't want to waste any more time than was absolutely necessary. Her family needed her, and she had to keep searching for clues.

Miranda decided to try finding Azuria with the technique her brother used to sense dragons from a great distance. She closed her eyes and reached out with her mind, imagining her vision spreading out from her like ripples on a pond. At first, she thought it wasn't working, but then she felt something. Anger. Boredom. Hunger. Hopelessness. It was almost overwhelming. But hidden behind all of those powerful feelings was a nervous expectation that made Miranda's stomach twist into knots. She concentrated on that feeling, and as if she were wiping fog from a mirror, all at once she could see the blue dragon's egg in her mind's eye.

Miranda opened her eyes and followed that same nervous feeling through one of the massive archways and down one of the dark, damp halls. As she walked deeper and deeper into the wilds' section, she was hit with a wave of putrid smells and gagged.

"Reeks, doesn't it?" said a familiar voice to her left.

Miranda recognized the speaker as one of the wild dragons that had tried unsuccessfully to shoot her with lightning the last time she entered this section of the Warren. The beast was looming just inside the open door to one of the hall's many lairs. Miranda felt terrifyingly exposed and vulnerable.

As if sensing Miranda's nervousness, the dragon added, "*Do not worry, human, we will not attack you... yet. Azuria is our alpha, and she has... forbidden it.*"

"What is that smell?" Miranda asked, pulling her shirt up over her nose.

Sadness flashed in the dragon's eyes, only to be replaced with something like contempt.

"*That is the smell of captivity, human. We protest our imprisonment. We refuse to let our jailor enter our lairs. However, he does not wish to negotiate our freedoms so that we can come to a compromise. So our conditions remain inadequate.*"

"*And our food is of the lowest standards,*" said another voice from another open lair to the right, which turned out to belong to a wild blue Miranda had not seen before. "*We are a coastal species,*" the beast continued. "*We use our lightning to shock the ocean waters, stunning pods of whales and schools of sharks. Here, they only serve us dirty land creatures to eat.*"

"*We should be free. To fly and hunt as we please,*" said a third who had crept up behind Miranda.

She realized she was surrounded. "You would be discovered in an instant. There are people everywhere," Miranda said, feeling both sad and defensive at the same time. "Trust me, if the rest of the world found out about dragons, you would be a lot worse off."

The dragon to the left chuckled. "*Spoken like a true dragon jailor. You have learned very quickly, dark one. We had hopes when Azuria was spreading tales of a young girl with powers to block lightning and to hear and speak to us that the legends had come true. That after centuries of our confinement, our queen was returning to liberate us. But now we can see you are not the one. We will have to wait longer. But we can feel her. She is coming. And when she rises, we will follow.*"

The hairs on Miranda's neck stood on end. "You're talking about Tiamat."

The dragons stared at her for a long silent moment, then turned and disappeared back into their dark lairs.

Miranda doubled her speed, walking as fast as she could, heading again toward the feeling of nervous anticipation.

She soon came to a closed lair door and knew Azuria lay just on the other side. Miranda took a deep breath to steady her nerves and raised her hand to knock.

"You may come in, human. I could smell you as soon as you entered our realm."

Miranda pulled the door open and stepped inside. The room was darker than she had expected, and it had a strong, stale, animal smell mixed with something like rotting vegetation. The domestic lairs were all clean and well kept by comparison. There was a large pool at the rear of the room and a sparse pile of hay that appeared in the room's dim light to have been smashed flat long ago. Miranda also noticed that the wilds' lairs were equipped with the same automated waste removal system that the domestics used, which Billy referred to as the "potty portal," in one of the far corners.

"My grandfather wanted me to check to see if the egg—I mean, your *child* is okay." Miranda stammered.

Azuria inspected the egg carefully and nodded. *"It should be a matter of seconds now."*

"What do you mean, 'a matter of seconds now'? For what?"

"For my child to emerge, and join this world." Azuria's last words came with a wave of sadness that took Miranda's breath away.

"And that makes you sad, why?" Miranda asked.

"You have seen with your own eyes, human. You can feel the despair, the anger. You can taste the stench of this place on your tongue. Generations of my line have been born here. Born in captivity. Never knowing the salty air on our faces. Never relishing the sweet flesh of the oceans' bountiful prey," she said and sighed. "I grieve for my child. He should not have to live in this... prison... that I was reared in."

"Why is this place in such a state of disrepair? The rest of the Warren isn't this bad."

"When that despicable human, DeSoto, let me out of our section of the Warren to hunt you down, I saw firsthand the additional privileges the mongrel dragons enjoy. It is only right that we be allowed the same degree of freedom. They are allowed to wander the Warren at will, and venture outside on occasion. Why should we endure a lesser fate? In protest, we are not allowing the humans in here until our conditions are met. We are not meant to live underground like this," Azuria concluded proudly.

"But my grandfather can't dragonspeak. How was he supposed to even know you wanted to negotiate?"

"*He understood well enough to send you, Miranda McAdelind. And now you can take our message back to him. We demand more freedoms.*"

"But if you were to go outside, you would be hunted to extinction," Miranda said with conviction. She wasn't sure if that was true, but she had to believe her family was doing the right thing by the dragons.

"*Perhaps. Perhaps not. A place where we can be protected and free must exist in this world.*" She turned her head back to the egg, which moved slightly. Miranda felt that nervous excitement again. "*I never wanted to have a child. Never wanted him to know an existence without freedom. But your family continues to breed us like some common domesticated beast. Always assuring us that our captivity is for our own benefit, to keep our bloodlines strong and healthy. I wanted to believe them, but when I saw that we were being treated worse than their meek little dragon pets, I began to question all their assertions. Now I wonder what I can do to make his life better than mine.*" Sadness spilled from Azuria, hitting Miranda like a wave of cold water.

A cracking sound drew their attention to the egg. Small fissures began to appear up and down its length. A triangular section of shell started to budge as something from the inside pushed outward. Azuria reached up with her razor sharp claws and gently brushed the fragment away. Soon a small head, the size of a full-grown cat's, pushed through the egg's thin membrane. It moved its head from side to side, eyes closed. Azuria continued to brush pieces of the shell away with the utmost care until the baby dragon was free from the egg's confines.

The large blue dragon scooped the baby up in her forepaws and licked him ever so gently clean. *"He's so beautiful,"* she said, and Miranda began to tear up as she felt the pride and love emanating from Azuria.

Miranda walked over closer to the baby to get a better look. He was indeed beautiful, with his bright-blue scales, small but sleek horns, and strong-looking wings tucked back tight against his body. But it wasn't until his eyes opened that Miranda felt something stir deep inside her. His brilliant blue irises, a near match to Miranda's own, looked at her with such wonder. She was connected to this creature. She could feel that now.

"I... I understand, Azuria. I'll talk to my grandfather about all of this and see what I can do. Will you, at least, allow them to come in and clean up a little? Fresh hay and water, washing out the lairs. This would make a much safer environment for him."

Azuria thought about this for a moment and nodded. She held her baby out for Miranda to hold.

Miranda gently reached up and cradled the newborn dragon in her arms. He leaned into her, making a soft cooing sound. Miranda's heart melted.

"He likes you, human. Since you saved my child, I shall allow you to name him."

Miranda looked up in surprise. "Are you sure?"

Azuria nodded.

Miranda considered this; she didn't want to be too cheesy,

he deserved better than that. Something to do with the ocean. Something that promised a fresh start. Something powerful and unpredictable. "How about… Tempest?"

Azuria inclined her head to Miranda. *"A fair name, even if it is a human name. Let it herald the return of lost freedoms, and a better life for my son."*

Miranda looked down at Tempest and his eyes met hers. Right then, she made a silent vow to make his life a better one. One day he *would* be free.

CHAPTER 6

MIRANDA
Dream Walking

MIRANDA TEETERED ON THE EDGE *of a cliff overlooking a cavern so vast, its walls and ceiling disappeared into infinite darkness. Hundreds, maybe thousands, of dragons swarmed high above her. The chamber below seemed alive, pulsing to a steady rhythm, as if the heart of the earth itself throbbed beneath it. But as she looked closer, Miranda realized it was not the floor that was moving, but thousands of robed figures chanting and swaying as one. She recognized this place instantly as the cave from the nightmare she and Justin had shared before they came to Colorado.*

Ugh, *she thought.* Not again. *She tried to move, to take control of her dream self, but she couldn't.*

She descended a steep stone staircase to the floor below and approached an ornately carved altar. And just as before, there was the long curved knife and three cracked stone tablets lying on it. The same scaly hand reached out and placed the one missing piece into the gap on one of the tablets, and instantly they all began to glow, causing the cracks to disappear entirely.

Miranda's gaze traveled past the altar to a wall of green flames erupting from a rift in the cavern floor. Black smoke swirled and began to take shape. Her heart started to race. Now she knew who this was, and it terrified her. Then the earth shook with Tiamat's deep, menacing laughter. She felt panic surge through her, but no matter how hard she tried to fight, she could not avert her eyes from this vision.

She turned around to face the congregation. They fell silent, their last notes echoing off the chamber's unseen walls. Miranda looked at their partially concealed faces, seeing the scaly heads and lipless mouths hidden in the recesses of their shadowy hoods. Yellow-and-red eyes of the draconian horde staring back at her. She and Justin had fought dozens of these vile creatures with a lot of help and a whole lot of luck. How could they possibly defeat this legion to free their parents and their aunt?

Miranda's field of vision turned to take in the pair of stone pillars where before she had seen her father and her aunt shackled with rusty chains, but this time instead she saw an image of herself—her body slack and her head hanging down, dried blood matted in her hair.

Then, out of the corner of her eye, she spotted movement, and a wave of nausea washed over her. Miranda felt herself in two places at once. She had felt this sensation a couple of times before: when Storm had showed her the visions of what had happened the night Em was abducted, when she touched the stone shard in Justin's room, and the last time she had had this same dream vision in their apartment in New York.

Miranda turned her head and realized she was once again in control of her body. Standing next to her was Aunt Em. She looked exactly like the woman in the photograph Mr. O'Faron had recently gotten from a draconian. Maybe a little thinner, and with even darker circles under her eyes, but she was the same defiant woman Miranda had come to admire.

The woman gaped at Miranda, her blue eyes shining with hope. "Am I imagining you?" Em asked.

"I'm here, Aunt Em," Miranda said, her voice sounding strangely distant to her own ears.

Her aunt's eyes began to well with tears. "It worked!" she cried and ran to Miranda. Em reached out her hands, then stopped, seeming afraid that if she made physical contact, this illusion would end.

But Miranda threw caution to the wind and hugged her aunt fiercely. Em was warm and real, and Miranda could feel her heart racing. Her aunt's body began to shake as it was racked with sobs.

Em pulled back and regarded her lovingly. "You're the first person I've touched in so many years." She wiped her eyes with the back of her hands. "We don't have a lot of time. If you're seeing me, that means a draconian is dangerously close to you right now."

"I did what you asked me to do. I went to Storm. She is herself again. And now Grandpa... I mean, your dad, knows you are alive and is trying everything he can to find you—"

"Don't worry about me. I'm not important. You are. The last time they used me to locate your father, he was able to send me a simple message—"

"Where are they? Are they prisoners?" Miranda asked.

Em shook her head. "I don't know. Robin was in a cavern or something, but not here. It was someplace near an ocean."

Miranda's heart sank. She had held out hope that her parents were either on their way to help her, or they were with Aunt Em. This was worse. If the draconians didn't know where her parents were, that meant they weren't prisoners like Em either. Miranda's mother and father must be just off doing whatever it was they did all the time. They had abandoned their children—again. She couldn't let Justin know, it would break his heart.

"Well, that's just great," Miranda said, surprised by how angry she felt. "Hold tight. We're coming for you,"

"You can't!" her aunt said urgently. "Not right now at least." She reached up and put her hands on Miranda's shoulders. "Finding your parents and me isn't the plan. You need to listen—" She suddenly grabbed the sides of her head and fell to her knees in agony. Miranda could see blood flowing from her ears.

"What's wrong? What's happening to you?" Miranda knelt down to help, but her hands just went right through Em, as if she were a ghost.

"They are using me to pinpoint your exact location. You are the person they seek, Miranda. Not me, or your parents. You need to keep on this path. They won't be able to locate you through magic if you can get the spear—" She cried out in pain.

"Em!" Miranda screamed. "Tell me how to find you. I'll rescue you. We'll all rescue you."

Em shook her head emphatically. "There isn't... time. Your parents need you... to go to your... grandfather."

Miranda nodded. "I'm with him now. He's using every resource at his disposal to find you—"

"No. Your other grandfather. Kaya's father. The trail continues... there."

"Trail to what? To you? To Mom and Dad?" Miranda felt a sudden tightness, as if the world around her were collapsing in on itself.

Em squeezed her eyes closed tightly, whispering, "To your destiny. You must face... Tiamat." Then her eyes flew open, and she yelled. "Miranda! Wake up! They've found you!"

Miranda's eyes shot open. Standing above her, mere inches away—a cloth wadded up in its scaly claws—was a draconian.

Miranda screamed and kicked with all her might at the lizard-man. It stumbled back, and she rolled out of her bed in the opposite direction from her assailant. But now she was trapped between her bed and the wall opposite the bedroom door.

"Grandpa! Justin! Help!" she screamed.

The draconian hissed and lunged at her. Miranda could sense the move a fraction of a second before, and dodged to the side.

She heard heavy footfalls rushing in her direction.

The draconian jumped up onto the bed and was getting ready to leap when Miranda's bedroom door flew open, and her grandfather raced in, gripping his massive silver sword in both hands, charging at the intruder.

The drac turned just in time to see the sword flash in a blurring arc—severing its head from its body, and sending a spray of bright, dark-red blood shooting across Miranda and the ceiling, walls, and floor of her room. Miranda shrieked.

"Are you hurt?" her grandpa asked, breathing heavily.

Miranda stood on shaky legs, trying in vain to wipe her assailant's blood off her face and arms with a shirt she had plucked off the ground. "I... *Yuck!* I'm fine."

Her grandfather bent down, grabbed the cloth from the draconian's lifeless hand and smelled it. He pulled it away from his face quickly. "Chloroform. He was trying to knock you out. Probably to abduct you."

Miranda's throat tightened. A close call—too close. A second later and she would have been on her way to that cave she had seen in her dreams.

From down the hall, she heard sounds of a struggle. Her grandfather's face fell. "Justin!"

They turned and sprinted from Miranda's room. When they reached Justin's open door, they found him leaping from left to right on his bed, dodging thrusts of a draconian's knife and—laughing.

"Is that the best you've got?" he goaded his assailant while using his baseball bat like a sword, blocking and countering every attack the filthy creature threw at him.

The drac brought the knife down in what should have been a killing blow, but Justin, anticipating the motion, swung the bat up and shattered its wrist. The draconian cried out in pain and dropped the knife.

Justin flashed a smile at Miranda and their grandfather. "Hey, guys. Look what I found in my room."

The draconian pivoted and glared at Miranda. She could see a mix of fear and hatred in its eyes—could see that it was caught between a desire to flee and to kill.

There was a loud thud as Justin smacked the creature hard on the head from behind with the baseball bat. The drac's eyes crossed as it crumpled to the ground, unconscious.

Justin jumped down from his bed. "Did you guys see that? I was all over the place. That creep couldn't even come close," he said and hopped back, still wielding the bat like a sword, blocking and lunging at an imaginary enemy. Then he stopped and frowned. "But I guess it's not very fair when I can see every move they're going to make before they make it." He shrugged. "Oh well, I'll take *that* unfair fight every day of the week." He held the bat up and looked at it. "Good thing someone left this little baby in my room. I probably would have been dead without it, and it allowed us to take a prisoner. Did you put it in here, sis?"

Miranda felt the hairs on her neck stand on end. Mrs. Lóng had placed the bat in Justin's room earlier that day—as if she had known what was going to happen. "No, but I know who did—"

Just then the cook was at the door. "Is everyone all right? Oh dear, what do we have here?" she asked, looking horrified at the motionless draconian on the floor, swooning slightly, like she was going to faint.

"Ying. Call William. We need him here now," Grandpa Mac ordered as he quickly bound the draconian's hands together with a sweatshirt he pulled from Justin's closet.

Mrs. Lóng swallowed hard and looked pale, but Miranda wasn't buying the act for a second. The old woman knew far more than she let on.

"Yes, Mac. I'll call him at once," she said and left the room.

Their grandfather moved Miranda and her brother into the hallway. "Are you two all right? They didn't harm you, did they?"

Justin smiled. "It didn't even come close to touching me." Then his eyes shot to Miranda. "Wait. There was one of these creeps in your room too?"

Miranda nodded. "He was holding a cloth over my face when I woke up. I screamed for Grandpa, and he cut its head off."

Justin whistled. "Cool. Can I have a sword too?"

Grandpa Mac stepped outside Justin's bedroom to look back down the hall toward Miranda's room. "We'll see, son."

He reached up and stroked his thick gray mustache, lost in thought. "The one in Miranda's room must have been aiming at capturing her. But that one there," he said, pointing the great sword at it the drac Justin had knocked out, "was trying to kill you."

Justin frowned. "Yeah. That seems to be their strategy. Capture people named Miranda, kill everyone else. But why?"

Grandpa Mac stepped back inside Justin's room. "That's what we're going to ask him," he said and gave the drac a kick in the side.

"The last time we tried to interrogate a draconian, it didn't go so well," Miranda said, remembering the drac she and her brother had bested, which had somehow incinerated itself before their eyes.

"They do seem to have a tendency to burst into flames," Justin added.

Miranda snapped her fingers. "I've got an idea. Grandpa, do you think you can carry that no-good lizard into the bathroom?"

CHAPTER 7

JUSTIN
Twenty Questions in a Tub

JUSTIN HAD TO ADMIT that Miranda's idea of keeping the draconian from bursting into flames was elegant in its simplicity; throw the filthy lizard into a bathtub full of ice-cold water. He also had to admit that even the largest bathroom seems tiny when you have half a dozen people crammed into it. In addition to Justin, Miranda, and their prisoner, there were also Grandpa Mac, Mr. O'Faron, his son, Billy, Miss D—and, standing close to the door, looking like she was getting ready to hurl at any moment, Mrs. Lóng. Everyone's eyes were laser-focused on one thing: the submerged draconian in the tub.

"Are you sure this will work?" Billy asked, looking skeptically at the unconscious creature. His arm was still in a sling from the fight, when Justin had hit him with a can of bear mace and hyperextended his elbow. But in Justin's defense, that was when he had still thought the older boy was the thief stealing gold and dragon eggs from their family.

Miranda shrugged. "I imagine having a dozen fire

extinguishers would be better, but we only have this one from the kitchen," she said, holding up the small red canister Mrs. Lóng kept stored under the sink. "The rest are in the Warren, and we don't have time to get there and back before the drac regains consciousness."

"I say we go for it, and wake him up," Justin said. "Don't get me wrong, I love staying up all night with you guys, but standing around for hours staring at a bound lizard-man, up to his neck in water, is kind of weird, even for our family."

"Fair point, son. Everyone ready?" Grandpa Mac asked.

When they all nodded, Mr. O'Faron walked over to the edge of the tub and slapped the draconian lightly on the face. Nothing happened. He tried a little harder, but still nothing. "You did quite a number on him, Justin. Any other ideas on how to wake him?"

Justin stepped closer, but his grandfather held out his arm, barring him from touching the draconian. "That's close enough, son. This one was aiming to kill you less than an hour ago. I don't want you within arm's reach of this varmint."

"I know how to wake him up. And don't worry Grandpa, he can't hurt me," Justin said, more confidently then he felt, and gently pushed his grandfather's arm down. He walked over to the edge of the tub and placed a hand on the lizard-man's head. A shiver shot down his spine, and he had to focus hard on not withdrawing away from the creepy creature. Its fine scales felt like snakeskin, smooth and dry, not at all slimy, and his skin felt hot, almost feverish. Warm-blooded, like the dragons'. *That makes sense,* Justin thought. *Otherwise they'd be vulnerable at night and underground.* But that wasn't what was so unnerving about touching the draconian's skin, it was the fact he was this close to something that had tried to murder him in his sleep less than thirty minutes before.

Justin closed his eyes and pushed out with his mind until he felt it connect with some part of the draconian's consciousness, then he mentally shouted into its brain, "*Wake up!*"

The drac's eyes shot open. It tried to pull away from Justin's touch, but it only succeeded in splashing around, sending water sloshing in small waves onto the floor.

It looked around wide-eyed at the people clustered in the small room. It opened its mouth, showing rows of razor-sharp teeth, and hissed, "Let me go immediately. We only want the girl and the tablet fragment. Give us what we seek, and everyone else may live for a while longer."

"No deal," Grandpa Mac said, pointing his great sword at the drac's chest. "You're in no position to negotiate, lizard. However, give us some information, and we might let *you* live—for a while longer. It's in your best interest to start talking, and talking quickly. Let's start with why you were trying to abduct my granddaughter."

A flood of familiar images hit Justin: his sister chained to the pillars, the cracked stone tablet, the shadowy creature rising out of the flames. "Yeah, yeah, you guys keep thinking about that one scene over and over again. It's like a bad music video stuck in your mind or something. But why do you want her? What does Miranda have to do with Tiamat?"

The draconian thrashed side to side angrily. "Do not speak my queen's name, human! Your unworthy species does not have the right."

"My unworthy species has you tied up and our prisoner," Justin snapped through gritted teeth. "You need to start talking and talking quickly. What does *Tiamat* want with my sister?"

The draconian hissed again and tried to lunge up at Justin, but Mr. O'Faron jammed his hands on its head, pinning it down in the water. The creature glared at Justin for a moment before yelling at the top of his lungs. "Take me now, my queen!"

Suddenly, Justin felt a burning sensation in his leg and looked down to see the stone shard glowing brightly in his pocket.

The draconian's eyes became as wide as saucers, and it hissed out triumphantly, "You have the shard? We are so close. My queen will rise and feed on this world, making it anew."

Justin's mind was suddenly filled with the image of a monstrous dragon-like shape moving across the earth, leveling cities, devouring humans, and leading an army of monstrous creatures in her wake. His head started to pound as the apocalyptic vision began to overwhelm him. He opened his eyes again and saw the draconian grinning wickedly.

Justin felt a rage he didn't even know was possible surge to life and he sprang at the smirking captive, hands outstretched to close around its scrawny neck and choke the life from it.

His grandfather caught Justin in midair. "Easy, son. Simmer down now. We won't get any answers if we let this no good cave crawler get the better of us."

"You don't understand! They're going to destroy the world! All of it! They have to be stopped!" Justin spat, struggling to get free.

The draconian made that weird hissing cackle Justin recognized as its hideous laughter. "It's too late, human. Too late for all of you. Where my kind, the umū dabrūtu, have failed, Ugallu and Lahmu will succeed. Even now they come for you. The sky and the earth itself move against you. You are doomed. Doomed!"

"Okay. Enough of this crap," Miranda said. "Where is our aunt Em? Tell me, now."

The draconian became deadly serious as it whispered, "No need to worry, you will see her soon enough—*Miranda.*" Justin flinched, hearing his sister's name uttered in a well-practiced, menacing purr. "It is your destiny to liberate the Dark Queen from her prison. It is only a matter of time."

The pain in Justin's leg intensified, followed instantly by a mind-splitting headache. He grabbed the sides of his head, fearing it might break open at any second, overwhelmed by a vision of Miranda suspended by chains between the two stone pillars they had seen in their shared nightmares, some kind of bluish energy pouring out of her, and feeding a huge, shadowy creature as it coalesced into something tangible. Miranda slumped forward, completely drained, her head lolling listlessly on her chest. The beast, no longer a shadow, reared up on its back legs, spread its colossal wings wide, and let out a chilling cry of victory.

A scream snapped Justin out of the vision and drew his attention to Mrs. Lóng. The old cook was shaking violently, her hands on the sides of her head, blood trickling from her nose.

"She's... too powerful!" the cook screamed, collapsing to the floor.

Justin felt the pain in his leg radiate outward to the rest of his body. The stone shard was now glowing so brightly that he could even see the cuneiform script right through his jeans.

A deep menacing voice echoed in the small room: *"You have done well, my child. Go in peace."*

"Yes, my queen!" The bath water began to boil. The draconian screamed.

"Move!" Mr. O'Faron shouted, throwing himself at everyone, knocking them all back into the hall.

A thick cloud of steam erupted from the bathroom. Grandpa Mac flung himself on top of Justin and Miranda, protecting them from the blast of superheated water as it shot out toward them.

Fire alarms began to blare throughout the house.

Mr. O'Faron grabbed the fire extinguisher Miranda had somehow managed to keep clutched in one hand and ran back into the bathroom. The shower curtain was on fire, but within a matter of seconds, he had ripped it down and covered it with a thick layer of foam.

He looked at the tub and shook his head. "It's… gone."

Justin stood up shakily and took a step forward on trembling legs. His headache had stopped, and the burning sensation from the shard had subsided, but he felt very weak. Miranda helped steady him as they both stumbled back into the bathroom. The curtain was a charred mess, black smoke hung heavy in the air, there was the pungent smell of burned meat, and all that remained in the bathtub of their draconian prisoner was a ring of ash. "I'm *never* taking a bath in there again," Justin said. "So… What do we do now?"

"First things first. We need to immediately clean up this filthy mess," Mrs. Lóng chimed in, coming up next to them. "It is going to take a week just to get those stains out of the tub."

"Are you… okay?" Justin asked. There wasn't any sign of the cook's bloody nose, and she looked as spry and unblemished as always.

"Yes, dear. Just a slight headache, that's all, but it passed," she said nonchalantly.

Grandpa Mac inspected the remains of the draconian and frowned. "This place isn't safe for you two any longer. We need to get you both out of here. Especially if there are other creatures coming after you, and we have no reason to doubt that there aren't." He motioned for all of them to move back into the hall, where there was more room and way less stinky air. "William, do you know anything about the names that pile of dust mentioned before going nuclear on us?"

Mr. O'Faron nodded. "According to legend, Ugallu's a sky demon and one of the eleven kinds of monsters Tiamat created to do battle against Marduk—"

"Eleven?" Miranda interrupted. "You've got to be kidding me."

"According to the notes Mom and Dad sent to us, draconians, wyverns, and dragons are just three of the types of creatures Tiamat made," Justin chimed in.

"But why did she make monsters in the first place?" Miranda asked.

"She wanted revenge for the death of her husband," Mr. O'Faron said. "All the other gods were terrified of her—"

"I can see why," Justin interjected.

Mr. O'Faron nodded. "But Marduk alone stood against her, defeating Tiamat in combat, and either vanquished the gods and monsters that had sided with her or used them to assist humanity."

"What about the other name it mentioned?" Grandpa Mac asked.

Mr. O'Faron nodded. "Lahmu is a name shared by two beings. The first was one of the primordial gods, the other was one of Tiamat's monsters. I'd have to imagine neither would be nice if they were indeed real."

"I think at this point we have to assume they are very real, very powerful, and very much heading this way," Grandpa Mac said. "But where can we hide the kids to keep them safe from such demons? Maybe if we hit the sky and keep moving, stay ahead of them, we can buy some time until we have a real plan."

Miranda shook her head. "No. We can't do that, Grandpa. We would just be placing all of you in danger." She paused and shot Justin a look that said, *Trust me,* then added, "The only place we will be safe now is with our other grandfather."

"What?" Grandpa Mac sputtered out, looking as if he had just been punched in the gut. "Where in Sam Hill did you get that crazy idea? I can protect you just as well as *he* ever could."

"I got that crazy idea from Em. She told me to go to him," Miranda said. "Right before the draconians attacked us, I had another vision—Em reached out to me again. They were using her to find me, and I think they inadvertently opened a connection between the two of us. She didn't have time to say much, other than that Justin and I need to go with our mom's father."

"How… how is she?" Mr. O'Faron asked.

"She's a fighter, and she's alive."

"Are Mom and Dad with her?" Justin asked hopefully.

A flash of anger seemed to darken Miranda's face, and she looked away. "I… I don't know. She was alone. If we're going to save her, we can't keep on having every lead literally explode in our faces. Em said the trail to… " Miranda hesitated for a moment, and Justin realized there was more she wasn't sharing. "To rescuing her starts with our other grandfather. Please, Grandpa, time is of the essence, we have to go."

Their grandfather's face fell, but he nodded. "All right. I'll call him. That will give us a couple of hours to sort all of this out before he gets here—"

Mrs. Lóng cleared her throat. "Actually Mac, I already phoned Paul. He is on his way right now and will be here in less than thirty minutes."

CHAPTER 8

MIRANDA
The Chief

"YOU DID *WHAT*?" Grandpa Mac bellowed. "That's not your call, Ying."

Mrs. Lóng walked over and placed her hand gently on his arm. "Mac, I am fairly sure you know that it is." Grandpa Mac's face shifted from bright red to its natural pink before he closed his eyes and nodded.

Mrs. Lóng turned to Miranda and Justin, her face uncharacteristically somber. "Kids, grab your belongings, you will be departing soon."

"How long should we pack for?" Justin asked.

"Pack light, but as if you might not be returning," Mrs. Lóng said matter-of-factly. Miranda could see the weight of her words hit her brother like a hammer to his chest.

"What is that supposed to mean? Are you saying we won't be coming back to Thunderbird Ranch?" Justin said. "What about Red? I can't just leave him."

Grandpa Mac held up his hand for silence. "Mrs. Lóng doesn't mean to imply that you won't be coming back. That was an unfortunate choice of words," he said, shooting the cook a disapproving look. "We don't know exactly how long this business with these new threats is going to last, so you need to pack for mobility and the long haul, just in case. Trust me. I'll get you two back under my wing as quickly as I can. And I'll make sure to look in on Red and keep him up to date on how you're doing. Now hustle. It's going to be a long night."

Justin lowered his head and trudged into his room, mumbling his disapproval the entire way.

Miranda noticed one more lingering glance shared between her grandfather and the cook just before he stomped off down the stairs to the ranch house's main floor.

Mrs. Lóng smiled at Miranda as she pulled a pair of bright yellow rubber gloves from the front pocket of her apron and pulled them on with a snap. "No time like the present to begin cleaning the bathroom, right, dear?"

Miranda crossed her arms over her chest. "How did you know Justin would need the baseball bat? Are you a witch or something?"

"Don't be silly, my dear. Witches aren't real." Mrs. Lóng giggled before returning to the filthy bathroom, where she began scrubbing the blackened tub vigorously.

Miranda shook her head. What in the world was going on with that woman? Not only had she placed the baseball bat in Justin's room just in time, essentially saving his life, but she had also screamed and fainted when Tiamat caused the draconian to explode. There was something very strange going on with her. And after everything they had been through so far this summer, Miranda still wasn't sure if she could entirely trust Mrs. Lóng.

When Miranda walked back into her room to pack her meager belongings, she almost tumbled over the headless body of her draconian assailant. She fought back gag after gag as she stepped gingerly over the corpse and avoided the still spreading pool of red-black blood to reach her things and begin packing. This is just too gross, she thought. Why didn't Mrs. Lóng start cleaning in here? Or why didn't one of the older men come in and drag the creature's remains out? Miranda glanced back at the body and shivered. Totally disgusting. How in the world was she ever going to sleep in this room again, knowing there had been a dead lizard-man on the floor?

Miranda got a sick feeling in her stomach as the reality of her situation began to set in. Maybe that was the point. Maybe this had been the last night she would ever sleep at Thunderbird Ranch. She clenched her fists. *No. I'll be back,* she thought. *I'm not going to let some stupid monsters stop me from finding my Mom and Dad and Aunt Em, being with Storm and helping the dragons here on the ranch.*

"You aren't going to scare me away," she said, glaring down at the draconian's body. "Nothing is going to stand in my way of freeing Em and bringing her home."

Miranda squatted down and pulled her suitcase out from under the bed. She threw every article of clothing she had brought with her from New York into the worn case, not even bothering to sort through some of the less practical articles. She then grabbed her overstuffed backpack, still loaded with the remnants from her last day of middle school, wadded-up papers and tattered notebooks filled with assignments and doodles from another life. A life when everything had just been... ordinary. A part of her wanted nothing more than to ignore all the craziness and go back home... just for one day... to feel like her old self again. But Miranda knew in her heart of hearts, that couldn't happen, and she had a sinking suspicion that no matter how all of this turned out, there would be no going back to her old life. Ever.

Miranda glanced back down at the draconian's corpse and

sighed. "What I wouldn't give for an ordinary life right now," she said and dumped the contents of her pack out onto the bed.

She reached over to grab the scroll she had taken from the warehouse, and the package her parents had sent them with all their notes—convinced there were clues in both that she just needed the right context to uncover—when she noticed a pair of blue cowboy boots standing by a chair in the corner of the room, with a matching jacket on the chair back, things she hadn't seen before. A golden sticky note was attached to one of the boots that read:

These were your aunt's. She would want you to have them.

The handwriting was most certainly Mrs. Lóng's. Miranda recognized the exaggerated strokes from the continuously updated list of chores the old woman maintained for her and her brother. When had she put them in here? They hadn't been there when Miranda went to bed the night before. *Oh well, that's one more weird thing to add to the ever-growing list of oddities about the strange cook.*

Miranda grabbed the jacket, the boots, and the package and crammed them into her now empty backpack, then picked up her suitcase and stepped over the drac's body on her way out into the hall.

Justin was already there waiting for her. He had his school backpack over his shoulders and his suitcase nearby, and he was wearing a tan cowboy hat and matching jacket that Miranda had also never seen before.

"Check this out," he said, indicating his new apparel. "They were in my closet. There was a note on them saying they were Dad's. Pretty nice, huh?"

"I don't know. It doesn't seem like you've earned the right to wear that hat yet," Miranda said, shaking her head.

Justin had just started to protest when knocking at the front door silenced him.

They listened intently to their grandfather's heavy footfalls as he went to the door and pulled it open.

Miranda cocked her head to one side and could just make out the hushed voices of two men.

"Must be our other grandpa," Justin said and looked around the hall with a sad look in his eyes. "I don't want to leave. Not now. What if this is an even bigger mistake and we are walking right into another trap?"

"Em said this is what we need to do. We'll just need to put our faith in her and hope for the best," Miranda said. "Come on, let's get going."

Justin nodded, grabbed his suitcase, and headed downstairs. Miranda was right behind him as they stepped down into the main hall.

Grandpa Mac was standing in front of the open door, his looming form blocking the other man on the porch from their view. "I don't want to talk about this now," Grandpa Mac growled. "We're never going to see eye to eye."

"Suit yourself, you stubborn old goat," said an equally gruff voice from the porch. "And that's the last time I'll ask."

"Good," Grandpa Mac shot back.

Miranda cleared her throat loudly, making her grandfather turn around, looking suddenly embarrassed.

"Oh… hey there," he said. "Ah, come on over here, kids, and let me introduce you to someone." He stepped aside and motioned for the other man to come in. "This is your grandfather, Chief Pa'na'lulu."

Miranda was a little shocked. The man didn't look old enough to be her grandfather. His hair was jet black, full and pulled back. His skin was slightly darker than either of theirs, and his eyes were the same striking light-brown color as their mother's. He smiled broadly at them, and Miranda couldn't help but smile back.

"My goodness. Look at you two. Good thing they favor my side, eh, Johnny?" he said and elbowed Grandpa Mac in the ribs. "Let's hope they dodge that white-hair gene of yours completely. No one wants to look like they're eighty when they're actually only forty."

Grandpa Mac shot him a dirty look and growled slightly.

"Wait. Your name is John? I thought it was 'Mac,'" Justin interrupted.

Their grandpa rubbed his temples with both hands as if he had the world's worst headache. "You actually thought my name was 'Mac McAdelind'? Mac is a nickname, Justin, short for McAdelind."

"Well we have a *red* dragon named Red, a *storm* dragon named Storm… " Justin said and shrugged. "So, yeah, *Mac McAdelind* didn't seem completely out of the question."

"It's John," Grandpa Mac said, then turned and exited into his study. "I need to grab something before you head out."

Their other grandfather came over and knelt down on one knee in front of Miranda and Justin. "You know, I'm not all that comfortable with this whole grandpa deal. I just found out I was one a couple of hours ago. So take it easy on me, okay? And you guys can call me by my English name, Paul Stone, until you get a little more comfortable with our tribal language."

"Okay… *Grandpa*… Stone," Miranda said, still not entirely believing the middle-aged man in front of her could be their grandfather.

He stood back up and grabbed their suitcases. "I'll take these to the truck. You guys say your goodbyes to the *old man*. But don't take too long. There's a nasty storm coming up from the south, and I don't want to get caught in it before we make it to the cabin," he said and smiled at them again before heading out the door.

"He's, like, Dad's age, right?" Justin asked. "How is that even possible?"

Miranda shook her head. "Totally weird."

"He is sixty-eight, same as Mac," said the familiar voice of Mrs. Lóng from behind, causing them both to jump.

Miranda spun around. "Would you please stop doing that?"

"Doing what, dear? Here are your toiletries. You left them in the bathroom upstairs." She handed Miranda her things, then walked over to Justin and gave him a tight hug. "Do be careful, child. If you have to start a fire, please keep it small." Then she stepped back and regarded Miranda for a moment. "Follow your heart, Miranda. It will not steer you wrong," she said and turned on her heels, disappearing into the dining room.

Miranda shook her head. "Okay, why is every adult here so weird?"

"Miranda. May I have a word before you leave?" Grandpa Mac yelled from the study. "And Justin. Be safe. Don't do anything stupid."

Justin rolled his eyes and made a slicing motion with his hand across his throat.

Miranda laughed and shoved her backpack into Justin's chest. "Take this for me, please? I'll be out in a sec." Then she turned and walked into the study.

Her grandfather was standing by his desk with a grim look on his face. There were several large boxes filled to the brim with papers, envelopes, and other personal items. Miranda walked over to one of the boxes and looked at the stack of envelopes inside bundled together with twine.

"Whose letters are these?"

Her grandfather grunted, "Huh? Oh, these. They are Mr. DeSoto's personal effects. Those letters are from his brother."

Miranda thumbed through the envelopes, noticing they

were all still sealed. "He never opened them?"

Her grandfather shook his head. "No. Not one of them. I thought there'd been hard feelings between those two for a long time. But it appears they were only on one side. Now, Lord DeSoto is asking for permission to come up here to collect his brother's body and all of his things."

Miranda was suddenly worried. What if the two brothers had been working together? What if this was just a ploy to get close to her and Justin? "What did you tell him?"

Her grandfather stroked his mustache, lost in thought for a moment. "I asked him to give me a couple of days to get everything together."

"Do you think that's a good idea?" Miranda was a little shocked that her grandfather would agree to let any member of the DeSoto family on Thunderbird Ranch, especially after what his head of security had tried to do—stealing and collaborating with the draconians and planning to have them all killed.

"Whether it's a good idea or not is irrelevant, Lord DeSoto is very upset. The least I can do is honor his wishes to bring his brother's body back home." He reached over and took the stack of envelopes out of her hands and placed it back in the box. "But this isn't why I asked you to come in here. Listen, I don't like letting you two out of my sight one bit. You're my responsibility to keep safe. Your parents sent you *here*, not to Paul. I feel like I've let them, and you, down."

"None of this is your fault. As I said before, no place is safe for us. We can't hide from Tiamat. But I trust Em, and believe her when she says we need to go with Grandpa Stone. Don't worry, I'm still keeping my promise, I won't stop until we've gotten our parents and Em all back. It's only a matter of time. And I won't let anything get in my way."

The old man smiled. "I know you won't. But the price for getting my kids back safe can't be the loss of my grandchildren.

You need to be careful. Don't take any unnecessary risks. You hear me?" Then he paused, reached behind his desk, and pulled out the long, flat leather scabbard containing his great silver sword.

"I want you to keep this safe for me while you're gone," he said and handed it to her.

"I can't take your sword, Grandpa," Miranda said, balancing the shockingly light weapon in her hands.

Her grandpa laughed. "What's changed? It's not as cool if you're not stealing it from my safe?"

Miranda frowned. "I didn't take the sword, by the way, but that's not what I meant. You'll need this to protect yourself while we're gone. I don't think the draconians will stop coming here after we've left."

The older man placed his hands over hers, pressing her fingers tightly around the scabbard. "Don't you worry about me, I'll be dandy. That's not the only weapon I have stashed around here. And where you'll be going is… special. The draconians won't be able to set foot there. Your aunt must have known this, and that's why she's sending you there. But once this threat has passed, I'll come for you two." He paused. "And in the meantime, I'm going to follow up a lead Lord Ddraig, Gwen's father, might have about your parents' disappearance. Who knows? Maybe this time we'll get lucky." He crouched so that Miranda was looking down at him. "Do an old man a favor, will ya? Don't take any chances, don't be a hero, and stay safe. Okay?"

Miranda didn't answer—she just placed the sword down on the floor and hugged her grandfather hard around the neck. He hesitated, just for a moment, then wrapped his arms around her tightly in return. She pulled back from their embrace and wiped a tear from her cheek. She quickly picked up the sword and ran out the front door.

CHAPTER 9

JUSTIN
People of the Unseen Land

JUSTIN YAWNED HARD and shook his head to clear the fogginess from his brain. It was the middle of the night, he should be dead asleep, but he was too anxious to relax. The entire three hours drive deeper into the mountains on dirt and gravel roads had been nerve-wracking, to say the least. Not only because some of the roads had sheer cliffs on one side with no guardrails but because Justin had fully expected draconians or wyverns or some host of terrible new creatures to jump out at any moment and try to kill them.

A big storm, moving in rapidly from the south, was illuminating everything in flashes of lightning as the roll of thunder vibrated the truck's cab like a drum. Justin also wasn't looking forward to where they were going either. He had finally settled into Thunderbird Ranch—just now, almost a month after leaving New York. He loved having his own space apart from his messy sister instead of the bunk beds they had shared in their apartment. He had friends…

Well, *one* friend, who happened to be a giant, rather sarcastic red dragon, but a friend all the same. And no one was picking on him any more since he and Billy had come to an understanding, of sorts. For the first time in a long time, Justin felt like things were looking up. Well, except for the fact his parents were probably being held prisoner and maybe tortured somewhere, and creatures out of someone's nightmares kept trying to kill him. On second thought, it all pretty much sucked. He was just feeling mad that the few things in his life that were positive were now all being taken away from him. It wasn't fair.

The truck turned hard to the left, snapping Justin instantly out of his dark thoughts.

"We're here," Grandpa Stone called out from the front seat of the old truck. "Welcome to the Oni'waz'legani tribe."

"The Uni-Was-Leggy tribe?" Justin asked.

"That was a joke right?" Grandpa Stone said and chuckled. "It looks like we're going to have to have a crash course in the better side of your DNA. Oni'waz'legani means 'The People of the Unseen Land.' That is what we call our tribe, and this is the entry way into our territory."

"So, does that mean we just left the United States and now we're in our own country or something?" Justin asked, and his sister hit him on the arm. *"Ow!"*

Grandpa Stone looked in the rearview mirror at Justin and frowned. "No. Not exactly."

"But we're on tribal land, right? Then federal laws don't apply."

The older man shook his head. "It's not like that for us. Because of our unique… situation, we are actually an undocumented and unrecognized tribe. We own our land, but we keep our identity somewhat hidden. It's better that way."

Justin slumped back into his seat and sighed. "I've never

been outside of the United States before. I was hoping this would be something cool."

Grandpa Stone threw his head back and laughed. "Oh, you just wait. I guarantee you'll be impressed once you see everything."

The truck's headlights reflected off a couple of broken-down vehicles and an old fruit stand in a sad state of disrepair on the side of the road. Just beyond the run-down objects in the woods, Justin could barely make out several small structures with dim lights. This was turning out to be worse than he could have imagined. "Is this it?" Justin asked, with a little more disappointment in his voice than he meant.

"No. All this… "—Grandpa Stone said waving his hands in the direction of the structures—"is what outsiders expect to see. We won't reach the tribal land until tomorrow."

Miranda leaned forward, resting her arms on the back of the front seat. "What do you mean *tomorrow*? How far do we have to drive? We don't have time to waste. Our aunt is trapped in a prison somewhere and our parents are… missing. We need to figure out why Em sent us to the valley. I don't think you understand—"

"I *understand* just fine, Miranda," Grandpa Stone said, shooting her a stern look in the rearview mirror. "It's my daughter who is lost too, remember? But first things first. We get you two to safety, and then we figure out what to do next. And just to clarify, we're not driving to the tribal land, we're walking to it."

"Walking!" Miranda screeched. "You're joking right?"

"No joke. It's back in the mountains, off the beaten path. In a place where your enemies can't reach you."

Miranda sat back hard and crossed her arms with a loud "*Humph*," glaring at the back of their grandfather's head. "I keep telling everyone that no place is safe," she said. "Our enemies are going to be coming for us while we keep playing this senseless game of hide-and-seek. We can't conceal ourselves from Tiamat. She can find us anywhere we go."

Grandpa Stone looked in the rearview mirror and laughed. "There's my little girl. I was wondering if I would see any of Kya'ho'ah in either of you, and there she is."

Justin had only heard his mother Kaya called "Kya'ho'ah" a couple of times before, mainly as a form of teasing by his father. "What does Kya'ho'ah mean exactly?" he asked.

"It means, 'wise beyond time,' which was very fitting for your mother. She was always knowledgeable beyond her years. However, the unfortunate downside of her personality was that when she got stubborn, then her name would take on a new meaning, 'little-know-it-all,'" he said, and laughed again.

They continued past the small houses, zigzagged up a steep slope, and came to a locked gate barring the road ahead. Unlike the Warren's massive, King Kong–size entryway and double razor-wire fence, this was just two simple green metal poles on hinges padlocked together with a small chain. Justin imagined the intent wasn't to stop massive creatures from coming in or out, but just to block the road from curious people.

Grandpa Stone put the car into park and hopped out. "I'll be right back."

Justin watched as he walked up to the gate, pulled out a key, and unlocked the padlock. He pushed both green bars hard, and they swung out of the way.

That's when Justin sensed something in the woods beyond.

He turned quickly to Miranda, and she nodded. "I sense it too. Are you reading anything? Can you tell what it is?"

Justin closed his eyes and let his mind spread out as far as he could. "*Hmmm.* Feels like a dragon. No ill will. Just… watching. How about you?"

Miranda shook her head. "Not even that much. You think it's all right? Are they dragons from Thunderbird Ranch?"

Justin shrugged. "Seems fine to me. It's not Red or Storm if that's what you're hoping. Beyond that, I'm not totally sure. They do seem… different… though."

"Different how?" Miranda asked.

"More like wild dragons than domestics. Remember when Miss D said there were dragons living in the mountains? I wonder if that's what we're sensing."

That's right, Miranda thought, and nervously scanned the forest again. But if there were wild dragons out here in the mountains, then why did the blue dragons of Thunderbird Ranch need to be kept underground in the Warren? Immediately after she had checked in on Azuria and Tempest, Miranda had talked to her grandfather about the changes the dragons desired. He said he would look into some options, but that they would be safest in the Warren. But if wild dragons were in the mountains already, Miranda wondered, why hadn't he just considered having them live out here?

Grandpa Stone returned, interrupting her thoughts, and pulled the truck forward just past the gate. After locking the gate back up again, he threw the truck into gear and continued to guide the vehicle cautiously up the steep path.

"Not far now," he said cheerfully.

By the time the ground leveled off, the lightning was strobing all around them, and the wind was gathering strength, pushing the truck from side-to-side as if it were made of canvas. Their grandfather kept looking at the sky, then checking on Justin and Miranda in the rearview mirror. He seemed more nervous than he was letting on.

They came to a sudden stop in front of a small log cabin just as the sky opened up and rain poured down in sheets.

"We're going to rest here until sunrise," Grandpa Stone

yelled over the thunder and rain. "Make a run for the porch. I'll grab your bags and be right behind you."

Miranda and Justin nodded and opened the truck's rear doors, then ran as fast as they could the short distance to the cabin. Even though it was only about ten feet away, they were thoroughly soaked by the time they reached the porch. The wind howled through the trees, and Justin shivered. He felt the presence of more dragons here. They were all focused intently on something. Something in the storm. He looked up as lightning flashed. A great distance away, he saw something hovering in the air.

Justin backed up quickly, pulling Miranda with him until they had their backs against the cabin's rough exterior wall.

"What is it?" Miranda asked urgently. "Did you see something?"

Justin nodded. "In the sky. Over there."

"Was it a... wyvern?" Miranda whispered.

Justin shook his head. "I don't know *what* it was, but it looked like a man with wings."

"That must be one of Tiamat's monsters. Why do you think it's just hovering up there?" Miranda asked and shivered.

"Good question, sis. We're in the open with little or no protection. It's like it's waiting for something."

"Maybe it's waiting for the other one to arrive?" Miranda said, but Justin had a sneaking suspicion there was more to it than just that. Without saying so out loud, Justin sensed Miranda agreeing with him to keep their thoughts and feelings to themselves.

Grandpa Stone came running onto the porch, water dripping from him as if he had just stepped out of the shower fully clothed. "What a downpour," he said, pulling out a key. He unlocked the door to the cabin and stepped inside.

Justin and Miranda were right on his heels, and as soon as they were in, Justin slammed the door shut and locked it.

Grandpa Stone flipped on a switch, making a small overhead light flicker to life, illuminating a space not much larger than Justin's room at Thunderbird Ranch. There was a cast-iron wood-burning stove, four folding chairs around a card table, a large wooden chest, and several cots stacked in a corner.

"Is it just this room?" Justin asked.

"Yep. We really only use this as a stopover, if it's too late in the day or there's inclement weather. Lucky us, we got both tonight. So, let's make ourselves comfortable for a couple of hours, and get some shuteye before we head out at dawn." Then he looked out the window. "Assuming, of course, this lets up by morning."

He walked over to the stack of cots and moved three into the only open space in the cabin, then went to the chest and pulled out three sleeping bags and laid them out on top of the cots. He then grabbed two aluminum-framed hiking backpacks and placed them on the table.

"Tomorrow, you'll need to move what you can from your suitcases and backpacks into these. We won't be able to make the hike with those suitcases. Anything that won't fit, stash in the chest. Oh, that reminds me. Do you guys know how to play golf?"

Miranda just stared at him. "How does hiking remind you of golf? No. We don't play golf."

"Everything reminds me of golf," he said, then sighed. "Too bad really, great game. Maybe we could hit a couple of balls around sometime. You know, get you two interested in the sport?"

Justin shrugged. "Sure. I guess, why not."

His grandpa clapped his hands together. "That's great. Can't wait to show you the ropes. My short game is excellent. Okay then, time to rest. We have a long walk tomorrow."

Justin looked around the small cabin, noticing something

for the first time. "Umm… where's the bathroom?"

Grandpa Stone shook his head and smiled. "City folk. No running water in this cabin. If you need to go, just wake me, and I'll take you outside."

Justin looked out the window and gulped. He could still sense several dragons nearby, and there was that flying man-thing in the storm too. "That's okay. I'll just hold it until morning."

* * *

Justin was having a bad dream… well, not actually a dream, a vision. After being around dragons for a while now, he could recognize when a dream was just a dream, and when it was something else entirely, even while he was still asleep.

In it, he had spent hours flying through wind and rain, chasing the shadowy figure of a winged man. Justin flew high above the clouds, looking down at the swirling eye of the storm, and at its vortex was the very creature he sought.

He tucked his wings back flat against his body and dove at the man at the center of the storm. He could feel the force of the wind struggling against him, trying to keep him away, but nothing was going to stop him from reaching his goal.

The flying man had his back turned to his approach. It would be a clean kill. So close now.

The man turned… but it wasn't a man at all. It was something out of a nightmare, with the body that resembled a human's, but the head of a… lion.

The creature roared out a single word: "Anzu!"

Justin's eyes shot open, his heart racing. He could not only still see the freakish creature, he could still smell it too: an overpowering musky animal smell mixed with fresh rain.

Calling it something like "wet dog" wouldn't do the stench justice.

Justin lay there for a moment, taking in deep breaths to calm his racing heart, when a sound to his right drew his attention to a man sitting in a chair, staring out the window. It took Justin a moment to remember where he was, and that the man was his Grandpa Stone.

His grandfather was perfectly still, not moving a muscle for a long moment. Justin began to wonder whether or not he was asleep in the chair, when he suddenly leaned forward and stared through the window up at the sky. A flash of lightning revealed a long silver knife in Grandpa Stone's hand.

Justin heard an echoing roar and trees cracking in the distance. His grandfather crouched low, still peering out the window. He stood suddenly, making a series of hand signals to someone—or something—outside. When everything had been silent for a little while, he noiselessly moved back into the chair.

Justin's heart was pounding against his chest. What the heck was happening outside? He concentrated, trying to sense anything beyond the tiny cabin's walls, but he could only pick up an overwhelming feeling of frustration coming from the woods surrounding the isolated dwelling—frustration, but there was something else too. Emptiness. Like a black cloak hiding something from view. The only other time he had felt anything like it before was in the warehouse in Denver, when the dracs had blocked his ability to communicate telepathically with the dragons. Were there draconians out there as well? No, this felt different. And what the heck was an *anzu*?

Justin pulled his sleeping bag up over his head, leaving a narrow gap through which he could keep his eyes on

Grandpa Stone and the window. He knew sleep was now out of the question. He willed the sun to rise, wishing desperately for this night to end.

CHAPTER 10

MIRANDA
City of the Ancients

MIRANDA DROPPED HER HEAVY camping backpack onto the narrow, rugged path with a soft thump, but kept her long sword strapped diagonally to her back. Grandpa Stone had offered to carry it for her several times already, but she felt safer having the mighty blade within arm's reach. She put her hands on her lower back and stretched, trying to work out the tennis-ball–size knot that had formed there. They had set off at sunrise and had walked for several hours.

The storm had done significant damage to the trees for miles around the cabin. Large branches, and in some cases entire trees, littered the ground and obstructed the trail ahead. Tiny rushing streams had cut fresh erosion tracks down the sides of the mountain, feeding into the normally small mountain creeks and causing them to swell to twice their normal size. Having to navigate around these obstacles made the journey even more challenging than it ordinarily would have been.

Miranda reached into her pack, grabbed a bottle of water, and drank from it greedily.

"How much… farther?" she asked between gulps.

Grandpa Stone, who didn't even seem the least bit tired, glanced around. Then he noticed something he liked and smiled broadly. "Come over here and look at this."

He motioned for them to follow him and led the way up a smaller intersecting path to the right.

Miranda shouldered her pack and followed Justin up a modest slope festooned with exposed tree roots that created a set of natural steps. Soon they reached a sort of plateau, which overlooked a broad valley.

"Where are we exactly?" Miranda asked. "I haven't seen any roads, electrical lines, or signs of people anywhere. The tribe doesn't seriously live this far away from civilization, does it?"

Grandpa Stone nodded. "We do indeed. Like I said, we want to keep a low profile." He pointed back the way they had just come. "Thunderbird Ranch is only about ten miles, as the dragon soars, in that direction, but with a whole lot of monstrous mountains in between here and there. Much, much longer and slower on foot."

He then indicated down the valley to the right. "That high point, there, is Mesa Mountain." Next he gestured down the valley to the left. "And we're headed, there, to that waterfall."

Miranda and Justin took a couple of steps forward, craning to see any such landmark.

"What waterfall? I don't see anything except trees," Justin said.

"Trust me, there's plenty down there. Mystic energy keeps our people hidden from unwanted eyes. I know it seems pretty remote around here—"

Miranda let out a sharp laugh. "You think?"

Grandpa Stone frowned at her but continued. "However, we are not so far away from hiking trails that the risk of exposure is out of the question."

"What's so special about the tribal land?" Justin asked. "Is it like Thunderbird Ranch, and you have a bunch of dragons hidden under a mountain?"

Their grandfather answered with a smile. "You'll see. Okay, we have another couple of hours of hiking before we get to our destination."

Miranda and Justin groaned in unison.

"Oh, come on. This is some of the most beautiful scenery in the world. Enjoy yourselves. Plus, it's all downhill from here," he said and quickly walked back down to the main trail.

"This stinks," Justin complained. "I'm so tired. Walking a million miles after getting no sleep the past couple of nights is the last thing I want to do."

"I know, but this is our best lead so far. I just wish we could get there faster. This is all taking too long," Miranda said and began jogging down the trail after her grandfather.

* * *

The last hour of the hike was spent in near silence, with grandpa Stone occasionally breaking the stillness of the pristine mountain valley by whistling one old-time tune or another.

That's a little weird, Miranda thought. *There are always sounds; birds, insects, wind through the trees, something.* Then, as if reading her mind, loose stones from one of the nearby cliffs broke off and tumbled down the sheer slope to her left.

Miranda froze and looked at the spot where the rocks had

broken free. Her heart was racing—she felt sure a half-dozen wyverns were perched above her, preparing to strike at any moment. She reached slowly over her shoulder and gripped the worn hilt of her Grandpa Mac's great sword, preparing to rip it out of its scabbard at the first sign of movement.

But there was nothing there.

She scrutinized the dense woods around her, not only with her eyes but also with her mind, scanning the trees and rocks. Someone—or something—was watching her. Fear started to creep slowly up her spine, and she shivered.

"I know, I feel them too," Justin said, coming up from behind her, and making her jump with fright. "They've been out there for about an hour now."

Miranda punched him in the chest. "Don't sneak up on me like that."

Justin rubbed the spot where she had hit him, an indignant look on his face. "We're walking single file on a narrow path. You stop walking, and I run into you. That's how it works."

Miranda ignored him and asked, "How many do you think there are?"

Justin glanced around the wooded area. "As far as I can tell, there are at least ten different dragons watching us right now."

"Ten!" Miranda said in disbelief.

He shrugged. "Maybe more. It's difficult to tell. Something up ahead is interfering with my ability to sense any details. It's like the opposite of what happened at the warehouse and last night. Then I couldn't sense anything, but here all I can sense is a huge energy field dead ahead. It's kind of like I'm trying to listen to a whispered conversation in a noisy room. You know what's crazy though? I know the dragons are close by, but I can't see anything. Not a trace. I've even reached out a couple of times to talk. I know they can hear me, but they haven't responded yet."

Miranda looked around nervously. "Do you think they're friendly?"

Justin nodded. "There is a kind of admiration mixed with uncertainty... or even a little... fear. It's weird."

Then Miranda remembered something her brother just said. "Wait, did you just say something blacked out your vision last night too?"

Justin nodded. "That thing in the storm had this emptiness surrounding it. It was more than not being able to sense it. I can't sense lots of things. This was more like someone turned off the lights in a room. There should be light, but there isn't any."

"Come on, kids!" their grandfather yelled from far ahead of them. "We're almost there!"

Miranda looked around once more, seeing nothing but the woods around her. "Come on. Last one there is a rotten egg," she said and ran down the sloping trail.

After a short distance the path leveled out, turned to the right, and moved farther and farther away from the valley wall. The trees became taller and lusher. Then Miranda could hear the subtle whooshing sound of fast-moving water in the near distance.

Grandpa Stone was standing in the path ahead. As Miranda walked up to him, she noticed that the trail turned slightly to the left, became a lot broader, and was paved with wide, flat stones. Purple, yellow, and white wildflowers adorned the ground under the protection of towering trees.

"Wow. This place is beautiful," Miranda said, and bent over, taking one of the delicate flowers in her hand. "What are these?"

Her grandfather knelt next to her. He looked at the flowers for a moment, then stared off into the woods, lost in thought. "They're called columbines. They are your grandma's favorite flower."

Justin came walking down the trail breathing heavily and holding his side. "Did I... ever mention... how much... I hate... running?"

"Once or twice," Miranda said. Then she felt something grabbing her attention, like a subtle vibration, coming from somewhere ahead on the stone walkway. "What's that?" she asked and started to walk down the flagstone path.

"What's what?" Justin said, following closely behind.

A large stone obelisk stood about six feet high to the left of the path. Miranda paused, holding out her hands toward it as if trying to warm herself by a fire in winter. "Do you feel that?"

Justin nodded. "Yes. That's what's putting out the noisy energy I was talking about. What is it?"

Their grandfather stood silently behind, watching them intently.

Miranda walked closer to the stone object, observing for the first time carved cuneiform script twisting around it in a complex, almost decorative pattern. She followed the script up toward the top of the obelisk and noticed a large polished blue stone set into it.

"What the heck is cuneiform script doing on an obelisk in the middle of the Rocky Mountains?" Justin exclaimed.

The pulsing force Miranda was feeling was emanating from this very stone. She reached out to touch it. But before her fingers could come into contact with its glasslike surface, her brother grabbed her arm, pulling it away.

"What the heck, Justin?"

He shook his head in warning. "I feel its power too, sis. But given your past with touching stones and passing out, I don't think that's a good idea."

She nodded and turned to Grandpa stone. "You've been quiet. What is this?"

"We call it the Lulu'na'waz'nani, which means 'the stone

of hiding,' or 'the protection stone.' That little baby is how we keep off the radar and part of the reason this valley is so extraordinary."

Miranda looked around, but other than the well-manicured path and the completely out-of-place obelisk with Sumerian script spiraling around it, there wasn't anything else out of the ordinary.

"So where is this tribe exactly? I still don't see anything. Please tell me we don't have to hike for a couple more hours," Miranda moaned.

Grandpa Stone walked past them, whistling softly, and as he was about to pass the obelisk, he turned around completely so that he was walking backward, gave them a wave, and disappeared into thin air.

Miranda looked over at Justin and raised an eyebrow. "After you, dear brother."

Justin bowed deeply. "That's okay, dear sister. Age before beauty."

Miranda shook her head. "Chicken," she said, goading him, and took several steps forward.

As soon as she was even with the blue stone—emitting the waves of power she could feel moving through her—the world started to warp and shift. Where there had been a densely wooded valley only seconds before, there was now something out of a very confused history book. The valley extended for a mile, but it wasn't sloped as it had appeared to be only seconds before, it was flat. Beautifully manicured gardens stretched out on either side of the broad river that looked engineered into some kind of stone-lined canal. Both sides of the valley rose up hundreds of feet, creating a natural shelter. In the cliff face itself were carved dozens upon dozens of stone dwellings. It looked like the pictures of Mesa Verde Miranda had seen, except these were still homes where people lived.

However, the strangest thing of all was at the very end of the valley. A long, narrow waterfall spilled over the cliff and disappeared into the roof of an enormous pyramid-like structure before continuing on as the river they were walking beside.

Justin ran into Miranda from behind. "That was… interesting…" he said, and then his voice trailed off completely as he took in the crazy scene. "Uh… um… is that a… ziggurat?" He stepped around Miranda and almost fell over with excitement. "What the heck is an ancient Sumerian temple doing in rural Colorado?"

Grandpa Stone smiled. "What indeed," he said, and spread his arms wide. "Let me be the first to welcome you to the City of the Ancients."

CHAPTER 11

JUSTIN
The Temple

JUSTIN RUBBED HIS EYES, blinking several times, and shook his head, trying to clear the apparent mirage from his mind. "Miranda. You're seeing what I'm seeing, right?"

She nodded dumbly, staring wide-eyed around the valley.

Justin's gaze swept from the completely out-of-place temple to twenty or so people working in lush gardens not far from where they now stood, tending to a crop big enough to feed a small town for over a year. His eyes continued around the valley walls, gaping the entire time, before settling at last on what looked to be some of the most well preserved mud-brick buildings in existence. Wooden ladders and ramps meandered up from the valley floor to the multilevel complex, looking like some Neolithic version of the Chutes and Ladders game.

Movement above the impossible structures caught Justin's attention, and he peered up higher along the canyon wall. Peppered along the cliff's face was a series of caves with small ledges where a dozen coppery-brown dragons that had just flown through the magical protection field were now perching.

But the most remarkable—and completely out-of-time-and-place—building was the giant step pyramid at the far end of the canyon. Justin loved looking through his parents' old books about ancient civilizations and had seen many images of ziggurats before. This type of temple was not only the "home" of the Sumerian god who was the patron of each particular Sumerian city, it was also the cultural center of each of those early city-states.

"This is a joke, right?" Justin said, pointing at the temple. It didn't make any sense that there could be such a structure here in the middle of the United States. "Someone built this recently as a tourist stop or something."

Grandpa Stone shook his head. "No joke. The temple was constructed just prior to any of the other structures built in the valley."

"But that doesn't make any sense. It looks brand new. All of this does," Justin said, waving his arms around the valley. "And besides, that style of ziggurat predates cliff dwellings by thousands of years."

Grandpa Stone laughed merrily. "You sound just like your mother. This used to drive her insane. From what she has told me, both the temple and the homes were built at about the same time. But from the pictographs, we know the temple was indeed erected first." He shrugged. "Not sure what that all matters, though. It's been here for as long as our people have lived in this valley. This is our home, and we protect it."

"So, are you telling me, someone built this temple around the time the first cliff dwellings started to appear? Like around five hundred AD?" Justin asked.

Grandpa Stone shook his head. "No, Justin, what I am

telling you is, all of this has been here since the time of Sumer."

"That's impossible. There is no way," Justin said, crossing his arms. "How did that knowledge get here? There is no record of any Mesopotamian civilizations reaching across the ocean. How could that have happened?"

"*Our* people got here. Why would it be such a stretch to think someone from the ancient Middle East couldn't make it as well?" Grandpa Stone said with a smile.

"'Our people' came over on a land bridge during the last ice age is how. That was like, twenty thousand years ago. And it doesn't explain how someone got from the ancient Middle East to here five thousand years ago," Justin said, exasperated.

"Your mom tells me this particular temple is closer to six thousand years old, and no it does not." Grandpa Stone looked at the cliff face where the dragons were perched. "But something does."

Miranda let out a bark of laughter. "You're saying ancient Sumerians flew here on dragons and built a temple? That's crazy."

Grandpa Stone pointed to the cliff wall. "Not Sumeri*ans*, just *one* Sumerian. Plus, there are dragons living here in a magically protected valley. So is it crazy for the continental United States to have a valley with a six-thousand-year-old Mesopotamian temple in it? Yes. But, it can be crazy, and still be true."

"But how?" Justin asked, now utterly exasperated.

The older man sighed. "I was going to take you to the house first, but I don't think your little minds are going to rest until I show you the temple." He dropped his backpack down on the stony trail and said, "Leave your packs here. I'll have someone take them to my place while we have a look around."

He motioned to one of the men working in the field, and Justin and his sister shook their heavy backpacks off their shoulders and onto the ground. Justin felt a hundred pounds lighter. He turned to Miranda and noticed she still had Grandpa Mac's sword strapped to her back. He was about to make a comment about how ridiculous she looked when he noticed her staring intently at the temple. "What's *that* look for?"

Miranda turned back to him, lost in thought. "*Hmmm*... Oh. Just thinking about—something."

"Care to clue me in?" Justin asked.

"Well. The style of temple is from ancient Mesopotamia right?"

Justin nodded.

"So is Tiamat. This has to be what Aunt Em wanted us to see. There must be a clue inside we need to find."

"I guess," Justin said. "Seems like a stretch to me. Em probably just wanted us to come here so we could be hidden from Tiamat."

Miranda gestured to the massive stone building. "There's a freaking Sumerian temple sitting in a mountain valley in Colorado, Justin. Of course it's a clue."

Their grandfather returned and clapped his hands together excitedly. "Okay, let me show you around a bit. As you can imagine, we don't get many visitors. So just shout out any questions you might have."

"We will," Justin and Miranda said in unison.

After walking for several minutes down the well-manicured stone path toward the temple, Justin asked, "How in the world did we not see this place when we were getting close to it?"

"The Stone of Hiding is how. Not only does it cast an illusion over the entire valley, it shields us from our enemies and keeps this vale in an ideal state. Crops always grow to their full potential. Buildings remain as they were originally built. And the people who live here don't age as they do in the rest of the world."

Justin's mouth fell open. "Wait. You mean you guys are immortals? No wonder you look so young."

"I wish," their grandpa said, laughing. "No, unfortunately, we die just like everyone else. We just look really good until we do. Everything must pass in time, no matter how old, magical, or eternal it might seem."

"How did the Stone of Hiding get here?" Miranda asked.

"Ah. Now that is tied directly to the story of the temple, so we'll come back to it." Grandpa Stone stopped and indicated a section of the wide canal that cut straight from the temple's waterfall down the center of the valley. "Here is where I met your grandmother."

Justin looked down at the quickly flowing stream and said, "You met our grandmother in the water?"

Grandpa Stone nodded. "Yes." Then he turned and kept walking down the path.

Justin and Miranda ran to catch up.

"Hold on a minute. You just can't drop something like that on us and then walk away. What is her name? Where is she? Why was she in the river?" Justin said.

He smiled slyly at them. "She is called Akena'tani. But that is all I'm going to tell you for now. I want to give you something to look forward to tonight."

"Our grandmother is here? Where is she?" Justin asked glancing anxiously around.

Grandpa Stone shook his head and looked off into the mountains. "No. She's not here right now. She's something of a free spirit and comes and goes as she pleases." Then seeing the disappointment on their faces, he added. "But you never know when she'll drop in. What I meant was, I'll tell you the story of how we met tonight at dinner. I think it will be enlightening to you both."

Next their grandfather stopped at an area of flat, smooth grass with several flags sticking out of the middle of small holes.

"Wait. You actually have a putting green here?" Justin said in disbelief.

"What can I say? It's one of the few vices I have. You can blame your great-great-grandfather McAdelind for introducing the game of golf to us. It was his idea to place this green here; that way he could play all year long." Grandpa Stone bent down to whisper, "Plus, I have a magic putter that can't miss. It used to drive Mac insane…." He trailed off, lost in thought. "Anyhow, it's a great sport. Your mom was never interested in it. Not even a little. No matter what I tried, I couldn't convince her to take a swing at a ball. She was always so interested in books and old ruins."

"So, the McAdelinds and the… Only-Was-Lappy… had a good relationship?" Justin asked, struggling to remember the unfamiliar tribal name.

"Oni'waz'legani," the older man scolded, shaking his head in disappointment. "You know what… just call us 'The People of the Unseen Land' or simply, 'The People' for now. And yes. We worked together. Traded. And were good… friends."

"You and Grandpa Mac didn't seem very *friendly*," Miranda said.

Grandpa Stone frowned and nodded. "You got that, huh? That's yet another story for later. Although, I'm not sure he would want me to—"

Just then, a large brownish-red dragon came gliding down from one of the caves, cutting their grandfather off in mid-sentence. Its thick hide was rough, like stone, and was the same color as the exposed cliffs. The horns along its back were dense and blunt, and its wings looked much more sturdy than the thin membranes of the other dragon breeds Justin and Miranda had seen so far.

The dragon turned in a tight circle, descending rapidly, and landed hard on the putting green.

Grandpa Stone let out a high-pitched shriek. "Not on the green, you big oaf! You'll ruin it! I'll never be able to putt accurately with those massive divots. We've talked about this!"

The dragon took two steps to the side, off the green, and sat down on its haunches. Its copper-brown eyes, similar to Justin's grandfather's and mother's eyes, came to rest on Grandpa Stone.

"And here I thought that magic putter you are always going on about could make a shot no matter what obstacle was in its way?"

"He said, he thought your magic putter was good enough to make shots no matter what," Justin translated.

His grandfather shot him an annoyed look. "Thanks, Justin, but I can understand his lame excuses just fine without your help." Suddenly, Grandpa Stone's face lit up. "Wait. You can understand him too?"

Justin's jaw dropped. "Yeah. But we were told that *we* are the only humans who can dragonspeak."

"You might well be. For me, it's not speaking or even understanding words per se. I sort of see what he means, just fleeting images in my mind really. That along with spending, pretty much, my entire life around this big klutz has morphed into a kind of speech over the years." Grandpa Stone turned back to the dragon. "I can understand you, right?"

"Like a kindergartener at a college lecture."

Grandpa Stone shook his head. "See. He just put the image in my mind of me as a baby sitting in a classroom. Nice. Anyhow. I can understand old Rockgobbler here pretty well, but not any of the other dragons."

"And that's why they keep sending me to talk to this dolt," the dragon said, and hissed out a laugh.

"Ha ha. Graceful and loyal, I'm so lucky," Grandpa Stone said and walked over to the dragon, scratching him lovingly under the chin. "We've been friends for as long as I can remember."

"Indeed, we have," the dragon added. "Since we were hatchlings."

Justin let his concentration move from the words he heard to the thoughts the dragon was sending out. After a short time, he could clearly see the images the dragon called Rockgobbler was sending to his grandfather. A boy about six years old was playing in this very garden with a young brown dragon. They were happy.

What Justin was seeing was like a snapshot in time, the condensed image of a shared memory. When he and Miranda talked to the dragons, each dragon spoke directly to them in his or her own unique voice.

"Why do you call him Rockgobbler? Is that some kind of dragon insult or something?" Justin asked.

"The dragons of the valley—call them brown, copper, or earth dragons—can chew up stones and boulders and spit them back out as superheated gravel. Very deadly. When I was younger I thought I was being quite clever giving him the name Rockgobbler."

"And here I thought Justin got his bad-naming gene from Dad," Miranda teased. "Can others in the tribe communicate with dragons too?"

"Some others in our direct line have shown a similar talent, but we never actually hear *words*," Grandpa Stone said, and jerked his thumb at Rockgobbler. "Wait. Are you telling me you can really understand this joker?"

"Yes, like he's speaking to us in English," Justin said, tapping the side of his head. "But it sounds like it's coming from in here and from the dragon simultaneously."

"We can also sense the dragon's thoughts and feelings and intentions," Miranda added. "But to be honest, Justin is far better at that than I am."

Their grandfather nodded thoughtfully. "Interesting. I think that's unique." Then he turned back to the dragon. "Did you want something other than to ruin my golf game?"

Rockgobbler rolled his eyes and said, *"The winged lion-man is still near, but he does not advance."*

"Post sentries around the perimeter of the valley, and when night falls we will drive him away from here."

"There is more. The earth rumbles. Something else is coming this way."

Their grandfather knelt down and placed his hands on the stone path. "That is odd. What could it be?"

"When we were questioning the draconian, he said the sky and the earth would come for us. That flying thing you mentioned is most likely the sky demon," Miranda said and knelt down to feel the ground. "I can feel a slight vibration in the earth… and something else too. A sort of electric feeling moving up my arm."

"I'm willing to bet the earth-demon-dude is the source of that," Justin said.

"I must inform the Ancient One, immediately," Rockgobbler said, and leaped into the air. He made a beeline for one of the cliff's caves and disappeared inside.

"What does he mean by 'the Ancient One'?" Justin asked.

Grandpa Stone seemed lost in thought for a moment. "*Hmmm?* He actually said, 'the Ancient One'? That's odd. I only ever get an image of a large cave with purple geodes and pools of water. I figured it was a place for the dragons to commune with their ancestors or something. That's interesting. Maybe one day I'll be allowed back there and see for myself."

"Don't the dragons work for you? Aren't they domestics?" Miranda asked.

Their grandfather laughed. "There is nothing domestic about those beasts. No. We are two species, but one tribe. Rockgobbler no more listens to me than I do to him." He stood, looked back down the valley and frowned.

Justin and Miranda turned to see what their grandfather was looking at so intently. Black clouds covered the horizon, moving down the length of the valley directly toward them.

"Come on, kids," Grandpa Stone said, placing his hands on their shoulders and steering them toward the temple. "It looks like we're going to have another rough night ahead of us."

CHAPTER 12

MIRANDA
The First One

By the time Miranda had walked to the top of the temple's stairs, she was breathing heavily. Even in this mountain valley, she figured they must still be at a pretty high elevation.

No one had said a word while they were climbing the steep stone stairs. The sound of the waterfall was almost too much to shout over. Plus, it felt like if she took her eyes off the steps even for a moment, she would fall to her death.

She took a second to look back at the valley below. It was magnificent—truly a utopia—but as she lifted her gaze to the gathering storm, she wondered if it still would be the same paradise after tonight.

Miranda felt Grandpa Stone's hand on her shoulder. "Don't worry. The magic will hold. We'll take care of whatever nasty things are hiding in there. As a people, we have been warriors for thousands of years. When our tribe works as one, nothing can stand in our way."

Miranda nodded, terrified by the idea that there existed

something so powerful, it could create storms, and that it was hunting her. "I hope you're right."

Her grandfather laughed. "I usually am. Just ask your grandmother. Oh wait, she isn't here. I suppose you'll just have to take my word for it. Come on, let me show you the inside of the temple before we head home for dinner."

Grandpa Stone led Miranda and Justin through an ornately carved entryway and into a well-lit circular chamber. In the very center of the space, the waterfall entered through the ceiling, then disappeared again into the floor, with no more than a slight *whoosh*ing sound. It fell so straight, it looked like a column of water. Miranda wondered if this had been accomplished by some clever feat of engineering, or by... magic. The walls were punctuated by six evenly spaced torches in brackets, reflecting light off the glossy tile mosaics covering every inch of the room.

Miranda wandered around, quickly looking at the images. A woman, her hair streaked with silver, was riding on the back of a dragon as they flew low over a vast mountain range. On the next panel, the same figure was standing at the end of a valley looking up at a waterfall. This must be an image of the City of the Ancients, Miranda reasoned. Well, an image of the view before the temple or the adobe structures had been constructed.

Miranda walked across the room to another pair of mosaics. The next image in the series also featured the same woman, now holding up a small mallet to the sky. Two spirit figures hung in the air above her. One glared menacingly down at her, while the other's eyes were locked firmly on the angry one. In the final image, the woman was standing before the ziggurat. Her shoulders were slumped and her hair was completely white. She was leaning on a short staff for support.

"Kids, come over here," Grandpa Stone said.

Miranda wanted to inspect the images more closely—after all, the reason her aunt had sent her to the valley might be hidden somewhere in these mosaics—but Grandpa Stone had walked to the other side of the room, opposite the entry.

Once Miranda rounded the pillar of water, she was stunned to see a beautifully carved and painted statue of a woman that had been totally obstructed by the waterfall. The woman looked to be maybe in her thirties or forties, with long silver hair and bronze skin. She was dressed in a simple tunic made of cloth and cinched around her waist with a piece of rope. On one side a thin piece of dark wood was tucked into her belt, and on the other side, a small mallet. Her head was tilted back and turned to the sky. Her hands were spread wide, palms up, as if she had either been praying or holding something for a sacrifice.

The last thought caused Miranda's stomach to lurch. Having seen herself chained to a pillar, marked for sacrifice to the queen of monsters, she didn't like thinking about that possibility.

Not far in front of the statue was a small pillar about three feet tall and festooned with cuneiform script.

Grandpa Stone looked up at the statue, and said, "This is Api'onu, the First One. Our line is descended directly from her. It was she who gathered the wild *kosa'sinu*, which means 'winged snakes' or simply 'dragons,' from all over the mountains to this very valley. She came riding on the back of a mighty earth dragon, named Ya'ne'unde." Grandpa Stone turned in a slow circle, indicating the images on the walls one by one. "This is her story depicted here."

Justin giggled. "What does 'Yanni's undies' mean?"

Grandpa Stone lowered his head, shaking it slightly. "I'm about to revoke your tribal membership, Justin. It's pronounced Yah-nay-oon-day, and the name means, 'lighthearted' or 'mirthful,' but if it helps, we'll simply call him Ya'ne. You two would have gotten along quite well. Now please, let me finish the tale." He cleared his throat and continued. "When Api'onu came to this valley, she knew it was the place she was meant to be. So she pulled out her mighty hammer, and erected this temple."

Justin raised his hand. "An old woman built this temple by herself, with a *hammer*?"

"Yes. A *hammer*. And she wasn't old. Anyhow, not long after the temple was built, a nomadic people from the northwest came to this valley seeking refuge from terrible beasts that hunted them, the *unktéhila*, or 'horned serpents.' You might know them better as wyverns."

Miranda felt a shiver go down her spine and whispered, "I *hate* wyverns."

Grandpa Stone nodded. "But the tribes of men and dragons did not trust one another. The dragons looked too much like the wyverns, and the dragons had only agreed to come here with the First One to escape their war with mankind. It was she and Ya'ne who united the tribes of man and dragon together, showing them that when they worked as one, no wyvern could ever stand against them. That is when we became one people, the Oni'waz'legani"

"To this day, it is the right of passage in our tribe that man and dragon must go on a quest together, working as one, to honor this union and renew the vow our people swore to the First One to protect this valley for all time. When they return successfully from their quest, they are made full members of the tribe. We call the humans Bino'kosa'sinu, or Dragon Riders and the dragons Naya'kosa'sinu, or Dragon Warriors."

"*Man* and dragon?" Miranda said crossing her arms. "Please tell me you aren't excluding women."

"My goodness. Kya'ho'ah, when did you get here?" Grandpa Stone said with a smile. "Our tribe was founded by a woman,

Miranda," he said, indicating the statue. "I'm sure the ancestors would remove the magic of this valley and cast us out if we were ever so close-minded as to exclude women—from any of our quests."

"What kind of quests?" Justin asked, although he seemed distracted by something on the small pillar in front of the statue.

"Securing something that would be beneficial to the tribe. Finding an artifact of the past we can honor. Or, for the very brave, slaying a horned serpent and bringing back some part of the beast as a trophy," Grandpa Stone said.

"Kill a wyvern? Been there, done that. I guess I'm all quested up then. You can just call me Mr. Dragon Rider from now on." Justin said, and then pointed at the top of the pillar. "What went here?"

Miranda walked over and saw that her brother was looking at a slight depression in the rock. It looked as if something small and flat should have been placed there.

An angry look shot across their grandfather's face. "One of our ancestral relics is what. Someone came here and stole it."

"I thought the valley was hidden and safe from your enemies? How did someone come in here to steal it?" Miranda asked.

"How indeed," Grandpa Stone growled.

"Aha! An inside job," Justin said. Throwing around terms he had learned from TV crime shows and movies was one of his favorite pastimes. Miranda rolled her eyes. "Do you know who the perpetrator was?"

"I have my suspicions. As you know, only people who know this temple is here and have no ill intent can enter the valley. And no one from the tribe would ever take something so sacred as this artifact," Grandpa Stone said.

Miranda thought about who else must have knowledge of the valley, and a disturbing thought struck her. "You don't actually think the McAdelinds took it, do you?"

"It could be no one else," Grandpa Stone replied with a solemn nod.

"Is that what you and Grandpa Mac were arguing about?" Justin asked.

"That and... other things," he said, looking suddenly sad.

"What was this artifact exactly?" Miranda asked, sure that there was no way in the universe Grandpa McAdelind would ever steal anything.

"It was a small, flat stone with ancient script covering it, about so big," Grandpa Stone said, holding his fingers several inches apart.

Justin choked and started coughing.

Miranda looked at him and shook her head. "I didn't see anything like that at the ranch. Why do you think he took it?"

"Because I know the McAdelinds had one similar to ours. I also know their sacred stone went missing when Mac's daughter was killed by the wyverns. It seems fairly logical to me. There has always been a bit of jealousy between Mac and me."

Miranda saw the image of Aunt Em holding a similar piece of the tablet that Justin carried in his pocket at all times. That shard had been taken by the draconians almost twenty years before. "When did this artifact go missing exactly?"

"Not sure how that matters," her grandfather said. "But sometime in late May of this year."

Miranda looked at Justin, and she could tell he was thinking the same thing. It was their parents who had taken the shard. About a week before they sent Miranda and Justin to Colorado, their mother and father had gone on a trip somewhere. And not long after they got back, the draconians knew exactly where to find them. What didn't make any sense was: Why would they remove the shard if it was so well protected here? Was it possible that their parents had set this whole mess in motion by taking the shard from this temple in the first place? If so, that would just be one more thing to add to the ever-growing list of mistakes they had made.

The wind howled outside as the storm grew in intensity. Their grandfather looked back at the entryway and said, "We should get to the house and have some dinner before the storm hits. The magic shield should protect the valley. Typically, the weather stays in an ideal state here all year round. A little wind, an occasional rain shower, but never snow or storms of any kind penetrate its magic. But there is something different about this storm, I can feel it. The wind is greater than I can remember. It too seems magical, not natural. We may be in for a rough one tonight."

"Can't I just stay a little longer?" Miranda asked, scanning the walls for any clue or hint, anything that might point her in the direction of her aunt.

Grandpa Stone shook his head. "There will be time later. Let's get moving." Then seeing Miranda's look of disappointment and misinterpreting it, he added, "Don't worry. I have some other good stories lined up for you tonight."

Miranda was slow to follow her grandfather and brother out of the temple. There was something here; she could feel it. But where? She needed to stay and figure out what it was.

"Come on, Miranda!" her grandfather shouted. "The wind is making the steps treacherous. We need to leave, *now*."

Ugh, Miranda thought. It was like no one felt the same urgency to help her family that she did. She was beyond frustrated. But fine. She would just have to sneak back here tonight after dinner.

"Coming!" Miranda yelled and cast one more glance at the statue of the woman with her face to the heavens. This was where she was supposed to be—she could feel it.

CHAPTER 13

Justin
The Tale of River

Justin followed Grandpa Stone across the field toward the cliff dwellings on the side of the valley to their left. They continued past frantic workers trying to protect the crops from being damaged by the high gusts of wind. Occasionally one would stop, shout something to their grandfather in the tribal language, then continue working.

"Is everything okay?" Justin asked after the fourth person yelled something.

Grandpa Stone didn't turn around but shouted back over his shoulder, "Everyone is worried, and they are asking me if they should be."

"What are you telling them?" Justin asked.

"The truth," he said flatly and continued across the fields until they stood at the bottom of a series of ladders made from heavy logs. "Follow me," Grandpa Stone said and scrambled quickly up the thick rungs.

After climbing three consecutive levels, Justin was winded.

He felt like he had just completed an army obstacle course. "Do you have to do that every time you come home?"

His grandfather chuckled. "No, I usually take the ramps, but I thought you guys would like something a little more authentic."

"I'm good, let's stick to the ramps from now on," Justin said, leaning over the cliff to help his sister up and over the last rung.

As he reached over, a huge gust of wind came whipping down the valley. The people working below yelled and ducked as low as possible. The squall was strong enough to move the ladder away from the rock wall with Miranda still on it. She screamed and wrapped her arms around the top rung, holding on for dear life.

Grandpa Stone dove for the ledge and grabbed the top of the ladder. He held it in place, grunting with the effort as his arms were stretched under the heavy weight. "Hurry... help your sister."

Justin reached over and grabbed Miranda's hand, pulling her across the distance. As soon as she had jumped across the small gap to the ledge, his grandfather let the ladder go, and it flipped down the steep cliff, breaking apart as it crashed into the valley floor below.

"That's not good," Grandpa Stone said, pushing himself up into a sitting position. "Great. That will take a couple of days to fix and get back up here."

"Shouldn't we be more concerned about how that much wind is getting past the shield?" Miranda shouted, pressing herself flat against the rough stone wall.

Grandpa Stone looked around, shouted something down to several men and women who were running toward the dwellings for shelter, then turned to Miranda and Justin. "I'm sending out a couple of scouts to see what's going on above the storm, maybe get a sense for what this thing is exactly. We'll just hang out here until I get word."

Justin nodded. "Sounds good to me. Plus, I'm starving."

Miranda rolled her eyes. "Are you always hungry?"

"Only when I'm awake," Justin said and smiled.

They struggled against the wind, following Grandpa Stone along a wide ledge, keeping close to the sides of the buildings nestled into the rock wall. All of the human-made structures were constructed with some red, brick-like stone that Justin had initially mistaken at a distance for mud bricks. Justin looked up and could see rows of thick log ends barely sticking out from the wall surface where the second floor and the roof must be.

Their grandpa stopped at a brightly painted green door and pulled forcefully on the handle, fighting the wind that was pushing to keep it shut. He stood back and quickly motioned them both inside.

Before Justin went through the doorway, he paused and looked at an area of the sky where the clouds were spinning like a cyclone. The eye of the storm was directly above the Stone of Protection. When he closed his eyes and reached out with his mind, he was met with that same blackness he had experienced the night before. The demon *was* there.

His grandfather put a hand on his shoulder and guided him inside. "Don't worry about it, Justin. It will be okay. We'll take care of this tonight."

Justin nodded, but in his heart, he knew it wasn't going to be that easy.

The interior of his grandpa's house was not at all what Justin expected. The textured walls were painted a soft brown, and there were dark-leather couches and recliners draped with pillows and blankets of gold and white. Family photos hung on the walls, along with images of exotic locations and famous landmarks from all over the world. As Grandpa Stone had promised, his and his sister's heavy backpacks had been brought up to Grandpa's home and were leaning against the wall in one corner. But the thing that most caught Justin's attention was the enormous flat-screen TV against the back wall. "No way. You have a TV?"

"Of course I have a TV. I'm not Amish. How else do you think I watch golf and the Broncos?" Grandpa Stone said. He walked over to one of the recliners and plopped down, indicating with a gesture that Miranda and Justin should have a seat too.

Instead of sitting down, Justin walked around, looking at the walls. "How are you getting power and television stations? This place is completely in the middle of nowhere. I didn't see any cables or power lines outside." Then his eyes lit up. "Wait, is this all magic-powered?"

His grandpa laughed. "It is indeed. The magic of solar energy and satellite dishes." Justin started to ask another question, but his grandfather held up a hand and continued. "On top of the mesa above the valley," he said pointing toward the ceiling. "We have an extensive solar- and wind-energy operation. Operated under the name Hidden Valley Power. We take what we need for the people here and dump the rest into the electrical grid for profit. It's an excellent deal, really. We continue to live off the land as our ancestors did, without polluting the Earth, and we make enough on the side to ensure our people are well provided for."

Miranda smiled. "That's ingenious."

Their grandpa bowed. "Thank you very much. That was all my idea. Well... My and John's idea... If I'm being completely honest. We both went to college together and studied engineering."

"Then you and Grandpa Mac used to be friends," Justin said, matter-of-factly.

"The best of friends." Justin saw a flash of sadness in his eyes. Grandpa Stone looked toward the corner of the room and smiled. "Hey. That reminds me. I want to show you something."

He walked over and grabbed an old wooden stick that was propped against the wall. "Check this out," he said, holding it up so they could see it. The wooden stick was about four feet long, and on one end there were several feathers tied to the pole with leather straps, while on the opposite end, held in place with what looked like an entire roll of duct tape, was the head of a golf putter.

Justin smirked. "*That's* your magic putter?"

"I know it doesn't look like much, but trust me it's got it where it counts," Grandpa Stone said, swinging the club as if taking a long putt. "I almost never miss with this baby. All I have to do is think about where I want the ball to go, tap it lightly, and—*wham-oh!* A small breeze shoots out and the ball goes straight in the hole. Tomorrow I'll let you try it out. But I have to warn you. It only seems to work for me."

"Sure it does…." Justin said, narrowing his eyes suspiciously.

Miranda had walked over to a picture on the wall. "Is this Mom?" she asked.

There weren't many photos of their mother and father around the apartment in Manhattan, and Justin couldn't remember a single instance of seeing an image of his mother as a child. So he rushed over and joined his sister. Like everything else in the magical valley, the photo looked as if it had just been taken. It was in black and white and depicted Grandpa Stone with his arm around a young woman who looked a lot like his mother, holding a child of about three in her arms and smiling broadly. They all looked so happy.

"Yes. That is our little Kya'ho'ah," he said, grinning proudly. Then he looked at the woman in the photo, and even though he was still smiling his eyes filled with sadness. "And that is your grandmother."

"You said you met her in the river? What happened?"

Miranda asked.

"Yes. About forty-five years ago in fact," he said, and sighed. "It was such a beautiful summer day. John and I were going to hunt down a wyvern that had been spotted in the area, when we came across a young woman unconscious on the riverbank. As you can imagine, this was something unheard of. No one ever accidentally wandered into this valley. The stone not only keeps this place invisible and preserved but it also encourages unwanted eyes to look elsewhere."

"What do you mean?" Justin asked.

"There are people who are supposed to be here, and those who are not. The ones who are not suddenly get the idea to head in another direction. I've seen it a couple of times with park rangers and hikers. They start walking down the trail into the valley, then when they get within sight of the stone, they suddenly turn around and walk back up the hill."

Miranda frowned. "Why didn't that happen to us?"

"Because you are *supposed* to be here," he said. "Up until that point, no outsider had entered the valley without our permission. And such a beautiful one to boot." He sighed deeply before continuing. "When she woke up, she had no memory of who she was or how she'd gotten there. Over the next several days we checked missing-persons reports and asked any of the other tribes nearby if anyone had disappeared recently, but none had. When we asked her what she wanted to do, River insisted on staying here. She said there was something about the valley that felt right, like she was being called to this place."

"Did she ever find out who she was and where she was from?" Miranda asked.

"She did, but that story will be for *her* to tell you someday." He winked at them and continued. "The village elder at the time named her Akena'tani, which means River Daughter. But we just called her River."

"Did you guys get married then?" Miranda said.

Their grandfather shook his head sadly. "It was a little more complicated than that. I wasn't the only one who liked her."

Justin slapped his knee. "Oh, snap! Grandpa Mac had a thing for her too. Did you guys fight over her?"

"We didn't fight. We were the best of friends. We made a gentleman's agreement not to pursue her unless she wanted to be, and if she did in fact fall in love with one of us, the other would just have to live with the consequences. But like so many things in life, fate had a different idea. John's older brother died unexpectedly, and it fell upon him to become Dragon Lord."

"Wait. Grandpa Mac wasn't supposed to be the Dragon Lord?" Justin asked in disbelief.

"No. In fact, he wanted nothing to do with the title and politics of the dragon families. He much preferred being here, in the mountains, living a less complicated life. But duty and his new level of responsibility forced him into an immediate year-long internship with the Drake family."

"No way our grandfather spent a year with those slimeballs," Miranda said, her arms crossed over her chest.

Justin knew the reason for her hatred, and he too had a hard time believing Grandpa Mac would ever spend a year with that bigot, Lord Drake.

"Keep in mind that the current Lord Drake was just a teenage boy, and his father was not nearly as big of an idiot as he has become. But you are right. John didn't want to go. Things were complicated, and if you know him at all, subtlety isn't one of his strong suits." Grandpa Stone smiled and sighed. "Then word came that John was going to extend his trip by another year, and things moved along. River and I grew closer, and we were soon married."

"Is that the other reason you and Grandpa Mac are mad at

each other?" Justin asked.

"Partially. He cared more for River than he let on, and he was devastated to learn we had married."

"What do you mean, 'partially'? What else happened?" Miranda said.

"Your parents happened," he said, anger flashing across his face. "John didn't want his son to have anything to do with us, and trust me, the feeling became mutual when Robert took my daughter away."

"Yeah. You keep on telling yourself that. I can't think of a single instance where Dad was able to talk Mom into anything she didn't want to do," Justin said, and walked over to another family picture. This one was similar to the first; however, their mother was about ten years old now. Immediately Justin could tell that something major had changed in these people's lives. None of them looked quite as happy as they had in the last picture. This time, Grandpa Stone had one arm on their mother's shoulder and the other at his side. Their grandmother was not standing as close to her husband and daughter as before. She was just standing there, staring straight ahead, a sad look in her eyes, absentmindedly touching a large pearl necklace around her neck. Something about the gesture looked so familiar.

There was a knock at the door, and they all turned quickly around.

The door opened, and a man poked his head in. He was drenched, and the wind and rain forced its way through the small opening. "Pa'na'lulu!" He shouted. "Something is happening you need to see at once!"

Their grandpa rushed over to the door, depositing the putter he had been holding in the corner again. "What is it, Mana'doe? Did you see something while scouting?"

The man named Mana'doe looked back over his shoulder.

"We must go. The protective shield is weakening. The storm demon has been joined by another, one made of earth and mud. Their combined attack is… devastating. If we don't stop them soon… the valley will be lost."

CHAPTER 14

JUSTIN
Grandpa Stone's Magic Putter

GRANDPA STONE PUSHED PAST Mana'doe and peered outside. "By the ancients," he whispered. "I can actually see the barrier. That's not good. Not good at all."

He turned and ran to a tall cabinet resting against one of the room's rough walls. Inside was an old blue golf bag. He reached in and pulled out a long silver sword.

"Wait a minute. That sword looks identical to Grandpa Mac's," Miranda said.

"That's because the McAdelinds gave us the sword as a gift, and we, in turn, gave them this—" He indicated the worn black leather strap wrapped around the hilt. "That's what makes them so light. Another good story for later.

"Golf must be a little more… dangerous… than what I've seen on TV," Justin said. "You keep a sword in the golf bag and the putter in the corner? That's really weird."

Grandpa Stone grinned at him. "Not really. I use the putter more often," he said and swatted Justin on the butt with the flat of the blade on his way back to the door.

"Now you two stay here… unless the shield falls, then move as quickly as you can to the Temple. All the others will gather there for protection. But don't worry, we're going to deal with this once and for all." He motioned to Mana'doe, and they both quickly ran outside and into the raging storm.

Justin followed them to the door, pushed it back open slightly and peered outside. The sky was almost completely black. Clouds swirled about the eye of the massive storm. There was a low thumping sound that sent vibrations through him. He looked up at the usually invisible shield. With each quake, it shimmered with bluish energy, allowing sheets of torrential rains to rush through.

His grandfather and Mana'doe were standing near the edge of the cliff dwelling, staring up at the cyclone. Grandpa Stone put two fingers to his lips and blew several shrill whistles. Within seconds, Justin could sense the dragons quickly approaching. He watched in stunned silence as his grandfather took several steps back, and then hurled himself off the ledge.

Justin's heart nearly stopped, until he saw his grandpa Stone on the back of the earth dragon, Rockgobbler. "Okay, that was pretty darn cool."

A moment later, Mana'doe executed the same maneuver, and Justin watched as the two dragon riders joined several others in a tight formation as they left the shield and flew head-on into the storm.

A gust of wind hit the door from the outside and slammed it shut, knocking Justin back and into the couch. "Whoa. That's completely crazy. You should have seen the move Grandpa Stone just made… uh… What are you doing?"

His sister had pulled on a blue jacket and was unsheathing the long silver sword Grandpa Mac had given her. "We need to find answers before those creatures break through the shield. We've run out of time."

Justin put both hands out in a *stop* gesture. "Grandpa Stone said they can handle this and to stay put. We should do as he says."

"You don't really believe they can handle what's out there do you? Come on, Justin. No one has a clue about what these things are, and if the dracs were scared of them, I don't want to wait and find out why."

"So what are you saying, you want to run away?" Justin asked incredulously. "If anything, we should be out there with them fighting. You didn't see what I saw in the mind of the draconian we captured. Tiamat is going to kill *everyone*."

"No! That's not what I'm saying at all." Then Miranda relaxed a little. "We need to check out that temple again. I know that's where we are supposed to be. I can feel it. Once we find what we were sent here for, we go back to Thunderbird Ranch, get Grandpa Mac and the dragons, and rescue our parents and Aunt Em. *Then* we worry about Tiamat." She sighed. "But if we wait too long, those things hunting us will be here, and it will be too late. It's now or never."

Justin shook his head. "This is sounding very familiar. Our family is in danger, and you want to snoop around."

Miranda nodded. "And how did that work out for us last time? We found out our family is a bunch of dragon ranchers, and we met Storm and Red."

"Point taken. Plus, Grandpa *did* tell us to go to the temple if the shield falls. I imagine it wouldn't hurt to get a head start," Justin said, grudgingly. "All right, let's go."

Miranda smiled. "Grab your coat, and look around for something you can use as a weapon if we need to defend ourselves."

Justin ran over to his backpack, pulled out his father's light-brown jacket that someone had left for him back at Thunderbird Ranch, and put it on. He quickly scanned the room, looking for anything to use as a weapon, when his eyes fell on his grandpa's magic putter. "Grandpa will kill me if I break that."

Miranda followed his eyes to the putter. "Look at it. You'd probably be doing him a favor. The thing has been duct-taped together a hundred times already. Now take it and let's go."

Justin walked over to the corner and reached out to grab the wooden shaft, but stopped abruptly. He felt a pulsing energy emanating from it, just like the energy he had felt expanding from the protection stone.

"What's wrong? If Grandpa gets mad, I'll take the blame. Come on." Miranda shouted from the door.

Justin took a deep breath and grabbed the putter with both hands. Instantly he felt the energy move through him, and all the hairs on his body stood on end. The shaft was warm and cool at the same time, and he could feel a strange force swirling around inside the staff. The putter felt almost... alive. What in the world was happening? Was it truly magic, or was he just imagining all of this?

"Justin. Now!" Miranda yelled, straining to hold the door open against the wind and rain.

They ran outside and onto the cliff as a small quake shook the ledge, sending dust and loose rock from the overhang above. "Okay, time to go!" Justin shouted, and they sprinted to the left and down a series of ramps that led to the valley floor.

The earth shook again, and the sky flickered a brilliant blue, as sheets of rain came pouring through the breach in the protective shield, soaking them instantly to the bone.

"Let's run for it!" Miranda shouted over the downpour.

They started sprinting down one of the long pathways that cut diagonally toward the temple when they heard a series of blood-curdling screeches in the distance. Justin and Miranda stopped dead in their tracks and looked down the valley.

Justin couldn't see anything through the thick black clouds and heavy rain, so he closed his eyes and reached out with his mind. He pictured his vision spreading like ripples on the surface of a lake, focusing his thoughts down the valley. On the other side of the shield, there was a dark spot, just like the one that seemed to surround the flying lion-man demon. That must be the other creature, the one made of earth and mud that Mana'doe had mentioned.

"Can you sense anything? Are there wyverns out there?" Miranda asked. Justin could hear the terror in the question.

"All I can sense so far is another one of those dark areas like before.... No, wait. About a mile beyond the shield, there are a bunch of wyverns and draconians."

Miranda closed her eyes too. "Are you sure? I can barely sense anything."

Justin nodded. "Very sure, they're fighting with the dragons from the valley. Oh no, the dracs are trying to lure them even farther away."

The ground shook again—even more violently than before. The shield rippled, and a loud cracking sound to the right drew their attention to the cliff dwellings. Justin watched in horror as a massive piece of stone broke off from the overhang above and demolished several small structures, before crashing down to the valley floor.

Dark, ominous laughter shook the earth. "I'll tear this place down brick by brick if I have to. Save me the trouble, little girl. Come, bring the tablet shard to me. *Now.*"

Justin closed his eyes again and concentrated as hard as he could, trying desperately to see past the dark veil blocking him from reading the creature's thoughts. Then, far beyond the demon, he sensed Rockgobbler turn in the sky, making a beeline for the village.

"Come on, Justin! We don't have a lot of time left. Let's move," Miranda said, pulling him toward the temple.

But Justin held his ground. "Grandpa is coming back this way." He could feel the rage and anger building in Rockgobbler as he approached his target. Justin concentrated even harder and could sense the dragon diving at his intended prey.

"Come on. Why are you standing there," Miranda said, pulling on him again.

Justin shook her off. "Hold on a sec."

Rockgobbler was closing in. He could feel the excitement of the imminent kill building within the dragon. Then fear, followed immediately by pain, then—nothing. Justin sucked in a quick breath.

"What is it, Justin? What happened?"

"It's Grandpa Stone and Rockgobbler. I think they might be hurt. They went down when they attacked the creature on the ground. We need to help them." Justin started to walk toward the obelisk but stopped dead in his tracks when Miranda grabbed onto him and spun him around to face her.

"I know this sounds cruel, but we need to stick to the plan and rescue our family."

Justin couldn't believe what he was hearing. "He *is* our family too! Mom and Dad wouldn't want us to sacrifice Grandpa to get them back. No, I'm going to see if Grandpa needs help." He pulled free of her and started back down the path toward the protection stone. "You can come if you want."

Justin heard Miranda sigh in frustration, then run to catch up to him. When they were about thirty feet away from the stone, he could see something colossal in size punching the obelisk with one oversize arm. With each strike, the shield would flicker and fade, allowing sheets of rain and gusts of wind through. Mad laughter followed. "It's only a matter of time. A few more strikes and I'll be in. Trust me, if that happens before you bring me the shard, I'll kill everyone out of spite. As a matter of fact, I'll start with this one right here."

Justin came to a running stop, shielding his eyes with his hand from the rain, and looked at the creature. One of its huge arms had morphed into a massive pillar formed out of rocks and mud, pinning a man helplessly to the ground, as if he had been caught in a landslide.

"I can sense you, boy. We're not after you. All we want is the girl and the shard, everyone else can go on their way," the creature said, and it struck the obelisk one more time, causing the shield to sputter and shimmer. It turned and looked at Justin. It was a massive figure, two times the height of an average man, and probably six times as wide. Two glowing yellow eyes were shielded under a rocky brow ridge, and a mouth that looked like a hole in the dirt curved up into a smile. "There you are, boy. Such a fragile young thing. It would take nothing more than a flick of my finger to turn you into a pile of mush and bone." A wicked grin formed again on its craggy mouth. "After I'm done with this one..." It said, and the pile of rock and mud sprouting from its side began to shift and form into a massive arm. It picked up the man it was holding down and dangled him like a marionette in front of Justin. Grandpa Stone's head lolled unconsciously side to side with each movement.

Justin screamed, "Let him go! Immediately!"

The creature turned their grandfather to look at him and said, "What do you think, chief? Should I let you go?" Then out of the corner of his mouth, it said in a low voice, "Not until they give you the girl and the shard, great Lahmu." It turned to Justin and Miranda and smiled its evil smile yet again.

"Put the man down and then we'll talk," Justin commanded, gripping the putter tightly. He could feel the energy pulsing through the makeshift weapon, and it felt warm and tingled in his hand. "Drop him now, or I'm coming out there and making you do it."

The creature named Lahmu laughed and swung his arm with his grandfather down to the ground, covering him with mud and rock. Dirt crawled and spread over Grandpa Stone's prone body, covering every inch of him like an earthen cocoon. Then Lahmu said in a booming voice, "Brother! We can reserve our energy. You see, these two children have delivered what we have been tasked with recovering."

A lightning strike hit just behind the mud-and-rock monster, and Lahmu glanced over his shoulder at a figure descending from the storm clouds above. It looked like something out of a mix-and-match animal game, with the head of a lion, the body of a man, and the legs and wings of a falcon. It was wearing nothing more than a simple kilt, with a glowing talisman around its neck. It carried a huge mace in one hand and a long knife in the other. And when it spoke, its voice came out as a soothing purr. "It is a good thing you two younglings had a change of heart and decided to come to us. I am not sure I would have been able to quell my brother's lust for blood much longer. It would have been a shame for him to slaughter all of your kind needlessly."

"Needlessly? Of course, there is never a need, Ugallu. But I think if they do not get moving and hand over what we have come here for, we can do it for fun," Lahmu said with a rumbling laugh. "As a matter of fact, I've changed my mind. Now I *am* going to kill them all, every one."

The lion-man growled. "Steady your hand. We came here to finish what the umū dabrūtu and their scorpion-tailed steeds, the bašmu, have been too weak to achieve. Nothing more. Quell your bloodlust." He turned and glared at Miranda. "Plus, I have need of the girl. She will accomplish a task for me before we deliver her to our queen."

The rock-and-mud man slammed his other fist hard into the ground. "I will do as I please. If I wish to grind their bones to dust, leaving them nothing but puddles of flesh, it is my right as one of Tiamat's chosen. You will be wise to remember that, dear brother."

The lion-man's lips curled into a snarl, but he said nothing.

"Time's up," Lahmu said, and mud started to flow over their grandfather's head and face. "This one dies first."

CHAPTER 15

Justin
Reinforcements

"No!" Justin yelled, and charged through the protective barrier and directly at the mud monster. He swung the putter hard at its pillar-like arm and felt a massive amount of energy release.

A burst of wind erupted from the end of the stick, striking the creature with enough force that it brought down several trees as it tumbled through the forest.

"Holy cow!" Justin said. "The putter *is* magic."

Justin looked up at the flying lion-man to make sure he wasn't about to attack from the air, but he was just hovering in the sky, about twenty feet off the ground, staring at the staff. His eyes went wide for a moment before narrowing back to slits. "She's not there," he growled, looking almost… disappointed, as if he had been expecting Justin to fight with some other weapon.

Lahmu pulled himself up slowly, using one of the toppled trees as a brace. The wet earth surrounding him began to ripple as he drew it into him—quickly doubling his already substantial size. He stomped one of his tree-trunk like legs into the ground, making the earth shake.

The mud on the end of Lahmu's arm began to bulge and form into a huge ball. "That was a grave mistake. You will regret that, human."

"I guess we'll see who… regrets… what. That sounded way cooler in my head," Justin said, holding the long stick like a baseball bat. "Bring it on, squishy."

Lahmu roared and hurled the large mud ball at him.

Justin felt the energy building again, and he swung with all his might at the fast-moving mass. It split in two, both halves soaring past him and colliding with the ground making loud thumps. Justin tapped the stick on the ground a couple of times and took the batting position again. "You missed. Is that the best you've got?"

Lahmu's face split into a wicked grin. "I didn't miss."

"Justin! Look out!" Miranda screamed.

He turned in time to see each half of the mud ball morph and rise from the ground, taking on a humanoid shape, roughly resembling a smaller version of Lahmu. *This isn't good,* Justin thought. "Miranda. Grab Grandpa and help him back to the shield. I'll hold these two… err, I mean… four… off."

Miranda tried to make it to their grandfather, but the lion-man blocked her way. "Not so fast, little girl. You are the one I seek."

Miranda brought up her long silver sword into a defensive position, and Ugallu laughed. "Didn't your parents tell you that little children should not play with sharp objects?" he cooed, bringing his sizeable mace down in a wide arc.

Miranda swung the great sword up to meet the blow that sought to disarm her, sending sparks flying in every direction, and stumbled backward from the force of the strike. "Never got that message, my parents weren't really around much," she grunted.

Justin swung the putter at the winged lion-man, striking him on the side, knocking him temporarily off balance. But that time the effect wasn't as strong. Justin could feel the power within the putter becoming more erratic with every use.

"We need to get Grandpa out of here before—" Something hit him hard from behind, sending him to the earth. Justin struggled to roll over, but when he finally did, he saw that one of the mud clones had landed on top of him, pinning him to the ground. It seemed to melt onto him, the mud swiftly crawled up over his legs and waist, spreading like thick chocolate pudding over his body.

"Miranda! Help!" he screamed, struggling to keep his arms and hands free.

Miranda sprinted over and tried to drag him away from the creeping mass. The mud stopped spreading up his body as it shifted and moved. Long spider-like legs shot out from the sides of the blob, trying to get a grip on the surrounding soil.

Miranda dropped Justin's arms, and swung at the creepy legs with her sword, severing several. However, as soon as she removed a piece, another one would grow instantly in its place. She was relentless in her desire to cut the creepy mud-spider-thingy to bits, futilely hacking chunk after chunk away. But it wasn't until she removed one of the legs with enough force that it shot into the river, and dissolved into a cloud of muddy silt, that Justin had an idea.

"Pull me into the water! Quickly!" Justin shouted as the mud creature spread up to his chest. His sister grabbed him with one hand and swung the sword at the snaking tendrils with the other. With one last surge of effort, she tugged them both into the swiftly rushing river.

As soon as Justin plunged into the water, the mud-clone

dissolved and was swept away. Justin broke the surface of the river gasping for air. "I think if we stay in the water, the earth-dude will have a hard time getting to us."

Miranda nodded toward Ugallu flying not twenty feet away with his arms raised to the sky chanting something. "But Mr. Flying Lion over there will be able to fry us with lightning... well, at least fry you, I'm pretty much immune."

"That doesn't make me feel any better."

"Sorry. On dry land, we can try to grab Grandpa Stone and make a run for the shield. Here, he just needs to hit the water near us," Miranda said, then yelled, "duck!" As another massive mud-and-rock boulder was hurled in their direction.

Justin looked at the opposite bank to see another mud-monster clone forming, cutting them off from seeking protection there. "He's trying to trap us. That's not good. I think you're right. We need to get out of the water, now. Maybe I can clear a path with the putter."

"Worth a shot," Miranda said.

Justin grasped the shaft of the putter, but this time the power wasn't building as it had before. It seemed out of control and unfocused. Justin bore down and tried to force the wild energy to his will. His hands throbbed painfully as the power in the putter seemed to fight back.

Something hit him hard in the side and sent him stumbling back farther into the river, and he lost all control over the staff. There was a massive explosion as the building energy within the putter released suddenly. Justin and Miranda went flying in opposite directions, propelled by the mysterious force within the staff.

Justin lay splayed on the riverbank, not far from his grandfather, gasping for breath, the wind knocked out of him. He used the putter as a crutch, trying to get back to his feet.

Out of the corner of his eye, Justin saw something lunge at him—one of the mud-clones—and he retreated back and into the river.

Miranda resurfaced about ten feet to his right, a pained look on her face as she held the massive sword in one hand and her side with the other. She looked unsteady, as if she might pass out.

Lahmu stood on the riverbank, his overly elongated arm shrinking back into his body. He must have shot it out like a giant yo-yo, hitting Justin in the side and breaking his concentration. "What's the matter, little human? Is the power of the staff too much for you to handle? Brother, subduing these two children is going to be very easy. I told you we should not be concerned."

The lion-man flew over closer, his mace crackling with lightning. "Perhaps you are correct, Lahmu. They appear weak and unprepared. However, it would be foolish to underestimate them. After all, they aren't quite *entirely* human."

Justin splashed over to Miranda, who was now waist deep in the water, and helped to steady her. "Sorry about that, sis. I lost control of the energy. We're trapped. I still can't read either one of these guys' thoughts. Can you block the lightning?"

Miranda shivered. "I think so. Only if it's close to us, though. And like I said, he doesn't need to be close to kill you." She looked back over her shoulder. "We're about ten feet away from the shield. I can see the protection stone. We can still make a run for it."

"And leave Grandpa out here defenseless? No way," Justin objected.

"*We* are what they're after. Maybe we can buy some time for Grandpa to wake up," Miranda said.

Justin shook his head. "There has to be another way. What

if we—" He stopped mid-sentence when he saw the lion-man's eyes shoot open; they were now glowing with energy. Lightning was whirling rapidly around his mace. He began to advance slowly toward them. Mighty beats of his wings were keeping him hovering just inches above the water's surface.

Movement to his left and right caught Justin's attention as two of the mud-clone creatures stalked along the shore, flanking them, cutting them off from either riverbank.

"I've got a bad feeling about this," Justin said and looked to where their grandfather was lying on the ground, motionless. They could really use some of those other warriors and dragons right about now. Had they all taken the bait and chased the wyverns and draconians down the valley? He and Miranda were outnumbered and overpowered. Without any help he'd be dead in seconds.

Justin closed his eyes one last time, reaching out with his mind to see if he could sense any of the warriors or dragons near enough to help. But he couldn't detect any of them. They were either dead or out of his range.

Then he felt it. Small at first—just a familiar feeling in the pit of his stomach—but with every beat of his quickening heart, hope began to grow.

"You know," Justin said, addressing the lion-man. "Those… what did you call the draconians?—yabba-dabba-doo, or something—are kind of jokes compared to you two. If they had started with you… er… guys, we would have been captured a month ago."

Lahmu chuckled. "Truer words have not been spoken for millennia, human. Our queen depends too much on those weak umū dabrūtu. They are pawns—fodder for battle. They should be used as they were intended—to clean up after the real warriors, leaving the actual work to us, the mighty Lahmu and Ugallu."

Justin looked over at his sister and shrugged. "I'm sorry, but I don't recognize those names, are you guys famous or something?"

Miranda leaned in and whispered, "What are you doing?"

"Stalling. Reinforcements are coming," Justin whispered back.

"No reinforcements are coming to save you, boy," Ugallu, purred. "But have no regrets on that score. No human can stand against our might."

Lahmu shrugged his great shoulders. "We are feared, not famous. We were created to do battle against gods, not children. You two are nothing but a nuisance, and eliminating you is nothing but a task to be completed."

A bolt of lightning shot from Ugallu's mace and struck a nearby tree branch, setting it instantly on fire. "Enough talk. You will surrender now or I will incapacitate the girl and roast you alive, boy. You have three seconds to comply." He raised the mace over his head.

Something large landed behind the two creatures, placing itself between the demons and Grandpa Stone, and Justin couldn't help but smile. The enormous form of a red dragon spread his wings and arched his back, letting out a bone-shattering roar.

This was instantly followed by another dragon—a blue—landing on the opposite bank behind the mud-man clone. Her wings tucked back along her sleek body, crouching low, as her tail thrashed back and forth, readying to pounce.

Justin almost laughed with glee knowing that Red and Storm, their friends and protectors, were with them now.

He sensed something else too. A third dragon, moving swiftly and impossible to see. It swept past overhead, flying through the gale wind as if it were nothing. Maybe Argo, or Thunder.

No, it was Nightshade. Was Billy here too?

He looked up into the night sky—squinting into the wind and rain, just in time to see something red, white, and gold plunge off the black dragon's back. It did a flip in the air, and then there was the sound like a sheet caught in the wind, flapping hard.

Both Ugallu and Lahmu followed the plummeting object closely with their eyes. Justin grabbed Miranda's elbow and pulled her back and away from where it was going to crash into the river.

A plume of water blasted high into the sky.

Standing in the middle of the water, poised between Justin and Miranda and the two monsters, in her red dress and white apron, was… Mrs. Lóng?

The mysterious cook glanced over her shoulder and said, "Do be a couple of dears and help your grandfather to safety." Then her eyes began to glow with a golden light. "I will deal with these two."

CHAPTER 16

Miranda
Retreat

Miranda was losing her mind. That was the only explanation. The freezing water was causing her to have hallucinations. There was no way in the world that Thunderbird Ranch's crazy cook had just plummeted out of the sky off the back of a dragon and landed gracefully in the middle of a storm-swollen river.

But there she was. Miranda shook her head vigorously—she had to be seeing things. But when Miranda looked again, Mrs. Lóng was still there.

Something was tugging on her shirt from behind, and Miranda turned to see Justin guiding her to the riverbank toward Red and their grandfather. But Miranda couldn't avert her gaze from the scene playing out. Mrs. Lóng was moving her arms in sweeping circular motions around her body, like a very slow hula dance.

Ugallu let out a mighty roar and pointed his large, storm-charged mace directly at the cook.

Miranda screamed out a warning and tried in vain to

move in front of Mrs. Lóng, hoping to block the lightning from turning her into a crispy fossil. But Justin held Miranda tight, dragging her farther onto shore and completely out of the water.

The tip of the mace exploded with energy, followed by a cracking of thunder, as the zigzagging lightning arced wildly toward Mrs. Lóng.

The old woman barely slowed her swirling motion as she flicked her wrist, launching a giant ball of river water high into the air. It intercepted the lightning bolt, which exploded into a cloud of steam.

Miranda's jaw dropped open. What the heck had just happened?

"Duck!" Justin yelled and pulled down hard on Miranda, forcing her into a low crouch. She felt a blast of wind as Red's tail swung swiftly over her, missing her head by mere inches and colliding with one of the mud-man clones, which had snuck up on them from behind. The force of the impact sent it flying through the air and into the whirlpool.

The water around the cook began to spin faster and faster as she drew it to her and forced it to rise into the air. Mrs. Lóng was creating a waterspout, standing calmly in the eye of the vortex, and as the water continued to recede from the riverbanks, Miranda could just make out the cook's pristine golden shoes, somehow untouched by the mud and muck at the bottom of the river.

Suddenly everything stopped; the cook, the water from the cyclone, even the rain seemed to hang in the air motionless: time stood still. Mrs. Lóng, her glowing golden eyes crackling with energy, snapped her head to the side to look at Miranda. "Don't just stand there, dear. Grab your grandfather and get him behind the shield," she said, her voice deeper than normal, almost menacing. "Move. Now!"

She threw her arms out toward Lahmu, launching the

waterspout toward him with tremendous force and striking him like a tidal wave.

The monster tried to hold his ground, fighting against the deluge of river water as it blasted whole chunks from its body. Lahmu raised his arms in a vain attempt to block the assault, but those too were washed quickly away. As the demon's chest was slowly being ripped apart, something small and shiny was exposed, but only for a second, before the rest of his form vanished.

"So. That's how you want to play, creature!" yelled the disembodied voice of the mud-man. It seemed to come from all around them at once, echoing off the canyon walls.

Ugallu took advantage of this distraction to come swooping down at Mrs. Lóng, swinging his wicked mace hard at her head.

The old woman moved ever so slightly to the left, dodging the massive club by inches, only to step directly into the path of the curved knife's follow-up stroke. She threw one arm up in a block, stopping the knife's momentum with strength no human, let alone a person who was almost seventy years old, should possess.

Ugallu's eyes opened wide in shock, and he paused for a fraction of a second—clearly confused by his unlikely opponent. But that was all the cook needed. She jumped high into the air, spinning at the same time and sending a kick hard into the flank of the flying lion-man. Ugallu let out a scream of pain and frustration as he pinwheeled into a patch of shrubbery some twenty feet away.

Justin had managed to guide Miranda back away from the riverbank and over to their grandfather. He was bending over the unconscious man, trying to revive him, but Grandpa Stone was unresponsive.

Miranda crouched down next to them and said, "I think we're going to have to drag him back."

Justin nodded, and they each grabbed hold under one of the unconscious man's arms. They both strained hard, but their grandfather was too heavy to move. "Red. When you're done making mud pies over there, we need your help moving Grandpa behind the shield!" Justin yelled over the wind and rain.

"*Does it look like I'm playing?*" the massive red dragon grunted, his voice strained as he struggled against three new mud-clones that had popped up out of the riverbank and were grabbing onto his tail and front legs. "*These guys are stickier than snot.*"

Then Miranda felt it: a massive buildup of electricity. She looked back over her shoulder and saw Ugallu rise into the air and hover about thirty feet off the ground. The storm clouds were swirling around him as tiny bolts of electricity illuminated the flying monster in the center of the vortex.

"Mrs. Lóng! Get out of the water!" Miranda screamed.

Mrs. Lóng turned and started to wade quickly toward Miranda and Justin, but then she stopped dead in her tracks. She was straining to move, pulling hard against something under the surface. Miranda watched in horror as thick mud began to climb out of the river, holding her feet in place.

The old cook crouched low, then sprung high into the air, but thick tendrils of mud and rock shot up and grabbed her, pulling her back down into the water even deeper than before.

Ugallu smiled wickedly. "Time to die, creature!" he yelled over the roaring wind.

Mrs. Lóng looked back over her shoulder at Miranda, and for the first time, she could see fear in the old woman's eyes.

Miranda called out to Storm with her thoughts. "*Storm! The lion-man is going to use lightning. You need to get Mrs. Lóng out of there now. Hurry!*"

The blue dragon didn't hesitate, but leapt right at the cook, cutting effortlessly through the vortex of wind and lightning, and grabbed Mrs. Lóng by her outstretched hands. Storm pulled her up and out of the river just as Ugallu brought his mace down, pointing it at the spot the old woman had been standing a moment before, and unleashed a massive burst of electricity.

Red was able to shake the mud-men off and bound toward Miranda and Justin, his massive paws scooping them both up and tucking them under one forelimb while gripping their grandfather under the other. Red tucked all three into a ball, forming a protective shield to insulate them from the shockwave of superheated steam exploding from the river. He hit the ground hard and rolled through the barrier and into the City of the Ancients.

Storm soared in and dropped the cook near Red.

Mrs. Lóng took a couple of deep breaths, looking more tired than Miranda had ever seen before. "That shield isn't going to last long. We need to get to the temple," she said and strode over to their grandfather. She placed a hand on his forehead, then gently moved it down to his cheek.

Grandpa Stone's eyes flickered open, trying hard to focus on her face. "River?..." he whispered and closed his eyes again.

"The river is fine, you old fool," Mrs. Lóng added quickly. "Your grandfather's leg and a couple of ribs appear to be broken, and from the sound of it, he also has a concussion. We need to keep him safe while we deal with this situation."

"Is Rockgobbler... okay?" Grandpa Stone whispered.

"I sent Billy off to retrieve him, they should be here shortly," Mrs. Lóng replied softly.

No sooner had she spoken the words than Billy and Nightshade came flying in high through the shield. Nightshade was straining to carry the great brown dragon gripped tight in his forepaws. Even with the added weight of the full-grown dragon, Nightshade was able to land softly a few feet away. Rockgobbler was bleeding in several spots on his forelimbs, wings, and stomach, and he had a huge gash on his neck.

Billy tipped his baseball cap to Miranda and flashed her an impish grin. Miranda felt heat starting to rise in her cheeks and forced herself to look over at her grandpa.

Mrs. Lóng pointed at Billy and said, "Don't just stand there gaping like an idiot, Billy. Come over here and make yourself useful."

Billy shot the cook a dirty look but dismounted quickly and ran over. "I *was* being useful. There are a dozen wyverns out there. I had to fight them off before I could grab the dragon."

"Are the other warriors okay?" Miranda asked, concerned for the other dragons and tribesmen that she had watched fly out to fight off the attackers pursuing her and her brother.

Billy nodded. "They were right behind me. They should be here any second."

"We should wait for them, we can regroup and attack those two creatures as a team," Justin said.

"No. We cannot delay," Mrs. Lóng said. "We must get to the temple and try to repair the damage done to the shield before those demons break through."

"But you were beating them on your own. We could end this once and for all," Justin objected.

Mrs. Lóng vigorously shook her head. "I was not beating them, child. I was barely holding them off."

Several dragons in formation flew through the shield all at once and landed not far away. All of them looked beaten and bruised and ready to collapse.

"Look around you, Justin," Mrs. Lóng continued. "They will take over this valley and destroy everyone. The shield is our only hope—for now."

The earth shook. Miranda looked over at the protection stone and saw the reformed Lahmu hammering it with fists made of solid rock. "How can we repair a magic shield? Don't we need a wizard or something?"

"We don't need to repair it, dear. We just need to recharge it," Mrs. Lóng said. "I believe we have everything we need to accomplish that task right here. Now, let us move before all is lost."

CHAPTER 17

JUSTIN
Recharge

"**M**RS. LÓNG. WAIT UP!" JUSTIN SHOUTED, sprinting to keep up with her shockingly fast pace.

"We must hurry, dear. Those demons will not honor you by calling a 'timeout.'" Mrs. Lóng gestured back toward the failing shield surrounding the valley. "It is now only a matter of seconds before the protective field that has kept this valley safe for millennia will fall. It is up to you and your sister to ensure the protection remains… even if it is for just a bit longer."

Justin let out a humorless laugh. "What in the world are Miranda and I supposed to do?"

Mrs. Lóng stopped and regarded him for a second. "Honestly, I am not entirely sure. But I will know once we get there." Then she turned and redoubled her speed, heading for the steep steps of the ancient ziggurat.

Justin looked over his shoulder to make sure Miranda, Red, and Storm were still following. Billy had remained with the tribesmen and their dragons. If the shield was going to fall, they were going to stall the two demons long enough for Justin and Miranda to attempt—whatever it was—the cook had in mind.

Mrs. Lóng reached up and touched her pearl necklace, and her eyes narrowed for a moment. She looked as if she had seen something horrible up ahead, and stopped so suddenly that Justin stumbled past her. When he turned around to ask her what was wrong, she pointed to the buildings on either side of the cliff walls and said, "Did you know that some of these bricks were made by *baking* mud?"

So I was right, thought Justin, *some of them are mud brick after all!* But had Mrs. Lóng lost her mind? Now was not the time for an anthropology lesson. "What does that have to do with anything?" he asked.

Mrs. Lóng tapped the side of her head. "Just something to think about, dear."

When they arrived at the temple stairs, Red gently lowered Grandpa Stone to the ground. Mrs. Lóng knelt down beside him, checking his pulse and gently pulling his eyelids apart. "Your grandfather will be all right so long as we can reinforce the barrier."

Justin noticed strands of his grandfather's long black hair streaked with gray. "Uh… why is Grandpa's hair turning white?"

Mrs. Lóng motioned around her. "Without the magic of the protection stone the valley is dying. Its power to preserve is fading fast. Soon time will catch up to all things here—the crops, the buildings, and the people." She turned and addressed the dragons. "Can you two remain here and make sure the chief is protected?"

When Red and Storm nodded their great heads, she stood and brushed her dress and apron down flat and said, "Come along now, children. We have much to do."

When they got to the top landing of the ziggurat's stairs, right outside the entrance, Mrs. Lóng stopped and looked back down the valley. The rain had turned to hail and was now coming through in waves as the shield continued to pulse out of existence. Justin could see the men and women down below seeking shelter under their dragons' wings.

Mrs. Lóng reached out toward Justin. "We have run out of time. Hand me the staff."

Justin hesitated, feeling a lot safer with the magical putter in his possession, but tossed it to her reluctantly.

She grasped it and spun it in her hands several times, testing its weight before—to Justin's horror—she ripped off the feathers and the golden golf club head held tightly in place by a cocoon of gray duct tape and colored string.

"Hey! What are you doing? You're breaking Grandpa's putter!" Justin yelled and tried to take the staff back.

Mrs. Lóng slapped his hand away. "This is no putter, child. And it certainly does not belong to your grandfather. It needs to be in its original form if this is going to work properly. Now come," she commanded, and headed quickly into the large circular room inside the temple that they had visited a few hours earlier.

Mrs. Lóng came to a stop in front of the statue of the woman their grandfather had called, "the First One." She paused for a moment, staring up at the statue, and bowed her head in what Justin could only describe as reverence. When she turned back around, Justin was shocked to see tears in her eyes. Who was this woman to Mrs. Lóng? There was no way they could have known each other, yet Justin had the feeling that they were connected somehow.

Mrs. Lóng handed the putter to Miranda. "Do be a dear and place the staff there," she said, indicating the statue's outstretched arms.

As Justin glanced down at the small pillar in front of the

statue, his hand instinctively slipped to the stone shard in his pocket. This had to be where it belonged. He pulled the small piece of rock out and placed it in the slight indentation: a perfect fit. As soon as the small stone made contact with the pillar, the cuneiform script began to glow with a soft bluish light.

Mrs. Lóng nodded approvingly. "Excellent."

With both objects now in their respective places, the room began to shake slightly.

"What's happening? Is the temple going to collapse? Did you activate the self-destruct or something?" Justin asked, looking around nervously.

Mrs. Lóng frowned. "Please, child. Would I really put you two in a dangerous situation like that?"

Justin shrugged. "Maybe."

Miranda nodded. "Probably."

The cook shook her finger disapprovingly. "I have half a mind to—" The earth began to quake, cutting her off. Dust and rocks rained down from the slipping seams in the stone ceiling.

Justin ran back to the entrance. "Uh oh! One of those mud balls just got through the shield. If we're going to do something, we need to do it now."

"Quickly, both of you, don't remove the staff from the statue's hands, but grab hold of either end and face the entrance to the temple," Mrs. Lóng instructed.

As soon as Justin touched the staff, his fingers began to tingle. A tremendous energy surged through the smooth wooden pole. "Whoa! It's been supercharged."

Mrs. Lóng took a step back. "Excellent. Now concentrate on that feeling. Let the energy from the staff build and flow into you—through you. Feel it move into every cell in your body."

Justin closed his eyes and let the strange feeling spread.

"It's kind of like when Red used his breath weapon... except different. This is gentler. It doesn't feel like I'm trying to contain a bunch of fire, it feels like... air or wind... trying to escape in every direction at once."

"You are feeling the elemental forces trapped inside the staff, dear. We are going to use them to transfer the power of the temple to the protection stone, and hopefully, recharge it enough to live another day. Now stop the chitchat and concentrate," Mrs. Lóng snapped.

Justin could sense something and looked over at his sister. She was sweating, straining with concentration, but he could also feel that she was worried too, and he didn't blame her. The last couple of times he had tried anything to do with dragon's breath or fire it hadn't gone quite as planned. As a matter of fact, at the warehouse, it had all gone horribly, horribly wrong. It seemed like every time he tried to exert any control over something he didn't entirely understand, he almost killed someone. The truth was, Justin was scared. He didn't want to be responsible for hurting anyone, and controlling these forces seemed well beyond anything he would ever be able to do.

But what choice did he have? If he didn't try, if he just gave up, a lot of people would die. Miranda wasn't giving up. He was just going to have to be brave like her. Plus, Justin had sworn to himself days ago that he would no longer be a coward. If he had learned anything over the past month, it was that he had to be brave. Not just for himself, but for his whole family. So he took a deep breath, closed his eyes, and let the energy soak in.

Justin soon felt the power flowing from the staff through his arm and into his body. It felt warm and familiar, as if a missing piece of him was returning home. He felt powerful and strong. He wanted nothing more than to let these feelings wash over him, to become the person he had always dreamed he could be. To be as strong as his sister. No, stronger: a superhero.

The energy was swirling faster and faster inside him, building in intensity and power. But then something happened Justin did not expect. In the very center of the cyclone, he felt a fire begin to burn. The same fire he had felt when Red used his breath weapon for the first time, and again at the warehouse when he had tried to control the strange greenish flames. He could feel it building inside him, growing and strength and intensity, and he began to panic. He was going to lose control, and someone was going to get hurt.

"Justin. You need to stay calm," Mrs. Long said. "Do not force the power, guide it. Use the energy within yourself as a conduit."

Nothing she was saying made sense. How was he supposed to guide it? Instead, he tried to stop the flow of energy, stop the cyclone from twisting inside him, stop the flame from growing and spreading, but he couldn't. The more he tried, the more it grew. Fear took over, and Justin attempted to release his grip on the staff, but his hand refused to respond.

He forced his eyes open. Mrs. Lóng's forehead was creased with worry.

Justin strained to look at Miranda. Her hair was standing on end, wild with electricity, as arcs of blue-white energy danced across her body.

Justin's vision began to cloud over with a shimmering orange haze, and he realized he not only felt that he was on fire but he was in fact literally on fire. His breathing became erratic, and he felt he couldn't draw air into his lungs. It was happening again. He needed to stop it. He was going to burn it all down.

"No!" Mrs. Lóng yelled. "Do not stop. You are almost there. Fight through the pain." Justin heard his sister groan, but she said nothing. "Concentrate on the feeling, the power awakening in both of you. Try to keep it there for just a moment longer."

Justin closed his eyes again, but the fire was too intense, he was going to burn up if he kept it inside him a second longer. He screamed, and fire burst out in all directions.

Mrs. Lóng jumped back quickly. "Justin, if you don't hold it together, all is lost. You are almost there. You can do it!"

Justin felt the fire building even stronger, and it felt like his eyes were burning from the inside out. "I can't!" he yelled, and another burst of flames surged from him. He heard his sister scream, and he forced his eyes over to see her. Her shirt was on fire. He was going to kill her.

Mrs. Lóng made a quick motion with her hand, and a stream of water from the waterfall shot onto Miranda's arm, extinguishing the flames. But as soon as the spray touched her, bolts of electricity traveled its length, one arcing out, hitting Mrs. Lóng in the chest and sending her flying back against the wall.

Justin gasped as the old woman remained motionless for a moment. He saw a hole burned through the fabric of her red blouse, just below the neck. He wanted to run to her, to help, but he was locked in place by the mysterious force flowing through him. Then he watched in stunned relief as the old woman shook her head and stood on shaky legs. She reached up and touched the pearl necklace, sighing in relief. The material of her red blouse began to weave itself back together, becoming whole again.

Mrs. Lóng straightened out her white apron, brushed off her skirt, and strode back over to them, placing herself between Justin and his sister. She had a sad look in her eyes. "You both can do this. I know you can, because you have to. There is no other option. You need to learn control, or all is lost," she said. "Do not give up, do not give into your insecurities and fears, everything is depending on you." She reached out and placed her hands on top of theirs.

As soon as she touched him, the pain was gone. Justin could feel the strength and determination of the cook's will. She was not going to let the fire and lightning and wind out of control—they were her servants. Justin latched onto that feeling and forced the fire back inside, containing it.

"Good. Now move it into the staff," Mrs. Lóng grunted, her voice laced with pain and determination.

Justin focused on pushing the intense inferno swirling inside him into the wooden pole. He could feel it moving from his chest, through his arm, and into the staff. That's when he felt something else there too. Another presence entirely. Other spirits were in the temple with them. He felt one of the beings nearby, a being that wanted only to protect this place. It seemed to be residing in the very statue of the silver-haired woman, holding the magic staff in her outstretched arms. But beyond that, in the deep recesses of the temple there was something ancient and very angry.

"That's it. You can feel the spirit's energy. Force it out of the statue and into the protection stone," Mrs. Lóng whispered.

"What is it?" Miranda asked.

"A protection spirit. That is all I know. Concentrate. Now is the time. Your energies are one with the staff. Envelop the spirit. Pull it out," Mrs. Lóng directed, her voice harsh with pain.

Justin could feel it, fighting against them, struggling to stay. He forced his fire to connect with the electrical energy flowing from his sister. The second the three primal forces mixed within the staff, he heard the spirit scream, and a beam of intense energy shot from the statue of the First One's eyes and out through the entrance of the ziggurat.

The spirit cried out, *"No, don't. He will get free. He can't get free!"* Then it was gone from the temple. Sucked from its home of more than six thousand years.

There was a pulsing sound all around him, and Justin could feel the protection stone lapping in the energy it so desperately needed to keep the shield in place. He could feel the barrier becoming stronger, and the attack from the two demons weakening against its restored might.

When the beam finally stopped, he could move again. Justin let go and looked over at Miranda. She smiled weakly at him. They had done it. They had restored the shield. The City of the Ancients was safe—they were safe.

Mrs. Lóng let go of the staff and looked at Justin and Miranda with unseeing milky-white eyes. "That was… adequate… children," she said, in no more than a whisper. Then her eyelids fluttered shut, and she collapsed to the floor.

CHAPTER 18

Miranda
Tabrati

MIRANDA WATCHED as her brother dropped to his knees, cradling the old woman in his arms, shaking her ever so slightly. "Mrs. Lóng! Can you hear me?" But she was unresponsive.

"She'll be all right, Justin. You saw what she could do. She's magical. A witch or something. She'll be fine," Miranda said reassuringly, trying to ease her brother's fears.

But Mrs. Lóng did not look well. She looked fragile and spent. All the natural color had been drained from her face. Miranda bent down next to the woman and touched her arm lightly, feeling how cold it was. She then took Mrs. Lóng's wrist and felt for a pulse. There was a slow, gentle beat. She was still alive. "She'll be fine, Justin."

Her brother lowered the old cook's head to the stone floor. "We need to get help. She seems frail, and she never seems frail. I'm not sure how much damage was done to her. This is my fault. She'd be okay if I hadn't lost control."

Miranda shook her head. "This was her idea, she knew the risks."

Justin's brow furrowed, like he was about to give her a lecture, when his eyes came to rest on something behind her. Miranda spun, half expecting to find an evil creature or spirit creeping up on her, but instead saw that a section of wall next to the statue had moved, exposing a dark hallway that disappeared deep into the temple.

"When in the world did that happen?" Miranda said.

"We must have done something to open it when we charged the shield. Where do you think it goes?" Justin asked.

Miranda shook her head. "I have no idea. But I think this is what we're supposed to find. Let's go."

"What about Mrs. Lóng? We just can't leave her here," Justin said.

Miranda nodded, ran over to the temple entrance, and yelled down, "Billy! We need your help!"

A minute later the older boy came running into the temple, out of breath. "What is it? Are you okay?"

"Yes, we're fine. We need somebody to watch over Mrs. Lóng while we see what is back there," Miranda said, motioning to the passage behind the statue.

Billy looked down at Mrs. Lóng, and his eyebrows knitted with worry. "What happened?"

"Long story. I'll fill you in later," Miranda said, grabbing her brother and pulling them to his feet. "We'll be back in a second."

Without waiting for a response, Miranda walked over to one of the lit torches attached to the circular room's wall and pulled it out of its sconce. "Come on. Let's check it out."

Justin stood up and followed her over to the dark entrance. "Whoa," Justin exclaimed. "That looks like it's going right to the center of the temple."

Miranda grabbed his arm. "Well... let's find out." And she

pulled her brother down the stone corridor.

After only a short time the hall opened up into another circular room, but much more massive than the first. Small reflective stones diffused the light of the torch all around the space, illuminating the chamber. Cuneiform script covered the walls, forming complex patterns over every surface. And at the opposite end of the room from where they had entered stood a large rectangular stone table with two items resting upon it.

Miranda and Justin crossed the room until they were standing in front of the two small objects. One was a large, beat-up wooden mallet, which looked to be about as old as the temple itself. The other was a simple wooden stick not much bigger than a pencil.

"Hey, these are the two things the statue of the gray-haired lady had tucked into her belt," Justin said, and before Miranda could stop him, grabbed the mallet.

"Justin. Put that back! Who knows what that will do," Miranda said, trying to snatch it out of his hands, but he moved it out of reach and swung it back and forth several times.

"It's getting warm and tingly, like the magic putter… er… I mean, staff. Wait a minute. Do you think this is the hammer that the old lady used to build the temple? I bet it's totally a magic hammer, like Thor's." Justin held it toward the ceiling above his head and closed his eyes. Nothing happened.

"You can open your eyes, O almighty god of thunder," Miranda said.

Justin tentatively opened one eye, looked at the wooden mallet, and frowned. "I guess not. Bummer." He placed it back where he had found it.

Miranda crossed her arms over her chest and scowled at him. "You're lucky that wasn't booby trapped or something. You could have been shot by a hundred arrows or crushed by a giant stone." Then she got a wicked smile on her face. "But since it's not…" She snatched the thin cylindrical object off the table. As she inspected it more closely, she noticed that it had a small triangular shape on one end, while the other ended in a sharp point.

"What do you suppose this is?" Miranda asked.

Justin leaned over and inspected it carefully. "*Hmmm*. That looks like a reed stylus—the tool used to write cuneiform script. The wedge end made the triangle shapes, and the other end made the lines. You really never listened to Mom and Dad, did you?"

Miranda shrugged. "They were always so boring. But trust me, I wish I had paid more attention now." She was just about to place the stylus back down again when it started to glow and grow warm in her hands. The cuneiform script on the walls started to move and shift, like ants marching through the tunnels of their colony, and began to form shapes.

Justin wandered over to the nearest wall. "Cool! Are you doing this?"

Miranda walked next to him. "I don't think so. I don't know. The stylus became warm and started to glow. It must be magic, like the staff."

All around the room the script was moving, forming detailed images for a moment, then shifting slightly to show another similar picture. It felt like being in the middle of a primitive animated movie, watching each frame being created on the fly. Each moving image repeated cyclically at first, like a short loop of film.

Miranda slowly walked back toward the entryway and stopped at what appeared to be the first in the series of shifting images, with Justin close behind. Now the "movie" started to unfurl in earnest, as they watched a man with a long curly beard and some sort of crown or headdress, walking with an unusual gait, entering an enormous cave. He was grasping a long stick, maybe a spear, with one hand, using it as a walking staff. In the other he held a scepter. As Miranda looked down, she noticed his feet were like a frog's. No wonder he was walking so funny. His skin also looked odd, not smooth like a human's but rough like a reptile's.

The frog-man was slowly approaching a woman sitting on a throne. All around her were pools of water with big fish leaping out of them in high arcs, only to disappear below again. When Miranda and Justin had drawn close enough to the figure, the moving cuneiform script shifted into a close-up of the man bowing down before the woman. She was both beautiful and frightening at the same time.

Miranda sucked in a breath. "Tiamat!"

Justin nodded. "Sure looks like the creepy statue of her."

"But who is that guy?" Miranda asked as the stylus in her hand began to vibrate, slender colored beams of light shooting out in all directions. Miranda thought about dropping the reed and running for her life, but something in her gut told her it wasn't dangerous. The light moved in weird and unexpected ways, zooming around the room randomly like out-of-control rockets, then converging on a single spot in the very center of the circular chamber.

A ghostly image began to take shape, made from the beams of light, unclear at first, like the reflection in a fog-covered mirror, but soon it outlined the form of the woman from the statue outside. She wasn't very tall, about Miranda's height, and she was thin, but athletic. The figure was dressed in the same tunic and rope belt around her waist, but this image also depicted her wearing a pair of high leather sandals. Her silvery hair cascaded down over her shoulders in thick flowing waves.

Miranda noticed that the figure held a ghostly version of

the same reed stylus tightly in her hand as it floated over to the animated image on the wall where she and her brother were standing.

Justin and Miranda backed away, not sure if this was a trap. Was the ghostly woman a demon, or something even worse?

The ghost stopped directly in front of the image and said in a voice that sounded both distant and right next to them, "His name is Apsu, god of the fresh waters. He is petitioning the Dark Queen, Tiamat, goddess of the salt waters, seeking her blessing and permission… to destroy their offspring."

"Offspring? You mean he wanted to kill his own children?" Justin asked.

"Some of his children, yes." The ghost-woman turned to fix him and Miranda with her glowing eyes. "Apsu could not find rest in the world any longer. The younger gods and their favored creature, man, were not only taking his waters but they were polluting them as well. They diverted his rivers and streams to nourish their animals and crops. They used his waters to carry away their waste. The gods had shown men how to enforce order upon chaos, how they might bend the natural world to suit their needs. This greatly offended Apsu, and he wished to end it." The woman made a sweeping gesture with her arm. "What you see before you is an account of the events that led up to the rise of Marduk and the fall of Tiamat."

Miranda quickly looked around the room, its walls displaying panel after panel of moving images made from cuneiform characters. In the next panel, Apsu appeared to be lying dead at the feet of a man wearing a pointed hat that resembled something you might see on a wizard. Next, Tiamat—fighting through angry tears—created an army of monsters, some familiar, some so terrifying that Miranda wished never to see anything like them again. Then that image pulled back, revealing a boy and a girl watching from a distant hill as the legion of monstrous creatures and elemental beings assembled.

Now the panel on the far wall began to transform rapidly, portraying two eagles with lions' heads stealing a stone tablet. They fled toward a distant mountain range. There they rested until the same girl and boy from the previous image surprised them in an ambush. The boy stabbed one of the birdlike creatures with a spear and it disintegrated, while the other fled with the tablets. Miranda could see that the boy was angry at his failure to kill both the lion-headed eagles. Suddenly the earth began to shake all around him as water erupted from the ground in towering geysers. But the girl bravely walked over to him, placed a calming hand on his shoulder, and the jets of water receded.

Was this boy depicted here Marduk? It couldn't be. Marduk, Miranda remembered Justin explaining before, was the Zeus of the Mesopotamian pantheon, the king of the gods. He couldn't have been just a boy.

As interesting as the weird animation was, Miranda doubted an ancient history lesson would bring her any closer to finding Em, so she turned her focus back to the apparition of the woman who appeared to be an incarnation of the First One. But that couldn't be true either. She would have been dead for well over five thousand years. This had to be some trick, a hologram or something.

"Who are you?" Miranda asked.

The woman, who looked both foreign and oddly familiar, bowed slightly. "My name is Tabrati. I am the architect of this temple and guardian of the sacred weapons, and I have been waiting a very long time to meet you, Miranda."

CHAPTER 19

MIRANDA
The Call of Destiny

"WHAT DO YOU MEAN, you've been waiting a long time to meet *me*? How do you even know my name?" Miranda asked, unable to stop her voice from shaking.

"It was foretold that you would come one day—a young woman of my line—and that you would wage war upon the Dark Queen reborn—vanquishing her once and for all," the apparition said with an absolute air of certainty. "It was also foretold that your name would be Miranda."

"Foretold by whom?" Miranda asked.

"By Marduk, chief of all the gods."

Justin stepped in front of Miranda, placing himself between her and the apparition. "I'm Justin. I imagine you were expecting me as well."

The image of Tabrati regarded him for a moment, then shook her head. "Not at all. Are you Miranda's servant?"

Miranda laughed dryly. "No. He's my brother. Trust me, he would make a thoroughly terrible servant."

Justin turned and punched her in the arm. "What? Who is always keeping our room clean? Who folds and puts away his clothes as soon as they're washed? And who do you know that can clean up an entire acre of burned-down woods so quickly? Plus, who keeps saving your butt all the time?"

"Excellent points, dear brother. You are entirely correct. You may now be my servant."

Justin ignored this comment and turned back to the image of Tabrati. "Well, it's weird you've never heard of me, because I'm kind of involved in all of this too."

Tabrati nodded. "Of course, you are correct, little one"—at this, Miranda saw Justin's eyes flare—"for we are all involved. It is an eternal battle between the forces of order and chaos."

Justin's face flushed. "That's not what I mean—"

Miranda put her hand on his shoulder, silencing him. "What my brother is trying to say is, we're in this together. I'm not here to fight Tiamat, or anyone else for that matter. I need to find information on how to rescue Aunt Em."

"And our Mom and Dad," Justin said, shooting her a questioning look.

"Do you know where they are?" Miranda added.

Tabrati cocked her head to one side. "You can not deny your destiny, Miranda. Whether you accept its call or not is irrelevant. Your destiny is already written in stone."

"I don't believe in destiny," Miranda said with a scowl. "Everyone can choose his or her path in life. And no one can tell me otherwise… not even a ghost."

Tabrati crossed her arms, just as Miranda and their mom always did when they were annoyed. "I am no spirit—I can assure you. I am a shadow of the past, one of many, a part of the woman who was Tabrati. When she recorded this script"—the apparition gestured to the images on the walls—"the stylus of Nidaba, goddess of writing, it not only created a living vision of the history depicted here, it also brought into being a glimpse of the person who recorded those words."

Tabrati looked at the images on the wall with a pained expression. "I, however, represent the last of the stylus's waning power, which renders me weaker in knowledge the living Tabrati, and limited in the time I have to impart it."

The temple shook, sending dust and stone from the ceiling in small brown clouds.

Justin ducked, covering his head with both hands. "Is the shield under attack again?"

The image of Tabrati looked up at the ceiling and shook her head. "My time is not the only thing limited by the magic, it seems. This temple was constructed with the last portion of the wicked god Kingu's divine energy. Because Kingu was so powerful, to imprison even this small fraction of his soul required more than what the Stone of Hiding could manage while keeping this valley safely hidden for centuries. So I bound him to this structure with a powerful protection demon. That spirit is gone—wisely siphoned off to restore the shield around this valley. However, now that it has left the temple, Kingu's parsu is breaking free of its prison, and as a result this structure, forged from that very soul, is breaking apart."

"What the heck is a *parsu*?" Justin asked, still eyeing the ceiling suspiciously.

"Never mind. We don't have time for this." Miranda interrupted and stepped closer to the apparition and said, "Tell me what you know about our aunt Em."

"*And* our parents," Justin added, this time scowling at Miranda.

"As to where these members of your family might be, I told you, I do not know. But Miranda, your family does not matter, they are only distractions from your true destiny. This is your burden to bear, as it was foretold, and so it shall be. My purpose here is coming to an end. I am to set you on the correct path so that you will fulfill your destiny completely. You must recover the divine weapons needed to vanquish the Dark Queen."

Miranda stomped her foot down in frustration. "I told you, I am not interested in fighting some ancient dragon-lady—" The temple shook more violently this time, making a big stone break free from the ceiling; it fell to the floor and smashed into a hundred pieces.

Justin placed a hand on Miranda's shoulder and pointed to the image of Tabrati. "Look. She's disappearing."

The vision of the woman was becoming more translucent. "I do not have much time with you, Miranda. I am… so very tired," Tabrati said and sagged slightly. "The task I was set by Marduk has depleted me more than I can ever convey." She looked down at her hands, which were almost entirely gone now.

"You said you were one of many. What do you mean? Could another version of Tabrati tell us where the hostages are?" Miranda asked.

Tabrati sighed, nodding to the stylus in Miranda's hand. "In each of the sacred temples, this same story is recounted: Marduk's triumph over Tiamat and her legion of monsters. The tale will help you on your journey—if you take the time to learn the lessons it can teach you. To gain access to this lore, you will need to take the stylus of Nidaba with you to each of the temples. It is the only thing that can open the way to the knowledge you need, and is the only thing able to conjure the other incarnations of myself." Miranda noticed that Tabrati's legs and arms were now fading away quickly, but she continued to speak. "You must go to the four remaining temples and retrieve all of the divine weapons of Marduk. If you face Tiamat without their combined might, you will fail, and the world you know will cease to exist, as the Queen of Chaos restores everything back to the old ways."

Miranda felt her stomach tighten. The only thing she cared about was finding her aunt and her parents and freeing them. Once she accomplished that, they could all figure out what to do about Tiamat.

"Wait. Let me get this straight," Justin said. "Miranda has to fight a god with a bunch of old weapons or the world is going to be destroyed?"

Nothing was left of Tabrati now but her chest and head. She mouthed a barely audible "Yes…"

Justin let out a nervous laugh. "No pressure there, huh, sis? And you were completely freaked out by math pop quizzes a month ago. My, how the world has changed."

Miranda gave her brother a shove. This couldn't be another dead end. There had to be something here she could learn from Tabrati that would help her locate Em.

"But—" Miranda began to protest, but she was cut off by the apparition.

"I have run out of time," Tabrati said faintly. "I need to tell you two things before the magic has drained away from here completely. First, the staff that allowed you to enter this room is one part of the Spear of the Winds. Lastly, the spearhead can be found in a temple located in a dense jungle upon a wide plateau. Follow the mountains to the south, then…"

The image of Tabrati faded into nothingness.

"You've got to be kidding me," Justin said in disbelief.

Miranda could only stare at the spot where the ghostly image of Tabrati had hovered only a second before. "That couldn't be it. Go to a temple in a jungle south of here? What kind of clue is that supposed to be?"

"Well, that would be a *cryptic* clue," Justin said. "But I think she just told us the next temple we need to go to *isn't* in the

United States."

"How do you know that?" Miranda asked.

"Duh. There aren't any jungles in the southwest. The nearest it could be is Mexico. But it could also be Central or South America too. It would take us a lifetime to find it. Where in the heck do we even start?"

Miranda didn't respond. She just continued to stare in disbelief. She had failed… again. There was nothing here to help her find Em and their parents. Only some stupid story about how she needed to fight a dragon-lady for the fate of the world. Like that could ever actually happen.

All of a sudden the walls of the temple began to shake again, sending a whole section of the ceiling crashing down, missing them by mere inches.

"Get out of there!" Billy shouted down the hall. "The temple's collapsing!"

Miranda hesitated for a moment, desperately scanning the script on the wall, searching in vain for anything she might have missed. She had not even witnessed the whole story. Maybe there was another clue there—like the location of where Tiamat's forces were gathering, or where the draconians kept their prisoners, or where an impossibly large cave existed with a couple of pillars, anything.

Justin ran over to the stone table, dodging falling debris along the way, and scooped up the mallet. He came running back toward Miranda, grabbed her by the hand, and ran, dragging her back down the hall. There was a thunderous crash from behind, and a cloud of dust erupted from the room they had stood in just moments before.

When they came sprinting back into the entry antechamber, they saw Billy carrying the still unconscious Mrs. Lóng out the temple entryway. Miranda reached up and grabbed the staff, yanking it out of the statue's hands, as Justin grabbed the stone shard from the top of the small pillar.

Billy was straining hard as he carried Mrs. Lóng down the stairs.

"Are you okay?" Miranda asked.

Billy nodded, sweat pouring from his face. "She's heavier... than... she looks."

When they were almost to the first landing, the roof of the temple collapsed, sending the waterfall—which had been so artfully integrated into the temple's design—spilling out in every direction. They were soon covered in a cold spray of water, soaking them to the bone.

"We need to get off the ziggurat. Now!" Justin yelled. "The whole thing's coming apart." They rushed down the rest of the steps, taking them two at a time.

They collapsed on the grass of the valley floor, barely reaching the ground before the whole building toppled in on itself. Miranda and Justin stood up as the last part of the temple crumbled with an echoing crash.

From somewhere deep inside the ruined structure there came deep laughter, and Miranda could have sworn she heard a raspy voice scream, *"I'm free!"*

What followed was absolute silence. Every human and every dragon in the valley was staring in shock at the spot where their ancient temple—the focus of the entire sacred valley—had stood for over six thousand years. Now it was nothing more than a pile of rocks and dust.

Justin let out a low whistle. "Oh man. When Grandpa wakes up, he's going to be *so* mad at us."

CHAPTER 20

JUSTIN
A New Lead

YELLING DREW JUSTIN'S ATTENTION to the stone path that traced along beside the river, where the small gathering of warriors and dragons had stopped to defend the valley if the shield fell. They were all gaping at the crumbled ziggurat, shouting and waving their arms. Justin couldn't understand what they were saying, and for the first time since they arrived, he was glad about that.

Two of the three dragons launched themselves into the air and flew directly to one of the caves in the valley wall, then quickly disappeared inside. Three of the warriors from the tribe were carrying a fourth dragon toward one of the longhouses. A lone warrior and dragon walked slowly toward them, never taking their eyes off the ruined temple. When they were close enough, Justin recognized the human as Mana'doe, the only other person their grandfather had introduced them to, and the battered brown dragon as Rockgobbler.

Mana'doe shook his head and said sadly, "This is why we

don't let outsiders here. They break things."

Rockgobbler limped over to Grandpa Stone and nudged him lightly in the side with his wide snout. *"I thought I had lost him for good this time,"* the dragon whispered.

"What happened out there?" Miranda asked.

"We flew directly at the two creatures attacking the shield," Mana'doe said, "when out of nowhere, a dozen wyverns attacked us, forcing us to engage them instead. We were doing well, holding our own, but your grandfather and Rockgobbler must have realized the wyverns were luring us farther away from the valley and turned back to engage the demons." His voice softened. "I saw your grandfather fall, but I was too engaged in battle to help. That's when everything went from bad to worse. The wyverns were working in concert to force us to the ground. It was a trap. Dozens of those filthy draconians were waiting for us. We barely got away with our lives."

Miranda shivered. "You said there are *dozens* of them out there?"

Mana'doe nodded. "Maybe more. They are some distance down the valley though, and are not near the shield."

Miranda turned to Justin. "Can you sense them?"

Justin closed his eyes and concentrated, reaching out with his mind, forcing it in the direction Mana'doe had indicated. At the very edge of his thoughts, he could feel malice. "Barely. They are just at the edge of my range, and I can only pick up strong emotion, nothing else. They must have learned their lesson, not to get too close to us." On a hunch, Justin spun around in a circle, sending his thoughts out in every direction. "There are *way* more than a couple dozen dracs out there though. Hundreds maybe. Completely surrounding us."

Red grunted. *"Makes sense. Eventually, that shield is going to fall, and when it does, those creepy dudes are going to sweep in and overpower everyone here by their sheer numbers."*

Miranda crossed her arms. "And even with recharging the shield, it won't last long under the constant onslaught. We may have only bought ourselves a day or two at most. After that, we're sitting ducks."

Justin looked down at his grandfather and Mrs. Lóng, both still unconscious, lying on the ground. "I wish they would wake up. We could use their help right now. Maybe we should get word to Grandpa McAdelind."

"He's gone," Billy said, speaking for the first time in a while. "He left this morning to meet with Lord Ddraig."

"Can he trust Lord Ddraig?" Justin asked.

"Of course," Billy said with a laugh. "The McAdelinds and the Ddraigs have been allies for centuries. They're all really nice. Granted, Gwen can be a pain from time to time, but her younger brother, Cedrick, is a good friend of mine…." Billy trailed off, lost in thought.

"What is it?" Miranda asked.

"Nothing," Billy replied. "I mean, he hasn't responded to any of my emails in a while. So, I *think* we're still good friends."

"Did Grandpa say where exactly he was going?" Miranda asked.

Billy shook his head. "No, but I think it's safe to assume it has something to do with your family. My dad is following Drake's men to make sure they leave the country and aren't hanging around to cause more trouble, and Mrs. Lóng… well, you know where she is."

"How did you guys know we were in trouble?" Miranda asked.

Billy shrugged. "We didn't… I mean, *I* didn't. Mrs. Lóng must have known, though. She said she needed me to give her a ride here and back because she needed to bring Storm and Red to you guys. Something about you two going on a trip somewhere and that you would need the dragons. Then, when we were flying in, we saw the earth dragons fighting wyverns. I wanted to help, but Mrs. Lóng said you guys were in danger and if we didn't get there quickly, Justin was going to die."

Justin shot Billy an angry glare. "What? I wasn't even *close* to dying."

Miranda smiled. "You would have been fried by lightning if Mrs. Lóng hadn't arrived when she did. I'm glad you guys showed up. Thanks."

Billy looked down at the ground. "Don't sweat it. When we were flying in and I saw the wyverns, I was worried. I'm glad you're safe."

Justin cleared his throat, changing the subject. "Who's running the ranch now?"

Billy laughed. "Gwen, if you can believe that, and a couple of the ranch hands we know who are loyal to the McAdelinds. That's it. I doubt any of them can help us, though."

Rockgobbler made a soft grunting sound, grabbing their attention. *"You must seek guidance from the Ancient One. He will know the correct course of action."*

"Who exactly is this 'Ancient One'?" Justin asked.

"He has been here since the beginning. The eldest of the elders. He will know what to do."

"What is he saying?" Mana'doe asked.

"He says we need to talk to some ancient dragon about what to do next." Justin translated.

Mana'doe shook his head. "Only the chief of the Oni'waz'legani is allowed to enter the caves of the dragons."

Rockgobbler looked sadly at Grandpa Stone. *"That is true. However, he is in no condition to meet with anyone. In the absence of the chief, the duties of his title fall to his heirs. Miranda and Justin will be permitted to enter."*

Justin translated for Mana'doe, who nodded slowly. "Okay.

Let's get these two back to the chief's house and see if we can wake them. At first light, I will escort you two to commune with the Elder."

Rockgobbler shook his head. "*I will accompany the young ones there myself. No one else may come.*"

"Sorry to burst your bubble there, pal, but the kid isn't going anywhere without me," Red said, rising on his haunches to his full height. "I don't care if the king of all the freaking dragons is up there, the boy is under my protection."

"And I will not leave Miranda's side again," Storm added, moving in close to Miranda.

Rockgobbler seemed to consider this a moment, then inclined his head. "*That is acceptable. I will call on the Ancient One. If he agrees to meet, I shall summon you.*" With that, the mighty earth dragon leapt into the air and flew into one of the caves high on the cliff wall.

CHAPTER 21

JUSTIN
The Ancient One

Justin leaned carefully over the edge of the cavern entrance to the dragon's domain. "This is a long drop. We must be a couple hundred feet off the ground. If you took a wrong step here... Splat! You're not walking away from that one."

"*Simple solution for you, kid. Don't fall,*" Red said flatly.

"Always the voice of reason," Justin retorted.

Miranda made a shushing sound. "Guys, you need to be quiet. We were told to wait here in silence while they check to see if this Ancient One is ready to meet us," she said, and shifted Grandpa Mac's sword, which was still strapped across her back, never far from reach.

Justin walked away from the edge of the cliff and sat down with a huff. "That was like a half an hour ago. How long does it take to check in on an old dragon?"

"*Apparently more than a half an hour,*" Storm said.

Justin, Red, and Miranda all turned to gape at the blue dragon. "Oh my gosh! Was that a joke?" Justin asked.

Storm peered deeper into the tunnel. *"I was merely stating a fact."*

Miranda smiled. "No. I think that *was* a joke."

Rockgobbler limped out of the dark tunnel, still injured from their battle the night before. *"The Ancient One will see you now."*

Justin stood up and brushed off the dust from his pants. "Finally."

The earth dragon led them down a series of interlocking natural caves. Justin could sense the presence of many dragons just off the main path. Most of them were resting quietly in extensive caverns, but he was also aware that a dozen or more were closely monitoring their progress through the labyrinth.

The farther down they went, the cooler and more humid the caves became. After they had walked for more than fifteen minutes, one of the broad passages opened slightly, and their way forward was blocked—guarded by two enormous and ferocious-looking brown dragons.

Justin could feel the suspicion and malice directed toward them and waved nervously. "Hi. We come in peace."

Rockgobbler swung his head around to face Justin and Miranda. *"What you are about to see no human has seen in a very, very long time. Do not approach the Ancient One unless he advises you to do so. Your presence here alone is a threat to him. No dragon in the history of our species has lived as long as he has. Any sudden movements by either you or your dragons that might be considered hostile will be met with immediate lethal force."* The dragon turned to Justin and added, *"Understand?"*

Justin glanced around at everyone else, then back at the dragon. "Why did you look at me when you said that?"

"Because he's smart, kid," Red said with a chuckle.

Justin crossed his arms and scowled.

Rockgobbler nodded once, then turned and led the procession through the entrance into the Ancient One's domain. The cave was larger and looked much older that any of the others they had passed through so far. Massive stalagmites and stalactites had melted together to form towering columns. Crystal-clear pools of water reflected shimmering waves of light from torches illuminating the room on every side. Here and there, purple and milky-white crystals formed large shrub-like structures. The whole space was eerily beautiful.

Rockgobbler motioned for everyone to stop and took a step forward. *"Ancient One. We have come for your guidance."*

When what appeared to be a small boulder, not twenty feet in front of them, moved, Justin jumped about a foot in the air.

There was raspy laughter followed by a fit of nasty coughing. *"Scared you, didn't I? But if you think that's scary, wait until you get a good look at my face,"* the rock said and laughed until it started choking.

Slowly the stone seemed to unfold into a long wrinkly wormlike being. It had no scales to speak of, just fold upon fold of wrinkled skin. The membranes of its wings were so thin, they appeared translucent. On its head, where great horns must have existed at one time, there was nothing left but empty sockets. It opened its eyelids and stared at them with milky-white eyes. *"Believe it or not, I use to be big and handsome."*

Justin took a step back. The creature before him was hideous. Not frightening, just plain hideous. "No… you still look… good," Justin stammered.

"Liar," the Ancient One said, and laughed. *"But I'll give you credit for not running out of here screaming your head off, or wetting yourself."*

"*I did wet myself,*" Red said, and his whole body shuddered involuntarily.

The Ancient One began sniffing the air, like a dog following the scent of a rabbit, and smiled broadly, exposing a mouth void of teeth. "*Now that is someone I haven't smelled for a very long time. Marduk, has my time finally come, can I join the others of my kind in the afterlife at long last?*"

Rockgobbler glanced down at Miranda and Justin, a sad look in his eyes. "*No, Ancient One, Marduk is not here. These are two children, descendants of the First One.*"

"*Would you* please *stop calling me 'Ancient One,' it makes me feel bad.*"

The earth dragon bowed deeply. "*My apologies, Ya'ne'unde.*"

The old dragon snorted. "*Better. And her name was Tabrati, not this 'First One' nonsense. I swear I don't understand why everybody has to come up with these ridiculous nicknames all the time,*" he scolded.

"Wait a minute. You're *the* Ya'—ne'—unde?" Justin stammered. "The lighthearted dragon, Tabrati's dragon? That would make you like, six thousand years old."

"*And I don't look a day over five thousand and one, do I?*" The ancient dragon laughed. "*For the record, I'm no one's dragon. Tabrati and I were friends. My original name before coming to this valley was Neperdu. But you can just call me 'Ya'ne' or 'Hey You'—anything other than 'Ancient One.' Oh man, I just hate that.*"

He swung his head back toward Rockgobbler and said, "*And I may be blind, but I can still see. Marduk is there.*" He pointed at Miranda and Justin, his clawed paw shaking violently. "*A god's parsu never changes, it's eternal. And those two, right there, are Marduk, as sure as I look like a worm with a sunburn,*" he said, laughing himself into another coughing fit.

"That's the second time someone mentioned a 'parsu.' What is that exactly?" Justin asked.

Ya'ne laughed. "Oh, by Anu above. You're as good as dead for sure. I can sense the end is quickly approaching, and you two don't even know the basics yet?"

Justin blushed. "We are kind of new to this whole thing."

The ancient dragon nodded. "Fair enough, but you'd better get up to speed quickly if you hope to survive. When we fought against Tiamat, we didn't know much either. Sometimes not knowing that you can fail is the only thing keeping you from falling flat on your face." He coughed deeply before continuing. "Parsu is the stuff that makes a god a god. The soul, if you will. It is the source of their power and what makes them 'special.'" Ya'ne made air quotes with his claws as he said this last word. "But it also exists in nature as well. Perhaps it is some energy left over from when this world was created. Marduk's father, Enki, had the power to take parsu and bind it to other objects, essentially enchanting that object with the powers of the parsu bound to it."

Miranda pointed at the magic putter in Justin's hands. "You mean like that staff?"

Ya'ne shook his head, turning to Rockgobbler. "She does know I'm blind, right? What staff are you talking about?"

Miranda blushed. "Sorry, I meant the shaft of the Spear of the Winds."

Ya'ne swung his head back to Miranda. "Well, why didn't you just say that in the first place? Yes, exactly so. Except Enki didn't create that weapon, Marduk did. He inherited that particular power from his father, plus he had a whole slew of his own." Ya'ne sniffed the air again. "There are two other objects infused with parsu present."

Miranda touched the sword her grandfather had given her. When her hand came in contact with the leather-wrapped hilt, the ancient dragon smiled. "Good. Yes, that is one."

"The sword?" Miranda asked.

Ya'ne shook his sagging head. "*No, not the sword—although it is forged from a unique metal—but the leather on the hilt. That is a strip from Tabrati's boots. They were enchanted with parsu from the wind itself, making anyone who wore them swift and light. Some time ago, one of the Oni'waz'legani chiefs cut her boots into strips and wrapped his warriors' weapons with the leather, giving the tribe an advantage in battle. Quite ingenious actually. Alexander McAdelind was given one of those strips as a token of friendship when he first came to this part of the world, and as soon as he knew what it could do, he wrapped it tight around the hilt of that ridiculously large blade of his.*" He paused for a moment, lost in thought. "*You know, those boots were what brought Marduk and Tabrati together in the first place. If that had never happened, I don't believe Tiamat would have been defeated.*"

"Are you saying a pair of boots saved the world?" Justin asked.

"*I suppose I am,*" Ya'ne said with a chuckle.

"So breaking apart something that has parsu in it doesn't destroy the parsu?" Miranda asked.

"*No. Parsu is bound to every ounce of the object, it always remains part of it.*"

On a hunch, Justin pulled the stone shard out of his pocket. Ya'ne's face darkened, and his upper lip lifted in a toothless snarl. "*Yes. That is the other.*"

"What is it exactly?" Justin asked. "I mean, we know it's a piece of some old tablet, but it's also something else too, right?"

"*That 'something else' is a part of Tiamat's very soul. After she was vanquished, Marduk placed her parsu into the Tablet of Destinies and smashed it to pieces, giving one to each of his human warriors and sending them to the four corners of the earth, so that she would not be able to return easily.*"

Justin looked down at the stone. "Gross! I've been carrying around a chunk of that dragon lady's soul in my pocket?" He quickly shoved the fragment back into his pants pocket, wiped his hands on his shirt, and shivered. "So, those three tablets we see in the draconians' visions are all called the 'Tablet of Destinies'?"

"Three? No. There is only one tablet. The other two must be other stones inscribed with the incantation that will bring Tiamat back."

"If Marduk killed Tiamat, why even worry about trapping her soul in a tablet?" Miranda asked.

"Because you can't destroy parsu. Eventually, Tiamat's soul would have formed a new body and been reborn. The only way to ensure this wouldn't happen for a long time was to divide her parsu up into many pieces and spread them around the world far apart from one another. The closer the shards are to one another, the stronger Tiamat's influence becomes."

"Wouldn't having a piece of Tiamat so close to us be a bad thing?" Miranda asked.

Ya'ne nodded. "Indeed it is. However, I believe that given the alternative of its falling into the hands of one of her servants, it is safest with you. There is a lot of Marduk in both of you. More than I have sensed since the ancient times. That power will shield you from the influence of Tiamat. It will keep the dark things at bay."

"What do you mean, 'the dark things'?" Justin asked.

"I mean, if you did not have the power to block Tiamat's influence, you two would already be under her control. The more pieces of the tablet that are united, the stronger she becomes. Someone who can sense parsu—like the two of you—can fall under her power and not even realize it. When each of Marduk's warriors was given a piece of the tablet to safeguard, the effects were minimized because Marduk also gave them a bit of himself to protect them from the tablet's influence. But *now that all but one piece has been reassembled, her soul is almost whole again, making her very, very dangerous. And that fragment right there in your pocket is a direct line to the Dark Queen herself."*

Justin remembered the first, and the only, time Miranda had held the stone and the impact it had had on her. Somehow it never affected him the same way. To him, it was just another rock. Well, a rock that on a couple of occasions got really, really hot. Oh, and caused a couple of draconians to explode into flames. But a rock all the same.

"The wild dragons at Thunderbird Ranch said Tiamat's call is getting harder for them to resist. Is this what they mean?" Miranda asked.

"*Yes and no. The dark queen's creations are compelled to serve her. She holds ultimate dominion over them. I do not believe many of them wish to be under her control—save the draconians,*" Ya'ne said with distain in his raspy telepathic voice. "*They serve Tiamat without question because of her promise to them.*"

"What promise?" Justin asked.

"*Dominion over all the lands. Once all humans has been wiped from the earth, the draconians will take their place.*"

Justin looked nervously around the dragons around the cave. "Do you guys hear her call too?"

"*No, child. The protective field shields us from her influence.*" Ya'ne's focus abruptly shifted to Red and Storm. "*Hmmm. There is something different about you two. Can't put my claw on it, but you seem more like one of us than one of the new breed of dragons.*"

"They can use breath weapons," Justin said, patting Red on the arm.

The old dragon just stared at them a moment. "*That's interesting… but I'm not sure if that's a good thing or a bad thing,*" he said, then sighed and added, "*The time of Tiamat's return is approaching."* He was seized by another coughing fit, his entire body racked by spasms. When the fit finally subsided, Ya'ne lay down, and tried to steady his breath. When he spoke, the words came out in little more than a whisper, *"Time runs short for me as well. You must depart at once for the next temple."*

"We can't leave now. We need to defend the valley until Mrs. Lóng and Grandpa Stone are better. We would be leaving them at the mercy of those two monsters out there," Justin said.

"I'm reasonably certain that Ugallu and Lahmu are after only you two," Ya'ne muttered drowsily. *"If it makes you feel better, the valley will be safer without you in it."*

Justin frowned. "That actually makes me feel *way* worse. Plus we don't even know where to go next."

"Didn't that creepy ghost version of Tabrati in the temple tell you where to go?" The old dragon asked.

"She disappeared before she had the chance," Miranda said.

"Ha! I told Tabrati that wouldn't work, Nidaba was such a hack." He laughed hard, had a coughing fit, then added, *"Just follow the mountains south for three days. You'll find a vast forest of clouds. Follow the two rivers to a big plateau. The temple will be sitting there somewhere, hidden by one of those blue protection stones."*

Ya'ne laid his head on the ground and closed his milky white eyes. *"Now go... seize your... destiny."* He let out a long rattling breath and fell completely silent.

They all stood there motionless for a long moment, not sure what to do, until Justin looked over at Rockgobbler and asked, "Uh. Did he just... die?"

Rockgobbler lowered his head in reverence, and Justin and Miranda followed suit.

"I'm not dead, you idiots."

They all jumped. Ya'ne was staring at them with a frown

on his sagging face. *"That is called a dramatic pause. I was trying to be profound."* He sighed heavily.

Miranda cleared her throat and stepped forward. "Ya'ne'unde, I was hoping you could tell us where Tiamat might be holding the hostages from our family. I was told the path I need to be on starts here in the Valley, but I haven't had much success in finding any clues about their whereabouts."

The ancient dragon regarded her for a moment. *"You still seem to think that your path and the hostages are related. I think you know they are not."*

Miranda's face flushed, and she shot a worried look at Justin. "There is no one right path."

"You don't believe any of this destiny stuff, do you? A war between gods and the end of the world is just a bunch of mumbo jumbo."

"It doesn't matter right now. I made a promise to save our aunt and our parents first. Once they're safe, we can figure out the rest."

"It is indeed important to honor and protect one's family." The old dragon nodded knowingly. *"As I am sure you have heard already, it's a right of passage for the Oni'waz'legani to go on a quest and prove their worth to the tribe… to their family. When the person comes back successful, they are given the title of Dragon Rider—that is the nickname Marduk gave to Tabrati so many centuries ago."*

"We did sort of ruin the valley. It's only right that we try to help our people if we can," Justin said. "Maybe we should see if there's a way to recharge the protection stone permanently, or bring the one at the other temple back with us? That could be our Dragon Rider quest—"

"We have more important things to do than some *stupid* quest," Miranda scolded.

Justin scowled at her. "I'm perfectly aware of that, sis. But since we have to go to the next temple anyhow, we might as well kill two birds with one stone."

"The quest is not simply a task," Ya'ne intoned. "*It is a way to honor your ancestors, and to give hope to the next generation. But it is also more than that too. It is through the journey that we learn about ourselves—a way to discover your place in the universe. Your mother did this, as did your grandfather, as has every member of the Oni'waz'legani stretching back to Tabrati. I can tell you with some degree of certainty that in every instance the warrior discovered what they were seeking, even if they weren't entirely sure what that was. As will you, Justin and Miranda.*"

Miranda crossed her arms. "But we need to save the hostages. We made a promise. A vow."

"*Listen, if you're not ready to face your destiny yet, that's fine. But I've seen enough in this long life to know everything is connected. If you are meant to save your family, then I believe that particular path begins by making the Spear of the Winds whole again.*" Ya'ne curled himself back into an earth-colored ball and whispered, "*I believe you have it in you to accomplish great things. You have the power of a god within you both. Now go. Find your path, honor Tabrati and become Dragon Riders, and save this world… or don't. Either way, this will all be over with soon enough.*"

CHAPTER 22

MIRANDA
Quest of the Dragon Riders

"Explain to me again what happened to our sacred temple," Grandpa Stone said. He was sitting upright on the couch in his living room, a tight bandage around his chest and a cast on his leg. In the short time the protection field had been down, he had aged physically—by ten years at least, Miranda thought. Deep wrinkles now creased his forehead and framed his eyes.

Miranda sighed. "Like I said, Tabrati, or the First One, told us it collapsed because the spirit of some old king was holding it together. And when we recharged the shield, we sucked out the magic spirit holding him in there."

Justin shook his head. "His *name* was Kingu, and he was a god, not some 'old king.' According to Mom and Dad's notes, he was the general of Tiamat's army."

Their grandfather frowned. "That's not the part I'm confused about. You said you really spoke to the First One, and she told you to follow the mountains south to another temple in the jungle?"

"That's the gist of it," Justin said.

"Where exactly is this temple again?" Grandpa Stone asked.

"Ya'ne said if we follow the mountains south, we will reach a forest of clouds. The temple is somewhere close to that," Miranda said. "As best Justin and I can figure, he's talking about someplace in southern Mexico."

"Why Mexico?" Grandpa Stone pressed.

"Because Mom and Dad have been there several times recently. We think they were looking for the temple too," Justin added.

Miranda sighed. "Plus, after closely inspecting the hodgepodge of postage stamps on the package they sent us, I think it originated from some place called Jaltenango de la Paz, which is close to mountains and jungles. I looked it up. All the clues seem linked."

Their grandfather shook his head. "Well, I can't let you two go down there alone. Once I'm better, we'll go together and see what we can find."

"Unfortunately, the shield will only last a couple more days, at most, if those demons attack again. Which we know they will. There is also a vast army of draconians lurking in the mountains surrounding us," Miranda said, looking nervously around. "If we wait, there won't be anything left of this valley or the people in it. We have to go before then, for everyone's safety."

"As a matter of fact, we're going to see if this other temple has a protection stone too. If it does, we'll bring it back here and restore the valley," Justin added hopefully.

Miranda scowled. "But that might be a long shot, and not really the goal of our mission."

Grandpa Stone looked down at the back of his now wrinkled hands. "As much as that would be appreciated, it would be completely irresponsible of me to let you two out of my sight." He leaned forward and grimaced in pain.

"We don't know for a fact that the shield will fall, but even so, you're safer here with us. I'll be well enough to ride in a couple more days."

Miranda stood up and began pacing around the small room. After a moment, she stopped, crossed her arms, and said, "As I keep telling everyone, there is no place safe for Justin and me. No matter where we are, we keep getting the people around us hurt." Miranda punched one of the plush chairs in frustration. "Actually, today humans and dragons both got hurt because of us. You and Mrs. Lóng almost died today, because of *us*."

Grandpa Stone shook his head. "Not because of you, because of those things out there. You can't fight something like that on your own. I'd be sending you to your deaths. No, there has to be another way."

"As much as I want to agree with you, I think our only hope is to find Mom and Dad," Justin said. "They have been working on this for a long time now. They must know how to stop the attacks and keep us safe."

"We can't count on Mom and Dad, Justin. We're on our own," Miranda said, her voice rising an octave. When her grandfather and brother looked at her with concern, she took a deep breath and added, "I believe that once we find the next temple, we'll know what to do."

"Well, you can't go alone. At least let me send the rest of our warriors with you," their grandfather pleaded.

Miranda shook her head. "We're not risking anyone else's life. We'll be with Red and Storm. That will be enough. Once we draw the demons, draconians, and wyverns away from here, you and Grandpa McAdelind can figure out some way of protecting all of us."

Their grandfather looked back toward the bedroom and said, "Once Mrs. Lóng is awake, she'll also have some good ideas about what to do next."

Miranda scowled. "Maybe. She seems to have her own agenda and secrets."

Grandpa Stone chuckled. "You have no idea." Then, seeing their questioning looks, he added, "So, what's your plan?"

"Our plan is to rest now, eat dinner, pack, and hit the skies at nightfall," Miranda said.

Their grandfather sat forward, his eyes wide. "Wait. You mean you're leaving *tonight*?"

* * *

As soon as the sun had set over the Rocky Mountains, Miranda and Justin walked down the series of ramps to the valley floor where the dragons were waiting for them.

But, to Miranda's dismay, Billy and Nightshade were there as well.

"So, where are we headed?" Billy asked.

"You're heading back to the ranch. I'm sure Miss D needs all the help she can get," Miranda said, her hands on her hips.

Billy turned to inspect a strap on his black dragon's saddle, tugging it to make sure it was securely in place. "Oh, she'll be fine. I'm sure Gwen has the place running in tip-top condition. I think I'll just tag along with you two for the time being."

"You can't do that," Miranda said in a panic. There was no way she was going to put Billy's life in danger. "I won't let you."

The older boy just laughed. "You won't *let* me, huh? You see, I made this promise to Mrs. Lóng that if anything happened to her, I would watch out for you guys. So, like it or not, I'm coming with you."

Miranda thought her head was going to explode. Who did he think he was? "We don't need a babysitter," she shot back.

Billy held up his hands in mock surrender. "That's not what I said. I said I would watch out for you guys. Which means help you out, have your backs, that kind of thing. Trust me, Miss McAdelind, by now I know I can't tell you what to do. But let me ask you a couple of questions first. Have you two ever camped out on your own?"

Miranda scowled at him. "Yes."

"Not successfully," Justin put in.

Red chuckled. *"I would say that's a resounding no."*

Billy continued. "Have you ever ridden a dragon on a multiday trip?"

"You know we haven't," Miranda said.

"I assume you're planning on traveling at night. How do you propose to navigate the terrain you can't see?" Billy asked.

"He is making excellent points," Storm chimed in.

Miranda glared at the dragon for a moment, then sighed. "Fine. But it's your funeral."

Billy smiled. "I'll take that chance." He turned and reached into one of the larger saddlebags strapped to Nightshade, pulled out a blue helmet, and tossed it to Miranda. "A present from Mrs. Lóng. That woman thought of everything."

Miranda looked back at the cliff-side dwelling where the mysterious cook was lying unconscious. "Yes, she did."

"Hey, we only use the helmets for fast flying. So… *nice*. Do you have one in there for me too?" Justin asked expectantly. Billy nodded and tossed him a red one. "Now, we should be able to get down there in a couple of days."

"It all depends on where we're going," Billy said.

Miranda reached into her backpack and pulled out a torn sheet of brown paper, with a hand-drawn map she had made of the southern part of North America. "We're going here, to Jaltenango de la Paz, Mexico."

Billy's face became pale. "That's dangerously close to the

DeSoto compound. Not a good idea, given what happened last week at Thunderbird Ranch. We should avoid a run-in with the DeSotos at all cost. For all we know, the entire DeSoto family is in cahoots with the creatures hunting you two."

"Wait. I thought they lived in South America?" Justin said.

"Sure, they used to. Lord DeSoto moved his family to Mexico about ten years ago."

"Why?" Miranda asked.

"Not sure. It was after his father passed away and he became the new Dragon Lord. If you're unlucky enough to run into him, you can ask him yourself," Billy said. "But why there? I thought you only had a vague idea about where the temple is located?"

She turned the map over and pointed to the canceled postage stamps on the brown paper that the package from her parents had been wrapped in. "Because this is our mom and dad's last known location. We think they were also looking for the temple." Her eyes narrowed. "But if you're worried, cowboy, you're more than welcome to stay here."

Billy frowned. "I think it might be a huge mistake, but a promise is a promise."

"Well then. That settles it," Justin said and quickly mounted Red. "Last one to Mexico is a rotten dragon egg!"

CHAPTER 23

MIRANDA
The Dragons of Latin America

Just as the third night was giving way to dawn, Miranda, Justin, and Billy landed outside the small village of Jaltenango de la Paz, Mexico.

Billy had spotted a small clearing on a mountain to the west of town, and they landed to make camp for the day. But after a long night of hard riding, Miranda needed to stretch her legs and walk firmly on the earth for a while.

Following a short walk down a narrow jungle path, Miranda found a large rocky outcropping with the clear view of the settlement below. She sank down onto one of the larger stones and stretched out, soaking in the warmth of the rising sun.

An elaborate sequence of church bells chimed, and Miranda propped herself up to look at the small collection of buildings below. The town wasn't wealthy, but the ceramic-tiled roofs and white Spanish-style church—whose bells were echoing off the surrounding hills—gave the village an old-world charm she had never experienced in New York City.

Miranda imagined that if the circumstances that had brought her here had been any different, she would be enjoying herself, but after the past couple of days of relentless pursuit by the two demons chasing them, relaxation seemed completely impossible.

Several times during their journey, she thought they had eluded the creatures hunting them, only to see thick storm clouds on the horizon and know that their pursuers were closer than ever. The only thing that seemed to be saving them so far was how much swifter the dragons were compared to the creatures trailing them. They hadn't spotted any sign of either Ugallu or Lahmu for almost a day and a half, but Miranda knew this was only temporary. At most, she imagined they had less than a day to find the temple and get out of here.

The jungle behind Miranda stirred, and she turned to see Billy approaching. He handed her a water bottle, and said, "Nice spot. Seems like a good place to collect your thoughts."

Miranda took the bottle and drank deeply. When she finished, she pointed to the village below. "Well, I was just thinking that I don't know a single word of Spanish."

Billy laughed. "You might have mentioned that before dragging us down to Mexico." He sat on the rock next to her. "Don't sweat it, McAdelind. I speak a bit of *Español*."

"Ever the Renaissance man."

"Nah. It's not really that impressive. Don't forget, I grew up in a part of the country that used to be a part of Mexico." He motioned to the village below. "We should be able to get around down there okay. But I think the bigger issue is going to be three unaccompanied minors walking around a small village near the Guatemalan border with no ID and only U.S. money."

Miranda covered her face with her hands. "I guess I get an F for not thinking this through, huh?"

Billy shrugged. "I don't know, Miss McAdelind. I would give you at least a D. I mean we are here—that at least earns you a passing score."

Miranda smiled. "You, Mr. O'Faron, are too kind."

Billy's face became very serious, and he asked, "What happens if we don't find anything that leads to your aunt and your parents?"

"We'll find something here. I can feel it. It will be something that leads us to Em."

"What about your parents? You keep talking about finding your aunt, but what about finding them?"

"Trust me. They don't need my help. They're off doing whatever it is they—" Miranda stopped in mid-sentence, realizing she was sharing too much. She didn't want to even think about her parents. They should be here with her now, helping her find Em, protecting her from these monsters, but they weren't. And were they really free, or were they captives too? The nightmare visions she and Justin had shared were ambiguous. "You know what? It doesn't matter. I swore I'd get my aunt Em back safely, and I'm not going to let anything stand in my way. Everything else is just going to have to wait."

Billy looked off to the horizon and nodded.

Miranda sighed. "So, what do you think our next move should be?"

"Well, as I see it, we have a couple of options. We could just walk right into town and ask if anyone's seen a strange temple around here, or—"

"Miranda. Billy. We've got a problem." Justin came running through the dense foliage and skidded to a stop in front of them.

"You didn't set the jungle on fire, did you?" Miranda

asked, with more genuine concern than sarcasm. Her brother had been practicing trying to exert some control over his growing abilities after a couple of nearly disastrous events. Twice since they had left Colorado, he had caused their small campfire to surge into a roaring blaze. And if it wasn't for the seemingly fireproof Red's stomping the flames out, Justin might well have been responsible for several devastating jungle fires.

He scowled. "No. Not this time. I'm sensing a ton of dragons, coming at us from all directions."

Miranda and Billy jumped off the rock and followed Justin quickly through the dense forest to their meager camp. Red, Storm, and Nightshade all had their backs to each other and were facing outward in different directions. They obviously could sense the dragons approaching.

"Should we risk flying out of here?" Miranda asked.

Billy ran over to Nightshade and pulled out a length of silver rope and a long knife. "The sun's up. Flying now would be way too risky. Our families just got out of trouble with the Council of Twenty. The last thing we need is to show up on their radar again. No, I think our best chance is to see what's coming at us and decide from there."

Justin likewise grabbed the magic putter, holding it at the ready. "Didn't you say this is close to DeSoto territory?"

"Not close to, it *is* DeSoto land. As soon as we crossed the border into Mexico we were in their territory. What I said was, this place is close to the DeSoto compound, their version of Thunderbird Ranch."

"They are close. I can smell them," Storm growled, crouching low, her tail lashing back and forth.

Nightshade suddenly became focused on a dark area of the forest directly before him. *"I don't get it. I can smell them right in front of me. But I can't see anything except shadows."*

Miranda pulled out the long silver sword Grandpa

McAdelind had lent her and looked over at her brother. He had his eyes closed and was moving his head back and forth. "Justin. Can you sense the dragons?"

"They're all around us. I can see them with my mind. There are nine of them, equally spaced out around us and hiding in plain sight. But they're waiting for something."

Miranda closed her eyes and tried to see the dragons in her mind's eye. At first, she was only aware that there was indeed something lurking in the woods. But as she concentrated on that feeling, images started to form in her mind. Large, sinewy, snakelike creatures lurked in the trees and bushes. She remembered a conversation with Mr. DeSoto back at Thunderbird Ranch. He had said the dragons in Latin America were very different from the ones in the north, that they resembled feathered snakes with wings and were masters at blending into their environment—so much so that people believed they were magic.

Miranda opened her eyes and looked directly at the spot where she had seen one of the dragons in her mind: nothing. She took a step closer and squinted, concentrating on the area where the head should be. And then she saw it: one horn. Then another. Soon she was able to make out the dragon's entire head. "I have one right in front of me," she whispered.

"I still can't see anything," Billy said nervously. "What should we do?"

"I think you should drop those weapons," said a deep male voice with a thick Spanish accent. "You have three seconds to comply, or I will command my dragons to attack."

Miranda stomped her foot down with frustration but dropped her sword to the ground. Billy and Justin followed her lead.

"Now tell me what you are doing here, and if I smell a lie, I will command my dragons to attack," the man continued.

Miranda took a step toward the voice, but it said, "That's close enough, *chica*. I do not like spies on my land. Any closer and—"

"And you'll command your dragons to attack. I got that already. My name is Miranda McAdelind. We've come here looking for my parents, Kaya and Robert. We received a package from them, addressed from this town, right before they disappeared."

There was a rustling in the brush directly before Miranda. Two feathered snakelike reptiles, their bodies longer than a school bus and thicker than an old oak tree, came slithering toward her. In between them walked a man in a dark-gray suit. His copper-colored skin was accented by dark-brown hair with just the slightest bit of gray at the temples, but his eyes were hidden behind a pair of nearly black sunglasses.

He came to a stop not ten feet away from Miranda, frowned, and removed his glasses. Miranda almost gasped when the man's eyes seem to change color as he regarded her suspiciously. When those strange eyes met hers, they settled into a more natural-looking deep brown, and his frown was replaced by the blank expression he had been wearing moments before. "I can not deny those eyes. You are unquestionably a McAdelind, and you look enough like Kaya to pass as her daughter. But Robert is a dear friend, and he has never mentioned you before."

Justin ambled forward until he stood next to Miranda. "We get that a lot."

The man's eyes shifted colors briefly before saying, "A son too?" Then, as if noticing that there was someone else nearby, he said, "Billy O'Faron. Is that you back there?"

Billy walked around the far side of Nightshade and bowed. "Yes, Lord DeSoto."

The man scowled at the boy. "You know that you are not supposed to enter another dragon family's territory without first gaining their permission."

"Yes sir, I do know that is our tradition."

"It is more than a tradition. It is a *law*," Lord DeSoto scolded. "I just expelled Lord Drake's men out of here two days ago, and I am not interested in any additional unwelcome visitors."

"I don't care if it's a law or not," Miranda grunted, her hands clenched into fists. "My parents are missing, and I think you know what happened to them."

The man took a step back as if she had just punched him in the chest. "How dare you come onto my land throwing accusations around—"

"How dare I? I dare, because a DeSoto, your brother, not only attempted to take over Thunderbird Ranch, but he tried to kill all three of us!" Miranda yelled, sending a dozen or so birds in nearby trees retreating into the sky. "I dare because that same brother hid a package our parents sent us—a package mailed from this town, before they disappeared."

This made Lord DeSoto pause for a moment. He put his sunglasses back on. "I'm not aware of the circumstances surrounding my brother's passing. I was hoping to gain a better understanding of what occurred, but Lord McAdelind is not returning my calls." Miranda started to object but he silenced her with a raised hand. "I mean no disrespect. I am merely stating a fact."

Miranda took a deep breath, trying to calm the anger that was surging out of her. Their parents had said they had been essentially betrayed by someone they trusted, and here was Lord DeSoto claiming to be their friend. But she wasn't going to find out anything if she didn't calm down first. She took several deep breaths, and when she no longer felt like attacking the man in front of her, she said softly, "Please, Lord DeSoto, any help you can give would be appreciated."

Miranda could feel the surprised stares her brother and

Billy were shooting her way. But she had to follow the path Em had set her upon, and this seemed like the best course of action open to them at the moment. She would just have to snoop around under Lord DeSoto's nose, and possibly draw the location of the temple out of him.

The Dragon Lord of Latin America nodded to her in acknowledgment, but she could sense the same level of distrust she felt toward him reflected back. "I suppose my... errand... will have to wait one more day. You will all come back to my home as my... guests, until we can get this business sorted out."

CHAPTER 24

JUSTIN
Lord DeSoto

Justin leaned over to Miranda and whispered, "Are we really just going to blindly follow this guy? He's probably leading us into a trap." They had been hiking down a narrow path on the opposite side of the mountain from the village for over an hour.

"He most likely knows where the temple is. So yes, we're just going to follow him," Miranda whispered, never taking her eyes off the man in the gray suit.

But Justin wasn't going to drop this so quickly. "We can't trust him, Miranda. I mean, he's wearing a *suit* in the *jungle*. You know who wears suits in jungles? Crime lords, or hit men, that's who."

"We don't have to trust him. As a matter of fact, I don't think we should. He knows more than he is letting on. I can feel it."

Justin knew he wasn't getting anywhere with Miranda. She was in one of her stubborn moods again. And since reasoning with her never seemed to work when she was like this, Justin was just going to have to play along.

At least the terrain was a lot easier than during some of the hikes he had been on in Colorado recently. There was a weird mix of tropical and nontropical trees and plants all around him. The forest was full of life. Signs and sounds of a multitude of living organisms were everywhere. If he hadn't felt like they were walking to their certain death, he would almost have been enjoying himself.

Almost.

Justin had finally achieved his dream of going to another country, but the overwhelming number of bugs and creepy-crawlies he was either batting away or kicking aside was kind of ruining the experience for him.

"From here, we will fly the rest of the way," Lord DeSoto said. Justin looked up and saw they were approaching the edge of a massive ravine. "Mount up, and follow me through the valley to the compound." He shot Justin, Miranda, and Billy a stern look before adding, "And don't get any ideas about trying to fly away. You know our rules. No one can see us."

Justin wasn't sure if that was a thinly veiled threat or merely a reinforcement of the pledge they had all taken, but the statement was unsettling nonetheless. He walked silently back to Red, climbed into the saddle, and secured the safety harness around his waist. From his slightly higher vantage point on the dragon's back, he watched as Lord DeSoto climbed bareback onto one of the massive feathered snakes that had been slithering along unsettlingly behind them.

The man made a slight motion with his hand, and the serpent dove off the side of the ravine and took flight. It was followed by Billy on Nightshade, then Miranda on Storm, and finally Red and Justin. The dragons glided effortlessly through the winding valley as it descended farther and farther into the mountainous terrain. Before long, Justin noticed a significant change in the atmosphere. The air became so thick with moisture that it felt like flying through a cloud. A thick fog hung all around, and Justin could barely make out his sister in front of him.

The valley split, and they followed the fork to the left. Not long after they made the turn, the fog lifted, and Justin could see a wide clearing with many buildings, surrounded by an imposing wall. The architecture was similar to some of the older structures he had seen in the village nearby. Smooth white-stucco buildings with red-tiled roofs were laid out around a central courtyard. It was in this courtyard that Lord DeSoto motioned for everyone to land.

When they touched down on the ground and dismounted, the man in the gray suit said, "Welcome to my home."

Justin turned in a slow circle, looking around the courtyard, getting a sense of his surroundings. The buildings looked ancient, yet very well maintained. Cut stones, connected by a spider web of soft green moss, blanketed the courtyard in an expertly arranged and intricate pattern.

"Carlos? What are you doing home so soon?"

Justin turned to the source of the voice. Standing on the porch of the largest structure around the plaza was one of the most beautiful women Justin had ever seen. She was tall, with mocha-colored skin and a bright smile that reached up to her eyes. When she walked down the stairs, she lifted her vibrantly colored patterned dress just enough so it wouldn't come into contact with the ground.

"Unfortunately, *mi amor*, I had to put my errand on hold for another day. We had some unexpected visitors arrive," Lord DeSoto said, and turned back to the kids. "Allow me to introduce my wife, Hanaa Nrgwenya-DeSoto."

The woman appeared to glide as she strolled across the courtyard to where they were waiting. She regarded them with suspicion at first until her large almond-shaped eyes fell upon Billy. "Why, Billy O'Faron, is that you hiding back there behind that black dragon of yours?"

Billy stepped around Nightshade and ambled slowly forward. He removed his baseball cap, cast his eyes down to the ground, and answered softly, "Yes, ma'am."

She beamed a smile at him. "My goodness, how you've grown in the last year. And what a handsome man you're becoming. Maybe I should have a talk with that rogue-of-a-father of yours and see what he thinks about a match with our Leyla."

Billy's face blossomed bright red. Justin had never seen anyone quite so visibly uncomfortable before, and he laughed.

However, Billy wasn't the only one who shot Justin a nasty look. Miranda didn't like the way this conversation was going either.

"And who are these two?" Lady DeSoto asked, indicating Justin and Miranda.

Lord DeSoto stroked his chin thoughtfully, and said, "Now, that is an excellent question. They claim to be the children of Robert and Kaya McAdelind."

The woman took a step back and regarded them for a moment. "That cannot be, can it? All the time we spent with Robert and Kaya, not once did they ever mention kids. But to look at them, they could very well be related." She shook her head insistently. "No, no, there is absolutely no way they would be able to keep the existence of two such lovely children a secret."

Billy ventured a peek up, but as soon as he made eye contact with Lady DeSoto, his face flushed, and he quickly averted his eyes again. "I can vouch for them, ma'am. Their parents kept them isolated from the dragon world."

"Carlos, why would they do such a thing?" she asked.

But it was Miranda who answered. "We're not completely

sure why, but based on the events of the past month, they were probably trying to protect us."

The woman snorted and threw her arms wide. "Protect you! Protect you from whom?"

"Believe it or not the list just keeps growing," Justin said, his eyes resting on Lord DeSoto. "But we're pretty sure who we can and can't trust."

Lord DeSoto met his gaze and said, "The children will only be staying with us for the night. Tomorrow I will escort them back to Colorado."

Miranda shook her head. "We're not going anywhere until we get some answers about where our kidnapped family members are."

Lady DeSoto looked confused. "What are you talking about?"

It was Justin that answered. "About a month ago our parents sent us to our grandfather's ranch while they took a trip of their own. We haven't seen them or heard from them since. Well, that's not entirely accurate—we did hear from them—they sent us a package postmarked from that town back there. Mr. DeSoto… umm… the other Mr. DeSoto… his brother," Justin said, indicating the Dragon Lord, "hid the package from us. And now our parents are missing. Since this is their last known location, we came here looking for clues to where they are now."

Lady DeSoto seemed genuinely taken aback. "I had no idea. They were just here, doing research. Has it already been four weeks? Well, it is settled. We must help the children find their parents, Carlos."

Lord DeSoto seemed to think about this for a moment before saying, "They have a day. It is imperative that I continue on my errand."

She lowered her head. "Yes, dear. I understand." Then she looked up and smiled warmly. "After you take your mounts to the stables, return to the main house, and I'll show you to your rooms. I'll also make sure Consuela adds four more places for lunch."

Lord DeSoto shook his head. "Only three, *mi amor*. I still have much to do."

She shot him a stern look. "I will have a place set for you, and you will be there, Carlos DeSoto. Your work can wait. Family and guests come first in this household."

The older man sighed. "I suppose I can check in on the wild dragons now, and do my other tasks after lunch."

"What's wrong with the wilds?" Lady DeSoto asked.

"Eduardo left me a message this morning saying they were growing more and more agitated. I'm going to go talk to him to see if he has any ideas why."

Lady DeSoto made a motion with her hands as if trying to ward something off. "*Ack*. You know how I feel about Eduardo and his kind. We'd be better off without any of those... *things* around. We can care for the wilds all by ourselves."

Lord DeSoto was silent for a long moment before saying, "Come, children." He led his snakelike dragon across the courtyard to some large buildings that Justin assumed were the stables. All the buildings in the compound were made of the same white-stuccoed walls and red-tiled roofs. To Justin's surprise, these stables were strikingly similar to the horse stables back at Thunderbird Ranch, only much larger—nothing like the dark lairs deep in the belly of the Warren.

"Your dragons can rest here tonight. We will make sure they are fed and watered. Now come, I'll escort you back to the house," Lord DeSoto said.

Red walked into one of the roomy stalls, spun in a circle, and plopped down with a sigh. "*O-o-o-oh yeah. This will do nicely.*"

"Are you sure you're going to be okay out here?" Justin asked, looking around suspiciously.

Red chuckled. *"You don't have to worry about me, kid. I'm not the one those demons are after. As long as I'm a good distance away from you and your sister, I think I'll be just fine."*

"You know, you never make me feel better about the situations I'm in. How about some optimism?"

Red closed his eyes. *"That was optimistic. I did say I was going to be just fine, didn't I?"*

CHAPTER 25

JUSTIN
Leyla

JUSTIN RECLINED BACK IN HIS CHAIR after eating more food at one meal than he had the entire week before. "*Ugh*... what did I do? I'm going to pay for that one later. Why did I eat *so* much?"

Miranda shook her head. "I ask myself that question about you all the time."

"I'm a growing boy. What can I say? Now I think it's time for a long siesta."

Lady DeSoto laughed. "I believe Justin has the right idea. The secret to a good life is eating well, followed by a good nap. Some people..."—she shot a look over at her husband—"take life *way* too seriously. We are here, we are alive, let us celebrate those two facts. Everything else can wait."

"I like the way you think, Lady DeSoto," Justin said, then groaned, massaging his stomach.

"However, in your case, perhaps a little more restraint is in order," she said with a smile.

"Are you also from one of the Dragon Families?" Justin asked.

The beautiful woman nodded. "I am indeed. My family—the Nrgwenya family—is from Tanzania. There we have a vast reserve, full of all sorts of animals, both common and... uncommon."

"Really? What are the dragons like in Africa?" Justin asked.

She threw her arms wide, and said, "They make all of the dragons around here look like itty-bitty little things. African dragons are indeed great beasts. Wings that can block out the sun. Heads so massive, they can eat a zebra in one bite. And claws so big that carrying a bull elephant back to their lair is no effort at all." She snapped her hands together for emphasis, causing everyone to jump.

"Wow! They sound very... interesting." Justin looked over his shoulder nervously. "There aren't any of them... around here... are there?"

Lady DeSoto laughed merrily, but it was Lord DeSoto who answered. "No, *chico*. None of the African dragons are here. It is much too humid. They would not thrive." Then he looked to his wife, and for the first time, Justin saw a smile creep to the corners of his mouth. "My wife is prone to *slight* exaggeration."

Lady DeSoto threw her napkin at her husband playfully. "What? I *never* exaggerate." Suddenly her expression became deadly serious as she glared at something behind Justin. "Leyla Marie Nrgwenya-DeSoto. You were supposed to be back from your ride an hour ago."

Justin craned his neck around to catch a glimpse of the newcomer and almost fell out of his seat.

Standing in the doorway was the second-most beautiful person he had ever seen. The girl... Leyla... seemed to be a little younger than he was, but she walked with the confidence of a high school student. She had smooth light-brown skin, deep-brown eyes, and sun-kissed curly hair that cascaded from her head like the bending boughs of a willow tree.

Her eyes met Justin's, and he felt his face burn through at lease four different shades of red.

Leyla cocked her head slightly and scowled at him. "¿*Quién es este muchacho?*"

"English please," Lord DeSoto commanded. "Our guests do not speak Spanish."

The girl rolled her eyes. "Fine. Whatever." Then she walked over to an empty chair, plopped down, and started grabbing food off the table and piling it onto her plate with significantly less grace, Justin thought, than someone so beautiful should have.

"Leyla, I asked you a question," Lady DeSoto said sternly.

"Oh, Mama. La Barbita and I were having fun. You don't need to worry about me. I'm old enough to be out by myself," the girl said, her words dripping with a sweetness her eyes didn't reflect. She then ripped a tortilla in half and used it to scoop up a handful of rice before shoving it into her mouth.

Miranda leaned over and whispered to Justin. "Now that's your kind of girl."

Justin's face felt like it was going to explode from a massive surge of heat, and he stomped down hard on Miranda's foot.

Lord DeSoto looked sternly at his daughter. "Leyla. We have discussed being home promptly many times. You have made your mother worry, and let the food go cold. I expect a sincere apology and for you to be home when you are expected. It is important that we keep our word. ¿*Entiendes?*"

The girl looked down at the table and mumbled, "I'm just following in your footsteps, Papa."

Lord DeSoto's face flashed with anger. "Excuse me?"

His daughter glanced up from the food and smiled sweetly at her parents. "Yes, Papa. I understand. Sorry, Mama. I will not do it again."

Lady DeSoto shook her head disapprovingly, then looked over at Justin and Miranda. "Do you cause your parents such anguish?"

"No. Well... I don't. But Miranda sure does," Justin said, indicating his sister with his thumb.

Miranda responded to this offhand comment with a swift kick to Justin's shin.

Both adults stood up and began to exit the room. Miranda quickly got to her feet and said, "Wait. Where are you going? We need to talk about what our parents were doing here."

Lady DeSoto looked at Miranda sympathetically, but her husband just gave a slight nod. "We will. However, I need to go into town to pick up some supplies for my trip." Seeing the frustration on Miranda's face, he added, "While I am there, I will also enquire about your parents. If anyone saw them or has information on their whereabouts, I will be more successful at discovering it than you." Then he exited out of the room without another word.

Before Lady DeSoto followed him, she turned to her daughter and said, "But until he returns, Leyla would be overjoyed to show you all around the compound."

Leyla didn't even turn to acknowledge her mother; she just groaned and slammed her head down on the table.

* * *

After lunch, Justin, Miranda, and Billy followed Leyla out of the extensive main house and into the courtyard where they had first landed. She stopped in the very center of the large cobblestoned area and gestured to all the buildings. "This is the compound. Any questions?"

"I don't think that's what your mother had in mind," Justin said.

The girl narrowed her eyes, placing her hands on her hips. "Excuse me, stranger boy. Who's giving the tour here? You or me?" Justin started to answer, but when Leyla continued, he realized the question was merely rhetorical. "I don't even know who you are. All I want is to be left alone, and not play *babysitter* to three stupid Americans."

"Okay. That's just rude," Miranda said. "Trust us, curls. We don't want to be here with *you* either. We're running out of time and need to find some answers of our own."

Leyla clenched her fists and stomped over to stand directly before Miranda, glaring up at the older, taller girl. "'Curls'? Do you have a problem with my hair, *chica*? Because it sounds like you do."

Miranda didn't budge. "What's your deal? Why are you so mad?"

"Gee. I don't know. Maybe I'm so mad because, for an entire year, Papa and I have been planning a trip to survey the territory, checking on the indigenous dragon populations, and making sure they are well hidden from the rest of humanity. This will be my first time doing this duty, and I've been studying hard to make sure I did it well. That was supposed to be this week. But no, he would rather go on some stupid business trip to the United States than be with me. Now, with you three showing up, he will need to push our trip back even further." Her eyes began to well with tears. "Now he will have to postpone our inspection until after the Council of Twenty meeting. You know what that means? That means it's not happening, and I have to wait until next summer."

"Why can't you just go after the meeting?" Justin asked. Which in retrospect was a huge mistake, because now the angry girl's fury was directed back at him.

"Because, American boy, I have *school*. And my mother won't let me skip school for… anything. She does not believe it's a lady's place to be a Dragon Lord, that those duties belong to the men of our world." Leyla spit on the ground. "Times have changed, even here. And I am going to be Dragon Lord one day." She turned back to Miranda. "So why am I mad? Because instead of spending time with my Papa learning about the family business, a business I *will* take over, I am stuck here babysitting you three, and after you leave, Papa will be on some stupid trip."

Miranda took a deep breath. "You don't know why he's going to the U.S., do you?"

Then the same thought occurred to Justin too. Leyla didn't know her father was going to Thunderbird Ranch to collect his brother's body and bring it home. "Miranda, don't—"

She waved him off and said coolly, "His brother—your uncle—died, Leyla."

She glared at Miranda for just a moment before tears began to trace her cheeks, then she turned and ran away.

Justin stood rooted in stunned silence watching the girl as she disappeared into the stables. What the heck had just happened? Why had Miranda blurted out bad news like that?

Billy frowned and said in a disapproving tone, "Smooth, Miss McAdelind. You probably could have handled that a *million* times better. And not just better… *smarter*. If you're serious about gaining any information, why are you actively sabotaging the effort?"

"These people don't matter. They can't help. We're losing focus. Leyla is at best a distraction, and at worst a diversion to keep us occupied while our enemies catch up to us. Her parents are probably involved in this somehow. We can't trust them and we're running out of time." She grabbed

Justin's arm and said, "Let's look around and see what we can find out."

He shook her off, glaring at her. "I'm not going *anywhere* with you until you apologize to Leyla."

Miranda let out a small laugh, and then realizing that he wasn't joking, scowled. "Why should I apologize to *her*? She was treating us like crap."

"Because she's very disappointed that her parents put a higher priority on something else other than spending time with her and that they kept her in the dark about what they were doing," Billy said. "Sound familiar?"

Miranda fumed for a second, then to Justin's amazement, Billy's words seemed to sink in, and the tension melted from her. She looked back over her shoulder, then sighed. "Okay, fine. I'll apologize."

The three of them jogged to catch up to Leyla. When they got to the stables, Justin wasn't even sure where to begin to look for the girl in the massive structure. He could feel the anxiety of the dragons around him, their empathy and concern for Leyla, and he decided to try to use those thoughts to pinpoint her location.

"She's this way," Justin said, pointing down one of the long corridors that split off from the main hall. He stepped quietly along the concrete path, listening for any sounds of the girl, but it was the perception of deep concern emanating from one of the dragons that caused him to hesitate in front of a stall.

"Leyla? Are you in there?" Justin asked softly, pushing the door ajar.

"Go away, American boy. I want to be left alone." She was sitting in the protective coils of one of the dragons. Even though it looked smaller than some of the others Justin had seen today, he could tell from its narrowed eyes and tensed muscles that he should probably keep his distance if he wanted to live.

Miranda stepped around Justin, ignoring the dragon completely, and said, "Listen, Leyla, I want to apologize. I didn't mean to come off so harsh. It's just... complicated... I guess, but I should have been more sensitive. The truth is, Justin, Billy, and I understand what it's like to have our families keep us in the dark about stuff—lots of stuff, as a matter of fact—and ditch us for something more important. My parents did that very thing a month ago when they came here."

Leyla looked up, her eyes red and swollen from crying. "They did? Wait, Robin and Kaya are your parents?" She shot up, brushed the straw from her pants, and said, "Well why didn't you say so in the first place. I always look forward to their visits. They've taken me on several archaeological digs in the jungle around here."

"What? Wait... they took *you* with them?" Justin stammered. He felt like he had just been punched in the chest. He glanced over at his sister—her face flushed with anger—and he saw that she was having a similar reaction. Their parents had *never* taken them anywhere. No matter how many times they begged, or threw tantrums, their parents always flat-out refused—telling them it was much too dangerous to take kids to the sites they were going to. But in reality, they knew now, their parents just didn't want to take *them*.

"Just that. They came here several times recently looking at the old Mayan ruins in this area. I mean, they are nothing special, nothing like Tulum or Chichen Itza, but sometimes they would find something interesting. When they did, they would bring Papa and me along so we could catalog the location," she said, then seeing the reaction on Justin and Miranda's faces, added, "Surely you have gone on many digs with them, and these small sights are just too boring."

Miranda glowered at the younger girl and said through clenched teeth, "Actually, they've never taken us anywhere."

Despite his feelings of jealousy and abandonment, something Leyla had said caught Justin's attention. "Wait. You and your father would catalog the sites? Does that mean there's a record of where our parents have been in the jungle?"

Leyla nodded. "Of course. We have a special section in our library where we house all sorts of things related to the ancient peoples of this region. There is also quite an extensive portion of our collection dedicated to the dragon families' histories and dragon lore as well."

This revelation jarred Miranda slightly out of her bad mood. "Can we see it? There may be clues in there we need to find my aunt."

Justin shot his sister a look. "And our parents."

"Of course. It's actually where Robin and Kaya spent most of their time when they stayed here." A concerned look shot across her flawless face. "What do you mean? Has something happened to your parents? Are they okay?"

Justin shook his head. "We're not exactly sure. But we think they are in danger—"

An overwhelming sensation of malice washed over him from behind, and Justin spun around to peer at the stall's entrance.

The silhouette of a humanoid figure was crouched low and glaring at them. It quickly pulled back the hood of its robe exposing the bald scaly head of a draconian.

Leyla smiled and waved. "*Hola,* Eduardo. What are you doing here?"

This Eduardo of whom Lady DeSoto had spoken at lunch turned out to be none other than a draconian. The drac ignored the girl, and his eyes narrowed menacingly at Miranda and Justin. "It *is* you!" he hissed, then took off at a full sprint.

Justin, Miranda, and Billy ran out of the stall and watched the drac dash through an open gate and into the dense jungle beyond the compound's high wall.

"Well, that was weird. What do you think that was about?" Leyla asked. "I've never even heard one of the dracs speak. I wasn't even sure they could."

Miranda spun around to face Leyla, her eyes wide with fear. "Wait. You've seen draconians before? Of course you have. You even called that one Eduardo, like he was your friend or something. Are you working with them?"

The young girl frowned. "What are you talking about? He's not my friend, he's a draconian, a wild-dragon caretaker. I was just surprised to see him, is all. The dracs are never around the compound. They spend all of their time tending to the wild dragons out in the jungle." Then she regarded Miranda suspiciously. "What did he mean by 'It is you'?"

"It means our enemies will be here soon," Justin said and looked around anxiously. "Leyla, we need to see that library, now. We've run out of time."

CHAPTER 26

MIRANDA
X Marks the Spot

MIRANDA TOSSED ANOTHER THREE-RING binder onto the table in frustration. "This is hopeless. These are *actual* Mayan ruins. There's nothing in here that even slightly resembles a Sumerian ziggurat."

Leyla, who had been watching them intently with a mixture of curiosity and amusement, laughed. "Are you *loca*? Of course there isn't a Sumerian anything around here, you're completely in the wrong part of the world. I can't believe you are really Robin and Kaya's daughter."

Miranda shot the girl a murderous look before snatching up a tattered journal and quickly thumbing through its pages. Even though she was trying to read as much of the information as possible, hunting for any hidden clue contained within the text, she found herself fighting to concentrate. Her mind kept drifting, and she realized she had flipped through several pages without remembering a single word she had just read.

Miranda let out a sigh of frustration and turned back to the first page. The truth was, she was mad at her parents. No, not mad, furious. It was bad enough that they continually abandoned her and Justin while traveling the world, but to leave her stuck in New York City while they were with this snotty little girl was just too much to take.

Miranda glanced over at Leyla and couldn't help but glare at the younger girl. Could her archaeologist parents really like this mop-haired tween better than their own daughter?

Miranda was never interested in any of this ancient civilization stuff her parents loved so much. Is that why they left her all the time? Because she wasn't the daughter they wanted? She stole a glance at her brother, the *ubernerd* of the family. No, that couldn't be it. They left Justin behind too.

Miranda slammed the book shut and added it to the ever-growing pile of useless information they had amassed in the DeSoto family library.

Maybe they liked Leyla better because she was prettier, or more refined? No, that was just stupid. Her mother had been a tomboy, just like Miranda—that couldn't be it either. But why? Why would they leave her, and to spend time with this… this—

"A-ha!" Justin shouted. "Eureka!"

Miranda almost fell back over in her chair. "What is it, Justin? Did you find something?"

He walked over to her and pointed to a large map he had found in one of the binders. "See this. There is a cloud forest not far from here."

Miranda frowned. "So? What does that have to do with anything?"

Justin shook his head disapprovingly. "Lucky for you I pay attention. Remember when Tabrati and Ya'ne told us we needed to go to the next temple?" Miranda nodded and motioned for him to get to the point. "Well, they said to follow the mountains to a forest of clouds. I thought that was a metaphor for the peak of a mountain or something, but they must literally have meant a *cloud forest*: you know, a moist tropical or subtropical forest with persistent low-level clouds."

Leyla glanced at the map over Justin's shoulder. "I've been all over that area. Trust me. There is no ziggurat there," she said, giggling slightly. "I still think you guys are teasing me."

Miranda rolled her eyes. "Believe what you want, curls. I trust my brother's guesses, way more than anything *you* have to say."

Leyla glared at her. "Why are you so mean? What did I ever do to you? Your parents are so kind. Why aren't you?"

I don't like you, because my parents were kind to you, Miranda thought, but instead she said, "Listen, we're not making this up. And pretty soon, the two demons that have been trying to capture us, the demons that draconian friend of yours has most likely just contacted, will be here soon. If we don't find the location of this temple, and fast, we'll probably never again see our family members who are being held hostage. So are you going to help us or not?"

"This looks eerily familiar," Lord DeSoto said as he entered the room. "But Leyla, I thought you were going to show our guests around the compound?"

"I was, Papa, but when I mentioned that Robin and Kaya spent a lot of their time in the library, our guests insisted on seeing the research we helped them with firsthand." Her face brightened. "Since you have returned early, can we still go on our inspection?"

Lord DeSoto looked away. "I am still far too busy. It will have to wait until I return from my trip abroad." Leyla's hopeful expression vanished instantly.

"Did you learn anything when you went into town?" Justin asked.

"Nothing important. A couple of people remembered seeing your mother, but that is all," Lord DeSoto said. He motioned to the massive pile of books and papers. "Find anything interesting?"

Miranda shook her head. "Not really. Did Mom and Dad ever mention anything unusual around here? Anything that was completely out of place?"

He cocked his head to one side. "Like what exactly?"

Leyla laughed. "Like a Sumerian temple."

Lord DeSoto's face became hard as stone and his eyes rapidly shifted like a kaleidoscope through a rainbow of colors. "How do you know about the temple?"

Miranda pushed herself back from the chair quickly, causing it to fall over with a loud crash. "If you know where it is, you need to tell us."

Lord DeSoto held her gaze for a long moment. "Your parents would indeed spend hours here… in this very room… searching for the location of an ancient temple, an impossible temple, a Sumerian ziggurat—"

"Papa, that's just crazy—" Leyla interrupted.

Lord DeSoto held up his hand, cutting off his daughter. "I would try to help them when I could, but the demands of this job would prevent me from being with them most times. When they were last here, something had changed. Their enthusiasm had been replaced with… disappointment."

"They probably didn't find what they were looking for," Miranda said.

"No. That's just it. I think they did locate the temple. Your parents are forever optimistic, and what I saw in them that day was nothing less than utter defeat. Something happened. Something that broke their spirit. They made me swear never to tell anyone about what they were doing here." He motioned to the piles of papers and books amassed on the tables and floors of the library. "I fear you are wasting your time, though. They would not have been so careless as to leave clues to the temple's location in here."

"Maybe they came back and went straight to the temple?" Justin said hopefully.

"I wouldn't hold onto any hope for that possibility," Lord DeSoto said. "Robin and Kaya always follow the protocol for the dragon families and would check in with me first before venturing deeper into my land."

Miranda watched Justin's optimism deflate slightly, but she wasn't so sure the older man was correct in his assertion. After all, her parents had stolen the Tablet of Destinies shard from the City of the Ancients.

"No, I don't imagine they're there now," Justin said sadly. "But perhaps they left a clue at the temple about where they were heading next, or maybe they left you a hint before leaving here?"

Lord DeSoto met Justin's gaze, and he sighed. "They did not. As I have told you, I have no idea where they are."

"But you do have an idea where the temple might be," Miranda said—a statement, not a question.

"Or, where they might have left notes to its location," Justin added quickly.

Miranda watched as Lord DeSoto's eyes darted quickly to a shelf in the corner of the room, then back to her. "As I have said before, you are wasting your time."

Miranda began to say something, but was cut off by Lord DeSoto's raised hand. "Once I reach your grandfather, and verify everything you have told me, I will take you to where your parents were last searching for the temple."

"He will be furious to find out we're here and not with Grandpa Stone, but I'm okay with a little yelling if it helps us find Mom and Dad," Justin said.

Lord DeSoto paced over to one of the windows in the large room, staring into the darkening sky. "I have been trying to reach him since you arrived. At first, no one answered at Thunderbird Ranch, and now that storm is causing so much interference, I can't get through at all. I will just have to try him again first thing in the morning."

"We can't wait until the morning," Miranda protested, knowing the monsters contained within that approaching storm.

"You don't have a choice in the matter," Lord DeSoto said flatly, then turned and walked out the door. "Dinner is in an hour. Don't be late!" he called back, before disappearing down the hall.

Miranda stomped her foot down in frustration. They didn't have until morning. Ugallu and Lahmu would be there by tonight, and without the protection stone, they would be quickly captured—or killed.

Leyla sauntered over to Miranda and said with an air of confidence, "We don't need my papa's help, I can lead you to the cloud forest myself. I know the way."

Of course she does, Miranda thought. Mom and Dad probably took her along with them. "That's okay, curls. I think we'll manage on our own."

Leyla's face reddened, and she muttered something in Spanish before pivoting on her heels and stomped out of the room.

Justin came marching over to Miranda and shoved her hard in the chest. "What's wrong with you? She was trying to help. We could use all the *help* we can get at this point."

Miranda grabbed her brother and spun him around so he was facing the window. "I was saving her life, dork. See that storm coming? It's not just bringing rain; it's bringing two demons that don't care who gets in their way." Miranda knew this wasn't the entire reason she didn't want Leyla to help them, but it was certainly a true statement.

"Okay. Fair point," Justin said grudgingly. "But how are we

going to find the temple's location without their help?"

Miranda let go of her brother and marched over to the bookshelf she had seen Lord DeSoto glance at. It was stuffed full of dusty old books, with titles all in Spanish. She grabbed one of the nearby chairs, pulled it over, and hopped up to get a better look at the contents toward the top.

There was a long tube, resting on its side against the wall above the bookshelf. It would have been impossible for anyone to see that was shorter than seven feet tall.

Miranda grabbed the cylinder, jumped off the chair, and inspected it carefully. It was about two feet long and made of metal. On one end there was a small padlock, similar to the one Miranda had on her school locker back in New York City.

"How in the heck did you know that was up there?" Billy said in awe.

"DeSoto glanced over here when we were talking. I followed my gut," Miranda said, giving the numbered dial on the padlock a couple of spins to clear it.

"That seems a little too convenient, doesn't it? Like he wanted us to find it. Why would he do that?" Justin asked.

Miranda shrugged, and spun the dial back and forth a couple of times before clearing it again and trying a couple other combinations.

Nothing worked. She had exhausted the birthdays for her family, and her parents' wedding anniversary, when a number sequence popped into her mind, and she entered 3-1-2.

The lock clicked open.

Justin whistled. "Nice one. It was my birthday, wasn't it?"

Miranda shook her head, then frowned. Leyla's birthday had better not be March 12, or Miranda would never speak to her parents again. "Remember that key Mom and Dad sent us in the package with three-one-two written on the side? That was the combo. Weird huh?"

Justin nodded. "Very strange. Don't stand there patting yourself on the back, open it already."

Miranda yanked off the metal cover and pulled out a rolled-up sheet of yellowing paper. She walked over to one of the tables, spread it out flat, and used several books to hold the corners down.

It was a very detailed topographical map with their father's handwriting covering it. Miranda's eyes rapidly jumped around, looking for anything that would indicate the temple's location. There was the town, the river valley, the DeSoto compound, half a dozen marked archeological sites, and the cloud forest, but what caught her eye almost immediately—near the top corner of the map—was a small red X.

Miranda smiled, and whispered, "Gotcha."

CHAPTER 27

MIRANDA
The Deal

MIRANDA GLANCED QUICKLY over her shoulder as her loose hair whipped around her face, partially obscuring her view. "Are you sure? I don't see anyone behind us." It was almost impossible to see anything more than thirty feet in front of them. At this altitude, flying through a cloud forest was like swimming in a thick fog bank.

"Definitely!" Justin shouted over the roar of the wind. "I can't see them either, but there's a dragon following us."

"What about you, Billy?" Miranda asked.

Billy shook his head. "I can't see anything. But it has to be Lord DeSoto. He's the only one who could be tracking us at this speed, and in this environment."

They had only been flying for about ten minutes now, moving as quickly as they could, skimming the top of the jungle canopy. Less than a minute before Justin had sensed a dragon on their tail. If it was DeSoto, why was he following them in such a hurry? Was he trying to stop them from reaching the temple?

"Storm. Can we fly any faster?" Miranda asked.

"*We can. I should be able to navigate through the clouds without colliding with obstacles. But without your helmets, breathing will be a challenge,*" the blue dragon said as she banked around a tree jutting up higher than the surrounding canopy.

Miranda regretted not grabbing all of their gear before fleeing the DeSoto compound. They had had just enough time to saddle up the dragons and grab their weapons but were forced to leave behind most of their saddlebags, including the ones containing their camping and travel equipment, their parents' notes on Tiamat, and the scroll Miranda had saved from the fire at the warehouse. They couldn't afford to be spotted. Every second was critical. Her eyes shot to the angry clouds to the north—a roiling gray wall that would engulf them in a matter of minutes. "I think it's worth the risk."

"*As you wish.*" With those words the dragon surged forward, beating her wings rapidly. The air was now rushing so quickly past Miranda's face that she could hardly breathe. She put her head down as close as she could to the dragon's muscular neck and took a series of short, sharp breaths. While the experience was extremely uncomfortable, it certainly beat the alternative: death.

"*I think that's it,*" Red said, and Miranda looked over to see the place the immense dragon was indicating with a tilt of his nose. Just ahead of them, rising above the mist, was a plateau surrounded by thick jungle and flanked by broad rivers on either side. From this distance, there wasn't anything that resembled a ziggurat or any other ancient structure visible.

"*Slow down for a sec,*" Miranda thought to Storm, and the dragon instantly pulled back from her breakneck pace, falling into a glide. This had to be the location. But where was the temple?

As if reading her mind, Justin bellowed, "The ziggurat must be cloaked, like the one in the City of the Ancients."

Duh, Miranda thought. *Of course.* Ya'ne had told them there would be another protection stone here. "Okay, let's set down and see what we can find," Miranda yelled over the wind. "Justin. Are we still being followed?"

"Yep. But that little burst of speed did put some distance behind us. I think if we do this quickly, we can be in and out before Lord DeSoto catches us."

Miranda pointed to a small clearing in the dense jungle where they would be able to set down. Storm landed lightly on the ground, followed closely behind by Red and Nightshade.

Miranda unstrapped her safety harness and dropped to the earth. As soon as her feet came into contact with the ground, she felt a slight tingling sensation, like electricity, moving up her legs and into her body. "This is totally the place."

Justin dismounted Red and ran over to her. "Sure is, sis. Whoa. This protection stone's energy feels even stronger than the other one. Ooh! I bet it's because it only has to use its power to conceal the temple, and not preserve the land surrounding it."

"Yeah, that's fascinating… nerd," Miranda said, then waved for Justin and Billy and the dragons to follow her. "Come on. There's a path over here, and it looks like it heads farther along the plateau."

She was running now full speed down the wide jungle path when Justin yelled after her. "Miranda, wait up! I have a bad feeling about this."

Miranda came to a skidding stop as Justin, Billy, and the three dragons caught up to her. "What is it? We're almost there."

Justin was looking nervously at the dense foliage. "Something isn't right."

"Do you sense dragons around here... ?" Miranda asked, following her brother's gaze. "Or... draconians?"

"Actually, that's the problem. I can't *sense* anything. No draconians, no dragon following us..." He regarded Red with concern. "I can't even sense *our* dragons. It's like at the warehouse. Something is blocking my ability to communicate.

Miranda turned to Storm. "Try saying something to me." Storm looked at her for a minute. Nothing. Miranda shook her head. "I can't dragonspeak now either," she said. "Can you and Red still communicate with each other?" she asked her dragon. Storm nodded.

"Whatever it is, it's blocking our ability to communicate with the dragons," Justin said.

"Guys," Billy said, crouching down, examining something on the trail. "This isn't good."

Miranda looked down and noticed an enormous three-toed track in the mud. "Is that a—"

"Wyvern print," Billy said, finishing her sentence. "And not just one, several of them. And they're big. And they're fresh. We need to get out of here immediately."

Even though she was terrified, Miranda shook her head. She couldn't give up now. Not when they were this close. "Let's make a run for it. All we have to do is make it to the temple. The shield will protect us."

Billy gave her a look—as if she were speaking another language. "What? No. We could be running directly into a trap."

Miranda nodded. "Probably. We've come too far, and I

can't turn back until I get answers. You can take off if you want." Then she motioned to Storm and turned, running down the trail as fast as she could. Miranda heard Billy and Justin yelling for her to stop, but she couldn't, not now. Em was depending on her. She wasn't going to let her aunt down.

After a couple of moments, the trail widened into another clearing. Miranda and Storm came to a skidding halt as the forest opened up in front of them. The energy field was even stronger here. She could feel it pulsing with power directly ahead. She had made it.

Miranda glanced back as Justin, Billy, Red, and Nightshade burst into the clearing behind her. This was it. She just knew this temple held the answers they needed.

Miranda smiled and took another step forward.

The jungle erupted as wyverns and draconians came rushing out from all directions at once, cutting off their retreat. The ground grew dark as a shadow fell over the sun. Miranda gazed up and saw that the storm had arrived faster than she had thought possible. There was something descending rapidly from the turbulent clouds above. Ugallu had arrived.

The three dragons quickly formed a circle around Miranda, Justin, and Billy, protecting them as best they could.

"I hate to say I told you so…." Billy said.

"I knew it was too convenient that Lord DeSoto just happened to tip us off. He was pushing us toward this trap the whole time," Justin said, and reached up to grab Grandpa Stone's magic putter from Red's saddle, gripping it tightly in both hands.

Miranda, realizing this was probably their only chance to arm themselves before the inevitable fight, pulled her sword from the scabbard hooked at the rear of Storm's saddle. She glanced quickly over her shoulder at where the temple must be. If they could just make a run for it, push their way through the wyverns and draconians, they could reach safety behind the protective shield. She was getting ready to say so, when she remembered something important. If they did make it inside the temple, she would need to talk to Tabrati again. Miranda reached up, pulled the small reed stylus out of her backpack, and shoved it into her pocket for safekeeping.

"I really need a weapon of my own," Billy lamented.

"You can just disarm people with your good looks," Miranda said, and blushed when she realized that those words had actually come out of her mouth.

"Uh… thanks. But I'd rather have a sword or a bazooka or something useful in a fight."

Ugallu landed not too far away and surveyed the small army of draconians and wyverns with what looked like a sneer. He let out a low rumbling growl. "I am in command here. All of you. Umū dabrūtu and bašmu alike. Back away. Give our prisoners a little breathing room, while I conduct… negotiations."

The draconians looked at one another but held their ground, apparently confused by the lion-man's assertion of leadership. When the dracs didn't move immediately, he brought his mace down and pointed it directly at one of the draconians nearby. A bolt of lightning shot down from the swirling sky and struck the unsuspecting drac dead. All the creatures stepped back instantly, giving Miranda and her friends a wide berth. Ugallu nodded and walked slowly over to the circle of dragons. He considered them with his red eyes for a moment before saying, "I have you now. You are at my mercy. Your mission is over. There is no escape."

"I don't know. Without your little mud friend… what was his name? Lame-o… I think we can probably beat a flying kitty cat," Justin taunted.

The lion-man laughed. "I love the bravado, child. Really,

I do, but that is all that it is: bravado. Take stock of your situation. You are vastly outnumbered. The umū dabrūtu priests have eliminated your ability to sense their warriors' thoughts," he said indicating a group of draconians huddled together chanting and rocking back and forth just beyond the clearing. "And Lahmu will be here very soon." He took another step closer, making Red growl deeply, but the demon didn't even flinch. "As a matter of fact, that is why I want to speak to you now, to propose a deal before Lahmu arrives."

"What kind of a deal?" Miranda asked.

Ugallu leaned closer and whispered in a hushed voice, "I have no interest in Tiamat's return. As a matter of fact, I would be happy for all of these so-called *gods* to disappear from this realm forever. I tire of being their servant. That would indeed be a blessing, and I wish you the best in that task. However, I am not here for a revolution. I have come for the only thing that has ever actually mattered to me. I need you to free my mate from her eternal prison."

"Anzu," Justin said.

Ugallu nodded approvingly. "You are very knowledgeable, child. How do you know of her?"

"The night at the cabin, you said her name."

Miranda looked at her brother. "Well, I for one have no idea what you're talking about. I've never even heard of something called Anzu before."

"Marduk imprisoned her soul in an artifact before his battle with Tiamat and used her as a tool to defeat the Dark Queen. The only reason I volunteered for this mission to retrieve you was because of the legends that the Spear of the Winds—the artifact she is bound to—is located in a hidden temple, a temple only you can access. Believe me, if I had wanted to, I could have taken you both that night when you were cowering in that small wooden structure, but I needed you to lead me to her resting spot."

Ugallu pointed at the magic putter Justin was gripping tightly. "When the boy brought forth the spear shaft, I thought my search was over, that at long last I had found Anzu, but alas, she was not there. It appeared the legends were only just that, legends. And the location of my mate would remain a secret for all time. Then again, this was only a single piece of the accursed weapon. The only explanation being that she must be bound to the spearhead. My hope was restored, and I knew that if I gave you enough space, creating a false sense of security that you had evaded us, you would lead me directly to her. And here we are. I can sense her close by. After countless centuries, I will have the means to escape Tiamat's control… and to have my mate back."

"Let me get this straight. We bring you the spearhead, and you'll what, let us go?" Miranda asked suspiciously. "That seems too easy."

"You are correct, human. There is more to it than just that of course. I will also need you to free her from her eternal prison. Only Marduk, and his father Enki, had the ability to bind divine energy to objects. It is a power I cannot only sense within you, but witnessed first hand when you transferred parsu from the temple to the shield, recharging it. That unique power has been passed from that wretched god onto you, and I will need use of it." He pointed his curved knife at Justin's leg and said, "Last, you will relinquish the final shard of the Tablet of Destinies to me. With Anzu's help I will keep it safely hidden from Tiamat for all time, ensuring she never rises again. Do those small tasks, and I shall let *all* of you go free."

"Even if I did believe you, what's stopping you from turning the shard over to Tiamat and hunting us down a week from now?" Justin asked.

"Fair question. Nothing is. I can offer you my apologies for trying to, well, kill you and your kind back in the valley. I hope you understand the necessity of keeping up expected appearances before Tiamat's minions. You will be free to leave here unmolested. You have my word."

"What do you think the word of a storm demon is worth these days, Justin?" Billy asked.

"A little less than the paper it's printed on," Justin replied. "Oh, wait—there isn't any paper,"

"We'll do it," Miranda said, stepping forward.

"What?" Billy and Justin said in unison. Even Storm gave her a questioning look.

"We'll do it. If you agree to let us all go… and tell us anything you know about where my aunt is being held prisoner. If you do those two things, we'll give you the shard and set your mate free."

Ugallu's lip curled back into a snarl, which Miranda quickly realized was actually a smile. He nodded and said, "Agreed. Now if I were you, I would commence your task. Lahmu will arrive soon, and even if I let you go, he will not honor the terms of our arrangement."

Miranda nodded. "Let's go, guys. The faster we get this done, the faster we can get out of here."

She turned and marched toward where she knew the invisible energy field was located. When Miranda could feel the pulsating shield directly in front of her, the ground began to shake violently. She turned and saw tendrils of mud and rock fused together shoot up from the earth, snaking their way around the dragons' and Billy's legs.

Miranda was shoved hard backward as the ground opened up where she had been standing a second before. Glancing around, slightly dazed, she realized she had landed on the other side of the protective shield, out of harm's way. Justin was next to her, having just tackled her and sent her flying clear of the expanding sinkhole.

Miranda quickly scrambled to her feet, pulling Justin up with her. Standing on the far side of the clearing now was Lahmu. He looked similar to how he appeared in the valley, a massive creature made of mud and stone.

"You move too swiftly, brother," the mud-monster said. "But I did catch up to you quickly. And look what I found on my way here: a little bird and her snake." He let out a deep, menacing laugh, then thrust out his two massive arms. In his fists—the size of boulders—he held a petite Latin American dragon that was writhing from side to side, trying desperately to twist free, and in the other, a young girl with long cascading curly hair.

"Leyla! No," Justin whispered. "*She* was the one following us, not Lord DeSoto."

"This is a pretty little birdie, don't you think? But so… *fragile*," Lahmu said, and Leyla let out a shriek of pain as his massive rocklike hand tightened around her. He threw his head back and laughed. Then he tossed her like a rag doll, and she landed limply near Billy. Thick slabs of stone shot up and completely surrounded them in a box-like structure, with only one small opening, facing the temple. Miranda could barely make out Billy and Leyla in the dark recesses of their rocky prison.

Miranda took a step forward, gripping her sword tightly, and screamed. "We had a deal!"

Lahmu shrugged. "Deal? What deal? Oh, the one where I won't kill any of these people if you surrender the stone and yourself to me. Sure, we can still have that deal. But, if you think that is unfair, I can just kill them all now and wait here for you to come back out. Hunger and thirst will drive you to me eventually."

"I'm not speaking to you, rocks-for-brains!" Miranda shouted back. Even though the two demons were looking right at her, she knew they couldn't see her through the protective shield. "I'm talking to lion-breath over there. Are you going to honor our arrangement, or not?"

Ugallu walked as close to the shield as he could—mere inches from where Miranda was standing. When he was sure Lahmu couldn't hear him, he whispered, "Reunite me with my mate, and I will have the ability to deliver you to safety. Until then, consider these"—he waved an arm at the captured humans and dragons—"as insurance guaranteeing that you will keep your word. And remember, child, I will do whatever it takes to get my... *family*... back. If that means destroying everything you hold dear, so be it. Do you understand?"

Miranda stood there for a long moment. "I understand, demon. More than you realize," she said through clenched teeth, and marched with a newfound determination toward the ancient jungle temple.

CHAPTER 28

JUSTIN
Temple of the Spear

JUSTIN SPRINTED to catch up to his sister. Looming before them was another massive stone ziggurat, nearly identical to the one in the City of the Ancients. If he hadn't been so furious at Miranda, he would have loved to ponder the possible meaning of this ziggurat's influence on the pyramid-building Mayan civilization. But he *was* furious. "What is wrong with you? It's not your call to make deals with our enemy. Especially bad deals."

Miranda spun around. "We were captured. Game over. What did you want me to do? Fight?"

"Yes!" Justin yelled. "That's exactly what we should have done. Not agree to give that *thing* what it wants. His mate could be even worse than both of those losers put together. We don't know anything about her. If she's been trapped in the spear since the battle with Tiamat, then I can imagine she will be pretty upset when she gets out."

"We're out of options, Justin. Plus I'm willing to bet he knows exactly where Em is being held. Getting her back is worth the risk."

"Em? What about Mom and Dad? You seem to be missing the obvious here," Justin said, exasperated. "We're not going to get them back, Miranda. Not like this at least. We're being manipulated—*played*—by creatures that are thousands of years old. We need to fix the spear, blast these guys to kingdom come, and save our friends first. Then we grab the protection stone from this temple and take it back to the City of the Ancients and save the people that are suffering—because of *us*. We use whatever information we find here to locate our parents and Aunt Em. Not sacrifice everyone along the way."

"No, Justin. We only have one goal—to get our family's hostages back. We swore that to Grandpa Mac. That's it. Everything else is just a distraction."

"Distraction! Rescuing innocent people from the forces trying to get at *us* is a distraction? Doing everything we can to stop Tiamat is a distraction? We should be focusing all our energy on saving as many people as possible—on the greater good."

Miranda turned away from him and continued her march to the temple. "Like you know what the greater good is."

Justin wanted to slap his sister. She could be so pigheaded. Tiamat wouldn't stop until she had everything she needed to return to Earth, and even if the lion-man-bird-thingy was telling the truth, there was no way he could honor their deal with that mud-dude and the dracs close by. She had to know this. So why was she so dead set on this terrible course of action? Justin sighed and muttered under his breath, "I *do* know what the greater good is—and so does our family."

As they approached the ziggurat, Justin was stunned by its many similarities to the one in the City of the Ancients. If it weren't for the lack of a waterfall cascading through the center of the structure, he would have thought this was indeed the same building.

Miranda was already halfway to the top, taking the uneven steps two at a time, when Justin reached the first step. *Ugh!* He hated stairs. "Wait up!" he shouted, and ran after her as quickly as he could.

By the time he reached the top landing, Justin was practically crawling on all fours. He rolled over onto his back, staring up at a sky blanketed by thick, dark clouds, and moaned, "I really need to exercise more." He stood up and stumbled through the ornately carved temple entrance.

The room was lit by the same strange always-burning torches they had encountered before, and the walls were covered in mosaic images depicting the journey Tabrati most likely had taken before reaching this temple. But that was where the similarities ended. Instead of a circular pool of water in the center of the room, there stood a tall stone obelisk—an obelisk almost identical to the one that had stood watch over the City of the Ancients for six thousand years. And like its twin back in Colorado, mounted toward the top of the structure was a similar blue polished stone, the mystical source of the protective shield.

Justin walked over to the first image on his left. Tabrati was riding on the back of Ya'ne as they soared over an ocean, away from a small island. The next image showed them standing on a sandy beach: Tabrati had her hands on her hips, and a group of what looked to be indigenous people were kneeling with their heads bowed. But the look on her face was one of frustration, while Ya'ne appeared to be laughing. The last panel on this half of the room showed them flying toward this very plateau.

Where the statue of Tabrati, holding her arms out wide and looking to the sky, had stood in the previous temple there was instead an immense stone door. Miranda was standing in front of it, moving her hands over every inch of the stone and inspecting it closely.

"Find a way in?" Justin asked.

She shook her head. "Nothing. I can't read any of this script either. This is so frustrating!"

Justin stood beside her and gave the door a once-over. There were indeed cuneiform texts inscribed over every inch of the stone, but at eye level, he discerned the image—the indentations actually—of two large handprints, one mirroring the other. "Did you try touching those two places?"

"Duh. That was the very first thing I did. But nothing happened."

"Or maybe you just don't have what it takes," Justin said, and motioned his sister to move aside.

Miranda stepped out of the way. "O great wise one: show me how it's done."

Justin cracked his knuckles dramatically, shook his hands as if getting the kinks out, then thrust them into the indentations on the door. He stood like that for several seconds, but nothing happened. He pulled his hands back and tried again. Still nothing.

"Well, at least you did that with flair," Miranda said, smirking slightly.

Justin looked at the indentations again. They were much larger than a normal person's hands, almost as if they were the prints of a giant's—or a *god's*—hands. "*Hmm*. I don't think this door is supposed to be opened by humans."

"Well, if that's the case, then we're in a worse place than I thought," Miranda said.

Justin shook his head. "No. That's not what I mean. Actually, I think we're the only people who can open this door." When Miranda gave him a quizzical look, he continued. "Both Ugallu and Ya'ne said they could sense Marduk in us. Like we are carrying around the essence of a god."

"So?"

"So maybe we're not supposed to do this alone," Justin said and put his right hand on the corresponding indentation. Miranda seemed to understand what he was suggesting, shrugged, and placed her left hand against the other. As soon as she touched the door, it began to glow. They removed their hands and took several steps back. The stone split in half vertically and both halves swung outward, exposing a dark hall beyond. Soon after the door opened, torches flared to life along the corridor, beckoning them to enter.

"Boo-yah! Who's the genius now?" Justin quipped.

"I figured out the code to the lock in Lord DeSoto's library."

"Okay, so genius runs in our family—" He paused. "I bet this is what Mom and Dad were trying to do, to get through this door. They must have gotten this far, but weren't able to open it. We are the only people who can access this area."

Miranda's face flushed red. "Yippee for us. That's something they would have known if they had spent more time with their own kids, and not some mop-haired… You know what? It doesn't matter what they were trying to do. Now come on," she said, and stomped off down the torchlit corridor.

"Why are you so darn stubborn!" Justin yelled, as he ran to catch up to her.

After walking down a series of passageways and a couple of flights of stairs, they came to a large square room. As soon as they entered, several torches, high up on the wall, ignited. The flickering lights reflected off mirrorlike tiles, illuminating the entire room. Near the center of the space were two small pillars, each about three feet high, with a bronze bowl perched on top of each. At the opposite end of the room was another enormous door.

As they approached the center of the room, a massive stone slammed down behind them, cutting off the way they had just come.

Justin heard the sound of water and spun in a circle to see that several of the tiles on the walls had popped off and water was now rushing swiftly into the room. There was also the sound of stone scraping against stone near the ceiling, and he glanced up in time to see a long rock column jut out horizontally from the wall. It had a ball of what appeared to be raw electricity, spinning and twisting at its tip.

Miranda was frantically looking around the room for any way out of the trap they had stumbled into. "All right, Justin. Time to tap into that inner god you were going on about."

The water was already spreading across the floor rapidly; in seconds, their feet were totally submerged. Justin looked up at the arcing ball of electricity. Even if they floated their way to the top of the room, hoping to find an exit up there, as soon as that electricity came in contact with the water, they'd be toast.

"Got anything?" Miranda asked, her voice trembling.

Justin kept staring up at the ball of lightning. "Yep. I've got a bad feeling about this."

CHAPTER 29

JUSTIN
Trial by Lightning and Fire

JUSTIN QUICKLY WADED over to the stone door that had slammed shut behind them and tried to push it back up, but it was about the size of one of the pillars at Stonehenge and probably weighed several tons. That wasn't going to work.

Maybe he could force it open enough to let the water out? He reached his hand down into the cold water, searching for a gap he could jam something into, but it was completely seamless. Justin tried to fight back the feeling of desperation threatening to cloud his mind as he ran his fingers around the door's edges, searching for a secret switch or something to release them from this deathtrap.

Miranda splashed over and said, "Try using the staff to blast the door open."

"Good thinking, sis. Stand back." Miranda quickly moved out of the way and behind him. Justin held the staff just above his shoulder, as if waiting for a baseball pitch. When he swung it at the door, a massive amount of energy was released from the end of the staff, forming a cone of wind that pushed the rising water aside—as if it were being parted by two huge invisible hands. When the blast struck the closed entrance the room shook slightly, but nothing more happened.

"Huh? That didn't—" Justin was cut off mid-sentence as the wind rebounded off the wall, sending him and Miranda flying backward. They landed with a splash near the center of the room by the two strange pillars.

Justin scrambled back up out of the water. "Any other ideas?"

Miranda was using one of the posts behind her as leverage to hoist herself up, when something caught her eye, and she waved Justin over. "Check this out. Something's carved on the side."

Justin leaned in close to inspect the symbol. "It looks like fire."

Miranda moved quickly over to the other bowl, and said, "Here's another one that looks like lightning. Fire and lightning. Those are the breath weapons our dragons have."

"Not only that, but you're pretty much immune to being killed by lightning, and fire doesn't affect me. That can't be a coincidence," Justin added.

Miranda looked up at the ball of electricity suspended near the ceiling. "So there's one of the pieces to this puzzle, but where's the fire?"

Justin quickly glanced around the room and saw the torches lining the walls. But they were well out of reach, suspended in brackets high up, near the ceiling. Even if they could get to them, what exactly was he supposed to do with the fire once he had it?

"Somehow the torches and that ball of energy up there are the key," Justin said. "See these symbols on the bowls?

I think we need to get fire into this one, and lightning into the other."

Miranda looked up. "Okay, but how? That's, like, twenty feet off the ground. If we wait until the water floats us up that high, the bowls will be totally submerged."

Justin closed his eyes for a second, trying to think through the puzzle. There had to be a way out of this. If he could only concentrate for a second. Often, if an answer seemed out of reach, he would try clearing his mind, but something was distracting him. It wasn't the cold rising water, or the sound of his chattering teeth, but something pulling at him. An almost nagging vibration or movement. A vibration he had felt before. Then it hit him.

"I can feel the flames!" Justin said. "Just like in the temple when we were trying to recharge the stone, just like the campfires that would suddenly burst out of control, and just like at the warehouse. I can *feel* them."

Miranda nodded. "You should be able to do more than just feel them. You should be able to control them. I was able to block and absorb the lightning when those two blue dragons attacked in the Warren while we were returning Azuria's egg, and at the warehouse you were able to push the fire back at the dracs."

Justin shook his head. "But I can't control it. You saw what happened at the warehouse. I set the whole place on fire and almost killed everyone. The last thing we need right now is for me to set this whole room on fire by accident."

Miranda motioned to the rapidly rising water. "Lucky thing we're standing in a couple of feet of water. You need to try. If you don't, we're already dead."

When Justin hesitated, Miranda said, "Look, I'll go first. Just do what I do."

Miranda closed her eyes in concentration. She reached

her hand out toward the spinning ball of energy. "I can feel it," she whispered. "The little bugger is fighting me."

Justin watched as the ball of lightning began to dance excitedly, reaching out toward Miranda, crackling and surging sporadically. It leaped toward her like a snake striking at its prey. But she held her ground, bringing up her other hand and forcing the energy back. Sweat began to drip down her face and lines of concentration creased her brow.

Miranda clenched her fists and slowly drew her hands back toward her chest. The lightning was slowly moving toward her, fighting her the entire way. Soon the ball was hovering above the brass bowl; at that moment, her eyes sprang open as she swept her hands in a downward arc. The lightning responded to her will and exploded into the bowl. As soon as it made contact, the symbol on the side of the bowl began to glow with a bright bluish light.

"Okay. That wasn't so bad," Miranda said. Then she must have sensed Justin's anxiety, because she quickly added, "Don't worry. It's not as hard as it looks. You can do this. It just takes concentration. Grab onto the fire and make it bend to your will."

Justin nodded, but he didn't feel very confident or will-bending. Everything always came easily to Miranda. He took a deep breath and focused on the closest torch. *Be like Miranda. Be like Miranda*, he repeated to himself, over and over again.

The more Justin relaxed, the more he could feel the flame. It began to move slightly from side to side, and he felt his body move in unison with it. He reached his hand up toward the light, and the torch flared slightly. He clenched his fist, and the flame died back down. Then he threw his palm open wide, and all the torches on the walls surged.

"Okay, that's pretty awesome," he said, feeling a little more confident. Justin tried to bring the fire back down again, by clenching his fist, but this time, the fire didn't respond—instead it flared even brighter. He tried again, concentrating even harder to make the fire bend to his will. But the flames continued to refuse him, instead bursting into small bonfires. He could feel the heat now, and knew if he didn't figure this out soon, he might end up boiling them both alive.

"It's not working. I'm losing control," Justin said, his rising panic causing his voice to shake slightly.

"You're almost there, just a little longer," Miranda encouraged.

"I can feel it, but I can't control it. The more I try to make it bend to my will, the more it resists."

"Maybe fire isn't like lightning. It might need a different approach," Miranda said.

That's it! A different approach. When he had lost control at the temple, Mrs. Lóng had told him not to force the power, but to guide it—to use the energy within himself as a conduit. He thought back to the old cook standing in the river. She had used her fluid motions to guide the water. Maybe if he tried leading the fire instead of forcing it, he could direct it where he needed it to go.

"I don't mean to rush you," Miranda said. "But if you don't hurry, we're going to be doing the doggy paddle in about one minute."

Justin lowered his head and drew his arms slowly backward, breathing in deeply the whole time. When his hands were nearly at chest level, he could feel the fire within him begin to build—but this time, it didn't frighten him. He exhaled, letting his air out slowly, and pushing his palms outward toward the flames. He could sense the energy within him reach out to the torches and feel how they were immediately drawn to it.

He opened his eyes, drew in another breath, and repeated

the motion. To his delight, the fire from each torch arced through the air like a flaming fountain. He concentrated on the empty bowl, and when he exhaled again, he guided all the arcing streams of fire into it. And once again, the corresponding symbol on the side of the pillar began to glow brightly.

Justin dropped his arms to his sides, letting out a sigh of exhaustion. "Whoa. That takes it out of you, doesn't it?"

Rumbling shook the room, followed by the noise of water rushing down hidden drains. Within seconds, all that remained of the deadly trap were a few puddles on the slick stone floor.

Miranda put a hand on her brother's shoulder. "We did it."

Justin looked up and saw that not only had the door opened on the opposite end of the room leading deeper into the temple, but that the stone blocking their path back had also risen, allowing them free access to the exit. "Yes, we did. Now let's get moving, we have a spearhead to find."

CHAPTER 30

Miranda
The Temple Sanctuary

MIRANDA WALKED CAUTIOUSLY into the next chamber, not wanting to set off another trap before they had a chance to figure something out. But her caution appeared not to be necessary. The next chamber was similar to the one in the temple back in Colorado, the room that held Tabrati's ghostly apparition. The walls were etched from floor to ceiling in cuneiform script, and there was also a small stone table toward the rear of the space.

Miranda pulled out the reed stylus from her pocket and gripped it tightly in her free hand. She felt the now familiar vibration of energy in the small stick as it began to glow. All around her the writing began to move and rearrange itself on the walls, forming animated images of scenes long past.

But Miranda wasn't here for a history lesson. "Tabrati," she said. "I need to talk to you."

Blue light erupted from the tip of the stylus and spiraled throughout the room, converging on a spot directly in front of Miranda. Slowly Tabrati's image appeared, but this time she was somewhat younger. Her pure gray hair now showed streaks of brown, and there were fewer wrinkles on her stoic face. She held her head high, shoulders square: the weight of the world had not quite beaten her down yet.

The otherworldly image smiled slightly and said, "I have been waiting a very long time to meet you, Miranda—"

Miranda held up her hand. "We've already met. I'm here only to ask you one question."

Tabrati looked confused. "But you must have many questions for me. How else will you prepare yourself for the upcoming battle with the Dark Queen?"

"See, that isn't all that important to me right now. Tiamat has taken some members of my family hostage, and I want to get them back. I need to know if you have any information on where they might be."

The apparition took a step back away from her. "I don't understand. Your destiny is to slay the Dark Queen and save the world."

"I don't believe in destiny. I told the other… *you*… that already. Tiamat can't rise, we still have the last shard. As long as we keep that out of her hands, the world is safe. She can become someone else's problem to solve. You must know something, a location where the draconians have a prison or the big cave where Tiamat is supposed to be, something that can help me."

Tabrati regarded her for a long moment before nodding. Miranda felt her heart begin to race. This was what Aunt Em had been leading her toward. "What is it? What do you know?"

"I know that you are scared."

Miranda felt her face flush with anger. "I'm not scared. I will do whatever it takes to get Em back safe."

"That, I do not doubt. But you are scared nonetheless. The

Dark Queen will continue to use that fear and self-doubt against you, manipulating you. You will be nothing more than her puppet," she said and pointed a shimmering finger at Miranda's chest. "You are conflicted because your heart is telling you one thing, but your head is telling you another."

"You don't even know me—"

"Oh, but I do, Miranda." Tabrati closed her eyes, and the reed stylus began to glow even more brightly in Miranda's hand. "I am connected to you through the stylus of Nidaba. Your thoughts and experiences are as open to me as mine are to you."

Miranda tried to drop the small stick, but her hand wouldn't let go. She tried throwing it; still her fist held onto it tightly. "Don't you *dare* read my mind," she said, trying to hide the panic she was feeling behind a veil of anger.

"You have felt abandoned by your parents... unloved even. When Leyla told you how they would take her to look for ruins, all those pent-up emotions came back to you, but you said nothing. You turned them into anger directed at the girl."

"You're wasting precious time. I need to save some prisoners, not talk to a psychologist."

Tabrati continued. "When your aunt reached out to you through the vision, she didn't say where she was located, she didn't even ask for you to come and rescue her."

"There wasn't time. The dracs were about to kidnap me—"

"Em has been a prisoner there for a very long time. She is smart and resourceful. Don't you think she could have given you information on her location?"

"No—yes—I don't know—" Miranda stammered. She didn't like having someone in her head. "It doesn't matter. She's in danger, and I need to save her."

Tabrati closed her eyes again. "She said to you, 'Don't worry about me. I'm not important. But you are.' Then she sent you to the valley. Why did she send you there, Miranda?"

Miranda felt tears begin to well in the corners of her eyes. "It doesn't matter. We need to—"

Justin walked over and stood next to Tabrati. "Miranda, what did Em say to you?"

Miranda looked up at the ceiling. "She told me it was the start of the trail."

Justin looked confused. "The trail to find Mom and Dad, and Em, right? That's what you told me. Were you lying to me?"

Miranda met her brother's gaze. She had been keeping things from him this whole time, and the weight of the deception all at once felt too much to bear, but she couldn't let him know about their parents, it would crush him. "No, Justin. To my destiny." She spread her arms wide. "Okay? This is the path I'm supposed to be on. Going around the world collecting old weapons and talking to long-dead people to face the queen of monsters. I am supposed to battle Tiamat." She started to laugh, not at the humor of anything in particular, but at the absolute absurdity of the statement. "I, Miranda McAdelind, am supposed to fight and defeat a goddess and save the world. Do you know how completely stupid that sounds? I can't do that. No one can do that."

Tabrati shook her head. "It is not so absurd, Miranda. And you *can* do it. I know you can, because I was there the first time she was defeated."

"By a *god*. With all kinds of crazy *god* powers, not by a fourteen-year-old girl."

"A fourteen-year-old girl with the power of that same god, Marduk, coursing through her veins. You have now just only scratched the surface of what you are capable of, Miranda. But even without those powers, a human can defeat a god."

"Yeah, right," Justin said.

"No. It is true..." Tabrati looked critically at Justin, as if noticing him for the first time. "Who are you, by the way? Are you Miranda's servant?" Justin's face turned bright red, and the ghostly version of Tabrati smiled. "I am only teasing you, Justin. I have access to Miranda's thoughts. I know my older self said that to you already."

"You're hilarious. I can see where Ya'ne gets it from," Justin said.

Tabrati tilted her head for a moment, then smiled. "Ah, Ya'ne'unde, the Lighthearted, a very fitting name indeed. I knew him as Neperdu, which means 'bright' or 'happy' in Sumerian. I cannot believe he still lives after all these centuries. Marduk said he would need to stay around until his work was complete, but none of us thought it would be this long. He does not look well, does he?"

"Not at all. He's the kind of ugly you can't un-see either," Justin said, and shivered. "Anyhow, you were saying a human could defeat a god."

Tabrati nodded. "When Marduk faced Tiamat's army, none of the other gods stood with him."

"Why was that?" Miranda asked.

"Because of the Tablet of Destinies. Whoever was named on the tablet as king could control the fate of all others... well, all except Tiamat and Apsu, for they predated the tablet's creation. After Marduk's father, Enki, had vanquished Apsu, by tricking him into drinking poisoned wine"—she pointed toward the moving image on one wall of the god with the pointed wizard hat Miranda had seen at the other temple—"Tiamat declared war upon the younger gods, seeking revenge for the death of her husband. Over many years, she plotted and built her army. During that time she took a new consort—an elemental god, named Kingu—and made him general over her forces. But to ensure that his authority was absolute, so that no other god could oppose him, Tiamat needed to inscribe his name upon the Tablet of Destinies."

"If the tablet gave you control over all the other gods, how was Marduk not affected?" Justin asked.

Tabrati winked at him. "Now that is an exceptional question and one that will take too long to answer—story for another time, but one you will need to know before facing Tiamat. All the other gods viewed humans as insignificant tools... all except for Marduk. So when it came time to face Tiamat's army, he enlisted the help of humanity."

"Couldn't the Tablet of Destinies control humans too?" Justin said.

"Indeed. But in their arrogance, Kingu and Tiamat did not see humanity as a threat, ignoring them until it was too late. And when Kingu tried to exert his control over Marduk's small force, it didn't work. He had already thought of a way to protect the people who fought with him from the tablet's influence." Tabrati swelled with pride. "Marduk's small army of humans faced off against an unstoppable force of gods and monsters, and they emerged victorious." Tabrati met Miranda's gaze. "Can a fourteen-year-old girl defeat a god? Yes, because I was that age when I vanquished Kingu." Her expression softened. "I know how arduous this is, Miranda, truly I do. The path you have been set upon is harder than anyone will ever know, but it is not a path you have to walk alone," she said, indicating Justin with a small gesture of her hand.

"I don't want to put any more of my family in danger."

"Your family is already in danger, child. You know this to be true. You have already said as much many times before. That is not going to change until you embrace your destiny and defeat the Dark Queen. Sure, you might be able to prolong the inevitable for a month, a year, maybe even ten years, but until you do face her, more and more people you care about will be used as tools to defeat you. Yes, your parents and aunt are imprisoned, but how many more could still be? Your grandfathers, your friends from school, your brother, Billy? The longer you wait to embrace your destiny, the more people you care about will be hurt."

Miranda lowered her head. "I suppose you're right. What do I need to do next?" When Tabrati smiled, Miranda tried to move her hand again. Her fingers were now free.

"Take the spearhead and place it in the gap—" The image of Tabrati disappeared as soon as Miranda shoved the stylus into her pocket.

Justin stood there with his mouth agape. "What the heck did you just do?"

Miranda turned and walked over to the stone table, where the spearhead lay. She grabbed it, feeling the telltale tingling sensation of the trapped demon's parsu inside, then shoved it into her other pocket. "Come on, let's finish this."

When Justin didn't follow her right away, Miranda turned to see him glaring at her.

"Justin, come on. We need to find out what Ugallu knows."

"What is going on in that little head of yours?" Justin barked.

"I'm sticking to the plan. Why? What's going on it that little head of *yours*?" she shot back.

"How utterly disappointed I am in you." He stomped over until he was standing toe to toe with her. "Did you listen to *anything* Tabrati just said?"

Miranda crossed her arms over her chest. "Yes. Did you? Because what it sounded like to me was she didn't know anything about where Em and our parents are. That is why we're here, remember? To find out where they are, not to take off on some ridiculous quest to fight a god. As far as I can see, Ugallu is the only one willing to give us what we want. So, I'm going to honor our bargain with him."

"Mom and Dad would be disappointed too."

"You're completely clueless," Miranda spat. "Mom and Dad

don't even care about us, Justin. You know what? You were right, I was lying to you—not to keep you in the dark about what Em said, but to protect you."

"Protect me from what?"

"From the truth. When I talked to Em, she told me Mom and Dad weren't even there with her. They were in a cave someplace. They don't even care about us."

"Just because they weren't at the same location as Em doesn't mean they aren't prisoners. You're being stupid. Of course they care about us." Justin studied her for a moment. "No, it's something else. You're using Mom and Dad as an excuse. It's this destiny thing, isn't it?"

Miranda felt her face flush. "You don't know what you're talking about."

"That's it. Isn't it? I can't believe it. You really are scared." His face twisted in disgust. "I've spent my whole life looking up to you, wanting to be more like you. I would look in the mirror and say to myself: 'If only I could be brave like *Miranda*, I would stick up for myself. If only I was strong like *Miranda*, I wouldn't be picked on so much. If only I had a purpose like *Miranda*, then I would be special too.'" He shook his head. "I was such an idiot."

Miranda's heart was beating hard, and she found it hard to breathe. Justin's words hit hard. "Well… do what you want… but I'm sticking to the plan."

Justin shook his head, then headed out of the chamber. He bumped into Miranda slightly as he walked out of the chamber, knocking her off balance. She stood there, stunned for a moment, before pulling herself together and following him.

"Justin. Wait—"

Miranda had almost reached the exit when the magical staff came rolling along the floor into the room and the stone door slammed shut, trapping her inside the chamber.

Miranda ran over and tried to push the door back up, but it wouldn't budge.

"Justin!" Miranda screamed. "The door shut! Can you get me out of here?"

Her brother's voice was muffled. "You lied to me, Miranda. But worse than that, you are lying to yourself. I'll be back for you when this is over."

Miranda felt panic begin to build within her. She was trapped. "What did you do?"

"I put out the fire. I'm going to do what Mom and Dad would have wanted us to do. I'm going to find a way out of this without letting the bad guys win."

"You can't do that alone. You're going to get yourself killed."

There was a long pause before Justin said, "Perhaps. But I believe in myself, Miranda. Maybe you should believe in yourself too."

Miranda placed her ear against the stone door and listened. She could faintly hear the sound of her brother walking away.

"Justin!" she screamed. "Get back here! Don't leave me! Please, Justin. Don't leave me alone."

But her brother was already gone.

CHAPTER 31

JUSTIN AND MIRANDA
Higher Calling

JUSTIN WAS NOW BEYOND FURIOUS. How dare Miranda lie to him. How dare she manipulate him. They had made an oath to stick together. No matter what. And she had broken it.

Em hadn't wanted them to risk everything only to rescue her, not at all. She had wanted Miranda to learn how to fight Tiamat. He was so angry, he felt like screaming.

But what about their parents? Were they prisoners too? They had to be. Justin couldn't accept that they would have left their own children in such peril. Plus, they would have returned here by now to try to enter the temple again.

Justin was so lost in thought that he almost exited the temple without realizing it. "Focus, Justin," he scolded himself. "Get a grip, or you'll never beat these guys."

Actually, Justin knew there was no way he could beat Ugallu, Lahmu, the draconians, and the wyverns all by himself, even if he was part god. They would rip him to shreds at the first sign of aggression. After all, he wasn't anything special. There were no prophecies about Justin McAdelind saving the day. No ancient blue ghosts wanted to give *him* guidance. If he was going to be a hero, it was going to have to be on his terms.

He did have a plan, though. A long shot. He wasn't going to sit by while innocent people were used as pawns to manipulate them.

Justin took a deep breath—several deep breaths in fact—and felt himself beginning to calm down. Part of his martial arts training with Mrs. Lóng was meditation, learning how to quiet his mind to focus on the task at hand.

When he was satisfied that he was focused enough to continue, he reached up and grabbed two torches off the wall of the temple's main entrance chamber. He took one last deep breath and walked out of the building and down the steep stairs.

When he arrived at the edge of the shield, he looked back over his shoulder at the ziggurat and sighed. "I hope you know what you're doing, Justin McAdelind," he whispered to himself. "Because if you're wrong, you'll be dead, and your sister will be trapped in that temple forever."

Immediately he regretted acting out of anger. This was stupid. He needed to go back and talk some sense into Miranda, not storm out there, guns blazing and hoping for a miracle.

He had turned around and started walking back to the temple when he heard a low growl. "I can smell you, boy. Come out here where I can see you." It was Ugallu. "You have until the count of three, or I'm going to rip out this lovely little girl's throat. One…" *Crap!* Now he had no choice but to face them. "Two…" His plan was terrible. He'll just put everyone in more danger. "Three—"

Justin tightened his grip on the torches and stepped

beyond the safety of the protective shield.

* * *

"When I get out of here, I'm going to kill him," Miranda said, then threw her head back and screamed at the top of her lungs, "Do you hear that, Justin! When I get out of here, I'm going to kill you!" She pounded on the stone door with her fists, instantly regretting that decision as pain exploded in her hands.

She spun around and sank to the floor. "If you're not already dead."

Over the past couple of minutes, she had tried using the spear shaft, her sword, and yelling at the wall to open the door. Nothing worked. She was trapped in this room at the bottom of the ancient temple, all alone, imprisoned, like her aunt, with no way out and no one to talk to.

Then it hit her: she did have someone to talk to. Miranda reached into her pocket, pulled out the reed stylus, and gripped it tightly. "Tabrati. I need you."

The stick began to glow brightly, then beams of light shot out, forming the woman's ghostly image. When she had finished materializing, she stood in front of Miranda, her arms crossed high up on her chest and glaring down.

Miranda met her gaze, then looked down at her feet. "I'm sorry," Miranda said. When Tabrati didn't immediately respond, she continued, "I shouldn't have cut you off like that. You were only trying to help. I get that. I'm ready to listen now."

"No, you are not. You are hoping I can help you get out of this room."

"My idiot brother is going to get himself killed. If I don't get out of here soon, I'll... I'll lose him too."

Tabrati crouched down so she was eye-to-eye with

Miranda. "You will lose everyone if you do not embrace your destiny once and for all."

"I told you, I don't believe in destiny."

The apparition shook her head. "Whether you do or do not believe in it is irrelevant, because the people who are working against you unquestionably do believe. They will not stop, they will not hesitate, and they will do everything in their power to ensure that the Dark Queen rises." Tabrati tilted her head and added, "But perhaps I'm not the one you need to hear this from. There are others who also oppose Tiamat. They do not have the gifts you do, yet they have worked tirelessly to prevent the Dark Queen's rise. They have sacrificed everything for the sake of this goal. Perhaps their words and actions will move you where mine have failed."

Tabrati closed her eyes, and her body dissolved into a shower of light. The energy shifted and reformed, like fireflies dancing in the night sky. Instead of a young woman, Miranda now saw what appeared to be an image of the entry chamber to the temple in which she was not trapped. A man—her father, she realized with a start—came walking into view and carefully inspected the ornately carved stone door that blocked access to the temple's inner sanctuary. He traced his finger along the cuneiform text, his lips moving as he translated the inscriptions.

"Kaya!" he shouted over his shoulder. "Come here. This is it."

When the image of her mother came into view, Miranda felt a sob building deep in her chest. She missed her parents so much—she couldn't deny that, despite her anger. She watched as the image of her mother read the inscription as well, then nodded and said, "I can't believe, after all these years of searching, we have finally found one of the resting places of Marduk's weapons."

Miranda could see the excitement on her father's face. "We're close," he said. "I can feel it." He pointed toward the indentations on the door she and Justin had opened earlier by just pressing their palms against it. "I think all we have to do is touch these spots, and we should gain access to the inner sanctuary."

He reached up and placed both of his hands on the door. When nothing happened, he frowned but still appeared optimistic. "We probably both need to touch it, so all the family lines are represented." Miranda's mother nodded, and in unison, they each pressed a hand against the door.

Miranda watched over the next several minutes as her mother and father tried every combination of their hands they could think of to access the chamber beyond: his right and her left, her left and his right, both her hands with his behind them and vice versa... Miranda could see her father's frustration build with each failed attempt. He screamed and smacked the stone with both palms. "Nothing's working! Why is nothing working?"

"Honey, it's okay. We'll figure something out," her mother said, trying to soothe her father, angrier than Miranda had ever seen him before.

"It's—not—okay," he said through clenched teeth. "Kaya, if we don't figure this out soon, everything is lost. Everything we've fought for, everything we've sacrificed, everyone we've tried to protect: lost!"

Miranda watched as her mother slowly turned her father around to face her. "We knew this was going to be a long shot. This isn't our fight—"

"The kids can't do this. They're not ready," he said defensively.

Miranda's mother placed a calming hand on his arm. "Time is running out. Robin, I know this is hard." Tears were streaming down her cheeks now. "I can't bear to put our children in danger any more than you. But it is their destiny. We know that to be true. But even knowing that, we tried, we tried so hard to spare them the trials they must face. This is the second temple we've discovered and the second one that has yielded no answers to us. We have to assume Tiamat knows about Miranda and Justin now. It won't take her minions long to find the children, and if they do, all is lost. We have run out of time."

Miranda's father's shoulders slumped. "What are we supposed to do, Kaya? We can't give up now. We're the only thing standing between them and that monster."

She shook her head. "But what if we're only standing in their way from ending this once and for all? It'll be our job—no, our responsibility—to teach and guide the children, to help them succeed in the task ahead."

Her father turned around and faced the door once again. "I can't accept that right now. Not until we've tried everything. Please, Kaya. I know the answer is here. I'll make a copy of the text, and we can take it to the Great Library. Maybe there's something we've missed. Let me just try this one last thing."

Miranda's mother wrapped her arms around her husband's waist, hugging him from behind, and said, "Okay, dear. We'll try *one* more thing. But after that, it's time to tell Miranda and Justin about who they are."

Just then the figure of another man came running into the chamber, a man Miranda didn't recognize. "Any luck?" he said with a familiar accent: Miss Ddraig's. He was soaking wet, with water dripping freely from a thick mop of red hair.

"Nothing good," Miranda's father said. "I'm going to take a couple of photos of the inscription and see what information we can find at the Great Library. Do you mind getting our transportation arranged? We should probably leave tonight." Then her father pulled out his phone and took several pictures of the ornate stone door.

The other man shook his head, sending a spray of water in all directions at once. "We're goin' t' have t' wait a bit. It's rainin' old women an' sticks out there, it is. We'd be better off headin' out in the mornin'." The redheaded man looked around the chamber almost nervously before adding, "Let me make a couple o' calls an' get somethin' set up straight away."

As he exited, Miranda's mom watched him, her eyes narrowing, and she whispered, "Something's up with Gareth—something's not right."

Miranda's dad stopped taking photos of the door for a moment and turned to follow his wife's gaze. "I thought I was being paranoid. But yes, something's definitely wrong."

"I believe that it might be time."

His face became grim. "Okay, I suppose we don't have much of a choice. If we fail, it will be up to the kids."

Miranda's mom nodded. "I'll tell him I need to get some supplies from town. When I'm there, I'll mail the package."

"Be careful. I'll keep Gareth busy here."

She nodded once before jogging out the door.

Miranda's father placed his phone back in his pocket, then closed his eyes and rubbed his temples with the palms of his hands. "They're not ready to face their destiny yet. I've got to keep trying."

The image paused, and Miranda walked over to the apparition of her father. She tried to reach out and touch him, but her hand went right through. "They know. Our whole lives they've always known," she said. "All this time, I thought they were trying to find my aunt, but they weren't."

The lights swirled around, forming the image of Tabrati again. "No. They were trying to spare you the trials you would have to face. They were trying to protect you."

"That's why they kept us hidden from our own family—

why no one knew about us. If the wrong people found out, we would have been kidnapped... or... worse. But they couldn't stop it. Could they?"

Tabrati shook her head. "No, Miranda, they could not. It is not their destiny to face Tiamat. It is yours."

Miranda looked around the room in a panic. "I need to get out of here. Justin's in danger. There's no way he'll be able to fight those two monsters on his own."

"There is so much you need to learn first. They want you, not your brother. Stay here and let me teach you some of what you need to know," Tabrati pleaded.

"I can't. You're right. They want me. But like you said, Tiamat will use the people I love against me. I can't let Justin fall into their hands too. I promise, once this is all done, I'll come right back here and learn everything I can."

Tabrati's face fell. "Once you leave this room, there will be no coming back. You see, the only way out of this chamber is through the destruction of this temple."

CHAPTER 32

JUSTIN AND MIRANDA
Out of the Frying Pan…

About the only thing going for Justin at the moment was that nothing outside the protective field had changed. Everyone was exactly where they had been when he and Miranda had gone inside the temple. The dragons were still pinned securely to the ground, their legs and necks encapsulated in earth and stone; Leyla and Billy were still trapped inside their box made entirely from stone slabs. But more important, the draconian priests were still clustered off to one side, just inside the clearing at the edge of the forest.

Ugallu's eyes narrowed as he sniffed the air. "Where is your sister, boy? And where is the spear?"

Justin shrugged. "She was being a bad girl, so I had to put her in time-out until she realizes what she's done. Oh—and I left the spear with her, so you can't get to it."

The lion-man took a threatening step forward but halted when Justin knelt down to the ground. "Do you intend to grovel for your worthless life?" Ugallu growled.

Justin plunged the torches he held in both hands down into the soft earth, which as he suspected was void of rocks or stones, thanks to Lahmu's recent little construction projects. "One second. I'm busy. I'll be with you in a moment."

"I want the spear, now!" Ugallu roared.

Justin stood up and dusted off his hands. "I told you already, my sister has it." He looked down at the two flames flickering and dancing on the tops of the torches. He let the warmth in his body reach out and touch the fire, feeling the two forces merge into one. He clenched both his fists, and the twin fires began to die down.

The lion-man took another step forward and spread his wings wide, making himself look even more massive. Justin opened his hands, fingers splayed, and the flames responded instantly, lashing out with heat and light. Ugallu's eyes widened in surprise, but he did not move. "So you have learned a new trick, child. Know this: those puny flames will do little to harm Lahmu—or me. Only the power of a god can destroy us."

Justin smiled. "Oh, good to know, but they're not intended for you." He closed his eyes and poured everything within him into the two flames. He could feel the energy move from somewhere within his gut, stoking the torches into bonfires as if he had just poured gallons of gasoline upon them. When the heat was as intense as he could make it, he drew the fire back into him.

Leyla screamed, and Justin opened his eyes. He was worried that one of the creatures had harmed her, but she was staring at him in horror. Billy was trying to calm her, but to no avail. She just kept pointing at Justin and screaming. He looked down and saw why: his entire body was consumed in flame. He smiled at Leyla and gave her the thumbs up to let her know he was okay.

That's when she fainted.

Justin sighed. He had always had zero luck impressing girls, and here he was on fire and not getting burned, how awesome was that? *Oh, well.* He wasn't there to impress Leyla, he was there to save the day.

Justin concentrated, trying to force all the fire into his right arm. He watched as the flames danced and moved along his body, from his extremities, over his abdomen, and up to his chest. From there he concentrated the flames and guided them down the length of his right arm until he held a tiny, blazing ball of white-hot fire in the palm of his hand.

"This is for them," he said, and in one smooth motion, threw the fireball at the cluster of draconian priests.

* * *

"What do you mean I have to *destroy* the temple?" Miranda said. Surely she must have misunderstood the six-thousand-year-old apparition.

"Just that. When your brother reset the trap, he locked you in here. There is no other way out. But if you release the spirit that is holding this temple together, as the walls begin to crumble, you might be able to escape in time."

Miranda stood there, opened-mouthed. "Are you freaking kidding me? That's impossible." When she and Justin had been in the other ziggurat and it began to collapse, the way out was already open. "What if this door doesn't open before the ceiling comes crashing down? This seems like a terrible idea."

"Of course, it is a terrible idea. But it is the only idea. If you had simply embraced your destiny in the first place, this would have never happened. As long as you ignore what you need to do, you will continue to be plagued with misfortune and loss."

Miranda thought back to how much her parents had done to try to spare her from this very situation. They had lived in isolation from their own families for almost two decades, they had kept their children a secret from everyone, and they had sacrificed any life they might have had to take the burden off Miranda, so she wouldn't have to face any of this on her own. She had always believed that her parents had kept leaving her and her brother because they didn't really love them, but in reality, they had done it all because of how much they loved them.

And now Justin was trying to save her too, to protect her from her poor decisions. Tabrati was right: as long as she denied the person she was meant to be, the people she loved would continue to get hurt. She had to try something.

"Okay. What do I have to do?" Miranda asked.

"It is time for you to truly embrace your destiny. You must repair the Spear of the Winds, for it is both the key to your escape and necessary for defeating the Dark Queen."

Miranda took the spearhead out of her pocket with one hand, then grabbed the shaft with the other.

"Good. Now join them," Tabrati said and pantomimed bringing the two pieces together.

To Miranda's surprise, no matter how hard she tried to force them, the two parts of the spear would not join. It was like trying to make the same poles of two powerful magnets touch. "What's happening? I can't get these two together."

Tabrati smirked slightly as she said, "The parsu trapped inside is resisting you. It does not want to be made whole again. It wants to be free of its incarceration within the spear. Like the lightning, you will need to bend it to your will."

Miranda closed her eyes, reaching out with her mind until she could sense the forces at work within both parts of the weapon. The shaft felt wild, as if a windstorm or a cyclone were trapped inside it, while the spearhead felt angry and vengeful. "I can feel them," Miranda said. "They're very different."

"That is because they are indeed very different. Marduk bound the winds from the north, east, west, and south to the shaft of the spear. Those are *elemental* parsu, a force of nature, byproducts of creation," the apparition said. "Within the detached spearhead is the soul of a demon—"

"Anzu," Miranda said, and she felt the energy within the spearhead begin to surge and twist with hate.

"Ugallu's mate. Yes."

"Why did Marduk trap her? What did she do?" Miranda asked.

"She was a thief. Tiamat commanded the monster she had created, Ugallu, to steal the tablet from Marduk's father, Enki, who wisely always kept the tablet hidden so that no other god could attempt what Tiamat was trying to do. Ugallu watched Enki for years, hoping to discover the tablet's location."

"His opportunity arrived after several years of waiting, when Marduk wanted to show his new human friend the tablet that could free humanity from the control of the gods once and for all. Seizing the opportunity, Ugallu—forever a coward at heart—convinced his mate, Anzu, to steal the tablet right out of Marduk's hands."

"Is that how Tiamat got the tablet?" Miranda asked.

"Not exactly. Marduk and I caught up with them as they were trying to flee the land. Anzu has a… power… an ability to conceal herself from the gods. But Ugallu was overconfident and sloppy. You see, he never intended to deliver the Tablet of Destinies to the Dark Queen."

"What were they planning to do with it?" Miranda said.

"When we came upon them, Ugallu was trying to inscribe *his* name onto the Tablet of Destinies, making him god over all. But he was no god, and therefore could not write his name upon it." Tabrati smiled for just a moment, lost in her memory, before continuing, "Marduk was able to surprise Anzu, stabbing her with this very spear, and drawing her parsu into the spearhead. But Ugallu fled with the tablet, leaving his mate behind. He most likely tried to use it to curry favor with Tiamat."

"For his freedom?" Miranda asked, thinking back to her conversation with the lion-headed beast.

"No. Power. Ugallu did not always appear as he does now. He was at first simply an eagle with the head of a lion, like Anzu, before delivering the tablet to Tiamat. After that, he became what he is now, and was given the power to control and master the weather."

Miranda remembered the animated image from the temple in the City of the Ancients of the boy and girl surprising two lion-headed eagles and stabbing one of them with a spear. That must have been Anzu. But she hadn't died—Marduk had drawn her soul into the Spear of the Winds instead. And the other one that had flown away—leaving his mate behind—was Ugallu. "So instead of asking Tiamat to help free his mate, he exploited the situation for his personal gain?" Miranda asked, feeling the spear flair with anger again. *Now that's interesting,* she thought. "Why try to free her now, after all these years?"

Tabrati shrugged. "Perhaps guilt. Perhaps some power he or the Dark Queen needs. I do not know for certain."

The spearhead began to quiver with hate: Was this directed at Miranda or at Ugallu? "So, to get these two pieces together, I just have to push them a little. What happens once they touch? How do I keep them that way?"

"The two parts should become one as if they were never intended to be separate entities."

Miranda closed her eyes, feeling the two pieces struggling

against each other, and forced her will upon them. The more she tried to pull the two together, the more the force pushed them apart. It reminded her of the inner wall that blocked the domestic dragons from accessing their breath weapons. But now, instead of breaking something down, she was trying to repair it.

Miranda felt a stirring deep in her chest. Electric energy began to build within her. It was the same feeling she had experienced when she and Justin were trying to recharge the stone protecting the City of the Ancients.

"Yes. That is it. That is the divine parsu within you, Miranda: the source of your power and the legacy passed down to you by Marduk."

Miranda forced the energy through her arms and into her hands. The spirits within recoiled slightly. She was able to move the two parts of the spear closer together, but they still resisted her. On a hunch, she forced a thought into the spearhead: *"Anzu. Help me, please. I will make sure you get justice for what happened to you."*

All resistance vanished instantly, and Miranda was able to bring the two artifacts together. The spearhead had fused magically with the staff. The Spear of the Winds was whole again.

Miranda slowly opened her eyes to find Tabrati smiling at her. "Excellent work, Miranda. You have wisdom beyond your years. Now. Are you ready for the hard part?"

CHAPTER 33

JUSTIN AND MIRANDA
... Into the Fire

JUSTIN'S AIM WAS SPOT ON—maybe he should have played baseball after all—the fireball exploded right in the middle of the chanting, dancing, creepy lizard-dudes. Their clothes caught fire and they all started screaming and running around in circles, struggling to put out the flames. It didn't look like the fireball had killed any of them, but that wasn't Justin's goal—he just wanted them to shut up.

"Red. Can you hear me?"

"Loud and clear, kid," the dragon said in his deep, smoky dragonspeaking voice. "Now how's about you get me out of these rock handcuffs so I can bust some heads?"

"I'm working on it. One thing at a time," Justin said, barely dodging out of the way as one of the draconians flung a curved blade at him, missing his chest by mere inches. Justin could sense them now. All of them. The impact was almost overwhelming, but he learned quickly that the strongest feelings were coming from the closest of the creeps now advancing toward him.

Justin kicked out, catching the drac in the knee. There was a crunching noise, and the creature fell to the ground screaming in pain. Justin reached down and grabbed the knife the drac had dropped. It wasn't much of a weapon, but it was at least something.

"Okay, take your time, I'm not in a hurry or anything," Red lamented.

"You know what? I think I liked you better when you were silent."

"Behind you!" Red shouted, and Justin rolled to the left as the massive barbed tail of a wyvern came swinging down where he had stood a second before.

"Never mind. Keep talking. Never stop talking," Justin said, scrambling to his feet and racing to where the dragon was secured tightly to the ground. As he ran, stones shot up all around him, trying to trap him in a structure similar to the one that held Billy and Leyla prisoner.

Justin looked around and noticed two things. First, the more rocks that popped up, the fewer there were holding down the dragons and the two humans; and second, the less structure Lahmu himself seemed to have. Right now, the mud-and-rock monster appeared to consist almost exclusively of mud, as if someone had removed all of his bones. That gave Justin another idea.

"Hey, ugly!" he shouted at Lahmu. "Ugallu said you were slow, but not being able to catch me, a human boy, is just plain embarrassing."

"That's your master plan? Make fun of him?" Red asked.

"This is going to work—" Justin said, as he stumbled over a stone rising from the earth that almost sent him sprawling to the ground. "I hope. When the rocks around your feet start to feel loose, take off. Spread the word, and be ready."

"You got it, boss."

Two draconians remained in close pursuit of Justin as he ran in a zigzagging pattern, trying to avoid rock pillar after rock pillar exploding from the ground around him. But it wasn't until he saw Lahmu directly ahead of him that he realized what the demon was doing. He wasn't just reacting to where Justin was running—the mud-monster was actually herding him into a trap.

Something small and round glimmered where the creature's neck should have been, just for a second, before it was engulfed again by the shifting mud. Justin had seen that before, when Mrs. Lóng had fought him the first time by the river. Was that his heart or something?

Lahmu's mouth opened, a gaping hole, and he laughed. "Got you now, little mouse." Then his whole body rose like a cresting wave.

Justin skidded to a stop and fell into a backward somersault, rolling between the two pursuing draconians. He stood up and ran back the way he'd just came. The ground shook violently as the wave of mud came crashing down upon the unsuspecting lizard-men, crushing them alive.

Justin risked a glance over his shoulder to see if Lahmu was directly behind him, when he ran into something unyielding that knocked him to the ground. His whole body felt like it had broken from the force of the impact. He must have run into one of the stone pillars.

Justin shook his head and looked up to see Ugallu towering over him. "Enough games, human."

* * *

"Okay. Like this?" Miranda asked, holding the spear in both hands, and looking up at the ceiling, impersonating the statue of Tabrati from the temple in the City of the Ancients.

Miranda still held the reed stylus in her right hand—

without it, she would not be able to communicate with the six-thousand-year-old ghostly apparition. However, she would need to put the stylus away before she started the chain of events she had to initiate in order to escape the temple.

"Yes. And the feeling should be just like when you used your parsu to force the spear together, only this time you are going to combine your power with that of the spear and free the spirit of the temple. Do you understand?"

Miranda laughed. "No. Not really, but I'll give it a go. How do you know so much about this? Did Marduk show you?"

Now it was Tabrati who was laughing. "No, child, I'm the one that showed Marduk how to do this."

"I don't understand. You're a human."

Tabrati touched the side of her nose with a raised finger. "Ah. But a very clever human. I would sneak into Enki's temple to steal artifacts he had enchanted. On one of these nights, I spied on him as he bound elemental parsu from the wind into a pair of boots."

Miranda looked down at her grandfather's sword on the ground in front of her. Ya'ne had told them that the leather on the sword's hilt had come from a pair of enchanted boots. This had to be part of the same story. "But how did you learn what to do?"

"Because I was spying on him when he was explaining it to his scribe. Enki wanted the knowledge passed on to someone he trusted in case something happened to him before he could teach Marduk." She had a far-off look in her eyes for a moment, then said. "*Hmm.* Funny how that worked out, actually. Almost as if that sneaky old god knew I was there... Well, enough of that. Let us return to you getting out of here."

The apparition crossed in front of Miranda and said, "The parsu used to construct these temples is from a particularly evil god—"

"Kingu," Miranda said.

Tabrati nodded. "Yes. Kingu. Marduk enchanted a small mallet with the would-be-leader-of-the-gods' parsu. A piece of his divine soul is what allowed me to construct and hold these temples together—a fitting punishment for one who destroyed so much." She looked off into the distance for the briefest of moments, as if remembering something painful. "So trust me when I tell you he will want to be free of this place and one day to take his revenge. However, he will not be able to do this until he is whole again. All you will need to do is show him the way out, and he will gladly take it. The challenge will be, of course, that as soon as he leaves, the magic holding the temple together will be gone."

"And that's where the spear comes in?" Miranda asked.

Tabrati looked to the ceiling. "Yes. You will have only a matter of seconds to act. Do not hesitate. Are you ready?"

"I guess I'm as ready as I'll ever be," Miranda said, not wanting to say goodbye, but knowing the people outside the temple were depending on her. "I want to thank you, Tabrati for… you know… showing me the right path… and all."

Tabrati smiled. "You are very welcome, Miranda. And this is not goodbye. I will see you in the next temple." Then she snapped her fingers together as she seemed to remember something and closed her eyes for a moment. "Sorry. I just cross-referenced the location of the next temple with your knowledge of geography, which if I might say so is quite lacking."

Miranda frowned. "Okay, and?"

"The next temple is located on an island off the northwest coast of Great Britton. You will know it by a large cave in the north-facing cliffs."

"Can you tell me anything else that might help?"

"I am sorry, Miranda, but that is all I know."

Miranda nodded. "Goodbye, Tabrati," she said, and shoved the stylus into her pocket.

The image disappeared, leaving Miranda alone again.

"Okay. Here goes everything." Miranda grasped the staff in both hands and it hummed with power. She closed her eyes, looked to the sky, and felt the energy building within her. As soon as her parsu mixed with the spear's, she lowered the spearhead until it came in contact with the temple floor.

A searing pain shot through her body. Something very powerful and evil was there with her, and it wanted to attack her. Miranda fought through the pain, forcing her energy through her body and into the spear. "Leave this place!" she shouted. "Leave this temple and be gone!"

She could feel Kingu's evil presence push back. *"One day, I will be whole again. When I am, I will destroy everyone and everything you care about. Do you hear me, daughter of my enemy? I will destroy what you love most before my queen takes you as her own!"*

"Get in line," Miranda said, gathering her energy with the spear's, and pushed as hard as she could against the malicious being.

It moved slowly away. *"You don't stand a chance. You were right to be afraid. You are nothing compared to Tiamat. You are not even worthy to face me. You will fail."*

Miranda tried to fight back the fear and doubt threatening to bubble up to the surface, and screamed, "Get out of here!"

With an echoing laugh, the spirit retreated into the darkness beyond.

There was a moment of eerie silence. Then the temple began to collapse on top of Miranda.

* * *

Justin's mind was working frantically as he scrambled back to his feet. Lahmu was behind him, Ugallu was in front of him, stone pillars flanked him on either side: he was trapped.

"Red. I could really use you right about now."

Justin could feel the dragon straining against the rocks holding him in place. "Well, your plan kind of worked. I can wiggle my toes, and my hind legs are loose, but that's about it. My head is still pinned to the ground. I'm not going anywhere. Any other bright ideas, kid?"

"Maybe. Is now a good time to grovel?"

"You could try. Nothing to lose except my respect," Red joked, but Justin could feel how worried he was.

The lion-man spun his huge mace around in his hand several times. "I'll make this quick."

"That's nice of you. But I think I'll pass," Justin said, his voice shaking.

Ugallu snarled, "Bravado to the end. I can respect that, but it's not going to stop me."

Justin opened up his mind, trying to sense the lion-man's movements, but there was nothing there, nothing but an immense void, just like on the night at the cabin and when the monsters had attacked the City of the Ancients. Something was blocking him from being able to sense anything from either the mud-monster or the lion-man.

Then Justin realized all at once that the presence of a zone around the two demons where he couldn't sense anything meant something must be actively blocking him. It also meant that if the demons had purposefully taken that precaution, then Justin must be able to read these two just as he could the draconians and the dragons.

But how exactly was he being blocked? Justin glanced around quickly. The draconian priests were gone, either dead or running for their lives, so they couldn't be responsible.

And none of the other dracs were chanting. Plus the obstruction the dracs created felt different: when they were chanting, Justin couldn't sense anything at all, including the dragons. But when he was around Lahmu and Ugallu only, there was just a dark hole surrounding each of the demons.

Ugallu raised his mace high over his head. Lightning struck it several times, charging it with crackling energy, and it began to glow. The light began to reflect off the knife he held in the other hand and off the talisman he wore around his neck.

"It's the talisman!" Justin shouted out loud, then clamped his free hand over his mouth. At the center of the ornate necklace was a small shining stone, similar to the gleaming object he had glimpsed within Lahmu. *That* must be what was blocking him. He just had to stay alive long enough to get it off the scary lion-man before he was roasted alive.

Justin crouched, gripping the knife he had taken from the draconian tightly in one hand, and waited for his opening.

Ugallu swung the mace down at Justin, and he leapt to the side, rolling behind one of the stone pillars as lightning exploded all around him. The ground was blackened instantly, and exploding rocks sent small bits of stone into Justin's exposed flesh. Tiny cuts pocked his arms, neck, and face. When the shock wore off, the stinging started.

"*Ow!* That hurts!" Justin screamed, trying desperately to wipe the dirt and rock out of his wounds.

"You missed, brother," Lahmu said, laughing. "Now it is my turn."

The ground began to shake violently. Trees all around the clearing began to topple, the stone pillars around Justin tumbled to the ground, and the earth felt as if it would split wide open.

Ugallu looked over to Lahmu with a shocked expression and said, "Was that you?"

Justin looked back over his shoulder at the undulating heap of mud. Lahmu too had a look of wonder on his shifting muck-face. "No. Something is happening behind the protective field."

"How do you know? Can you feel it?" the lion-man asked.

Lahmu pointed a thick, dripping arm toward where the temple stood hidden. "No, brother. I can see it."

Justin craned his neck to get a better view. The protective shield was indeed gone. But that wasn't what caused his heart to beat wildly in his chest and the breath to catch in his throat. As he watched, the mighty ziggurat, so completely out of place here in the jungles of southern Mexico, collapsed in on itself.

Miranda was still inside. Justin had left his sister in there, all alone, trapped. "Oh no!" he wailed. "What have I done?"

CHAPTER 34

JUSTIN AND MIRANDA
Capture the Talisman

"OH MY GODS," LAHMU EXCLAIMED, with equal parts awe and laughter. "You did our job for us, little mouse."

Ugallu threw his head back and roared. "No, you idiot. We needed the girl alive. I… needed the girl alive. We have failed on all accounts."

"No, Lord Ugallu, Beast of the Big Weather," said one of the draconian priests—apparently the only surviving one not to have fled after Justin's fireball. "In fact, it is not necessary for the girl to be alive in order for us to complete the ceremony. However, we will still need to secure the body and deliver it to our queen before it… spoils." He slowly approached and bowed down before the raging lion-man.

Ugallu glared down at the robed figure. "I do not care what is *necessary*, you worm. I want to be free of Tiamat's hold over me once and for all."

"Why would you want to be released from our queen's will? When she makes the Earth anew, all who are under her command shall be rewarded. She shall bestow—" The draconian fell suddenly silent as Ugallu brought his mighty mace down upon his head.

"I do not care about this *Earth*, all I care about is my freedom," Ugallu whispered to the lizard-man's lifeless body.

Justin stepped out from around the pillar he had been hiding behind. "So. You were lying. You never had any intention of letting us go." His voice was shaking. Not out of fear—he no longer felt any—but from sadness, and from shock. His sister had just died because of him. Because of them. Because of Tiamat. And Justin was going to make everyone responsible for her death pay dearly.

Ugallu looked down at Justin. His lip curled into a snarl. "I do not need to justify myself to you, human. I do what I please. I am the *god* here, not you. You are nothing to me, and your sister was only a tool I needed for my own purposes."

Justin clenched the knife in his hand, readying himself to strike, when the sound of crashing stones drew everyone's attention back to the ruined temple.

Toward the center of the mountain of rocks, the heap of rubble began to swell, blowing up like a bubble, as if about to explode. Something was surging up from below. Then in a mighty burst that sent rocks flying for miles in all directions, a tornado blasted skyward before snaking its way down the massive heap of debris and to the ground below. At its center, suspended in the eye of the vortex, holding the spear in one hand and a silver sword in the other was… Miranda.

Justin was in shock. His sister had escaped. Not only that, but she had figured out how to control the power in the spear—which, Justin saw to his amazement, was now whole again. He was still standing there completely dumbstruck when Red said, *"Kid. If you're going to do something, do it now."*

Justin looked over at Ugallu, who was crouching down, head low, knuckles pressed into the smoldering earth. His wings were spread, readying to leap into the sky: from the look on his face, he had no intention of fighting, he was getting ready to flee. Red was right. It was now or never.

Justin gripped the knife tightly in his hand, coiled into himself, then sprang at Ugallu. He moved so quickly that the lion-man didn't even have time to react—all his attention was still on Miranda. With one swift stroke, Justin slashed the knife across the demon's throat, then retreated back toward Red.

Ugallu looked down at him, his lips pulling back into a snarling smile. "Stupid human. Mortal weapons can do me no harm."

"I wasn't trying to harm you, stupid—lion—thing. I was just getting this." Justin held up the talisman for Ugallu to see. "Thanks, pal!"

Ugallu reached up and felt his throat, then shouted at Justin, "Give that back to me!"

Justin dangled the pendant teasingly. "You want it? Come and get it."

* * *

Miranda allowed the energy of the Spear of the Winds to dissipate, floating like a feather until she landed on top of the massive pile of stone—all that remained of the temple.

She surveyed the chaos unraveling below. Justin had cut something from Ugallu's neck and was running around like a crazy person.

Billy was still trapped in the prison-like stone structure along with Leyla, and the dragons were still being held firmly down to the ground with thick stone restraints.

Miranda cast another glance at Ugallu. He was quickly

gaining on her brother. The first order of business was to deal with the lion-man. She knew what she needed to do, yet now she was even more worried that she was making the biggest mistake of her life.

It's the only way, Miranda thought. She squatted down and quickly sifted through the rubble until she found a bit of stone that was the shape she was looking for. She pocketed it, took a deep breath, and had started to stand when something caught her eye in the debris nearby. Resting near the now toppled and cracked stone obelisk was a shimmering blue rock. "The stone of protection!" Miranda gasped. "No way. It survived."

She grabbed it, and as soon as her fingers closed around the stone, she felt it pulsing with power. "Still fully charged," she said, and quickly stuffed it into another one of her pockets.

Miranda sprinted the rest of the way to where Billy and Leyla were being held.

When Billy saw her approaching, he ran over and reached out for her through the one narrow aperture in their stone cage. Miranda rested her sword against one of the slabs and tentatively took his hand. Relief washed over his face. "You're real. I'm really glad to see you. When the temple collapsed, I thought you were a… goner."

"So did I," Miranda said. "Are you and Leyla all right?"

Billy nodded. "A little banged up, but nothing too bad. Can you get us out of here?"

Miranda let go of his hand and pulled away. "Yes, but not just yet. There is something I need to do first. You'll both be safer in here."

Billy looked at her with concern, but it was Leyla who spoke. "Let us out. We can make a run for the jungle. We'll be safer there. Please, Miranda. Don't leave us trapped in here."

Miranda's heart sank. She knew how Leyla felt, but she couldn't risk their trying to interfere either. "There are still a lot of dracs in the jungle—I can feel them. Trust me. I have a plan. You'll be safer in here."

Leyla pounded her fist against the stone wall in frustration. "Plan? You mean that *loco* plan where you give those creatures everything? You're not really that dumb, are you? They'll kill us as soon as you give them what they want. You're leaving us to die—"

Billy put his hands on Leyla's shoulders, and the girl fell silent. He stared at Miranda intently—studying every inch of her face before saying, "Do what you think is best, Miranda. I believe in you."

Miranda nodded and slipped Billy her grandfather's sword through the small opening in their rocky prison. "Take care of this for me. If this all goes wrong, you're going to need it," she said and marched quickly toward where she had last seen Justin.

* * *

Ugallu growled and charged at Justin, swinging his mace in a wide arc.

Justin smiled and ducked low, avoiding a blow that would have knocked him into the next country had it made contact. But it hadn't. Justin's hunch had proven correct: once the talisman was removed, he could sense Ugallu's intentions, just like the dracs'. He just had to keep the monster engaged a little bit longer.

"Strike one. Hey batter, batter! Swing, batter!" Justin mocked.

The lion-man threw his head back and roared with rage, then launched himself at Justin. He swung his mace from the left, followed by a thrust of his long knife, and pivoted his body around in a tight circle, trying to knock Justin off balance with the tip of one of his wings.

But Justin could foresee all of his movements a fraction of a second before the lion-man made each one. He continued to back away from Ugallu, luring the demon into position, keeping him ignorant of his intentions with taunts. Justin felt his heel come in contact with a rock, and he stopped, smiling up at the winged beast. "That was like, strike four. You really stink at this. I thought you were supposed to be some formidable warrior or something."

Ugallu seemed about to lose his mind with rage. He brought the mace down in a high arc, intending to smash the little human's brains in.

Justin rolled out of the way at the last minute, and the mace came crashing down on a huge stone. The rock cracked, then split in two, and released the hold it had on Red's neck.

"You realize that if he had missed, that would have crushed my neck?" Red said, shaking himself free. He swung his head like a massive club, hitting Ugallu in the chest and sending the monster careening into a nearby wyvern.

"I thought it was worth the risk." Justin spun and blocked a thrusting stab by a draconian, who seemed to appear from nowhere. *Okay, must not have gotten them all...* he thought. Red slammed his tail into the creature, sending it flying fifty feet through the air.

"As much as I enjoy listening to your witty banter, I would prefer to be free to kill some of these vile creatures too," Storm said.

"As would I," Nightshade added.

"Working on it. Red, you got that? I'll keep these guys occupied. You get everyone free."

Justin spun around in a tight circle, surveying the chaos surrounding him. Draconians and wyverns were charging at them from all directions. Ugallu still lay on the ground from Red's attack, but he was already trying to steady himself enough to stand, and Lahmu was… "Uh-oh. Where did mud-man get to?"

In answer to his question, the ground in front of Justin opened up as a tower of mud and stone surged into the air.

"Here I am, little mouse," Lahmu said, and shot his arms directly at Justin, striking him in the chest and sending him flying back.

Justin skidded to a stop about twenty feet away, his impact cushioned by the softened earth, and stood up on shaky legs. "*Ow!* I really don't like this guy—" A long tendril of mud hit him from the side, sending him flying and skidding across the ground again.

After Red had freed the other dragons from their stone restraints by smashing them with well-aimed blows of his mighty tail, he turned and charged like a rampaging bull—ramming Lahmu in the chest with his horned head. The demon was ripped in half from the force of the impact, but Red shot through its body, as if it were made of whipped cream, slipping on the slick, muddy remains and tumbling right into one of the approaching wyverns.

Justin watched in dismay as Lahmu's form quickly reshaped, his body stitching itself back together and sucking in still more mud and earth from the ground around him.

"*Beating this mud-dude is going to be way harder…*" Justin said, trailing off as he looked up at the squishy mass of undulating dirt. Then he remembered something Mrs. Lóng had said to him in the City of the Ancients, when they were walking to the temple after their initial fight with the two demons: that some of the bricks used to build the structure around there were made by baking mud. *That's it. Hardened mud.*

"*You still alive back there, kid? You kind of trailed off,*" Red said, as he dodged to the left and spun around, trying to sweep the wyvern off its feet.

"I've got an idea. Come over here and get behind me!" Justin shouted mentally to the dragon. Red was critical to his plan.

"You can see I'm busy, right?" Red said as he dodged a thrust from the wyvern's scorpion-like tail. *"Give me a moment. I'll be ripping this little beast's throat out in just a second...."*

Justin watched as Lahmu formed two stone-and-mud boulders in his hands and sent them flying directly at him. He was able to dodge out of the way of the first missile, but the second one caught him on the shoulder and spun him to the ground.

"Okay, time's up. I'm coming to you, so please be ready," Justin said, as he rolled out of the way, dodging several more rock pillars as they exploded up from the ground. He scrambled to his feet and ran directly over to Red.

The dragon dodged to the left, barely evading the wyvern's snapping jaws, then sprang at the creature's overextended neck. Red's razor-sharp teeth sank into his adversary's armored flesh, making the beast howl in pain. Red shook his head back and forth several times, ripping a large piece of the creature's throat out.

"So what's this brilliant plan of yours?"

Justin rubbed his hands together and said with far more conviction than he felt. *"I want you to light me on fire."*

CHAPTER 35

JUSTIN AND MIRANDA
Reckoning

RED TILTED HIS HEAD to the side as if waiting for Justin to add something else. "Oh... that's it? That's the plan? Shoot you with fire. You really are a tactical genius. That's a terrible idea. We don't even know what will happen if I hit you with dragon fire."

Justin sprang to the right, out of the way of a mud ball rolling after him. "It will work. Fire doesn't affect me. But just in case, not too much at first, hold some back. I need less than an inferno and more than a smoke ring."

"No guarantees, kid. I haven't really been practicing much—or at all—so this could be a disaster."

Justin laughed. "What's new? At least this time, you're already on the ground, so no crash landings. But this seems to be our fighting style: desperate human, hurting dragon."

"Ugh. Now I really do want to light you on fire," Red groaned.

Justin glanced over his shoulder—Lahmu was closing in on him. "Then what are you waiting for, big guy?"

Justin heard a huge intake of breath. He narrowed his eyes

and concentrated on the fire building inside Red, churning and folding in on itself, becoming hotter and hotter. Justin skidded to a stop in front of the red dragon and turned to face Lahmu. Justin was out of breath, panting and exhausted. The demon continued his advance, holding a huge boulder in each of his hands. "Has the little mouse run out of energy?" he mocked. "Too bad. I was beginning to enjoy our little game of chase."

"Oh, I wasn't playing chase. I was luring you into my trap. But don't feel too bad, I got the idea from you."

Lahmu looked from Justin to Red. "Surely you know by now that I can not be damaged by creatures such as you—a human and a mongrel dragon."

"Don't worry. He isn't like other domestics," Justin said. "And I don't plan on *hurting* you. I plan on *baking* you."

Lahmu threw his head back and roared with laughter. "Ah, yes. I have heard talk about the mongrel dragon that could use its breath weapon. Sorry to disappoint you though, it will take more than a dragon's fire to destroy me, human."

Justin smiled. "I figured as much. But I'm not just human— I'm something else too. Now, Red!"

Red reared up on his hind legs, spread his wings wide, and exhaled.

Justin was engulfed in flames. Really, really hot flames. He tried to ignore the pain and discomfort he was feeling—Red had been correct; dragon fire was significantly hotter than anything he had felt before. But it wasn't hot enough. Not yet, at least.

Justin concentrated on ignoring the feeling that his body was being burned and let the flames move through him, drawing them into the center of his body. There they swirled, mixing with his own internal fire, becoming something new. He felt as if he were trying to contain the very sun itself.

Justin flung his arms out, palms open, as he had seen Mrs.

Lóng do in the river. A cone of blue-and-white flame shot out from his hands, engulfing Lahmu.

The demon cried out in pain, then fell silent, as its body hardened instantly into a blackened statue.

Justin dropped his arms, letting them hang loosely at his sides. They seemed to weigh a hundred pounds each. He stumbled over to Lahmu's incinerated form. Cracks were beginning to snake across its entire body in a spiderweb pattern.

Right in the middle of Lahmu's chest, just barely peeking out, was the shiny spherical stone talisman. Justin reached up and easily pulled it free. As soon as he did, the remains of the mud-monster crumbled apart, falling to the ground in a pile of hardened earth and dust. Justin looked down at the stone in his hand, then at the remains in front of him. He reached out with his mind for any sign that Lahmu had escaped into the surrounding earth, but there was nothing. The monster was gone.

Justin turned around and smiled at Red. "We did it. We actually did it!"

"That's great, kid. I always wanted to try my paw at ceramics. But just a heads-up, you probably want to put some clothes on before any of the others see you."

Justin looked down at his entirely nude body, scraped and cut and bruised, but not burned: the intense fire must have burned all his clothing completely off. He let out a yelp of surprise and dashed over to the dragon. "Don't just stand there like a gaping idiot. Hide me before anyone else sees my naked butt."

Justin scrambled to pull on a spare set of clothes he had stashed in one of Red's saddlebags. In the same pouch was his father's tan cowboy hat. Justin smiled and placed it on his head. "I think I've sufficiently earned wearing this now." Unfortunately, he realized, he had only brought a single pair of shoes with him on this trip, and those were now gone too. He would have to walk around barefoot until he came up with some other solution. But beyond that, something didn't feel quite right. He felt like something was missing.

"Oh crap!" he shouted.

"*What is it, kid?*" Red asked, quickly scanning the area for an imminent attack.

"I lost the piece of the tablet," Justin said in a panic. The Tablet of Destinies shard had been an ever-present item in his pants pocket since his mother had entrusted him with it, but since all his clothes had been burned off, it was now missing. "I must have dropped it somewhere. We need to find it before Ugallu or the dracs grab it, or—game over."

* * *

Miranda had just blasted three draconians fifty feet into the air with the Spear of the Winds when she felt Ugallu's presence a fraction of a second before he struck. The massive lion-beast leaped at her from behind one of Lahmu's stone pillars, swinging his mighty mace down at the spot where she gripped the spear in an attempt to disarm her. Miranda was able to pivot and block the attack at the last second. However, it struck with enough force to drive her to the ground.

Ugallu growled as he pressed down on Miranda with the end of his mace. His lip curling up into a snarl. "How did you survive that, human? You should be dead. Did you make a deal with someone else? Maybe another one of Tiamat's creations? Is Lahmu double-crossing me?"

Miranda tried to shift and throw Ugallu off her, but the beast was too strong. "Paranoid much? No. That was real, lion-breath. My brother trapped me in there, because he didn't want me to honor our deal."

His eyes narrowed suspiciously. "You mean to tell me, that you're here to... *honor* our agreement? Release my mate and hand over the tablet shard?"

"Yes. In exchange for information on the location of where my family members are being held hostage. That's exactly what I'm saying, you big oaf." Miranda grunted straining against the force the lion-man was still exerting against her.

He regarded her for a moment longer, then released her. Miranda stood up slowly and took a couple of steps back, putting some distance between them.

"I see the Spear of the Winds has been made whole again," he snarled. "And I can sense that my mate *is* truly there."

Miranda nodded. "She is. Tell me what you know about the prisoners."

"All in due time," he purred. "Did you secure the last piece of the tablet from the boy?"

Miranda patted her pants pocket. "It's right here. I couldn't convince him to give it to me, but luckily I was able to pick up the stone along the way."

"Excellent. And of course, you will also be coming with me."

"Why, so you can just turn me over to Tiamat?" she asked, staring at the demon defiantly.

"No, foolish child. So we can keep you safely out of the hands of the Dark Queen," he whispered. "Anzu has the power to hide us—to shield our existence—even from the eyes of gods. All I have ever wanted is to control my own fate. And as long as the gods control the Tablet of Destinies, I will only exist to be their slave. All of us will be their slaves." Then he pointed his curved knife at Miranda. "But not you. No. You will be dead. As will every human on this planet. Tiamat views humanity as a scourge. A corruption of the natural order. She intends to wipe this world clean of your species. There is only one way out of this, child, and that is with me."

"How can Anzu keep us hidden?" Miranda asked. "I thought she was just a wind demon."

"Our species can control the wind, yes, but she has a *very* special gift, unique to our kind. Anzu can also bend the sight of those around her with magic, rendering her—and those nearby—invisible to even the mightiest of the gods."

"Is that how you two stole the Tablet of Destinies?" Miranda asked.

"I'm impressed. Someone knows their history." Ugallu nodded approvingly.

"What about the rest of the people I care for? Can you keep them safe too?" Miranda asked, her eyes narrowing on the lion-man.

"They will be safer without you around."

Miranda looked back at the stone prison where Billy was trapped, and then over at her brother—who was now wearing a different set of clothes than before and a cowboy hat, and he was barefoot. *He's so weird,* Miranda thought. She turned back to Ugallu. She had to act now. If she didn't, so much more would be lost. There would be plenty of time to hate herself later for this decision.

"Tell me where my parents and my aunt Em are," Miranda said, closing her eyes.

"As soon as Anzu is free, and you hand over the shard, I will tell you everything I know," Ugallu purred.

Miranda lowered her head and said, "I don't believe in destiny. And I will do whatever it takes to keep my friends and family safe."

Ugallu nodded. "A wise decision. Now, free my—"

"However, my parents believed I was destined to defeat Tiamat. They loved me enough to try everything in their power to spare me from the hardships that fate would lead me to, but they knew that if they failed, this was the path I must walk upon. They believe this with all their hearts. My parents failed to protect me. Not because they didn't love me, not because they weren't capable of protecting me, but because this has never been their destiny. It has always only been mine."

Miranda took a deep breath, reached into her pocket, and looked up at Ugallu. "You want the shard? Here it is," she said and tossed a small stone to him.

Ugallu quickly sheathed his knife and caught the object in one clawed hand. "A wise decision. Now free Anzu, and together we will... wait a minute. This isn't—"

Miranda rammed the Spear of the Winds into Ugallu's chest, silencing him.

Ugallu looked down at the shaft protruding from his chest, then back at Miranda, shock twisting his face into a mask of fear.

"I saw my brother cut something off from around your neck. It must have been what was blocking us from reading your thoughts. So I know you are only telling me what I want to hear. I know you are lying to me, vile beast. I knew that you were only going to keep me alive until Anzu was free, then that by killing me and keeping the last piece of the tablet, you would be postponing Tiamat's rise. It would never have worked. Eventually she would find you. Eventually someone else like me would be born. Eventually Tiamat would destroy this entire world."

"I may not believe in destiny, but I do believe in my family," Miranda continued. "They loved me enough to try to spare me from having to accomplish the impossible, but now the impossible is exactly what I *must* do. I'm going to do everything in my power to defeat Tiamat. And I'm not going to do it because it's my destiny, I'm going to do it because it's my responsibility," Miranda hissed, forcing the energy within her to reach out and join the spear's. "And you're going to help me."

She could feel Ugallu's parsu. It was strong, but nothing like that of the spirit in the temple. She pushed her energy out of the tip of the spear and into the lion-man's body.

"What are... you doing?" he said, his voice filled with dread.

Miranda forced her energy to wrap around the demon's, encapsulating it like a cocoon. "You wanted to be with your mate? I'm honoring your request," she said, and pulled her energy back into the spear, bringing Ugallu's parsu along with it.

"No. Wait. Do not do this. I'll leave you alone, I promise—"

When all the energy had completely been absorbed into the spear, Miranda pulled it free of the lion-man's body. The physical form of Ugallu burst into a shower of sparks that hung in the air for a moment—glowing like a million fireflies—before pinwheeling into the sky on the swirling winds.

Instantly the dark storm clouds overhead began to part and rays of sunlight shone down upon the ground.

Exhaustion washed over Miranda, and she fell to one knee, leaning heavily on the spear for support. Her hand tingled with energy as the Spear of the Winds pulsed with newfound power. She leaned her head against the staff and said, "I promise you. When this is done, when I defeat Tiamat, you, Ugallu, and Anzu will both be free. *Everyone* who has been made a pawn in this ridiculous war will be free. But until then, you will help me do what must be done."

"I hope you enjoy your time together. But I don't think Anzu is all that happy with you. Talking her into stealing the Tablet of Destinies and then abandoning her was a total jerk move. I hope this time together helps you to make up for that mistake."

CHAPTER 36

JUSTIN
Reconciliation

"Do you see the tablet shard yet?" Justin asked urgently. If he had lost the one thing keeping the evil queen of darkness at bay, he was a dead man. Literally, a dead man.

"Keep your pants on, kid," Red said and hissed out a dragon chuckle.

"You're hilarious," Justin shot back.

"*Relax, I see it. It's right over there.*" Red said, pointing with one huge claw at a spot on the ground that looked like the epicenter of a massive explosion. The earth was scorched outward in a jagged fanlike pattern radiating out toward the petrified pile of rubble, all that was left of Lahmu. Resting undisturbed on that very spot was the shard. Justin picked it up and examined it closely—not a scratch or mark anywhere on it.

A commotion drew Justin's attention to a fierce struggle occurring a short distance away. Miranda was fighting against Ugallu and losing.

Justin quickly pocketed the stone and sprinted over to help his sister. He was about twenty feet away when he saw her plunge the Spear of the Winds into the lion-man's chest and watched the monster explode into a shower of light.

Miranda looked like she was about to pass out when he skidded to a stop in front of her.

She glanced up at him, and her eyes narrowed. "You left me trapped in there," she said, pointing back at the pile of rubble. "I almost died."

Justin looked down at the ground. "I know, sis. I'm sorry. I… I just was so *mad* at you. You are so important, and you just don't care, and… I guess… I want to be important too. I just wanted you to realize you were making a huge mistake."

"You also wanted to punish me."

Justin nodded. "A little bit. I'm sorry."

Miranda stood up on wobbly legs, wrapped her arms around him and squeezed tightly. "I know you're sorry, and I know I kind of deserved it. I'm sorry too. You were right about a lot of things, Justin."

She pulled out of the hug, but still held onto his shoulders with both hands. "And you *are* important. I know this all seems focused on me, but you have just as much of Marduk's ability in you as I do."

"I left you alone, and I promised I would stick with you."

Miranda looked back at the ruined temple, then back at Justin, and she smiled. "I wasn't alone. Tabrati was with me. She taught me a lot of things about parsu and showed me an image of when Mom and Dad were here. They were trying to find the weapons and face Tiamat so I—*we*—wouldn't have too. They have been traveling and keeping us a secret from their own families all this time only to protect us." Tears started to well in Miranda's eyes. "I was so stupid. I thought they didn't love us."

Justin punched her softly in the chest. "That is just stupid.

Of course they love us. I just figured they were dedicated to their job, is all. So what now? Do we keep looking for Mom and Dad?"

Miranda shook her head. "It's not what they wanted us to do. They set us on this path to stop Tiamat from destroying everything. Maybe we'll find out more information along the way, something that will lead us to them as well."

She reached into her pocket and pulled out a shiny blue stone, holding it up for Justin to see. "We need to get this back to the City of the Ancients. It still has a lot of power in it."

"The protection stone! Do you think we'll be able to restore the shield?" Justin asked.

"We need to try," Miranda said and gestured back toward the destroyed ziggurat. "Besides, I don't think anyone will miss it here."

"Wait. I thought you said the whole Dragon Rider quest was stupid?" Justin goaded.

Miranda let out a sigh. "You only get one 'I was wrong' per day."

"Per day? How about in a lifetime." Justin laughed.

Leyla let out a sudden scream and Justin and Miranda pivoted to see what new threat was upon them. But they quickly realized it was a cry of joy. Barbita—Leyla's bearded Latin American dragon—had knocked down several of the stone slabs holding the two humans prisoner. In an instant, dozens of snakelike dragons surged out of the jungle, slithering around the meadow, finishing off any wyvern and draconian still alive.

Lord DeSoto burst through the foliage, riding in on the back of his giant serpentine dragon, an anxious look on his face as he surveyed the carnage of the battlefield. Then his eyes fell upon his daughter, and relief melted away the worry as he saw that she was unharmed. As he continued to take in the entire otherworldly scene, he noticed the massive pile of rubble and his gaze narrowed in on Justin and Miranda.

"Before he comes over here and starts yelling at us, I have to tell you something else." Miranda leaned over and whispered into Justin's ear, "I don't think Lord DeSoto had anything to do with betraying Mom and Dad. There was a guy named Gareth with them when they were here last, and Mom and Dad didn't seem to trust him much."

"Why would they be traveling with someone they didn't trust?" Justin asked.

"I think that's an excellent question, and one I plan on asking *him*," Miranda said with a tilt of her head toward the approaching Dragon Lord. Lord DeSoto did not look happy. His eyes were lost in shadows created by a deeply furrowed brow, and his mouth arced downward in what looked like a permanent frown. Every muscle in his body was so tense that he looked as if he were trying hard not to fall apart with each quickening step.

Justin cringed. "He doesn't look very happy, does he?"

"No, he does not," Miranda said, smirking slightly.

By the time Lord DeSoto had reached them, he was breathing hard, like a bull readying to charge. "What were you thinking, coming out here in the jungle and bringing my daughter with you, right before the storm…" He trailed off, looking to the sky, evidently confused. "Wait a minute. What happened to the storm?"

"It's a long story, Lord Desoto. One we can tell you all about once we get back to your compound. And we didn't know Leyla had followed us when we came looking for the temple," Justin said and pointed at the large pile of rubble.

"How did you even find the ziggurat?" he asked, his body relaxing a little. "It took your parents years to pinpoint the location and then a week of wandering around this clearing just to break through the protective barrier."

"We found a detailed map, in a locked tube in your library," Miranda answered. "The code was… something Mom sent to us, but I'm still not sure of the significance of the numbers." She paused for a moment as if considering exactly how much she should tell him. Even though Miranda strongly suspected that this Gareth guy was responsible for their parents' disappearance, DeSoto could still be involved too. She looked to Justin for confirmation that she should trust him, and when her brother nodded, she continued. "But we were able to find the temple because we were *supposed* to. Mom and Dad were trying to protect us from the truth, but this battle was never their responsibility. It is ours."

An intense feeling of being watched pulled Justin's focus beyond the collapsed temple, past the edge of the jungle, and just above the tree line. Some animal, large and golden—twinkled in the setting sun, but for only a fraction of a moment—before disappearing from sight. "We're being watched."

Lord DeSoto followed Justin's gaze, straining to see the distant figure. He gave three shrill whistles, which sent all but two of his cohort of dragons vanishing into the jungle. "They are close to the compound. Whoever it is, my dragons will catch them."

Justin closed his eyes and reached out with his mind. Past the flight of Latin American dragons—zipping through the trees of the dense jungle like guided missiles, past where he had spotted the golden creature, and to the very edge of his ability. He could only sense that whoever it was had gotten what it had come there to find. "They're gone. But it was a dragon. A gold dragon."

Lord DeSoto's eyes narrowed. "Drake."

"I thought he left a couple of days ago?" Miranda said.

"So had I. The scoundrel must have been lurking around,

but why?" DeSoto asked.

Justin shrugged. "Whatever it was he was waiting for, he got it."

"He might have been after the information our parents had sent to us. I left the package back in the stables." Miranda said. "We should check to see if anything is missing."

Lord DeSoto looked confused. "How can you know this?"

"Because they are magic, Papa," Leyla said as she came running over to her father. "Miranda can shoot the wind out of her spear, and Justin can catch on fire and not burn."

The older man looked down at his daughter with a mixture of disbelief and humor. "What? No." Then, as if noticing it for the first time, he looked intently at the spear Miranda was leaning against. "That cannot be... how did you... and you can... but that means... you found the Spear of the Winds—it is real."

Miranda hefted the spear into the air and spun it around in her hands several times. A light breeze began to move around the clearing, stirring dried leaves and dust. She closed her eyes—a look of intense concentration on her face—as the breeze grew into a gale. A funnel-shaped whirlwind appeared in the middle of the clearing, building in intensity until it transformed into a small tornado.

Miranda stopped the spear's circular motion, and pointed it from one of their fallen enemies to the next. The vortex moved to each spot, picking up the bodies of draconians and wyverns like a giant vacuum cleaner. Then with a slight shove of the spear, Miranda sent the funnel up off the ground and far into the distance.

She exhaled and nearly collapsed, but Billy was there to steady her. Everyone continued to watch in awe as the tornado moved deeper into the jungle before dissipating and dropping everything it had picked up gently, silently, down through the dense canopy to the forest floor below.

"I told you, Papa. They are magic," Leyla said, breaking the silence.

"Robin and Kaya were right. This whole time they were telling the truth. They said this was going to happen, but it seemed too far-fetched. Even when they showed me this temple, I was having a hard time believing them." He shook his head in disbelief. "But it is true, isn't it?"

"It is, Lord DeSoto," Miranda said weakly. "When my parents were here, they were with... someone else. Do you... know a man named Gareth?"

"Lord Gareth Ddraig? He's the head of the Welsh house. I think you know his daughter, Gwen," Lord DeSoto said matter-of-factly. "The Ddraigs and McAdelinds have been allies for centuries."

Justin remembered something Billy had said before they had all left for the City of the Ancients. "Oh no! Billy said Grandpa Mac went to meet with Lord Ddraig to follow up on a lead. We need to get back to Thunderbird Ranch as quickly as we can."

"It will... have to... wait," Miranda said, her labored words barely a whisper. "I... need to rest... for a little bit..." Then her eyes closed, and she collapsed.

Billy, who had already been supporting Miranda, caught her as she fell unconscious and gently lowered her to the ground. "Miranda. Miranda. Can you hear me?" Billy said.

Lord DeSoto placed two fingers on Miranda's throat, then felt her forehead with the palm of his hand. "Her pulse is strong, and she looks healthy. I am no doctor, but I think she is just completely exhausted. Come. Let us get her back to the compound. Hanaa knows far more about such things than I do."

Justin was concerned for his sister, but he knew Lord DeSoto was right. Other than being completely unconscious,

Miranda looked perfectly normal. Almost peaceful. He glanced slowly around at the others gathered. Humans and dragons alike looked beaten up and tired. "I suppose we're no good to anyone if we die on the trip back, and I'll need to check and see if that slimeball Drake did indeed swipe something from us. Plus, I'm totally starving. Do you guys make chimichangas down here?"

Leyla rolled her eyes. "¡*Ay!* Americans."

CHAPTER 37

MIRANDA
Lord Ddraig

MIRANDA HAD SLEPT for almost twenty hours straight. She didn't remember anything that had happened after she passed out from the effort of wielding the Spear of the Winds. She simply woke up after lunch the following day feeling very rested and ravenously hungry. That same night, their party set off with all haste to Thunderbird Ranch.

While she had been asleep, Justin, Billy, Lord DeSoto, and Leyla searched the compound for anything that might have been taken by Lord Drake. And much to Miranda's relief, all of their parents' notes and papers were still there. The only thing that appeared to be missing was the weird scroll she had taken from the warehouse in Denver. She wasn't sure what Drake wanted with that old piece of paper, but she had a sinking feeling it couldn't be good.

Justin had also tried several times to reach Grandpa Mac by phone. Unfortunately he had only managed to speak once to Miss Ddraig. Other than two ranch hands, she had been left completely alone. When Mrs. Lóng and Billy had departed suddenly and not returned, she found herself in charge and completely unqualified to run an operation the size of the ranch.

To make matters worse, neither their grandfather nor Mr. O'Faron had come back when they had said they would. The short conversation quickly turned into Justin trying desperately to calm the frantic young woman down and promising her they would all be there in a couple of days to help out.

Originally, Lord DeSoto had insisted on escorting them back, but after the events on the plateau, it didn't take much convincing for him to agree to spend some promised time with Leyla. He said he would postpone collecting his brother's effects for a couple of days and asked Miranda and Justin to please let their grandfather know that he would be arriving later than expected.

That was two days before. Since then, they had made excellent time back to Colorado.

Miranda was able to use the Spear of the Winds to blanket the sky with a layer of thick clouds. She had learned that if she concentrated just right, she could coax out Ugallu's ability to create storms and Anzu's to magically mask their location from Tiamat—effectively making them invisible. By traveling day and night, they were able to make it back in almost half the time.

The worst part of the trip was not knowing whether or not their grandpa McAdelind was sitting comfortably back at the ranch or if he had become the next victim of some insane plot to cleanse the world of humanity.

After they had checked in at Thunderbird Ranch, they needed to make an urgent stop at the City of the Ancients. In the hours following the collapse of the protective shield, there had already been signs of the pristine land's deterioration, not to mention their grandpa Stone's rapid aging. They had been gone for about a week now, and there was no telling the level of damage that had occurred during their absence.

"We are almost there," Storm said. "Another couple of minutes. Do you think it wise to land by the house? It is still light outside. We might be spotted."

"Worth the risk. Bring us down right there by the river," Miranda replied.

"As long as Lord McAdelind holds you accountable for that decision, I will oblige," said Storm.

"Trust me, if the old man comes charging out of the house, red-faced and screaming, I will be overjoyed," Miranda replied, struggling to keep worry from her thoughts.

The blue dragon tucked her wings back and began to rapidly lose altitude. Within seconds, she fanned her wings out wide—hovering for just a breath—before landing silently between the tree-lined river and large white ranch house.

After Red and Nightshade had followed suit, Justin dismounted and came running to catch up to Miranda. She was almost on the rear porch when she realized Billy wasn't with them. She turned around to see him still mounted on Nightshade.

"Aren't you coming?" Miranda called.

Billy pulled off his helmet, exchanging it for his favorite purple-and-black baseball cap. "Nope," he said, as he strapped the helmet to his saddle. "I should get these dragons back to the Warren. You guys go on ahead."

Miranda nodded, but she knew the real reason Billy wanted to go was to find out if his father had returned. Despite all his posturing and criticism of his father, Billy loved him and had been deeply worried about him over the past several days. "Okay. I'll catch up with you later," Miranda said. "Oh, and Billy... If you see Indigo, please let her know I'll visit as soon as I can."

Miss D had let Justin know that Indigo's condition had improved: she had woken up a couple of days before, but her behavior was very erratic. It was Miranda's fault that the young dragon had been injured in the first place, and she felt obligated to help Indigo recover. But that, like so many other things, was going to have to wait its turn.

Billy tipped his hat to Miranda and kicked Nightshade softly in the sides, sending the dragon into the air, with Red and Storm close behind, all flying low toward the Warren's secret entrance.

Miranda and Justin entered in through the ranch kitchen's back door. The place was an absolute mess. Dirty dishes were haphazardly stacked in columns that made the leaning tower of Pisa look structurally sound. There was a half-eaten casserole of some kind just sitting on the counter and a mound of trash bags piled next to the back door.

Justin whistled. "Oh man. Mrs. Lóng is going to lose it when she sees this mess."

Miranda's foot stuck to something squishy on the floor and she gagged. "And you thought I was bad. Apparently Miss D puts cleanliness on the back burner when she's feeling overwhelmed."

They continued to pick their way around the clutter and out through the swinging doors leading into the dining room. Miranda came to a sudden halt when she saw a man sitting at the large table with his back to them.

The man turned around partway, and Miranda recognized him almost immediately. "Lord Ddraig," she hissed.

"Aye. Do I know you?" he asked in the same heavy Welsh accent he shared with his daughter.

Miranda and Justin made their way around the room, giving the table a wide berth. When they had reached the fireplace, Miranda could see that the man was sporting a severely swollen nose and two black eyes. "Where's Lord McAdelind? Did you harm him? Is he alive?"

"Simmer down, kids. I'm right here," Grandpa Mac said as he walked stiffly in from the hall.

Miranda ran over and gave him a huge hug. "We were so worried about you."

"Why in the world were you *worried* about me? And what in Sam Hill are you two doing back here? Does Paul know you've come back to the ranch?"

Miranda and Justin looked at each other and grimaced slightly before Justin said, "Well... no, not exactly. He probably still thinks we're on our Dragon Rider quest."

"Your what?" their grandfather yelled, his face burning instantly red. "That no good... I told him *he* was responsible for you two—and he sent you on some ridiculous quest. When I see him, I'm going to—"

"You're going to what?" Justin asked, and gestured toward Lord Ddraig. "Punch *him* in the face too?"

Grandpa Mac nodded. "At the very least that's what I'm going to do."

"Well, as fun as that would be to watch, it was our idea to leave. We can explain everything later," Miranda said, and narrowed her eyes at the man sitting at the table. "We came here to make sure you were okay. We weren't sure if this... traitor... here had done something to you."

Their grandfather walked over to the table, pulled out the chair opposite Lord Ddraig, and sat down with a grunt. "*Hmm.* You two figured that out on your own, huh? Very good." He pointed a finger at Lord Ddraig and said, "No, Gareth here and I have come to a little understanding. Haven't we, son?"

Lord Ddraig nodded. "Aye. That we have."

"What happened?" Miranda asked.

"Well, I went to meet Gareth in Newfoundland to hear what information he had on Robert and Kaya—"

"Wait. You flew to Newfoundland, Canada?" Justin asked.

"It's not like that's much farther from here than where we were in Mexico," Miranda said.

"Actually, Miss Geography, it's about eight hundred miles farther," Justin pointed out.

Their grandfather choked a little, but managed to say, "You two were in Mexico? I'm going to have words with Paul when I see him. Anyhow. Gareth broke down and told me… actually, why don't you tell them what you said?"

Lord Ddraig looked ashamed, but met Miranda and Justin's eyes as he spoke. "They have my son, they do. The filthy liars have my boy. They said that if I told 'em where your parents were, they'd let him go." His eyes welled with tears and he looked down at the table. "But they didn't. They're all gone, they are. Robin, Kaya, Cedrick—all of 'em. An' they'll keep on takin' an' takin' until they have what they want. You don't understand who you're dealin' with."

Miranda shrugged. "I think we have a pretty good idea."

"Queen of darkness, hoards of monsters, evil gods," Justin added.

"Yeah. I think we understand," Miranda said, and she slammed her fist down on the table. "So you're going to tell us everything that you know, or so help me, a broken nose will be the least of your worries."

Despite the threat, Lord Ddraig's mouth turned up into a slight smile. "I didn't believe your granddad when he said Robin an' Kaya had children, but I'll be a dragon's— rear end—if you two aren't carbon copies of your parents." Then his expression changed—serious now. "As I told Lord McAdelind, I don't know much. Dracs were the ones talkin' to me."

Their grandfather leaned over the table, staring at Lord

Ddraig. "But...?"

"But... I know Drake is involved too."

Miranda shot Justin a quick look and said, "How *exactly* is Drake involved?"

Lord Ddraig shook his head. "I can't say that I know. But I recognized one of the dracs who came to me—it was one I've seen at Drake's Island durin' the Council meetin's."

"Where is this island?" Miranda asked, the hairs on her neck standing up.

"Off the northwest tip of Scotland," he said.

Miranda's face felt hot. Tabrati had told her that the next temple they had to find stood on an island off the northwest coast of Great Britain. This had to be the same location. She could feel it.

"What is it, Miranda?" Grandpa Mac asked, sounding worried. "You look like you've seen a ghost."

"We need to go to Drake's Island. Right away," she said, with an urgency that drew concerned looks from everyone else in the room.

"The annual Council of Twenty meeting is in a couple of weeks, and it's held on Drake's Island—"

"We can't wait for a couple of weeks. We need to go now," Miranda insisted.

Her grandfather held up his hands. "Trust me, young lady, I understand. But we have to do this just right. Drake's Island isn't like one of the other Dragon Lords' ranches. It's an isolated fortress. We'll never get near it if we're not invited. So we need to approach this with level heads, not heavy hearts. You hear me?"

Miranda was disappointed, and she didn't really understand, but she did trust her grandfather. "Yes, sir."

He nodded. "Good. Now, Gareth over here is going to do everything in his power to help us once we get to the meeting, isn't that right, son?" When Lord Ddraig nodded,

Grandpa Mac stood up with a loud grunt. "Now do you two have any idea where my cook has gotten off to? I'm famished, and that kitchen is a downright pigsty."

"If she's not here, then that means she's still in the City of the Ancients. Actually, we should get back there as soon as possible. We need to complete our quest," Justin said.

Grandpa Mac scowled. "I'm going to give your grandpa Stone a piece of my mind. He was supposed to be watching over you two, protecting you. I should have known that was a big mistake."

"Actually, Grandpa, I think you'll understand more when you see the valley. But Aunt Em was right. We needed to go there—not for our protection, but to continue on the path we have been set upon," Miranda said.

Grandpa Mac stroked his mustache thoughtfully. "What path is that?"

Miranda looked over at her brother and said, "The path to our destiny."

CHAPTER 38

JUSTIN
The Dragon Riders

"ARE WE ALMOST THERE YET? I'm going to die of hypothermia if we don't get to the valley soon," Justin said through chattering teeth.

"Do you want me to light you on fire again?" Red asked.

"Ah… tempting, but no. I like my clothes right where they are." He pulled his father's jacket tighter around him, trying to retain all the warmth that he could. Just wearing the old tan coat made him feel as if his dad were there with him somehow.

"You know, kid. Whatever happens, he'll always be with you."

"We're going to get him back, Red. We're going to get everyone back. I mean look at us… a kung fu master, void of fear, so quick it seems like he can anticipate the moves of his enemies, with the power of a god, and… a dragon. No one can stand in our way."

"Nothing like a little modesty. Well, at least one of those two statements is true. I am a dragon, and we will get them back," Red said. "Okay, there it is. Let's get on the ground… and no *crash landings."*

"No guarantees there," Justin said, and leaned forward, grasping the gullet grips as the massive dragon fanned out his wings, slowing to a glide.

"Oh no!" Justin gasped when they were close enough to make out the valley below. It was much worse than he had imagined. The grass, once a brilliant green, was brown and dead in spots. The field crops and fruit trees had wilted away, leaving mere skeletons of their former selves. Even the walkways and buildings looked as if they might crumble at any moment. Justin watched as the entire tribe seemed to creep out from the shelter of the ruins, drawn by the spectacle of the five great dragons coming in for a landing.

Once the dragons had set down in a clearing by the river and everyone had dismounted, Grandpa Mac joined Justin and Miranda as they surveyed the devastated valley. "What in tarnation happened to this place? It used to be a paradise." He noticed the pile of stones that had once been a beautiful temple. "And what happened to the temple? Wait—did you two do this?"

"No. Well… not entirely," Justin said, watching as the dragons and humans of the Valley cautiously approached them.

"It wasn't completely their fault, sir," Billy said, coming up with his father. "The two monsters sent by Tiamat destroyed the shield. Justin and Miranda just destroyed the temple."

"Nice," Miranda said sarcastically. "Don't worry, Grandpa. We're here to make things right again… we hope."

One of the great earth dragons landed nearby; Justin recognized him immediately as Rockgobbler. *"You have returned. The Ancient One was correct. We are very pleased to see you again."*

"How is the old worm? We should probably fill him in on what's happened," Justin replied.

"*Ya'ne'unde, the Ancient One, oldest and wisest of our kind, made his journey to join the ancestors not long after you departed on your quest.*"

Justin was overwhelmed with an intense wave of sadness emanating from not only Rockgobbler but all the other dragons of the valley.

"Wait, you mean he... died?" Miranda asked in disbelief. "What happened?"

"*Moments after you departed, he called us all to him and said the magic of this valley, the magic that had protected us for millennia, the magic that had sustained him longer than any creature made of flesh and bone had any right to exist, was gone. He had fulfilled his obligation to Marduk and helped set you on the correct path. Then he said you would return to make things right again, and that it was our duty to help you in any way we could.*" Rockgobbler looked up at the sky streaked with purples and blues. "*He was laughing merrily as he passed, overwhelmed with joy at being able to rejoin the ones that have made the journey before him.*"

"I'm sorry to hear that... I mean, I'm happy for him... I guess. I just wish I had had a chance to say goodbye and let him know that we were successful in our quest," Justin said. Seeing the baffled expressions worn by Billy and Grandpa McAdelind, who had been following only the out-loud human half of this exchange, Justin added, "We'll explain later." He turned back to Rockgobbler. "Is Grandpa Stone okay?"

"*He comes now.*" Rockgobbler inclined his head, indicating two men drawing near. One was leaning heavily on the other, and they were making slow progress. When they were close, Justin was shocked to see that his grandfather was... old.

"Well, well, well. Looks like time has caught up to you, *old man*," Grandpa Mac said with a chuckle. He was right. Their grandpa Stone seemed to have aged by at least thirty years since they had left. "Finally, you look my age."

"Don't flatter yourself, Mac. You've always looked like you were in your eighties," Grandpa Stone said with a small smirk. When he was within arm's reach of Miranda and Justin, he let go of the person helping him and gave his grandchildren a hug. "I thought I had hallucinated that you were leaving, and then the next day, Mana'doe told me that you had indeed left. I was worried sick."

"Well, we had to complete our Dragon Riders quest," Justin said.

"Oh? And what did you bring back from this quest?" their grandfather asked.

Miranda reached into her pocket and pulled out a small blue sphere. "We recovered a new protection stone, which we hope will sustain this valley for centuries to come."

Grandpa Stone leaned down and examined the rock carefully, his eyes widening. "Will it work?"

"Only one way to find out," Miranda said, then she and Justin turned and headed over to where the obelisk stood like a silent sentinel by the river.

The pillar's crowning protection stone, which had once been shiny and smooth, was now charred and cracked. Miranda reached up and easily pulled it free, leaving an empty shallow cylindrical recess at the top of the obelisk. She tossed the old stone to Justin and placed the one they had retrieved from the temple in Mexico into the opening. As soon as the blue orb was cradled securely in the obelisk, the cuneiform inscription spiraling around the ancient stone began to glow. A wave of light shot out and curved over and around the valley, encompassing it in a shimmering cocoon.

The entire tribe, which had by now gathered in a great arc surrounding the obelisk, lowered their heads in reverence.

Grandpa Stone raised both hands to the sky and proclaimed, "Lulu'na'waz'nani, the Stone of Hiding, has been restored. May peace and prosperity be bestowed upon the Oni'waz'legani until the Earth crumbles below our feet."

Justin glanced down and watched as a second wave of energy washed over the valley floor. Brown grass was rejuvenated to a brilliant green, pathways were instantly remade whole again, and fields and orchards sprang back from the dead.

When the spreading energy field reached the ruined temple, the ground opened up and swallowed its remains whole, leaving only a crystal-clear pool in its place.

"Whoa! That's crazy. I wonder why it didn't restore the temple?" Justin asked.

"The ziggurat was built with the parsu of a god. When that left, the temple was nothing more than a pile of rocks," Miranda said. "Trust me. The valley is better for not having even the smallest piece of Kingu anywhere near."

Justin inspected the growing crowd. "Where is Mrs. Lóng?"

Grandpa Stone looked back toward the rear of the valley, and said, "She's in the longhouse. Some of the structures higher up on the cliffs became unsafe, so we relocated everyone there. Her condition hasn't changed. She's still unresponsive."

"I'm going to go check on her, if that's okay?" Justin said. When his grandfather nodded, Justin jogged across the still-transforming valley floor. Delicate columbines blossomed along the trails, decorating the way with yellow and blue dabs of color.

With the disappearance of the temple, the longhouse was now the largest structure in the valley. Justin took the half dozen steps leading up to it two at a time and pushed the wooden door open. The building consisted of one enormous room, which had traditionally been used mainly for meetings and ceremonies but was now filled with beds and provisions. A fire was burning in a circular hearth in the middle of the room, with its smoke vented through a hole in the ceiling.

Justin walked from bed to bed, looking for Mrs. Lóng. At the farthest end of the structure, opposite the entryway, he found the old cook, lying motionless on her back, just as she had been when he had last seen her. Her face was still a perfect mask of calm, with the slightest of smiles just visible at the corners of her lips.

Justin sat down on the edge of a small bed next to his teacher. Why hadn't she woken up yet? They should probably have taken her to a hospital by now. "I'm not sure if you can hear me, Mrs. Lóng, but we're back now. Everything went pretty well. We were able to beat both Lahmu and Ugallu and restore the protection field around the valley. I wouldn't have been able to beat Lahmu if you hadn't told me about how some of the bricks around here are made out of baked mud. How is it that you always seem to know what's going to happen before it happens, and what I need to know?" He reached out and gently took the old woman's hand in his own. Instantly he could feel a strange warmth beginning to radiate from his hand, which began to glow with a faint golden light.

Mrs. Lóng's eyes shot open, and she sat bolt upright.

Justin screamed and fell off the bed and onto the floor.

"Stop being so dramatic, dear. How long have I been asleep?" she asked.

"I wasn't being *dramatic*. You scared the crap out of me." Justin stood up and dusted off his pants. "You've been out for over a week."

Mrs. Lóng reached up and absentmindedly touched her pearl necklace. "How did you wake me?"

"We brought the protection stone from another temple and replaced the broken one here. The valley is okay now. The stone must have healed you as well."

Mrs. Lóng's face crinkled in thought. "No. That is not it. How odd." She stood up and walked over to the door. "Come, child. I need to get back to the ranch house before someone makes a complete mess of my kitchen."

Justin cringed, then ran over and joined her. "Yeah... we should probably... hurry. Oh, did I mention Miranda and I were in Mexico the whole time you were asleep, and absolutely were not at the ranch... at all."

* * *

Later that night, Justin, Miranda, Red, and Storm were standing near a roaring bonfire in the large clearing by the river. The entire tribe, scores of men and women and many earth dragons, surrounded them in a wide circle. Justin watched in wonder as the dragons used their thick tails to smack hollowed logs, creating thunderous drumbeats, while the humans sang and chanted in their ancient tribal language, humans and beasts working together to create an eerie symphony of rhythm and melody.

The music came to a sudden halt, the final notes echoing off the canyon walls. Grandpa Stone stepped forward with the assistance of a long walking staff. He raised his free hand into the air and said loud enough for all gathered to hear, "Tonight, we recognize four new members of our tribe, a tribe that unites dragons and humans to live together as one people. And in the tradition of our people, we celebrate the success of this sacred union. It is our tradition going back to Api'onu, the First One, and the great dragon Ya'ne'unde, who taught our two peoples the benefits of working as one, that we send our youth into the larger world to bring back a lasting symbol of this union. In recognition of their accomplishments, we bestow upon them membership in the Oni'waz'legani."

"As we all know, evil spirits from a far off land attacked the sacred Lulu'na'waz'nani, the stone that has for centuries protected our land from enemies and the ravages of time itself. Our valley was dying, and with it, our people."

"Tonight we recognize the overwhelming accomplishments achieved by these brave warriors. For not only did they defeat the enemies of the valley but they have restored the Stone of Hiding, healing our valley and our people. No other accomplishment in the long history of the Oni'waz'legani since our founding has been so important to our tribe's future."

Grandpa Stone paused for a moment, then pointed to the pool where the ziggurat once stood. "They did, however, manage to destroy our sacred temple."

Justin cringed and looked over at his sister, who flushed with embarrassment.

Their grandfather smiled. "But the elders have decided to overlook that little incident in light of the situation. As we have learned, the temple was not placed here for our benefit, but for theirs," he said, indicating his grandchildren with his free hand.

He limped over to them and smiled broadly. "So it is with great pleasure, and with the authority granted to me by the ancients, that I bestow the title of Naya'kosa'sinu upon Red and Storm, and Bino'kosa'sinu upon Justin and Miranda."

The crowd broke into cheers and hoots of joy and celebration while the local dragons beat their tails wildly on the logs.

After several minutes, Grandpa Stone held up his hand for silence. Then he spread his arms wide, and said, "Welcome home, Warriors and Riders. You are now, and will forever be, Oni'waz'legani."

* * *

After what seemed like several hours of eating, music, and laughter, Grandpa McAdelind pulled Justin and Miranda away from the festivities. He was silent for a while as they walked along the paved path that traced the river's edge.

"We have a little under two weeks to prepare for anything that might happen at the council meeting. I think it best we act the parts we are expected to play and keep our investigation hidden in the shadows."

"What did you have in mind?" Miranda asked.

Grandpa Mac stroked his mustache thoughtfully and said, "Well, I thought one of you could stick with me in the council meetings—"

"Not me!" Justin shouted.

Grandpa Mac frowned but continued. "And the other will compete in the Dragon Rodeo, representing our family. That will allow us to work both sides of the event, and look for clues."

"What will Lord Ddraig's role be? We can't really trust him, can we? Getting in close with us might be exactly what he was asked to do in order to get his son back," Miranda said.

"I've known Gareth his entire life. He comes from honest stock. He just has his head all turned around over his boy. I can't blame him for that. But trust me, I'm not taking my eyes off him. Plus, he's going to help me with some important council business when we get there."

"And I'll be at the stadium winning trophies and bringing glory to the McAdelind name," Justin said, rubbing his hands together excitedly.

"Right," Miranda said sarcastically. "I'm sure you'll be able to beat the competitors representing *all* those other families who have been doing the events for years."

Justin shot a hurt look at his sister. "Way to be supportive, sis."

"Why do you think Drake is spying on the families and

kidnapping people?" Miranda asked.

"Honestly, I'm not entirely sure. He could be working for Tiamat, but I've known Drake for fifty years, and I can't imagine him bowing down to anyone. He's certainly up to something though. William and I were discussing that scroll Drake took from you down in Mexico. William believes it might be the same one he traded with the dracs for information on Em. There seems to be more to that old scrap of paper than just some draconian spell. Also, every ten years we elect a new Dragon Lord to rule the council. It's time for that election again, and a Drake has been in charge for centuries. But kidnapping and extortion seem extreme for Archibald. Don't get me wrong. He can be a dangerous adversary when he feels threatened, and we shouldn't underestimate him. But that's enough business talk for tonight. We can worry about the details tomorrow. We should get back to the party and celebrate. It's not every day the title of Dragon Rider is bestowed."

Miranda rolled her eyes. "I feel like we're wasting time. Compared to what we need to accomplish, this is such a small victory."

Grandpa Mac placed a hand on Miranda and Justin's shoulders. "No, don't look at it that way. It's important to celebrate every win, every victory, no matter how big or how small." He indicated the members of the tribe dancing and laughing around the roaring bonfire. "You saved these people… your people. You restored the magic of this valley, preserving it and your tribe for generations to come." He paused, then added, "Don't get me wrong though. There's more than a small part of me that is pretty darn happy that Paul now looks his age. Maybe he'll finally stop teasing me about how old I look."

Justin laughed. "I wouldn't count on it. So have you two made up yet?"

Grandpa McAdelind glanced over at the silhouette of two figures chatting by the fire. Mrs. Lóng was busy scolding Grandpa Stone about something he was doing wrong. "Not yet, son. Some wounds take a long time to heal." He smiled down at his grandchildren. "I just wish your parents were here to see this. They would be so proud of you two."

Miranda smiled. "You really think so?"

"Sure they would. Look at all the good you've done."

"I'm not so sure. We did completely destroy what would have been the top two archaeological finds of the century," Justin added.

Grandpa Mac chuckled. "I think you did this valley a favor by getting rid of that big stone monstrosity. I always thought it was a bit on the ugly side. Now come on. Let's have a little bit more to eat, then head home. We have a couple of busy weeks ahead of us."

THE ADVENTURE CONTINUES IN...

Don't miss a moment of Miranda, Justin, Red and Storm's adventures as they try to save their family and stop the dark queen Tiamat from rising, by visiting www.aakerr.com and staying informed of upcoming book releases.

If you've enjoyed the *The Dragon Riders*, please help spread the word by telling your friends and leaving a review.

Thank you so much for reading!

GLOSSARY

Akena'tani — The Oni'waz'legani name meaning "River daughter."

Annunaki — The descendants of the Mesopotamian god Anu. The Annunaki were the gods of order who promoted the rise of civilization, and were more sympathetic to humans than their cousins the Igigi.

Anu — The Mesopotamian sky god. The descendants of Anu are referred to as the Annunaki.

Anzu — A Mesopotamian wind demon that had the body of an eagle and the head of a lioness.

Api'onu — The Oni'waz'legani name for the "First one."

Apsu — One of the two primordial gods that all the other Mesopotamian gods are descended from. Apsu was the husband of Tiamat and was the god of the sweet water or fresh water.

Argo — Grandpa McAdelind's massive gold dragon.

Azuria — A female wild blue dragon that attacked Miranda several times thinking she was the thief that stole her egg. But when the real thief, Cisco DeSoto, was discovered and the egg returned, Azuria recognized Miranda as dragon-kind.

Bašmu — The Mesopotamian name for Wyverns. One of the eleven monsters Tiamat created to do battle against the god Marduk.

Billy O'Faron — The son of William O'Faron. Billy is sixteen-years-old and has lived on Thunderbird Ranch with the McAdelind family most of his life. Billy is an accomplished dragon rider and has won many trophies at the annual dragon rodeo.

Bino'kosa'sinu — The Oni'waz'legani name for "Dragon Rider."

Francisco "Cisco" DeSoto — The former security chief of Thunderbird Ranch who was the thief stealing eggs and gold from the McAdelind family in an attempt to discredit them with the Council of Twenty and seize control of the ranch for himself. Cisco was killed by his co-conspirators, the draconians.

Council of Twenty — The ruling body of the Dragon Families. Currently, there are only nineteen families in the council since the O'Faron family was expelled.

Ddraig — The surname of the Welsh dragon family and masters of the Welsh Red dragon line. Members of the Ddraig family include Gwen Ddraig, who works at Thunderbird Ranch as the McAdelind's dragon trainer, Lord Gareth Ddraig, and Cedrick Ddraig.

DeSoto — The surname of the Latin American dragon family. Members of the DeSoto family include Cisco DeSoto, Lord Carlos DeSoto, Lady Hanaa Nrgwenya-DeSoto, and Leyla Marie Nrgwenya-DeSoto.

Draconian — Often referred to as Dracs, are one of Tiamat's eleven monsters she created to do battle against Marduk. Draconians resemble humans but are covered in scales, have no hair, forked-tongues, and eyes with slitted pupils like a snake. The original Mesopotamian name for draconians is Umū dabrūtu.

Drake — The surname of the English dragon family and masters of the Britannia Gold dragon line. Lord Archibald Drake is the High Dragon Lord and the head of the Council of Twenty. Another member of the Drake family is Lord Drake's son, Winston.

Dragon — One of the eleven monsters created by Tiamat to do battle against the god Marduk. Dragons are large, scaled, creatures with horns and wings. Not long after Tiamat was vanquished, humans began using friendly dragons to help hunt down and control the wild dragon population. Over time dragons split into two distinct subspecies; wild and domestic. Domestic dragons closely resemble wild dragons, except are often stockier, less vibrant in color, and lost the ability to use their breath weapons.

Dragonspeak — An ability to communicate with dragons telepathically. This ability is extremely rare. It is believed that Justin and Miranda are the only two people in thousands of years to exhibit this ability.

Em McAdelind — Justin and Miranda's aunt who everyone believed to have been killed by wild wyverns when she was a teenager, however, she is very much alive and is being held a prisoner. William O'Faron was Em's boyfriend at the time of her kidnapping.

Enki — Mesopotamian god of magic and wisdom. Enki had the ability to enchant objects with parsu giving them special power. Enki is the father of Marduk.

Flare — Gwen Ddraig's Welsh Red dragon.

Grandpa McAdelind — The Lord of the McAdelind dragon family, grandpa McAdelind is a large, strong, man with gray hair and a big bushy mustache. He also has three long scars down the side of his face from where he was attacked by a wyvern.

Gwendolyn "Gwen" Ddraig — Gwen is the daughter of the Welsh dragon family, the Ddraigs. She is on a yearlong internship at the Thunderbird Ranch to learn more about the different dragon species and how to care for them. Gwen is an accomplished dragon rider and is operating as both the ranches dragon trainer and veterinarian.

Igigi — The elemental gods and goddesses that are descended from Tiamat and Apsu. They differ from the Annunaki, as the Igigi want the world to be returned to chaos.

Justin McAdelind — An accident-prone, slightly nerdy, eleven-year-old boy, who along with his sister Miranda was sent to live with their estranged grandfather in rural Colorado. After discovering his family was a group of secret dragon ranchers, Justin realized he had the ability to communicate with and sense the intentions of dragons and draconians.

Kaya McAdelind — The mother of Justin and Miranda.

Kingu — An elemental god who Tiamat made commander of her army.

Kosa'sinu — The Oni'waz'legani name for "Winged snakes" or "Dragons."

Kya'ho'ah — The Oni'waz'legani name for Miranda and Justin's mother, Kaya. It means "wise beyond time."

Lahmu — One of the eleven monsters created by Tiamat. Lahmu is an elemental creature that is made of rock and mud.

Lulu'na'waz'nani — The Oni'waz'legani name for a small, blue stone, about the size of a baseball. The name translates to "the stone of hiding," or "the protection stone."

Marduk — King of the Mesopotamian pantheon of gods and goddesses. Marduk came to prominence when he was the only Annunaki to step forward to challenge Tiamat.

Mesopotamian — Mesopotamia refers to what is now a large section of modern day Iraq and means, the land between two rivers. As an author, I am using this term to describe the myths, legends and gods that were shared and built upon by the Sumerian, Acadian, and Babylonian civilizations.

McAdelind — The surname of the North American dragon family. Their family's home, Thunderbird Ranch, is located in southern Colorado. Some of the members of the McAdelind family are Grandpa McAdelind, Robert "Robin" McAdelind, Kaya McAdelind, Em McAdelind, Miranda McAdelind and Justin McAdelind.

Miranda McAdelind — A tough and brave fourteen-year-old girl, who along with her brother, Justin, was sent to stay with their estranged grandfather in rural Colorado. After discovering her family was a group of secret dragon ranchers, Miranda realized she not only had the ability to communicate with and sense the intentions of dragons but that she was immune to and had the ability to control lightning.

Mrs. Lóng – The unpredictable and mysterious cook that is more than what she appears. Mrs. Lóng is often appearing and disappearing seemingly at random and has an uncanny understanding of what is going on around the ranch.

Naya'kosa'sinu — The Oni'waz'legani name for "Dragon Warrior."

Neperdu — The original name of Ya'ne'unde meaning "bright" or "happy" in Sumerian

Nidaba — Mesopotamian goddess of writing.

Nightshade — Billy O'Faron's black dragon.

Nrgwenya — The surname of the Tanzanian dragon family.

O'Faron — The surname of a former prominent dragon family that was stripped of their title and holdings by the Council of Twenty. Members of this family are William O'Faron and Billy O'Faron.

Oni'waz'legani — The tribal name which means 'The People of the Unseen Land" or simply "The People."

Pa'na'lulu — The Oni'waz'legani name for Miranda and Justin's maternal grandfather, Paul Stone.

Parsu — The divine power of the Mesopotamian gods and goddesses. Parsu is also sometimes referred to as *Me*.

Red — Robert McAdelind's Welsh Red Dragon. Red feels a kinship with Justin and has offered to be Justin's dragon.

Robert "Robin" McAdelind — Miranda and Justin's father.

Sage — An ancient green dragon that belonged to Alexander McAdelind, the first McAdelind to come to the United States.

Steel — A brash, juvenile, blue dragon at Thunderbird Ranch.

Storm — Em McAdelind's Blue dragon. Storm has spent the years since Em's disappearance in a state of self-isolation, blaming herself for Em's death. Miranda was able to show her that it wasn't her fault and that Em was indeed still alive.

Tablet of Destinies — A clay tablet with the names of the past leaders of the Mesopotamian pantheon inscribed upon it.

Tabrati — Also called "Api'onu" by the Oni'waz'legani tribe, was the founder and builder of the City of the Ancients.

Tiamat — One of the two primordial Mesopotamian gods that all the other gods are descended. She is the goddess of salt water and creation. Tiamat is often depicted as a beautiful woman, but with horns and fangs, but her true form is that of a colossal dragon. During her war with Marduk, she created eleven different types of monsters to do battle against the young god.

Thunder — William O'Faron's blue dragon.

Ugallu — One of the eleven monsters created by Tiamat. Ugallu is a lion-headed man with the legs and wings of an eagle.

Umū dabrūtu — The Mesopotamian name for Draconians. One of the eleven monsters Tiamat created to do battle against Marduk.

Unktéhila — The Oni'waz'legani name for "horned serpent," or "wyvern."

Warren — The massive underground complex at Thunderbird Ranch where the dragons live.

Wyvern — Similar to dragons in form, but have two legs instead of four, do not have breath weapons, and are far less intelligent. Wyverns also have long scorpion-like tails tipped with a deadly stinger filled with poison.

Wyrmling — One of the five stages of dragon development. Wyrmlings are equivalent to human children age three to twelve years old.

Ya'ne'unde — The Oni'waz'legani name for Neperdu, which translates to "lighthearted." Ya'ne'unde is an ancient brown, or earth, dragon that lives in the City of the Ancients.

Ziggurat — A temple built in ancient Mesopotamia that is a form of step pyramid. They were considered the home and seat of power of the gods for which they were built.

ACKNOWLEDGEMENTS

This book wouldn't have been possible without the help and support of several very important people.

Always first, my wife Jenifer, who continues to encourage me to follow my dream and supports me in every way possible.

My alpha-readers: Jen and Mom. Your support and encouragement and great suggestions helped make *The Dragon Riders* a stronger story.

My beta-readers: Becky, Will, Alisia and Bonnie. Your excitement keeps me moving forward.

My family and friends: Andre, Lilia, and Alex, Mom and Dad, Ryan and Sarah, Becky and Will, Alisia and Sergio, Bonnie and Jim, Carrie H., the Hustwits, the DeRodeses, Kevin, Heidi, Maureen, Andrew, Rick, Michelle, Chay, Claire, Rachel, Christie D, Eric D, Sonia, and many others who were, and still are, supportive of me throughout the entire process.

The great fans, both young and not so young, who reached out to me with kind words and excitement for the series.

And last, my editor Christopher Caines. Without his help, guidance and support, *The Dragon Riders* would not have turned out to be a sequel that surpasses its predecessor.

ABOUT THE AUTHOR

Anthony A. Kerr has always been a storyteller. Whether it was acting out elaborate plots with Star Wars figures when he was little, writing really, really, bad movies in high school, or creating weekly comic strips at work. Stories are always swirling around in his head, yelling at him to put them down on paper.

The Dragon Riders is the second book in the *Cowboys and Dragons* series. To stay informed on further books in this series, as well as other series and stand alone novels, please visit *www.aakerr.com* and sign up to be alerted to upcoming publication dates and events.

Anthony lives in Denver Colorado with his wife and three children.

Made in the USA
San Bernardino, CA
17 November 2016